HANG ON ST. CHRISTOPHER

BOOKS BY ADRIAN MCKINTY

SEAN DUFFY SERIES

The Cold Cold Ground
I Hear the Sirens in the Street
In the Morning I'll Be Gone
Gun Street Girl
Rain Dogs
Police at the Station and They Don't Look Friendly
The Detective Up Late
Hang On St. Christopher

MICHAEL FORSYTHE SERIES

Dead I Well May Be
The Dead Yard
The Bloomsday Dead

LIGHTHOUSE TRILOGY

The Lighthouse Land
The Lighthouse War
The Lighthouse Keepers

STANDALONE NOVELS

Hidden River
Fifty Grand
Falling Glass
The Sun Is God
The Chain
The Island

AS EDITOR (WITH STUART NEVILLE)

Belfast Noir

ADRIAN McKINTY
HANG ON ST. CHRISTOPHER

BLACK
STONE
PUBLISHING

Copyright © 2025 by Adrian McKinty
Published in 2025 by Blackstone Publishing
Cover and book design by Stephanie Stanton

All rights reserved. This book or any portion
thereof may not be reproduced or used in any manner
whatsoever without the express written permission
of the publisher except for the use of brief quotations
in a book review.

The characters and events in this book are fictitious.
Any similarity to real persons, living or dead, is coincidental
and not intended by the author.

Printed in the United States of America

First edition: 2025
ISBN 979-8-212-90502-2
Fiction / Thrillers / Suspense

Version 1

Blackstone Publishing
31 Mistletoe Rd.
Ashland, OR 97520

www.BlackstonePublishing.com

We forget that we are all dead men conversing with dead men.

—Jorge Luis Borges, "The Book of Sand"
The Collected Fictions

Hang on St. Christopher with the hammer to the floor
Put a high ball in the crank case, nail a crow to the door . . .
There's a 750 Norton bustin' down January's door.

—Tom Waits, "Hang On St. Christopher"

CONTENTS

1. Never Go to Belfast in July ... 1
2. A Sort of Homecoming ... 13
3. A Straightforward Little Homicide ... 23
4. Quentin Townes ... 34
5. The Picassos ... 43
6. The Burnt-Out Car ... 53
7. The Art Forger ... 68
8. The Phone Box and the Tailor ... 77
9. The Caravan Site ... 105
10. Dead Reckoning ... 127
11. The Break-In ... 140
12. The Kill List ... 154
13. The 750 Norton ... 168
14. Superintendent Clare ... 174
15. The Wake ... 180
16. The Second Murder ... 186
17. Young Lochinvar's Return ... 196
18. The Interview ... 205
19. The Ferryhill Road ... 212
20. The Mortars ... 223
21. The Aftermath ... 230
22. The Last Interview ... 240
23. Killian's Intel ... 250
24. Belfast-Knock-Shannon-Inverness-Reykjavik-JFK ... 261
25. Middle Bay ... 271
26. Chez Mr. Wilson ... 275
27. The Basement ... 278
28. A Sort of Ending ... 291

1
NEVER GO TO BELFAST IN JULY

No Alibis bookshop was packed. All eight seats were filled, and six people were standing at the back. Ciaran Carson came out of a side room with a mug of tea, a few sheets of A4, and a book of poems. He was wearing a dark-blue suit, white shirt, and red tie. He was a trim, confident man with short black hair and oval glasses. He looked like a scholar of ancient languages, which, of course, he was.

He said good evening and launched into his first poem:

"*Suddenly as the riot squad moved in, it was raining exclamation marks,*

Nuts, bolts, nails, car keys. A fount of broken type . . ."

The event went very well. Seamus Heaney, Derek Mahon, and Paul Muldoon were in the audience, and everyone else was a serious poetry geek or wannabe writer. "It's like when the Pistols played Manchester's Lesser Free Trade Hall in here tonight," I wanted to remark to someone, but none of this crowd would have understood what I was blathering on about.

Carson read from *The Irish for No* and *Belfast Confetti* and from his brilliant translation of the *Táin Bó Cúailnge*.

Questions were called for, and the usual Ulster embarrassed reticence descended upon us.

"What are the difficulties of translating Irish verse into modern English?" I found myself asking, and after the launch of this frail bark,

I was quite relieved to get only good natured responses from Carson and then Heaney and then a funny and scholarly aside from Muldoon.

I got a couple of books signed and walked out, well pleased, onto Botanic Avenue.

It was early yet, only seven o'clock, and my ferry was at midnight. Maybe a quiet pint in the Crown Bar or Kelly's Cellars? Maybe a film?

I found a phone box and called Beth in Portpatrick.

"Hi, it's me."

"Hey, how are you?" she asked.

"Fine. I went to that poetry reading."

"Was it good?"

"Very good."

"What are you doing now?"

"Just killing time. I'm booked on the midnight boat."

"How were your days at the station?"

"Really, really boring."

"That's to be expected."

"Yeah, it is."

I came in to work six days a month now, which was the minimum you needed to do to get your full benefits and pension when you retired. I usually did three days in a row, then took two weeks off to be a stay-home dad in Scotland; then I got the ferry over and did another three days. Until a year ago, doing boring paperwork had only been my cover, because I'd really been a case officer in charge of handling an IRA double agent in the police, who we'd turned into a triple agent working for us: feeding the IRA false intelligence and trying to pick up tips. But the stress of playing for us and them had finally taken its toll on Assistant Chief Constable John Strong, who had a coronary event in his back garden, where he'd been pruning his pear tree with a chainsaw. The chainsaw had avoided killing him, but it had laid waste to several of his prized garden gnomes before the cutoff switch kicked in.

It had taken him an hour to die out there, gasping for breath in the summer heat among the severed heads of his gnome army, and those of us who knew about his crimes and betrayals had considered that justice.

He'd been buried with a full RUC honor guard, and a couple of days later a small, masked IRA team had fired a volley of shots above his grave to salute "one of their own."

But now with Strong dead, the fake paper shuffling had become actual paper shuffling. As a part-time policeman, I couldn't do any proper detective work anymore, so it was admin and the occasional bit of traffic duty for yours truly until that glorious day August 31, 1995, when I could retire with a full twenty-year RUC pension. If I could somehow survive these working conditions until October 31, 1996, I'd get a full pension at the higher long-service rate.

We'd see about that.

Get out as soon as I could, was my instinct.

"Boring is good," Beth said. "I like to hear that it's boring. Boring means you're not on riot duty or on foot patrol along the border."

"I'm not up to any of those things," I said. "I have the doctor's note to prove it. My knees are too creaky for riot duty and foot patrols."

"Are you going into the station tonight?"

"I am. Briefly. I have to hand in my time sheet."

"Say hi to Crabbie and Alex for me."

"If they're in, I will. How's Emma?"

"She's great."

"Can I talk to her?"

"She went to bed early. I can wake her up, though."

"No, don't do that. Let the wee lassie sleep."

"Do you want me to wait up for you?"

"No, you go on to bed too. I promise I'll be quiet when I come in," I said. The new SeaCat ferry from Larne to Stranraer in Scotland took only an hour to cross the North Channel, so if all went well, I could be in my bed in the house in Portpatrick by one thirty in the morning.

"Okay, love you, Sean . . . bye!"

"Love you too."

I hung up the pay phone and walked to the cinema on Great Victoria Street.

It was a big multiplex with many options to choose from. Strangely, four of those options were Irish-themed films: *Far and Away,* starring Tom Cruise and Nicole Kidman; *Patriot Games,* starring Harrison Ford; *Cal,* starring Helen Mirren; *The Crying Game,* starring Stephen Rea. *Far and Away* was the story of a conflicted Irish rebel who runs off to America to escape the evil Brits; *Patriot Games* was about a conflicted Irish rebel who tangles with Harrison Ford and the evil Brits; *Cal* was about a conflicted Irish rebel who kills an evil Brit and falls in love with the dead man's girl; *The Crying Game* was about a conflicted Irish rebel who kills an evil Brit and then falls in love with the dead man's girl, who then turns out to be a bloke. The only thing funnier than Brits doing Northern Ireland was Hollywood doing Northern Ireland so *Patriot Games* definitely had the greatest potential for camp comedy. *The Crying Game* was the most artistically interesting, but I'd been lifted in an IRA honey trap myself, and the whole thing was a bit too close to home.

I decided to have that quiet pint in the Crown Bar instead.

A well-poured pint of Guinness in the well-worn snug at the back of the beautiful Crown Bar, Belfast, is for many people their idea of heaven come to this earth. But I was undergoing my habitual end-of-duty existential event and wasn't quite so chill.

It was the misfortune of many veteran police officers to acquire a messiah complex and go through the youthful temptations, the missionary journeys, the revelations, and finally the agony. Definitely the agony stage now for me. With the death of my double agent, I was a useless part-time peeler in the police reserve. Paperwork, chickenshit, and beat duty were how they punished part-time over-qualified coppers who came in only a few days a month.

I was in the snug at the back right of the Crown when I heard the unmistakable whoosh of Molotovs whistling through the air and exploding in petroleum fireballs as they hit the street.

I got up and walked down to the long red-granite public bar. "What's going on, John?" I asked the big barkeep.

"Some sort of riot. The police have blocked the Orange Order march on the Ormeau Road, so they've come out with the old bricks and bottles. Fun and games, you know?"

This was what Belfast was like every July nowadays.

It used to be that the Orange Order could march anywhere they wanted in Northern Ireland and the cops would protect them, but in the past few years the police had been trying to be more even-handed and wouldn't let the Orangemen parade through heavily Catholic parts of Belfast. Sometimes, the Orange Order and their sympathizers would take the diversion off their traditional marching route with equanimity, but other times they'd try to force the police roadblock, the police would resist, and there would be a riot. Often, Catholic neighborhood watch groups would come out to attack the Orangemen, and the police would get sandwiched between the two groups of rioters and then everyone, as they always did, would attack the cops.

As an off-duty, part-time detective inspector, perhaps it was my duty to see if I could help.

Stuff that.

I ordered another pint of Guinness and went back to the snug. I read the Ciaran Carson poems I'd bought, and a new book of verse by Paul Muldoon. It was a pleasant enough way to spend an hour, drinking Guinness by the fire while cops and rioters battled in the streets.

When I was done with my beer and went outside, things were ominously quiet.

Helicopters (police and army) were hovering over the west side of the city, and everywhere was smoke from burning tires and vehicles. A brand-new Mercedes, dull and ignominious in death, was upside down near the cinema. Dandified men in balaclavas and denim walked proudly over the median on Great Victoria and Glengall Street.

I looked for the RUC and discovered them pulled way back out of the trouble zone, behind a cordon of Land Rovers at Belfast City Hall. Glistening in their shields and helmets, they were the bristling Theban legions on the parched fields of Leuctra.

I smiled at this romantic notion, but actually this was pretty disturbing.

If the peelers were way back there, who was in charge of the streets?

I soon found out.

I walked to the multistory car park near the cinema and discovered that the security barrier had been torn down, the guy in the pay booth was long gone, and several cars from the first level had evidently been nicked. Car thieves the world over loved Beemers, so I was pretty relieved to find my black 1991 325i still in one piece. Yeah, I know, I go on about the BMW 3 series, but this beast could do zero to sixty in seven and a half seconds, and 145 on the motorway, and sometimes in a crisis situation it was good to know that you could do 145 mph on a motorway.

I looked under the Beemer for mercury tilt switch bombs and, finding none, got in.

I put the key in the ignition, and the engine and the radio kicked to life. Nirvana came out of the stereo speakers. Say what you will about *Nevermind* being a compromised punk album with Pixies, Rainbow, and Boston riffs, but it was still good to hear decent music again on BBC Radio 1 after a decade of synth and bubblegum-pop darkness. And although in the UK the bestselling albums of the summer were still Simply Red, Annie Lennox, and Michael Bolton, it meant something that in the US *Nevermind* had knocked Michael Jackson from the number one slot on the *Billboard* chart.

I'd driven about half a mile on Great Victoria Street before I encountered the first paramilitary roadblock. A dozen men in balaclavas had thrown burning tires across the road and were preventing vehicles from heading north. They were wearing matching denim jackets and were armed with aluminum baseball bats, knives, and machetes, and at least two of them had sawn-off shotguns.

I couldn't see exactly what was going on ahead of me, but it was obvious what must be happening. The paramilitaries would be interrogating every driver at the roadblock. If they liked the answers the driver gave to their questions, they would let them go; if they didn't like the answers, they would order them out of their car, hijack the vehicle, and make the driver walk home.

I looked to see if I could do a U-turn, but the traffic behind me was dense with evacuees.

Everyone was trying to get out of the city. The police and army were nowhere to be seen.

It was something of a tight spot. If the paramilitaries were Protestant and they found out I was a Catholic, they would order me out of the car and they might try to kill me. If the paramilitaries were IRA men and they found out I was a Catholic policeman, they'd order me out of the car and almost certainly try to kill me.

That was Belfast in July: a poetry reading, a quiet pint of the black stuff, a lynch mob armed with baseball bats and guns . . .

The car in front nudged forward toward the roadblock. The acrid stench of burning tires came in through the vents. *Où sont les* burning tires of yesteryear? Everyone on this street was time-traveling and PTSD-ing. All those previous bonfires and riots in seventies Belfast, eighties Belfast, and now nineties Belfast.

I suppose I could have gotten out and made a scene and tried to arrest the lot of them. And if I were one of those crusading cops from off the telly, that's exactly what I would have done. But that wasn't my scene.

The car ahead was let through the roadblock, and now it was my turn.

A chubby man in a balaclava leaned in and tapped the driver's-side window with gloved fingers. He was holding an Armalite assault rifle. His mate had a 9mm pistol.

"Wind your window down!" he said.

I wound the window down and switched the radio off.

"Yes?" I inquired.

"Where are you going?" he asked.

"Who's asking?"

The man turned to a shadowy figure behind him in a gray denim jacket, who was holding a pump-action shotgun.

"He's asking who's asking," the man said.

"Who's he to be asking us?" the man with the shotgun said.

"I just want to know if you're IRA or UVF. I can tell you're not the police," I said.

The man with the shotgun came forward and slapped the windscreen.

"We're doing the bloody questions!" he said.

All the other men at the roadblock turned to look at me.

Jesus, I had screwed this up already with my big mouth.

The man with the shotgun had arms covered with tattoos too ineptly done to read. His pudgy lard-colored neck, however, was holding up a gold chain with Ulster in block letters. He was, therefore, a Loyalist paramilitary. They were all Loyalist paramilitaries. UVF or UDA. A delicious shiver of pure fear made its way slowly down my spine. If they were in a particularly bad mood and looking for a random Catholic to kill, I could be their man for today.

I was armed, of course, but a six-shot revolver against a dozen men holding shotguns and M16s? Not much of a contest there.

If they did lift me and take me away with them, I had one card up my sleeve—almost literally.

Ever since the occasion two years ago when an IRA cell had tried to execute me on the high bog, I had secreted a razor blade and a lock pick in the left sleeve in a specially tailored pocket of my favorite leather jacket. If they handcuffed me and took me away, I'd at least have a last-gasp chance. But if they just decided to shoot me in the street like a mad dog, I'd have no bloody chance.

"Now, pal, answer the question. Where are you going?" the first man asked, putting his big muddy boot on the Beemer's shiny blue bonnet and pointing his pump-action shotgun at me.

I reached for my gun. Stuff the last-gasp shit—I was going to shoot this arsehole if he kept messing with my wheels.

"Carrickfergus," I answered truthfully.

"Carrickfergus?" the man with the gun repeated.

"Aye."

"That place is a shithole," Pump-Action Shotgun declared.

I did not reply.

"Well, what do you say to that?" the man insisted.

"Even if I worked for the Chamber of Commerce, I'd be reluctant to contradict a man pointing a shotgun at me," I said to a mirthless silence.

"Where in Carrickfergus?" the first man wondered.

"Coronation Road, Victoria Estate," I said.

"Victoria Estate, did you say? Do you know Bobby Cameron?"

"I know Bobby very well."

"What's he look like?"

"Like a fat Brian Clough."

"Ha! Yeah! That's him. All right, then. You can go. Nice Beemer, by the way," the man with the gun said.

"Thanks very much," I said, and drove slowly through the corridor of burning tires.

A man from Carrick who knew Bobby Cameron? Not an ideal victim. If they hijacked my car, I might be able to complain to Bobby, and the complaint would get passed back up the chain . . .

I was thinking these thoughts when, just another two hundred yards farther on, I was stopped by another illegal paramilitary roadblock.

"Where are you going?" a masked man with an axe asked.

"Carrick."

"Carrick? They're all head cases up there," he said with what seemed to be envy in his voice. Where did you get the car?"

"Ayr BMW in Scotland."

"Scotland," he said incredulously, as if I had named a place from the white spaces on a sixteenth-century map bearing the legend "Here be dragons."

"Scotland," I said again to reassure him.

"Scotland, eh? What do you do for a living?"

"I'm an accountant."

"Accountant? Boring bastard, are you?"

That tic of his, repeating the last the last word I said in the sentence, had potential for comedy, but I knew that if I tried any comedy it would not go well for me or, in the end, for him.

"Yes. I'm quite the boring bastard."

The axeman laughed. "Boring bastard. This is probably the most excitement you've had all year, eh?"

"Yes," I said.

"Aye. I knew it. Go on, then, get out of there before you shit your pants!" he said, and all the other masked men laughed. This was probably the most excitement they'd had all year as well. A chance to exercise power over men and women driving home from work, men and women with actual jobs, men and women who drove fancy cars . . .

After the third roadblock, I decided to get out of the city west rather than north. Exit through the Catholic neighborhoods, where the UVF wouldn't have the nerve to string burning tires across the road.

I headed down Divis Street and the Falls Road.

Up Sebastopol Street and Odessa Street.

Quieter here. This district guarded by men in doorways wearing long coats . . .

Above me, there was a noise like Lemmy from Motorhead clearing his throat, which, in fact, was an army Chinook helicopter flying low over the rooftops. It was only a show of force. There was no way they'd send in the army against those goons on Great Victoria Street. The goons were liable to attack the soldiers, and the soldiers would shoot back, and it would be a goddamn bloodbath.

I finally made it onto the Springfield Road, where there were a lot of ways to leave the city. The mazelike streets and the roadblocks and the aggro had taken their toll. My hands were trembling. I clocked myself in the rearview. Fear in those gray-blue Duffy peepers. Never got used to being afeard, did you? That's what having a kid does for you. Suddenly, you have skin in the game. Something to lose.

I turned the radio back on, and a song called "Achy Breaky Heart," by someone called Billy Ray Cyrus, annoyed me so much that the fear vanished by the second go-round of the chorus.

I finally escaped Belfast on the dear old Crumlin Road in the far west of the city. I drove through the relatively benign northern suburbs and pulled in at a quiet-looking cinder-block pub in Jordanstown.

It turned out to be a locals-only joint with tough-looking characters hugging pints of Harp (always a bad sign) and listening to flute-band music from an ancient tape player.

Still, I needed a drink to calm my nerves and quench my thirst. Just a wee half a Bass would do the trick.

I sat on a barstool and caught the barman's eye.

He was a big lad with a handlebar mustache and a cutoff white T-shirt that showed his jailhouse ink to great effect. The jailhouse ink revealed that he liked his mother, a girl called Denise, Manchester United, and Ulster.

He seemed to be in a foul mood about something, like Van Morrison on any random Tuesday.

"All right, mate? Just a wee half a pint of Bass there, please. I'm off to get the boat," I said, sticking a fiver on the table. A couple of the locals looked up from their pints and then looked back down again.

The bar had a cigarette machine, but I hadn't had a smoke in over a year now and I wasn't going to give those thugs the satisfaction of seeing me fall off the wagon.

"Times are changing, eh?" the barman said wiping down the counter.

"What do you mean?"

"Used to be that if a stranger came into your pub and ordered a *wee half*, everyone would call him a poof."

"Aye, and nowadays you only attract a few dirty looks and some tedious conversation from the barman. Half a pint there, pal, and be sharpish about it, I have a boat to catch," I said.

The barman draped his cleaning rag over his shoulder.

"Maybe you should just sling your hook and go and get your boat, *pal*," he said.

I sighed. Why was everything such a bloody effort in this town?

I was not in the mood for this. Maybe after a few coffees following a morning sorting through parking tickets, I'd be up for a bit of argy-bargy, but not on the downslope of an adrenaline crash.

In the dark comedy of my life, I wondered how best to play the scene. The easiest thing would be to leave. Just take my money and go. The second-easiest thing would be to flash my warrant card and make him pour the bloody drink. But as old Marcus Aurelius was wont to say, "Πρὸ ἔργου γίνεται τὸ τοῦ ἔργου τούτου ἐφεκτικὸν καὶ πρὸ ὁδοῦ τὸ τῆς ὁδοῦ ταύτης ἐνστατικόν." Yeah, I know, just rolls off the tongue, doesn't it? He said a lot of things, but the gist is, what stands in the way becomes the way.

So I decided I wasn't going to flash my police ID *or* leave. No, the barman and his cronies had just become a special project of mine.

I slid the fiver closer and bent over the bar toward him.

"You seem to have mistaken me for someone else, pal."

"This is my estab—"

"I want you to do me a favor and look into my eyes and tell me what you see there," I said slowly and clearly.

"What?"

"Look in my eyes. Take a really good look and tell me what you see there."

"Are you some sort of fruit?"

"Look at me."

Reluctantly his eyes flicked up and met mine. He also had greeny-blue irises with a hint of dark in them. But his dark couldn't match my dark. I was not a man who habitually got dicked around with, and I had already been dicked around quite enough today.

I let him get a glimpse of all the men I'd killed and all the men I'd hunted and all the men I'd put away.

You didn't get to be a barman—even in a place like this—without learning a little something about human nature.

He saw.

He knew. I might be north of forty, I might be only a part-time cop, I might be getting soft in the middle, and I might not have worked a case in a year, but I was the scariest bastard he was going to encounter in a long time.

I smiled at him and relaxed.

The movie of my life cut from close-up to the two-shot. He took a step back, removed a clean glass from the rack, and poured the half a pint.

"On the house," he said.

"Thanks very much," I said, and drank it in one.

All this aggression and sectarian strife—can't he see, can't *we* see, that they love us at one another's throats? I went outside to the Beemer, looked underneath it for bombs, and got in.

I turned on Radio 1. "Coming up Michael Bolton, Kylie, and Simply Red."

Yeah, so much for the musical revolution. I killed the radio and gunned the Beemer along the A2 to Carrickfergus Police Station, where, incredibly, there was a murder case waiting for me if I wanted it.

2
A SORT OF HOMECOMING

I left the Beemer in the car park and went upstairs to turn in my time sheet. As a part-time reservist, I no longer had an office. Just a desk in the CID incident room that I shared with Sergeant McCrabban, another part-timer. Crabbie was a low-maintenance deskmate, and it was no problem to share a space with him if you didn't mind his pipe smoke, which I didn't.

I turned the sheet in to Mabel in admin.

"Oh, Inspector Duffy, everyone's been looking for you," she said.

"Have they?"

"Oh, yes, Chief Inspector McArthur was on the phone. Very particular, so he was. 'Where's Inspector Duffy, then?' he says."

"Me? He was looking for me?"

"Yes."

"What have I done?"

"I'm not privy to the details. I'm like the mushrooms here, Sean—they keep me in the dark."

I looked at my watch. It was nine o'clock now. "Sorry, Mabel, I'm catching the midnight ferry to Stranraer. Is it CID business?"

"He wants you, that's all I know."

I shook my head. "Like I say, I'm off the clock. Sergeant Lawson is the full-time CID officer here, as you know, so—"

"He's on his holidays."

"Is he?"

"He is. Tenerife."

"Tenerife? Who goes to Tenerife?"

"Everyone, Sean. Everyone goes to Tenerife. He won't be back till next week."

"Oh, well, then you'll have to get Sergeant McCrabban. I'm catching the ferry."

"He asked specifically for you," Mabel insisted. She rolled up her red sweater sleeves and crossed her arms in a way that made her seem a bit like Velma from *Scooby-Doo*. Early-1970s adorable Velma, not redrawn 1990s trying-to-be-less-of-a-dork Velma.

"Mabel, look, I have to go. You haven't seen me, okay?"

"Don't be starting that, now, Sean," she said, her brows furrowing.

"Starting what? It's our running gag. You pretend to be annoyed with me, but when I'm gone you mutter to yourself *tsk tsk, that Sean Duffy, what a character . . .*"

"That's enough, now. Wait in the chief inspector's office and I'll see if I can find him," she said, a cross, unpleasant sanctimonious note in her voice now.

If I waited in the office, I was doomed. I shook my head and pointed at my time sheet. "Sorry. I'm off the clock. I have a boat to catch!" I said.

Quickly back downstairs to the Beemer.

I drove to 113 Coronation Road, where there was a For Sale sign in the front yard—a For Sale sign that had been there for over a year. It was a nice three-bedroom house in the middle of the terrace on a pretty nice street in a pretty nice housing estate. The problem wasn't the house. The problem was the asking price. I wanted twenty-five grand so I could buy one of those fancy new apartments they were building down at the marina and have a bit of change. I lived in Scotland for all but six days out of the month, and all I needed was a little one-bedroom flat overlooking the water, where I could store a few select records, keep a few tins of soup and some clothes. But nobody, it seemed, wanted to give me twenty-five grand for a three-bedroom house in the middle of a pretty nice terrace on a pretty street.

Now, a part of me knew that this was all bullshit: if I wanted to sell the house, I could do it easily if I knocked six grand off the asking price. But the real question, the deep Freudian question, was whether I really wanted to sell the house. I told Beth I did, told the real estate agents I did, told myself I did. I imagined how great that little flat at the marina would be. But truth be told, I loved this house, this street, and these people. We'd been through a lot together: a bomb defused under my car, assorted calls for my assistance following domestic disputes, an attack by the Loyalists *and* the IRA . . .

I got out of the car and helped a staggering Harry Blackwell to his front gate.

"Bit early for you to be in a state like this, Harry," I said to him, for indeed the pubs were all still open.

"Wedding. Wife still there. She sent me home."

"Wedding? Which one of your brood was the lucky—"

"Irina. The redhead. The difficult one. Glad to get her out of the bloody house," Harry said, doing the worst Tevye ever.

I helped him in his front door and walked back to the street.

Yes, we'd been through a lot together, Coronation Road and me. This was the first house I'd ever owned. Crazy thing for a Catholic peeler to buy a house in a working-class Proddy housing development, but at the time I'd bought it in 1980, it was perfect for my needs. Close to the Carrick cop shop, a big living room for my records, three bedrooms upstairs, and a shed out the back where I could smoke Turkish black unmolested. Furthermore, back in the early eighties this was the very last street in the Greater Belfast Urban Area, which was kind of romantic. The last street in Belfast—who wouldn't want to live there? Head south and you were in the Belfast suburbs; head north and you were in untouched, ancient Irish countryside. Changed since then. Carrickfergus town had expanded into the fields north of Coronation Road, and a lot of new people I didn't know had moved onto the street, but still, as the cat in that singing-cat show was wont to say: "Memories . . ."

I walked down the path, put the key in the lock, and went inside.

Precautions to get you through life in Ulster: lock pick and razor blade embedded in jacket sleeve, always look under your car for mercury tilt switch bombs, never sit with your back to a window or a door, always check the front and back door for break-ins.

No bombs, no break-ins.

I picked up a couple of letters from the hall floor and scanned them for anything interesting.

Nowt.

I walked into the living room and checked my albums. I'd left about a fifth of my collection here (four hundred or so records) so that I'd have something decent to listen to on my six nights a month back in Ulster.

I checked the clock in kitchen. It was 9:15.

Plenty of time for a can of soup and one side of an album before the drive to Larne.

The soup was tomato, the album was Brian Eno's *Music for Airports*, which was good lie-on-a-rug-on-the-floor-and-chill music.

I had the soup, and I was lying on the floor and chilling when there came a loud banging at the front door.

Instinctively I reached for my sidearm, a revolver, and from the coffee table I lifted the rather more effective Glock 17 9mm Safe Action pistol. I crunched to a sitting position and peered through the living room window, holding both weapons. I didn't see anyone in the garden, and I could see only the very back of the person waiting on the porch. Usually, assassins came in pairs, but not always.

I crept down the hall and peered through the peephole.

The person standing there was Chief Inspector McArthur, my boss.

I took a step backward and began tiptoeing my way back up the hall again.

"I know you're in there, Duffy. I see your car and I can hear your music!" McArthur said.

I hid in the living room, keeping perfectly still.

"Duffy, open up! I know you're in there! No one but you would have put that record on!"

Back along the hall a third time.

I opened the door. "Yes?"

"There you are! I knew you'd be home, and I knew you wouldn't answer the phone!" he exclaimed.

"You're a regular Uri Geller. What playing card am I thinking of?" I said.

"Three of clubs."

"No, the jack of fuck off. I have a ferry to catch."

He was wearing jeans and an anorak and Wellington boots. He'd been in the middle of something outdoorsy when they called him to the crime scene. Which meant it had to be something serious. Had to be a homicide. And the reason he was here was to convince me to be lead on that homicide, what with Lawson being away.

No chance. I am not one of those men who pray for storms and believe that storms will bring them peace.

"Can I come in?" he asked.

"You can come in, but there's not much point. I'm heading out for the ferry."

He ignored that and walked into the living room. I put the revolver back in the shoulder holster under my sport coat, and the Glock back down on the coffee table.

He sat down on the sofa while I stood, and we stared at one another for a very uncomfortable fifteen seconds. "Nice evening in Belfast?" he asked.

It was a poor opening gambit. I was tempted to paraphrase Groucho: *I've had a very nice evening, but this wasn't it, and you showing up like Banquo's bloody ghost is the icing on the shitecake.*

I said nothing and glared at him.

I didn't even offer him a cup of tea—a hanging offense in most of Northern Ireland.

"I've helped you out many times, Duffy, when the higher-ups were gunning for you," was his second salvo.

"The way I remember it is that I've bailed you out with our overlords many times and when it came to my own problems with the higher-ups, you kept your bloody head down and let me sink or swim by myself," I said.

"Yeah, well, we could be Rashomoning the past all night if we wanted. The point is, we've helped each other."

The verb "Rashomoning" from his unlikely lips was sufficiently arresting to make me sit.

He looked at me for another ten seconds and took out his pack of Silk Cut. He offered me one and I shook my head. I gave him the Tuborg ashtray that I kept for guests I didn't like.

"What the hell is this music? *Is* this music? Can you turn it off, please?"

I switched it off.

The tea thing had become untenable. Even if it was your worst enemy, you couldn't bloody escape the tea-and-biscuit-asking ceremony.

"Tea?" I asked.

"No time. Look, Duffy, there's been a murder."

"I can't go. I'm off duty. My shift finished at noon. I've done my six days this month and I'm off until next month. I was going to take the afternoon ferry, but I stayed to hear a poetry reading in Belfast."

"Duffy, you don't understand the situation. There's been a murder and our head of CID, *your* protégé, isn't even in the country. Gallivanting in Italy."

"Spain."

"Doesn't matter where he is, does it? He's out of the country and we've got no detective to investigate a murder. What are we supposed to do?"

"WPC Warren. I know Lawson has recommended her for the CID branch, and I hear—"

"She's still in training in Belfast. Won't be available until the end of the year."

"Pity. She's smart as a whip, that one."

"Well, she's not here and neither is your chosen successor."

"Call in Sergeant McCrabban."

"Sergeant McCrabban has also done all of his days this month, and anyway he is at some kind of farm auction in Ballymena."

"That sounds like a likely story."

"Well, that's what his wife said."

"So I'm the only detective in all of Carrickfergus?"

"Yes."

"And like Cinderella, I'll be gone by midnight."

"It has to be you, Sean."

"I can't do it. I already solved Sean Duffy's Last Case. Everything else would be anticlimactic. You cannot, as Paul McCartney says, reheat a soufflé."

"If you won't do it, we'll have to call in Larne CID," he said, fixing me with his dark eyes.

"Larne CID?"

"What other choice do I have?"

"But . . . *Larne*? You know what they're like."

"I've already checked. Chief Inspector Kennedy is available."

"But he's a . . . you've met him . . ."

"If you won't do it, it's got to be him."

"You're trying to bait me."

"I'm not trying to bait you. If you won't do it, I'll have to call Larne RUC."

Easy, Sean, don't let him suck you in. This is someone else's problem, nothing to do with you.

But then again, I couldn't let Larne CID come into our manor and bollocks up a murder case right in front of our noses.

"What are the particulars?"

"It seems to be a straightforward little homicide. Joyriders stole a man's car from outside his house on the Belfast Road. Apparently he resisted, and they shot him in the chest. The neighbors think he's some kind of painter."

"A house painter?"

"A painter painter. Like Hitler, you know?"

"Interesting that that's the name you come up with out of thin air when you were trying to think of a painter. Not Monet or Van Gogh. Hitler."

"Christ, Duffy, do you always have to be such an arsehole?"

"So they shot him in the chest and took his car. What type of car?"

"Jag."

"Aye, makes sense. There have been a lot of carjackings tonight. There have been riots in Belfast. The joyriders must be racing each other. Jag is a good car to race."

"Shame a man had to die for it."

"Aye."

"So will you take the case?"

"Forensics are over there now?"

"Yup."

"When does Lawson get back?"

"Sunday, I think."

"Okay, I'll need to ask the missus if it's all right. And I'll need to be on at least time and a half for the course of the investigation. Every minute I work on it will be overtime."

"Time and a half?"

"Yes."

"All right."

"And if I can get Crabbie to work the case with me, he'll have to be on time and a half too. And when it's overtime or extra duty it'll be above that. You know the union rules."

"Bloody hell. How much is all this going to cost me?"

"I haven't said I'm going to take it. I'll need to see what Beth has to say."

"Well, can you call her, please?"

I went into the hall, took a discreet hit on my asthma inhaler, and called her.

"Hello?"

"Hi, it's me."

"Hi, Sean, where are you?"

"Coronation Road."

"Ooh, have we got an offer for it?"

"No offer. Beth, look, there's been a murder and Lawson's on holiday, so they want me to run it."

"A case. Well, well, well, this is your dream come true. A case. A murder case at that."

"I told them I'm getting the midnight ferry, but they're desperate. The chief inspector is standing here right next to me."

"Oh, tell Peter hi from me."

I turned to McArthur. "Beth says hi."

"Tell Elizabeth hello from me."

"He says hi back. They'll pay me time and a half while I'm working on the case if I take it."

"How long would you be over there?"

"I don't know. With a murder case, you never know. But Lawson will be back on Sunday, so I can hand it over to him if it goes on that long."

"I'll miss you and Emma will miss you, but I can't say no, can I? Looking at you moping around the house. You've been itching for a case for the last year at least."

"No, I haven't. I don't miss detective work at all."

"Ha! Are you a terrible liar! Go on, do your case. Come over for the day if you can."

"It's a simple one. I might even have wrapped it up by tomorrow."

"Okay, Sean, if you say so."

"Kiss Emma for me."

"I will. Love you."

"Love you too. Bye."

I hung up the phone and looked at McArthur.

"The little lady's given her permission?"

"Oh, that's rich coming from someone who has to get forms signed in triplicate from Tina to go on the piss with the lads."

"That is a willful slander."

"One more call," I said, and rang Crabbie's house and told Helen that I would need the big man's help in a murder investigation.

"He's done with all that now, Sean," Helen said.

"It's only for a few days, and they'll be paying us time and a half," I explained. "Double time if we go over eight hours a day."

The chief inspector grimaced, and Helen audibly brightened up.

"Well, we could do with a bit of extra cash," she said.

I gave her the crime scene address and told her to tell Crabbie to meet me there when he could.

I called forensics to see who they had assigned to the case and was relieved to find that it was Frank Payne, who, despite his dyspeptic demeanor, was one of the better FOs in the biz.

I hung up and caught myself grinning in the hall mirror. A man was dead, and the dead man was crying out for justice, and Inspector Sean Duffy of Carrickfergus RUC was going to go and get that justice for him. *Detective* Inspector Sean Duffy of Carrick RUC.

I slapped McArthur on the back. "Right, then, me old cock, let's go see this crime scene, shall we?"

3
A STRAIGHTFORWARD LITTLE HOMICIDE

There are many ways to tell this story. I could talk about the redness of everything in this world. The red wind. The red clay. The red stain on the ground where Mr. Townes fell with shotgun pellets in his chest. I could talk about the blue smoke curling from the chimney tops, the icy-blue eyes of the forensic officer, the white and blue Police Land Rover Tangi on its side, wheels spinning, its blue guts spilling men under the withering fire of a machine gun. I could talk about the yellow sun setting over the swamp milkweed by the Chesapeake, or the yellow wings of the goldfinches in the nests along the Portpatrick road, or the little yellow dog of that man who threatened Beth with a closed fist that time. There are, of course, many ways to tell every story. But let's do it chronologically, at least for now, to keep the facts straight in our heads, yeah? For this straightforward little homicide was, of course, to become something much more complicated . . .

I went into the station to set up the CID incident room and get a warrant card that said "detective" on it. Then I followed McArthur out the Belfast Road to find this murder scene. Him driving his Volvo station wagon, me behind in the Beemer. He was a hesitant, nervous driver who frequently rode the brakes, so I gave him a lot of space to mess up.

I didn't actually need him. The murder scene wasn't difficult to find at all, what with the flashing police strobes on the Land Rovers, assorted coppers milling around, and half a dozen forensic officers in white coveralls going about their meticulous work.

The victim's house was a big old Edwardian mansion on the lough shore. Willow and chestnut trees and a well-manicured lawn. Similar houses to the left, right, and opposite.

This was where you lived if you had a bit of old money or were an up-and-coming doctor or lawyer. Maybe not the sort of place you saw a lot of violent crime, but if you were kids looking to nick a fancy motor, this was as good a place as any to nab one.

McArthur parked his car and got out. He was offering me his hand, so I shook it. "Well, I got you here. Can I leave all this in your capable hands, then, Duffy?"

"I suppose so."

"You remember all the procedures?"

"I imagine it's like riding a bike, sir."

"Is it? Right, then, I'm off. I'll put the kids to bed and come back in an hour or two to check up on things."

"You can just go on to bed, sir," I said. "I'll close up the crime scene. I'm sure, as you said, it's all straightforward enough."

This was an example of my rustiness. You never said things like that, what with God, the jinx, and fate listening in. Never. What were you thinking, Duffy? You eejit.

"Nah, I'll come back, Duffy," he said. He lowered his voice. "My in-laws are over from Stirling. My father-in-law is . . . well . . ."

"Understand completely, sir."

I waved goodbye and looked at the end of the driveway, and there was the stolid, pallid face and the long Raymond Massey–like physique of Sergeant John "Crabbie" McCrabban getting out of a Land Rover Defender. If you were looking to cast a local version of *The Crucible*, you wouldn't cast Crabbie as the Reverend Hale, because he'd be a bit too forbidding and grave for the role. But once you got to know him, you realized that underneath that dour Presbyterian visage there was a dry—very dry—sense of humor that he occasionally trotted out, and a guy who would never let you down.

I hadn't seen him for a while. A month or so. I waved at him. He nodded back. "How you doing, mate?" I called to him.

Crabbie came over. I wanted to hug the big galoot, but that would only embarrass him, so we shook hands.

"How do, Sean?"

"Not bad, and yourself?"

"Mustn't grumble."

"Do you ever grumble?"

"Not much occasion to, no. The Lord has been kind."

"Not to this geezer," I said, pointing at the corpse.

"This is my first case of any kind in about six months," Crabbie admitted in low tones. He too had moved to the part-time reserve, so he could spend more time on his dairy farm. "An assist to Sergeant Lawson on an armed robbery."

"And how did that turn out?" I asked.

"We got them."

"How? Forensic stuff?"

"Easier than that. Lawson went 'round the car dealerships to see who had just bought themselves a flashy new car. It was like a trail of breadcrumbs to the gang's door."

"Well, mate, you've gotten more practice than I have. This is my first actual case in over a year. Wee bit nervous about it, actually."

"How are Beth and Emma?"

"Good. Your brood and your better half?"

"Good."

We stood in silence for a beat or two.

"I hope we know what we're doing here, Sean," Crabbie said at last.

"I hope so too. Apparently, it's a car theft gone wrong, so not exactly something that will tax our limited mental capacities."

"If you say so, Sean."

"Let's say hello to Frank, eh?"

Frank Payne, the chief forensics officer, had evidently finished his job, because he was drinking tea and taking a cigarette break under a little canopy his team had rigged up.

As I said, Frank was a big, splenetic, heading-for-a-violent-heart-attack kind of man. He had no hair now, and his pale cheeks had taken on a purple cast. The tiny ciggie in his big paw looked somehow comic.

I shook his free hand.

"Well, if isn't the late, great Sean Duffy," he said.

"Nice to see you, Francis."

"I wondered what happened to you. I haven't clocked you or Crabbie at a crime scene in years! Sergeant Lawson I've seen, but not your shining, skinny, backwoods, inbred goblin face. What happened to you, brother? Did you fuck the deputy chief constable's wife or something? You were caught and they sent you to some scary suicide post on the border?"

"It's a little more prosaic than—"

"Well, what have you been doing with yourself? Tell me!"

"I'm in the part-time reserve now."

He looked amazed. "Part-time reserve? *You?* Seriously, mate, what happened?"

"Nothing happened. I'm only serving out my time until I can get my pension."

Comprehension dawned, and Frank nodded. There was nothing untoward about it. Half the coppers he knew were marking time until they got their pension. "And they let you stay as a detective?" he asked.

"No, they didn't. I only come in six days a month. You can't do case work with that schedule."

"So what do you do?"

"Paperwork mostly. Admin and traffic."

"And what about you, McCrabban?"

"Same thing. Part-timer until I get my pension."

"Jesus Christ, the pair of you. If you're not detectives in this organization, you're nothing. I know you have your farm, Crabbie, but I'm amazed at you, Sean. This was your life."

"Used to be, mate. It was my choice. Beth and I moved to Scotland and—"

"The one that looks like a boy?"

"She has a certain boyish grace admittedly, but she's all—"

"Did you marry her?"

"Not yet, I—"

"Wise man. If you do a background check on her, I'll bet you find she wasn't born a woman. Smart move on your part, if you ask me. Won't be able to get her pregnant and have her tie you down."

"We have a little girl."

"Aye, well, wonders of medical science, eh?"

"How come it takes only thirty seconds of convo with you before everybody wants to punch you in the fucking face, Frank?"

"I have a talent for shithousery," he said.

"And how's your misssus by the way?" I asked.

"You know she left me, Sean."

"That's right and she sends her best," I said.

Frank grinned and suddenly slapped me on the back. "God, man, it's good to see you. Part-time reserve or no, it's nice to be dealing with a real peeler for a change!"

"Sergeant Lawson is a real—"

"Sergeant Lawson is too big for his bloody boots, and everyone else around these parts is a joke. Don't get me started on Newtownabbey RUC or Larne RUC. I'm swimming in a sea of septic incompetence, Duffy."

"Well, at least you've got the buoyancy for it, mate."

"Fat jokes are beneath you, Duffy. You'll be doing 'your mother' gags next."

"Uhm, wait a minute, I have one: your mother is so classless, I mistook her for a Marxist utopia . . . No? Anybody?"

Frank sighed. Crabbie stared at his boots.

"So I suppose Lawson is on his holidays?" Frank said.

"Nothing escapes you, mate. He's in Tenerife."

"Tenerife? Bloody hell, who goes there?"

"Everyone, apparently."

Frank nodded. "Well, you're lucky or, I suppose, *unlucky* if you were hoping for a week's overtime. Straightforward business. They wanted this bloke's car. He didn't want to give them his car. They shot him and took the car. Have you heard the term 'carjacking'?"

"Yes."

"Well, it was one of those."

"What evidence have you gathered?"

"Shotgun pellets."

"Anything else?"

"Not much."

"Tell me about the pellets."

"Twelve-gauge, both barrels, shot from less than four feet away. He had no chance."

"Victim's name, occupation—all that jazz?"

Frank sniffed. "That's none of my business; that's your job. Do you want to see the body?"

"Not really, but I suppose we have to."

Frank led me along the pavement to where a white sheet was covering the body. Forensic men (and one forensic woman) had chalk-marked the shotgun pellets that were in the ground and were taking photographs of the tire treads of the stolen car, which had been driven off with some speed.

"You can tell by the tread that the vehicle was a Jaguar," Frank said.

I raised a skeptical eyebrow.

For all his abilities, I doubted very much that he'd ascertained the make of the car from this tread. He must have canvassed the neighbors. And if he'd canvassed the neighbors, he probably did know the victim's name, occupation, and so on, but he wanted me to do my own bloody legwork, the hateful big shite.

I lifted the sheet to look at the body. I hadn't had to do this in a while, and I'd been glad of that. In a lot of ways, I hadn't been cut out to be an RUC detective—my problems with the chain of command, my issues with the priorities of the organization itself, and my distaste for many aspects of detective work, not least among them looking at recently murdered people.

This particular scene was a mess. A mess that once had been a thinking, feeling human being. Sawn-off shotgun at very close range. Exactly the sort of thing a panicky joyrider would do. Half the victim's face had been torn off, and the hole in his chest was enormous.

He was wearing a sport jacket, white shirt, and brown slacks with Nike gutties—bit of an unusual ensemble. I bent down to touch the jacket. It was a linen cotton blend, bespoke tailoring. I examined it more closely. The label said that it was from Thomas Browne and Company, an old-money tailoring firm out of Dublin.

I let the sheet fall and stood up to get some air. The sheet drooped over the hole in the victim's skull and began to absorb some of the only partially dried blood. A macabre, bloody silhouette. It was a gruesome thing to see.

"Oh, crap," I said, wincing.

Paperwork seldom gave you nightmares. This, however, might.

"Are you all right, Duffy? You've gone green," Payne said with a grin.

"Aye, not used to this. The integrity of my sleep has probably been compromised."

"Ach, this is nothing. I see shite worse than this every day. Some of the road accidents I have to go to . . . Decapitations. Partial decapitations. Fire. Kids, you name it. One time I was called to the scene of a fire in a van carrying handicapped kids—"

I held up my hand. "Save it for another time, brother, will ya?"

"You've gotten soft, Duffy."

"You say that like it's a bad thing, Frank. How long has he been out here like this?"

"About an hour and a half."

"Who found the body?"

"Report of shots fired to the confidential telephone. Carrick police arrived and they called forensics."

"The local cops didn't call an ambulance?"

"He was dead, Duffy; there was no point. I mean, look at him."

"Twelve-bore, close range—is that what you said?"

"Twelve-bore, *very* close range. Side-by-side double-barreled shotgun. Fired together or almost simultaneously."

"Are you sure about that?"

"'Course. Panicky kid stealing a car. Guy resists, wee shite gives him both barrels. Death would have been very quick if not immediate."

I shook my head and gave Crabbie a look. He had a skeptical expression on his dour face too.

"All right, Duffy. You've got your sergeant. The band's all here. Do you mind if I piss off? I've got half a dozen cases like this in Belfast," Frank said.

"Murders?"

"No. Joyriding stuff. There was some kind of big riot this afternoon after a Loyalist march up the Ormeau Road. We tried to stop them marching up the Falls Road, and the whole thing kicked off. They hijacked dozens of cars and burned them all out. Top brass is hoping there might be some forensic evidence in the wrecked cars. No chance, but it's going to be a busy night for us looking for fingerprints in all that lot."

"There won't be fingerprints. They were all wearing gloves," I said.

"How do you know?"

"I was there," I said. "They tried to hijack my car."

"Why didn't you arrest them?"

"Me against twenty thugs with baseball bats?"

"I would have gone for it," Payne boasted.

"Sure you would, mate."

"Look, do you have any more questions, or can I go? Some of us are busy," Payne said.

"Forensic evidence around the car, Frank?"

"Nothing that we found."

"No cigarettes, matches, beer cans—anything our crims might have left?"

"Nope."

"Victim's wallet?"

"Bagged for you."

"ID in there?"

"No, just money."

"No credit cards or driver's license?"

"No."

"How much money?"

"Five hundred quid or so. Like I say, I've bagged it for you."

"Let's see it."

He went over to one of his junior officers, who found the bag and gave it to me. I put on latex gloves before taking out the wallet and the cash. The wallet wasn't interesting in itself, but this was a lot of money. And there wasn't just sterling; there was also two hundred quid in Irish pounds: ten crisp twenty-punt W. B. Yeats notes. Also three French five-hundred-franc notes with a hideous facsimile of Blaise Pascal on them.

I showed the foreign currency to Crabbie. "He got around, did our mystery man," Crabbie said.

"I think he's originally from Dublin which is interesting," I said. "That jacket is a Thomas Browne, just off Connolly Street. Fancy place. If we can't ID him any other way, they'll have a list of their clients."

"You know, joyriders almost never kill anyone," Crabbie mused.

"But it does happen," Payne insisted.

"It does happen," Crabbie agreed. "Strange that they left that big wallet full of cash."

"They panicked and fled," Payne said.

"What happened to the shotgun-shell casings?" I asked.

"Gone," Payne admitted.

"Our panicky joyrider took the trouble to leave the money but pick up the shell casings?" I asked.

"And if they shot him twice at chest height, it's odd that none of the pellets hit the car," Crabbie said.

"How do you know none of the pellets hit the car? The bloody car's gone!" Payne said.

"Well, there are no paint chips and no broken glass that I can see," Crabbie said.

"And look at those pellets in the asphalt," I said.

Frank Payne crossed his arms. "All right, smart guys, what do youse think happened?"

"I'm not ruling out your joyrider theory, but to me it looks like an execution. They shot him in the gut with the first barrel, and while he was on the ground they blew half his head off with the second. Look at all the pellets embedded in the pavement. The gun was pointing down."

Crabbie nodded. "No broken glass from the car windows around the body. The first shot was low in the stomach; the second shot came when he was prone. If he'd been standing against the car for both barrels, the side windows would likely have been taken out."

Frank looked at the pair of us and then slowly nodded. "Well, you're the experts. I just gather the evidence," he said with fake humility. "If it was an execution, there'd be no possibility of pleading manslaughter, then, would there?"

"No, I don't think so."

"That's good. Them wee bastards, if they top someone and they're underage, they let him out after two years. It's a disgrace if you ask me. Bring back the rope, eh?"

"It might not be kids," I said.

"It's always kids. Whole country's going to the dogs! Bloody kids. There's no respect anymore. 'Course, the problem is with the parents; they—"

"Me and the Crabman will find them," I said to stave off the full juror-number-three-in–*12 Angry Men* rant.

"Make sure that you do. I drive a Mercedes. I don't want it nicked," Frank said.

"We'll do our best," I said, offering him my hand to show that the conversation was at its terminus.

He shook the hand and nodded. "All right, I'll collect the lads and head out. We'll be on until the wee hours tonight."

"No rest for the wicked, Francis," I said.

"Whom the Lord loveth he chastiseth," Crabbie added.

Payne gave us a weary look, opened his mouth to do some more moaning, changed his mind, and departed.

"I think that's it, you know, Sean," said Crabbie, sensing my thoughts. "The first shot put him on the ground, and while he was down there, they finished him off."

"Why would joyriders do that?" I wondered out loud. "Murder, I mean. That's a big step up from car theft."

"I don't know. Maybe they just panicked right enough?"

"And again, do panickers take the shell casings with them?"

Crabbie shook his head. "In general, no, they do not. But seeing a man die sobers you up quick, sometimes."

The medical examiner's crew turned up to take the body up to the Royal Victoria Hospital, and Crabbie and I talked strategy. The fact that neither of us had been lead on a major case in years was disturbing, but the procedure came back pretty easily: secure the crime scene; canvass for witnesses; ID the victim; search the house for anything incriminating; notify next of kin. Nothing to it. Oh, yeah, and find the killer. That too.

4
QUENTIN TOWNES

A constable told us that the stolen car was a gold 1989 Jaguar with a Dublin registration, so I put out an alert for the vehicle. The victim's keys were gone with the car, but getting access to his house was easy with a lock pick kit and a minute to spare.

We did a quick shoofty around to make sure there were no starving kids or starving pets inside—there weren't—and that the gas was off. It was. We'd do a thorough search later when the case warranted it. A note for the milkman on the front step said: "One Gold Top only—Q Townes," and when we went door-to-door canvassing for witnesses, we learned that that indeed was his name: Quentin Townes.

The next door neighbors on either side had barely exchanged two words with the victim since he moved in about two months earlier, but the lady across the street, a Mrs. Franklin, was more helpful. She was in her late sixties but still worked part-time at Glenview Secure Mental Hospital as a staff nurse. Observant, friendly, and sharp as a tack, Mrs. F. would have been the ideal witness were it not for a tendency to become prolix.

Unfortunately, she hadn't seen the actual murder, but she had heard the gunshots, and she told us a good deal about the victim. She invited us in for a cuppa, and although we were in a bit of a rush to make the notification, we could see that there was no way of dodging the tea.

Chintzy living room, china teapot, Ceylon tea, full-cream milk, Jaffa Cakes—bog standard fare.

"Oh, yes, Mr. Townes has been a very good neighbor since he moved in. Very nice gentleman. Well spoken. He was a painter; did you know that?"

"Yes."

"Interior decorator sort of painter?" Crabbie asked.

I shook my head, but before I could explain, Mrs. Franklin had leaped in. "Oh, no, nothing like that. A *painter* painter. He was a very classy gent, was Mr. Townes. He did wee portraits and landscapes. Watercolors and oils. Did one of me and my granddaughter. It's very good. That's it over the fireplace. Look at thon; isn't it something?"

Out of politeness, Crabbie and I had to examine the picture, and truth be told, it wasn't a bad representation, although maybe a little generous to Mrs. Franklin from a senescence point of view. But if an artist can't flatter his subject a little, he's probably not a very savvy artist—Graham Sutherland / the fireplace at Chartwell being a case in point.

"Is that how he made his living?" I asked, sitting back down on the sofa and scarfing a Jaffa Cake.

"I believe so. He had a studio in the conservatory at the back. He said he'd been painting for years."

"He's not from around here, is he?" I asked.

"No, no, no. He was from down south somewhere. Although he's been up in Belfast for a while, I gathered. He'd only moved to this house a few months back, but he said he'd been giving classes on and off at the Tech for a while."

"How long is a while?"

"He didn't say."

"Dublin accent?"

"I don't know. Perhaps. He was well spoken, though. Polite."

"How old was he, exactly?" I asked. "We couldn't really tell from the, ehm, body, and we haven't been able to recover his driving license."

"Oh, he was in his fifties. He looked younger than that, of course, but I think he was an older man. Very courteous. Always said 'good morning, Mrs. Franklin!' Always helped me with my bins. Getting the new wheelie bins in and out. Those awful, difficult new bins. Why we couldn't have just stuck with the old ones, I'll never know. The binmen used to come 'round the back of the house, have a wee chat with you, carry your bin to the bin lorry, carry it back. Now you have to do most of the work yourself with those new wheelie bins and forget about having a conversation with those young bucks! Let no new thing arise, my grandfather used to say."

"Aye," Crabbie agreed. "Now, what time did you hear those alleged gunshots, Mrs. Franklin?" he asked while I finished my Jaffa Cake.

"Four fifty-five. It was the last numbers game on *Countdown*, and I was looking at the TV when I heard the shots."

"Are you sure? Was there a clock on your TV?"

"No, but *Countdown* is always the same. They do the last numbers game and then the conundrum and then they wrap up the show. The last numbers game is always at four fifty-five."

"And did you know they were gunshots?"

"I did not. I thought it was a car backfiring. One of the students down the way there has a Volkswagen and it's always doing that. Backfiring, stalling. Mrs. McCallister told me the engines are in the back of those things! That can't be right, can it?"

While Crabbie tried to get her off the topic of Volkswagen engines, I found myself caught in a stare with the black lough water. Just to the left, you could see the distant twinkling lights of Scotland. One of them, perhaps, was the lights from my own living room, and I thought again how odd it was to be removed from that universe of domestic bliss into this unpleasant little world of joyriders and murderers and dead men in bespoke three-hundred-quid linen jackets.

"No, if I'd thought it was shots, I would have gone out. I might have been able to help poor Mr. Townes," Mrs. Franklin continued with a flutter of emotion.

To prevent that emotion from becoming an entirely unnecessary feeling of guilt, I shook my head. "He died almost instantly. There was nothing you could have done," I said.

"That's a relief. He was a nice man. I wouldn't want for him to have suffered."

"I don't think he did. Shots, you said, not shot?"

"Two bangs, one after the other, the way a car does sometimes, which is why I thought it *was* a car."

"How long an interval between these two bangs, do you think?"

She thought for a moment. "Two seconds."

"Two seconds," I said, and wrote it in my notebook. Crabbie and I exchanged a look and a psychic communication.

A barrel in the gut to gentle his condition and bring him down. A barrel in the head at close range to kill him. Take the keys, steal the car, burn the car out to make it look like a joyriding gone wrong.

But what motive could there be if it wasn't a botched carjacking?

"Did Mr. Townes ever speak about any enemies, threats against him, dissatisfied customers? Anything like that?"

"Mr. Townes was a very good artist. I can't imagine he had any unhappy customers."

"Human nature being what it is, though, I'm sure he upset some people," I suggested.

"He was a very easygoing man. A churchgoing man, I think."

"Which denomination?" I asked—always a loaded question in Ireland.

"Well, he was from down south, so you'd think he was a Catholic, but I don't think he was actually. I think he was Church of Ireland."

"Why do you think that?"

"Well, while I had the weans sitting for their portrait, Radio Ulster was on, and Dr. Eames was talking about something or other and I saw Mr. Townes nodding to himself. And Dr. Eames is the Archbishop of the Church of Ireland."

"Not completely conclusive evidence there, Mrs. Franklin," I suggested.

"Well, he wasn't *very* religious," she conceded.

"We'll need to contact a next of kin," Crabbie said to me.

"Yes, thanks for reminding me, Sergeant McCrabban. Did he have any family that he spoke about?"

"No. He never mentioned any family to me. I assumed his parents were dead."

I sipped my tea. "Did he mention a wife or siblings?"

"No, he didn't. Oh dear, oh dear, I hope there's someone that'll come up to bury him! I wouldn't like to think of him without anyone to speak for him."

I put my hand on her arm and gave her a reassuring smile. "We haven't searched his house yet. I'm sure we'll find an address book. And if we don't, we'll find out who he's been calling on the phone, and call them," I said.

"That's very clever. You're very professional," Mrs. Franklin said.

I looked at Crabbie. "Mrs. Franklin says we're very professional," I said.

"I heard."

I leaned in conspiratorially to Mrs. F. "This is me and Sergeant McCrabban's first case in a while. We're actually a bit rusty, so any help that you can give us would be greatly appreciated."

"I'll do all I can," she said, genuinely appreciating my honesty.

"So he didn't speak about siblings, parents, or old girlfriends?" I reiterated.

"No, but he was a handsome man, though. I imagine he left a few broken hearts along the way when he was younger."

"Did he charge a lot of money for his artwork?" Crabbie asked.

"A hundred pounds for a portrait."

"That seems reasonable," I said.

"And if you weren't happy with it, he didn't make you take it. He just got out the white spirits and reused the canvas."

"He sounds like a very even-tempered man."

"The very words I would have used. Philosophical."

"Did he have any hobbies? Golf, sailing—anything like that?"

"None that I knew about."

"And I know I've asked this already, but are you sure he never mentioned any enemies?"

"None that he talked to me about."

"Did it not seem strange to you that he never spoke of his family at all? He must have come from somewhere."

"I don't like to pry, and he didn't offer the information. Maybe Kenneth would know. He was over there once a week. He did Mr. Townes's lawn as he didn't have a mower of his own. He was only renting, so I suppose he never got 'round to buying a mower, and Kenneth didn't mind. Good exercise for him. Doctor said he needed to get out and about. He talked to him a few times."

Mrs. Franklin got up, opened the living room door, and yelled upstairs: "Kenneth! It's the police! It's about Mr. Townes."

"I'm watching the snooker, amn't I?" a voice bellowed down the stairs.

"It's the peelers, Kenneth. They need to speak to you!"

A long pause and then a reluctant "All right. But this better not take long. It's live."

Kenneth came down the stairs. He was a large, balding man in a white shirt and brown cardigan. His Freddie Jones in David Lynch's *Dune*–style eyebrows were upturned at a thirty-degree angle, giving a delightful surprised/indignant look to his countenance.

"I'm Detective Inspector Sean Duffy; this is Detective Sergeant John McCrabban. We're investigating the death of Mr. Townes across the road."

"I didn't see anything. I was watching the snooker. It's the finale. It's the UK masters."

"Your wife says that you went over occasionally to mow Mr. Townes's lawn," I said.

Mr. Franklin gave Mrs. Franklin a betrayed look.

"So I did. What of it?"

"Did he ever talk to you about any friends, relations—anything like that? We'd like to ascertain the next of kin as soon as possible."

Mr. Franklin shook his head. "Look, here's the thing. I offered to mow his lawn when I was out doing mine and he said yes. To be honest, I wasn't expecting him to say yes. Nobody around here would say yes. They might borrow your petrol mower, but they wouldn't actually let you mow the grass for them!"

"It was good exercise for you!" Mrs. Franklin insisted.

"It was exercise, aye. Good exercise? I don't know about that."

"But you spoke to Mr. Townes," I said.

"Yeah. He wasn't what I'd call a chatterbox, but we talked on occasion."

"What about?"

"The usual things."

"What are the usual things?"

"Football, weather."

The usual things men discussed when they didn't want to talk about reality.

"What was his team?"

"Liverpool."

I turned to McCrabban. "Clearly, he was a man of taste and discretion. The suit, the car, Liverpool."

"Liverpool is in long-term decline. That's what the *Mirror* says," Crabbie muttered.

I ignored this and turned back to Mr. Franklin. "He ever talk about siblings, next of kin?"

"Nah. Never spoke about it. But there were no next of kin. I sort of gathered that. No friends either. No one ever came 'round, did they? No wife, no kids, no mother, no brothers. A wee bit suspicious, if you ask me. Around here we like to know where somebody comes from, you know? But Mr. Townes, he arrives in the street, dead of night, moves in, sets himself up as a painter, and nobody knows him from Adam."

"You're talking a lot of nonsense, Kenneth!" Mrs. Franklin said. "He arrived on a Monday morning. I saw him move in myself."

"Paid for all his bills in cash. Said he didn't trust the banks," Mr. Franklin said.

"I don't trust them either!" Mrs. Franklin countered.

Mr. Franklin shook his head and tapped his finger to his nose. "You can't use a bank unless you have ID, am I right?"

"Aye," Crabbie agreed.

"Am I also right in thinking you haven't found a driver's license or a passport yet?" Mr. Franklin asked.

"We haven't done a really thorough search of the house," I said.

"You won't find any either. I was over there doing his lawn one Friday, and the detector vans boys came to check to see if he had a TV license. He didn't, and when they asked to see some ID, he said he didn't have any form of identification in the house. And they said he had a twenty-four-hour grace period to go to the post office and get a license and he said he would, but I don't think he ever did. Quentin, he called himself. That part I believe. If you're going to make up a name, you wouldn't make up Quentin."

Mrs. Franklin was deeply irritated now. "I am sorry I brought you down, Kenneth. These are police officers conducting a very serious investigation and you're filling their heads with a load of nonsense!"

"You're the one talking nonsense!"

"Kenneth, lower your voice!"

"I can raise my voice in my own house, so I can!"

Crabbie was looking uncomfortable now and wanted us away from this. He nodded his head toward the door. He was probably right. A thorough search of Mr. Townes's house would likely give us all the answers we needed.

I got to my feet. "Just another couple of quick questions and then we should head on," I said. "You don't know if Mr. Townes had any other source of income apart from the painting?"

"No. I don't think so. Why do you ask that?" Mrs. Franklin wondered.

"He was driving a Jaguar, and he was wearing a rather expensive jacket," Crabbie said.

"Oh, yes, he was always very well dressed, was Mr. Townes," Mrs. Franklin said.

Mr. Franklin shook his head. "Were youse listening to me? I don't think he even had a bank account. He was always paid in cash for his work, and he told me once that he went to Belfast to settle his electricity bill. But you don't have to do that if you have a bank account, do you? They do direct debit, don't they? Cash only. Very strange in this day and age."

Mrs. Franklin shook her head. "You and the banks, Kenneth, please."

"Indeed. Well, thank you both very much. Here's my card. Call me if you can think of anything else that might help us with our inquiries. Anything at all."

We left the Franklins to it and recrossed the road.

"Search the house?" Crabbie asked.

"Search the house," I agreed.

I sent off a constable to call the electric company and find out about these cash payments for his bills, and I called in the standard background check to HQ to see if we could locate Mr. Townes's passport, driver's license, game license, gun license, or any criminal record.

"We haven't discussed motive," Crabbie said as we walked through Mr. Townes's front door.

"Motive?"

"If it wasn't a carjacking gone wrong."

"Ach, it could be any number of things. Jealous husband? Financial troubles? Trouble with the local bookies?"

Crabbie didn't look convinced by any of those explanations. But it was way too early to speculate about any of that. I sighed. "Aye, Crabbie, might be a tricky one even if it is only a simple carjacking. I bet we find the car burned out with enough petrol in the tank to get a real inferno going and wipe out all the recoverable forensic evidence."

"That's a bet I wouldn't take," Crabbie said, quickly adding, "Not that I would ever take a bet."

"No."

Crabbie rubbed his hand across his chin. "With no forensic evidence at the scene, no eyewitnesses, and potentially no forensic evidence in the car, this may be a hard nut to crack."

"That's why they called for the best, isn't it?"

"Yes, but the best was on holiday in Spain, so they have to make do with you and me," Crabbie said with only the barest hint of a smile.

5
THE PICASSOS

The house was a big Edwardian job overlooking the water. It was a furnished rental, so the old leather sofa, stiff-backed chairs, and grandfather clock did not reflect Mr. Townes's personality. Neither did the fussy flowery wallpaper and the thick red carpeting, which looked prewar.

There were four bedrooms upstairs, but three of them had apparently been converted into storage rooms for canvases and paint. Townes's bedroom was a spartan room at the back, with a single bed and a chest of drawers. In a cupboard, there were some shirts, a black polo-neck sweater, a couple of T-shirts, and a raincoat. A second bespoke suit from Browne and Company. This one was also a linen cotton blend, cream-colored, light and soft to the touch.

The entire back area of his house had been converted into an art studio. It was in a rather nice conservatory with a huge skylight and big south-facing windows overlooking the lough.

Townes's paintings were all over the shop and weren't terribly interesting. Portraits of local people and landscapes in the mold of Jack B. Yeats. The colors didn't leap out at you, and the people in the pictures were rather lifeless (but then, in all honestly, so were most of the subjects around these parts).

Crabbie and I searched the house peeler-style: thoroughly, carefully, professionally. But it looked as though it had already been depersonalized thoroughly, carefully, and professionally. No passports, no driver's license, no video-club ID. We didn't find any letters or blackmail notes or gambling receipts. No little black book detailing affairs, no diary, no eye-opening porn stash, no regular porn stash.

I put on a pair of latex gloves and went out to his bin. Rummaging through that, I didn't find any receipts either, not even from a supermarket.

"He might be a man who just doesn't keep receipts," Crabbie said.

We looked in the fireplace but couldn't tell from the ash whether he burned his personal correspondence.

"This is bloody peculiar," I said. "Let's start over."

Again, we searched the house for anything that might reveal where Mr. Townes had come from, or even a clue to his provenance.

Nothing.

"Aye," Crabbie agreed. "Strange."

A second canvassing of the neighbors also revealed nothing. *Quiet man who kept to himself*, and in Ulster no higher compliment could ever be paid to anyone. You could be killing prostitutes by the score in some basement dungeon, but if you were a quiet man who kept to himself, the neighbors wouldn't badmouth you to the cops or the TV crews.

No basement dungeon, by the way. (We checked.)

Back inside to look at the pictures again. Half-finished portraits of local children and families. Still lifes of flowers and leaves. Some of the landscapes revealed a bit of information: he had extensively painted the County Antrim coast and the Fermanagh lakes, and he had made several attempts at Ben Bulben in County Sligo. There even looked to be one of Monet-style haystacks. So he got around a bit.

"Do you want a cup of tea, Sean?" Crabbie asked.

"Third cup of the night, but why not?"

Crabbie stuck the kettle on, and I retired to the living room, which had a well-stuffed bookcase. On top of it were a few big art books—Kandinsky, Roy Lichtenstein, Rothko, and Jackson Pollock. Not exactly the schools that Mr. Townes followed in his own works.

Above the bookcase were two *possibly* original Picasso etchings—which, if genuine, would almost certainly be the most valuable pieces of art in the house. They were tiny and they were signed, but I couldn't tell if they were prints from a shop, or the genuine article. I held them up to the light and looked at the back, but I couldn't figure them out. They were small and they looked old, but they could easily be prints or copies. Hmmm.

I examined the bookcase. Bookcases were better than nothing at pointing you toward someone's personality. Thrillers, art books, a few history books, and quite the collection of Penguin Classics. I thumbed through a few of them looking for receipts or bookmarks, but nothing fell out.

The last of the long summer twilight had gone now, and I flipped the lights on. At this time of year, full darkness didn't come until eleven, so it must be pretty late night now. I tapped my watch, but I had forgotten to wind it. The grandfather clock claimed it was 6:17, which I doubted. The living room had no TV or radio or stereo for me to flick on and find out what hour it was in the rest of the world.

"What time is it?" I shouted to Crabbie.

"Can't talk; I'm on the phone to the station!" he yelled back.

I went to the living room windows and looked out at the street. Eerily quiet now. I'd sent all the coppers back to the station, except for a constable I would keep outside to secure the crime scene, and one forensic officer finishing up her work.

Crabbie came into the living room holding two teacups and looking glum.

"What's up?" I asked.

"No sign of the stolen car yet. And no appearance of Quentin Townes on the electoral register, the central criminal registry, or the Interpol registry. He never applied for a passport under that name north or south of the border, and he never got a driver's license under that name either. Here's your tea. I told them to try every database we had, 'cause I knew you'd want that."

"Aye, I do. And?"

"It'll take them a bit. They'll call us."

I took the mug and looked at him askance. "No biscuits, mate?"

"Didn't seem right to nick his biscuits," Crabbie replied.

"You're drinking his tea."

"Tea's one thing; food's another," he said definitively. Crabbie had very firm moral boundaries, and if you didn't want to upset him it was best not to question him about the geographies of those boundaries.

He was looking off kilter, was the Crabman.

"Here's one for you," I said. "Why did the dairy farmer get his wife another acre of pasture for her wedding anniversary?"

"I don't know."

"Because love is a cattlefield."

Crabbie stared into his teacup. I could tell he'd missed this quality banter.

"You see those drawing things above the fireplace?" I asked.

"The wee ones?"

"Yeah."

"Picassos."

Even Crabbie knew who Picasso was. He almost choked on his tea.

"Originals?"

"I think so."

"They must be worth millions!"

I shook my head. "Nah. They're etchings. He printed thousands of the things in his lifetime. They've got to be worth some serious coin, though . . . but not millions."

"So Mr. Townes had *some* money."

"Oh, yes. He's driving a brand-new Jag. He's renting a big four-bedroom house overlooking the water in the nicest part of Carrickfergus. He's wearing handmade suits and he's got two Picasso etchings. Our boy had some change."

We sipped our tea and thought.

"I've got one for you. From our Johnnie. He said try this out on Uncle Sean."

"Go on, then."

"Which trombonist has the highest IQ?"

"J. J. Johnson?" I said immediately, as J. J. was known to be a genius on bone.

"Glenn Miller," Crabbie said with a twinkle in his eye, which meant that we were about to receive that rarest of things, a Sergeant John Mc-Crabban joke.

"Why Glenn Miller?" I said, playing my part.

"Because Glenn Miller came up with the big band theory," Crabbie said, and like an ancient ship breaking up on a reef, his face cracked into a smile.

You couldn't help but smile back.

"That's very good. Tell Johnnie he got me."

"I will."

"There's the phone."

I picked it up, and it was yet more negation from the station.

"No sign of Quentin Townes in any database known to man," I told Crabbie.

"What about the car?"

"Still nothing."

"Maybe's he's a forger," Crabbie said, looking at the living room paintings.

I ran with the idea. "Hmmm, I like that. He forges some masterpiece; the dealer takes the picture and then hires a hit man to rub him out so that no rumors about the provenance ever leak out."

"Could be."

I shook my head. "But wouldn't there be preliminary drawings and sketches of said masterpiece? And we didn't find any of those. No sketches in the style of a lost Rembrandt."

"He burned them like he burned all his receipts and letters. He's a cautious man."

"Aye, okay, I'll run with that. So let's finish our tea and take another look at his paintings."

We went back into the conservatory, but it was as we saw the first time. Commonplace, "easy-listening" stuff. No secret masterpieces or drawings or studies for such works.

Back to the living room.

In this, his personal space, his sanctuary, he preferred other people's art.

A framed Rothko print, a very large Gauguin reproduction, a National Gallery Later Impressionists Exhibition poster, and those bloody Picassos.

"What do you think of these?" I asked Crabbie.

He lit his pipe, had a good puff, and examined them with me.

"Not really my cup of tea, Sean," he said at last.

The Picassos were of a bearded man and a woman, both nude. Not really my thing either. They were about the size of a big hardback book, and surely if they were originals they'd be worth a few quid.

I went outside to the FO, asked to borrow her Polaroid camera, came back inside, and took pictures of both Picassos.

"What did you do that for?" Crabbie asked.

"I'll show them to Archie Simmons. He'll know whether they're the real deal or not."

"Or he'll tell you they're fake, and when they're having the estate sale he'll snap them up and sell them."

Archie was, admittedly, not the most trustworthy character on the face of the earth.

I looked at the large Gaugin reproduction. It appeared to be called. *D'où Venons-Nous? Que Sommes-Nous? Où Allons-Nous?* In other words: Where do we come from? Where are we? Where are we going?

It was the usual Polynesian scene with muted colors and oddly rendered people. "Is it just me, or is Gauguin a bit shit?"

Crabbie looked at the painting. "Well, I'm no expert—"

"But you know what you like—"

"Aye."

"And these?"

"Not my sort of thing at all either. Gauguin, you say? Name rings a bell."

"Friend of Van Gogh. Left his family to become a painter and moved to the South Seas." I stifled a yawn and looked out the window. It had begun to drizzle now, and the moon was covered not by a sixpence but by dark Ulster clouds. "What time is it?"

"A quarter to twelve."

"We should head on, Crabbie," I said. "We're achieving nothing here. Check the Picasso angle in the morning."

We were just cleaning the tea mugs and about to head out the door when we bumped into the chief inspector. Unlucky us.

"I'm surprised to see you, sir. I thought you'd gone home. I would have made you some tea."

"I did go home. I came back. I bring tidings."

"Glad tidings?"

"Middling tidings. Were you lads talking about art?" he asked, casting a mildly amazed glance McCrabban's way.

"A little bit of art criticism. A little bit of conversation about jazz trombonists."

"I heard the word 'Picasso.'"

I showed him the etchings we'd been jawing about. McArthur leaned forward to touch one of them.

"Careful, sir, we think they might possibly be originals," I said.

McArthur snatched his finger back like a scolded schoolboy.

"How much is this stuff worth?" he asked, gesturing at the pictures on the walls of the living room.

"We think it's all largely worthless except for these two."

"Who is the next of kin?"

"Unfortunately, we have no idea."

"No idea?"

"We reckon the name Quentin Townes might be some sort of alias."

"Really?"

"Yes sir. When we looked for him on the electoral role, he didn't make an appearance; and when we ran his name and address through the driver's-license system, it did not show up. No credit cards, no credit history, apparently no bank account. He appeared to have no National Insurance number, and there's nothing on the Interpol computer."

"How did he pay his bills? The lights work in here, don't they?"

"Everything in cash. Got paid in cash, paid his bills in cash."

"This is quite the mystery, isn't it?" McArthur said.

"Yes. Mr. Townes doesn't seem to exist."

"Why would he do that, do you think? Pretend to be someone else?" McArthur asked.

"To avoid paying alimony to the ex-wife?" I suggested.

"Some kind of life insurance scam?" Crabbie suggested.

McArthur frowned.

"But you said you had news, sir?" I asked.

"Ah, Duffy, yes. I am indeed the bearer of tidings. They found Townes's car burned out in the Glenfield Estate. Joyridden to death, say the forensic boys, and a Molotov tossed in the back seat."

"Prints?"

"No prints. Thing was burned to an iron skeleton. They sprayed accelerant before throwing in the petrol bomb."

"Very professional of these teenage hooligans," I said with a trace of skepticism.

"The weans today are smarter than the kids of yesteryear, Sean," Crabbie said. "And these ones know that they are compromised, not just in a carjacking but also in a murder, so it's no wonder they took precautions."

"Well, I suppose we should get over there, Sergeant McCrabban. Do you, er, want to come, sir?" I added reluctantly.

"Oh, yes!" he said enthusiastically. "If I wouldn't be in the way? I could do with a lift. I walked here from the house."

The chief inspector was a gifted administrator who had gone to the police college in Hendon and finished at the top of his class. He was Scottish, better-looking and younger than both Crabbie and I, but he was bound to be disappointed to still be a chief inspector and to still be in Carrickfergus after all these years. Still, navigating failure is a useful skill to learn, especially if you live in Northern Ireland

If I had his job, I wouldn't hang around damp crime scenes at midnight if I could help it. His in-laws must be worse than I thought.

"It'll probably be quite boring, sir," I added, but he only nodded glumly and followed us outside.

We left the house and were immediately intercepted by a young copper I didn't know.

"Are you Inspector Duffy?" she asked me.

"Who's asking?" I said cautiously.

"WPC Green. You asked for the BT call logs for this address," she said, holding a piece of paper.

"This is very efficient, thank you, Constable Green," I said.

"It's nice to meet you, sir," she said. "I've heard a lot about you."

"Have you indeed?" I asked.

A bob of black curly hair was stuffed under her policewoman's kepi, and her cheeks were pale and her eyes blue. Sensing danger, McCrabban took the piece of paper from her. "Thank you very much, Constable Green," he said. "Make sure you check under your vehicle for mercury tilt switch bombs before driving back to the station."

She nodded and walked back to her car. Crabbie handed me the phone logs. They immediately got my attention because they were very strange indeed.

I showed them to the Crabman. "That's a bit odd," he said.

"What is it?" the chief inspector asked. I handed him the piece of paper and then deciphered it for him in case he was slow on the uptake.

"The home phone has been activated for about two and a half months. He's made about a hundred outgoing calls, and he's gotten about the same number of incoming calls."

"Okay."

"The incoming calls have come from paint-supply places, the electric company, a newsstand, a plumber—the usual thing. And a few of the outgoing calls have gone to places like that too but look at this number here. Almost half the incoming and outgoing calls went to the same number. A phone box on Point Road in Dundalk."

"Dundalk?"

"Dundalk," I said again.

"Okay. Is that supposed to be significant or ominous, or something?" McArthur wondered.

"Yeah, I'd say it was a little bit ominous. What would you say, Sergeant McCrabban?"

"A bit ominous, aye," he agreed.

"Why, for heaven's sake?" McArthur asked.

"Well, Dundalk is in the Irish Republic—"

"I knew that!" McArthur claimed.

"And it's where the IRA Army Council has its HQ. A lot of the top guys in the IRA have left Belfast and moved to Dundalk. It allows them to be still pretty close to the action and they can get Northern Irish TV and radio, but they're completely immune from police or army harassment."

"The SAS have been over the border a few times," McArthur protested.

"Always on lightning raids to little villages or farms contiguous to the border. Never to a big town like Dundalk," I said.

"Even the local police won't hassle them. Dundalk is an IRA stronghold. It's basically their town," Crabbie said.

"So you see, sir, if our victim was getting a lot of phone calls from a phone box on Point Road in Dundalk, it's very suspicious indeed," I said.

"Could he have been working for the IRA in some capacity?" McArthur asked.

"He could indeed," I replied, pleased to see that he was finally catching on.

"Doing what?"

"Money launderer, quartermaster, forger—anything at all, really."

"And so you're thinking there might be more to this carjacking than meets the eye."

I bloody did at that.

I patted the chief inspector on the shoulder. "Well, let's not jump to conclusions. It's something to bear in mind, though. Let's check out this burned-out Jag first."

6
THE BURNED-OUT CAR

We drove up the North Road to the Glenfield Estate, where we found a couple of forensic men I didn't know doing their last bit of work on the torched Jaguar. The car was a real mess—beautiful like an abstract sculpture or some great prehistoric beast. J. G. Ballard would have bloody loved it.

I pulled the Beemer behind the vehicle. Fire brigade foam was still blowing around the street, and there was the usual crowd of gawkers.

"I'd be very surprised if we get any solid forensic data out of that," I said, killing the engine.

Crabbie nodded and started filling his pipe again, which reminded me to take a hit on my asthma inhaler. I'd given up the smokes for two years now and my lungs were doing much better, but I still had to take the odd dose of Ventolin.

"Where are we?" McArthur asked, looking around him like a frigging tourist.

"Glenfield, sir," I replied.

"Don't think I've been here before," he said.

This was an odd part of Carrickfergus. In theory, it could have been cute up here. As the crow flies, we were just half a kilometer from my manor, Victoria Estate, but this was much more rural. Two lanes leading deep into the Irish countryside ran through the neighborhood, and a really quite lovely wood and river dominated the eastern part of the housing development. The houses were concrete-and-brick jobs built after a slash-and-burn operation in the countryside, but they weren't bad houses. Despite all that, it was a pretty bad hood. From the graffiti, it was obvious that the place was overrun with Loyalist gangs, particularly the UVF. American evangelical churches also had sprouted like toadstools, and there were several such places: the Elim Church of God, the Church of the Nazarene, the Church of the Living Christ. There were also a few bunker-like newsagents and a bookie's.

I got out of the car and turned up the collar of my jacket.

"Look at that," Crabbie said with disgust, pointing down the street.

At the junction of Carson Avenue and the Marshallstown Road, a Confederate battle flag and some kind of Waffen SS flag were being displayed from a telegraph pole.

"That's, er, a Nazi flag, is it?" the chief inspector said.

"I think so."

"Dispiriting," the chief inspector said glumly.

I looked at the burned-out Jag and talked to the FOs, but they'd found nothing. The car had apparently been swept clean of anything incriminating and then had been set on fire with the accelerant.

"What does one do now?" McArthur asked.

"We canvass for witnesses," I said.

A gang of children had gathered around the charred Jag skeleton, and Crabbie and I went through them asking if any of the wee shites knew who had dumped this vehicle in the first place. No one had seen anything. We knocked on doors, but the Belfast omertà held sway everywhere. No one knew where the car had come from; no one had seen who torched it; no one saw which direction the hijackers had fled.

Crabbie and I examined skid marks on the road next to the burned-out vehicle.

"This is interesting," I said.

Crabbie concurred, and I ordered one of the remaining FOs to take a photograph.

The chief inspector looked at the asphalt. He didn't see what we were seeing.

"It's a motorbike," I explained.

Crabbie nodded. "A big one," he added.

The chief inspector examined the skid mark. "How can you tell that?" he asked, apparently amazed by this most obvious of forensic truths.

I cleared my throat. "Well, sir, there's only one tire tread, so, er, that makes it a motorbike. And if you look at it, it's clear that he took off from here in a hurry."

Crabbie knelt to examine the tire mark more closely. When the FO professionals looked at the photos, they should be able to tell us the make, model, and maybe even year from their book of tire treads. That ability was beyond me but not, apparently, the Crabman.

"British bike," Crabbie said.

"You can tell?" I said, impressed.

"I may be wrong, but that looks like a Roadrunner Universal Grand Prix tire. Nineteen-inch wheel, of course. Four-inch width."

"For a Norton?" I asked.

Crabbie nodded. "Norton Commando, I think. FO experts will tell us for sure, of course."

"Do car thieves often ditch their burned-out vehicles and then go off on a motorbike?" McArthur asked.

"No, they don't, sir. They usually ditch the car not too far from home and then leg it."

A bunch of wee muckers had gathered to look at us now.

"Anybody get a look at the motorbike that drove away from here?" I asked.

But again: zilch.

"There's a tenner in it for anyone who can tell me what make of motorbike it was. Or maybe you lot don't know your bikes."

My clumsy attempt at bribery and reverse psychology also met with complete silence.

It began to rain a little more heavily now, and the crowd began to drift away one by one until they almost all had slipped indoors. It was probably nearly one in the bloody morning now too.

"We're done," the final FO said, and off they went in their white FO Land Rover.

The three of us were alone now in the street. The proudly flying Nazi flag and the complete lack of cooperation from the general public had greatly deflated Chief Inspector McArthur. "These people—don't they know we're here to help them?"

"Yes, sir."

"How are you supposed to solve a case without a single bloody eyewitness willing to tell us anything?"

"Welcome to my world, sir."

"And look at that horrible flag."

I walked to the Beemer, unhooked the radio mic, and ordered a tow truck for the remains of the Jag. They'd bring it to the depot and keep it there for a few weeks and then take it to the wrecking yard. We'd get nothing more out of it.

"Shall we head on, then?" Crabbie asked, looking at his watch.

"What time is it?"

"It's midnight plus forty-five."

"I've missed my ferry now for sure."

"I suppose you're staying in Ireland, then."

"I suppose I am."

McArthur cleared his throat. I caught his eye. Aye, mate, there's nothing more to do here. We CID goons are mortals just like you. I'll go back to One-Thirteen Coronation Road, and you go back to your young wife Tina and her annoying parents.

"Okay, let's hit the bricks," I was just about to say when a big, tattooed skinhead dude in a red parka came down the street toward us. He was accompanied by what could only be described as henchpeople. Three other skinhead blokes in rain gear, and a couple of skinhead girls. They were all in their teens or early twenties, and rather than looking ridiculous, they actually looked like trouble.

At their appearance on the street, some of the wee kids who

should have been in bed long before drifted back out of the shadows.

"Look at these giant soggy pork scratchings," the large skinhead dude said, to great mirth from his comrades.

"And who are you?" I asked.

"I'm Pete," Pete said. "You might have heard of me."

"I have heard of you. You denied our Lord three times after he was arrested in the garden," I said.

"What? No. What are you talking about? That wasn't me."

"Well, then, I haven't heard of you," I said.

"Pete Scanlon. This is my wee neck of the woods. And youse boys have been here long enough disturbing the peace, annoying everybody, so I think it's time youse went on home. Get me?"

"We were just about to—" McArthur began but I cut him off.

"Did you put that flag up?" I asked, pointing at the Nazi rag.

"No."

"Do you know who did?"

"No."

"Did you see who drove a Norton Commando away from that Jaguar there a couple of hours ago?"

"No."

"Well, then, Pete Scanlon, you're fucking wasting my time. Take your baldy crew and go back inside your houses, or I'll have the fucking lot of you lifted for affray."

"Who's gonna do this lifting?" he said with a pretty fair amount of menace.

"Me and my mates," I said, getting a skeptical look from McCrabban, and a *no bloody way* look from McArthur.

"This is a Young Carrick Defenders street, and you're here on it by our grace and favor, and we the residents think it's time you fucking left, peeler," Pete said.

"I'm CID. I'm investigating a murder," I explained.

"I don't care what you're investigating. If you know what's good for you, you'll fuck off," he said.

Several more scary-looking dudes had appeared from various doorways and side streets, and the mob of wee kids had increased to about twenty now.

Crabbie wasn't going to let me lose face in front of a paramilitary thug, but I could see the concern knitting his forehead. He gave me a little shake of the head that meant *leave it, Sean, it's not important. We've done what we came here to do; now let's go home.*

I took a step closer to Pete Scanlon. "The Assyrians came down like the wolf on the fold," I said.

"What?"

"And their cohorts were gleaming in purple and gold."

"Is that fact?"

"Aye, well, it's in the Bible, mate, so while not a fact as such, it is at least invested with a venerable provenance."

"You think this is Sunday school. You think you can quote Bible at us, and we'll go the fuck away?"

"It's not the Bible. It's a poem. Don't you like poetry? Here's some more: the sheen of their spears was like the stars on the sea, when the blue waves roll nightly on deep Galilee."

"What are you talking about, peeler?" he said, confused.

"Sorry, I thought you'd be interested. It's about these fucking cunts who tried to fuck with the wrong people."

"Inspector Duffy, I think we should be heading on," Chief Inspector McArthur said. The mob was still about twenty people, and the Beemer was parked facing the wrong way in the cul-de-sac. Might be hairy if it came to—

Something hard struck me on the side of the head.

Crabbie was immediately at my side, his hand reaching for his weapon in his shoulder holster.

I touched my left temple, and although I wasn't bleeding, it hurt like hell. Something shiny was rolling between my feet. I bent down and picked it up. A ball bearing.

I addressed the crowd.

"Who fired that!" I demanded.

No one said anything, but the crowd parted a little to reveal a blond kid of about fourteen years, holding a slingshot.

"Right," I began, but before I could say anything more, the wee shite took off running.

It was way beneath my dignity, and a detective really shouldn't be distracted by stuff like this, but I couldn't help myself. I reached into my pocket, took an enormous drag on my asthma inhaler, and belted off after him.

"No, Sean!" I thought I heard Crabbie yell, but it was too bloody late.

I chased the wean down Glenfield Street, where he turned and sprinted across the top road and up one of the lanes into the countryside. He was scared and fast, but I was big and angry, bearing down on him like a bull in Pamplona. I slipped, almost went arse over tit, righted myself, and ran on.

Through a bramble hedge, around an apple tree, over into a field.

Rain, mud, sheep shit, frightened sheep.

He slipped on a gate as he tried to get out of the field and went backward into the muck.

"You wee fucking turd," I said as I reached him.

"Mister, that—"

I grabbed his collar, pulled him to his feet, and slapped him on the head.

"Aow! That's police brutality, that is!"

I slapped him again.

"It's what?" I asked him.

"Police bru—"

I hit him again.

"It's what?"

"Nothing."

"That's right. Now, I've got some questions for you, and there will be a fiver in it for you if you give me the answers, and it'll be a trip to the police station for assaulting an officer if you don't. Understand?"

"A fiver?"

"A fiver if you can answer all my questions."

"All right."

"Did you see who dumped that stolen car and burned it out?"

"I seen him."

"What'd he look like?"

"He was wearing a balaclava and a brown leather jacket."

"He rode off on what?"

"A motorbike."

"What type?"

"Don't know."

"He'd parked the motorbike here earlier, drove the car here, burned out the Jag, and drove off on the bike. Am I right?"

"Aye."

"Come on, lad, what type of bike?"

"I don't know! Big loud one."

"License plate?"

"Fuck knows. It was parked behind the old offy; nobody seen it until he came roaring out on it."

"This guy—he say anything to anybody?"

"No. He just dumped the car, burned it out, put on his helmet, and rode off."

"What type of helmet? Shoei? What?"

"No idea."

"And before that, he was wearing a balaclava?"

"Aye."

"He parks the car, burns it out, and he drives off?"

"Yup."

"Nobody said boo to him?"

"He was gone in under a minute."

"Describe the bike."

"Black. Loud."

"How tall was this guy?"

"Your height. No, taller."

"Fat? Thin?"

"I don't know. Normal. Lemme go!"

That, I knew, was all I was going to get out of him. It was a miracle that I'd gotten so much. It was clever of the murderer to make the killing look like a carjacking gone wrong, it was clever of him to dump the car on this street in this neighborhood where no one would talk . . . and it was just his bad fucking luck that this wee shite had fired a ball bearing at me, and I'd gotten him away from his peers in the madding crowd.

"All right, sonny, one other question: who put that fucking Nazi flag up?"

"Jonty Reed. He's big into the Nazis, so he is."

"Where does he live?"

"Number four. House with the blue door."

I reached into my wallet and gave the wee shite a five-pound note. He took it greedily.

"No more shooting catapults at policemen. You could get yourself shot by some of my more excitable colleagues."

I turned and walked back across the field and down the muddy lane.

When I got back to Glenfield Close, Crabbie and the chief inspector were visibly relieved to see me.

"Sean, thank God, are you all right?"

"Yes, I'm fine," I said.

"Let's go, for God's sake!" McArthur said.

"One more wee bit of business first, sir," I said.

I took another discreet hit on my asthma inhaler and marched across the street to number bloody four. I rapped on the door, angry-peeler fashion. I could see that the TV was on in the living room, its blue light casting ghostly images onto the living room wall. What was on at this time of night? Some foreign film on channel four? The Open University?

"Who is it?" a cautious voice asked.

"The Old Bill."

"The who?"

"The peelers!"

"Hold on."

A white, lardy slab of a man opened the door in pajama bottoms and a white singlet. He had thick black glasses and wild brown curly hair and fading swastika tattoos. He was taller than I by about six inches, and he must have been eighteen stone. An intimidating guy if you were easily intimidated.

Behind him in the hall were a dozen new rectangular boxes marked *JVC* and *SONY*. Video cameras and VCRs.

"What do you want?" he said, grinning dementedly like Bingo from *The Banana Splits*.

"Did you put that SS flag up there?"

"Who are you?"

"Detective Inspector Sean Duffy, Carrick RUC. Did you put that flag up?"

"I did."

"Why?"

"Solidarity."

"Solidarity with what?"

"White pride. Pride in the Anglo-Saxon race."

"What the fuck is that flag supposed to be?"

"It's the genuine article. Not a reproduction, mind. Genuine. So fuck you."

"What the fuck is it?"

"SS Heimwehr Danzig. Greatest military organization the world has ever seen."

"The only thing the SS were good at was machine-gunning unarmed women and children and shoving their bodies into pits."

"Propaganda."

"All right, fuckhead, go and get a ladder and cut that fucking flag down in the next five minutes or I'm going to punch you so hard it will rip a hole in the fabric of fucking space-time."

"You wouldn't dare."

"And then once space-time has been ripped a-fucking-sunder, I'm going to find your da on the day you were conceived and kick him in the fucking nuts."

"Aye, big talk for a—"

"And then I'm going to travel back to this fucking timeline and arrest you for possession of stolen fucking goods."

"You can't fucking do any that, so you can't."

"Have you got receipts for all those video recorders in your hall there? Must be three thousand quid's worth of stuff there. That's grand larceny, mate. That's not pay-the-fine-at-the magistrate's-court. That's three years in the nick if I was to arrest you."

He looked worried now.

"But I don't have to arrest you, do I? I could use my policeman's discretion and let this all go. What do you think, my little troglodyte friend?"

"In return for what?"

"Cut that fucking flag down. In the next five fucking minutes."

"It's freedom of expression."

"Four minutes and fifty seconds."

"Look, mate, I know people. I know people in the UVF high command."

"Four minutes and forty seconds."

"All right, all right! Hold your horses! I'll get my ladder!"

He ran out the back to get his ladder, and I took the opportunity to have a wee look-see. I walked past the stolen video cameras and had a look around his living room. A bookcase full of World War II books, a Nazi naval ensign on the wall—this guy was the real deal.

He walked past me carrying a metal stepladder, and I followed him outside to the telegraph pole.

The rain had dispersed most of the crowd, but Pete Scanlon was still there with his skinhead buddies.

"What are you doing, Jonty?" Pete asked the ladder man.

"It's none of your business," Jonty replied. He leaned the ladder against the telegraph pole, climbed up, and carefully began cutting down the SS banner.

"Is he making you do that, Jonty?" Pete said. "He has no right to do that. He has no right to make you remove that or any flag."

"It's none of your business, Pete," Jonty grumbled.

"Don't give in to the peelers! They can't make you do anything. It's a free fucking country, so it is!"

"I'm not making him do anything, Peter. He's doing this of his own free will. Aren't you, young Jonathan?"

"Yes. Own free will," he said in a monotone.

He finished cutting down the SS flag and carefully brought it down the ladder with him.

"Give it to me," I said.

"That's my property, that is."

"Give it to me," I reiterated.

"What are you going to do with it?"

"I'm going to use it as the lining in my cat's litter box. It'll give me a lot of fucking pleasure knowing that my cat is pissing and shitting on a genuine Nazi flag."

Jonty's bug eyes bugged even more, and a vein bulged in his neck. Pete and his crew took a step toward us.

"The flag," I insisted.

Jonty handed over the flag. "Thank you very much. Now, just to let you know, I'll be driving through here later on this week, and if anybody five streets up or five streets down puts up any kind of Nazi flag again, I'm coming back to you. Do you understand?"

"I might not have done it!"

"No, you might not. But it's going to be your job from now on to remove any Nazi flags that appear in the neighborhood. Do you understand? If I see any of them around here, I'm coming straight to you."

Jonty nodded.

"Now, get the fuck out of my sight."

Jonty picked up his ladder and carried it back to his house.

Scanlon was flabbergasted by all this. Jonty was clearly a man of parts around here, and he was leaving the scene like a whipped dog. I threw the car keys to McCrabban. "Turn the car 'round, Crabbie, will ya?" I asked.

"Will do," Crabbie said. He looked under the Beemer for bombs and then got in the driver's seat, put the key in the ignition, and did a three-point turn.

Pete's eyes hadn't left mine.

"Let me finish that poem for you. I'm sure you're curious how it all turned out: 'For the Angel of Death spread his wings on the blast, and breathed in the face of the foe as he passed.'"

"I get the message. You think you're a hardman," Pete said.

"Last verse: And the widows of Ashur are loud in their wail, and the idols are broke in the temple of Baal . . . You get the fucking picture, Petey boy?"

Pete got the picture. "What did you say your name was?"

"Sean Duffy, formerly and now again of Carrick CID. Here's my card if you want to complain about me," I said, and handed him my card.

"There won't be any complaints, pal. But there might be a knock on your door in the middle of the night," he said.

I shook my head. "There won't be any door knocks in the middle of the night. Ask around, son. I'm fucking unkillable."

Crabbie opened the passenger's-side door of the BMW. McArthur was sitting nervously in the back, no doubt vowing never to visit another crime scene with the CID.

I got in the car, and Crabbie drove us out of the subdivision, in the direction of the North Road.

"That was absolutely horrifying," McArthur said. "Is that always how you conduct your investigations, Inspector Duffy?"

"I forget. I haven't been on an investigation in a couple of years. Is that how it usually goes down, John?"

"With you, yes, it's usually something like that," he said with the merest fractional hint of a grin on his face.

"I thought those men were going to kill you," he said.

"They weren't men. Just wee slabbers who talked the talk," I told him.

"Well, that's enough excitement for me. It's very late now," he said.

"What time is it?" I asked him.

He looked at his watch and sighed. "It's after one," he said.

"Aye, long night. Let's call it."

"Now I remember why I stay behind a desk all day," he murmured.

We drove back to the station. McArthur went home and Crabbie went home, and I typed the full report and filed the paperwork.

A long night indeed.

I finally got back to the house on Coronation Road as the sun was coming up over Scotland.

I went in through the front door and took a can of Bass from the fridge, stripped off all my clothes, and had a very quick shower.

I sipped at the Bass and caught my reflection in the steamy bathroom mirror.

"You missed all this, didn't you, you stupid bastard?"

The Duffy in the mirror did not reply, but you could tell.

He was a forty-year-old man with a wife and child. He ought to be past this nonsense. But yeah, he did bloody miss it.

We were, after all, only thinking reeds, base creatures driven by our base instincts. And one of those instincts was to follow the chase across the savanna. A million years of evolution had ingrained that in us. It was going to take another million to get rid of it.

I went downstairs to the living room and threw kindling, an old newspaper, and a peat log into the fireplace. When it was going strong, I tossed the SS flag in and watched it burn.

I got my sleeping bag and a pillow from the linen closet.

I poured myself a glass of Jura whisky.

I looked through the records and found the one I wanted: "Spiegel im Spiegel," by Arvo Part. The version I liked, with piano and viola rather than piano and cello.

I lay down on the Persian rug in front of the fireplace.

The music and the smell of the turf and the taste of fourteen-year-old single malt Jura.

I got into the sleeping bag.

In Scotland I was safe. I was a different man. A postmodern man with the postmodern sickness: *la chair est triste et j'ai lu tous les livres.* Anomie. Weltschmertz. Entzauberung. Call it what you will. In that world of garden centers and hardware barns, that world of order and safety, the fate of men was to grow fat, old, complacent, and reactionary and eventually to die.

That was there. On that side of the sheugh. But not here. Things were different here on this side of the water. Here I had purpose. Here I had a case.

"A murder case," I said aloud.

Arvo Part.

Whisky.

Nazi flag burning in fireplace.

Perfect.

And I couldn't wipe the silly grin off my face as I drifted over into sleep.

7
THE ART FORGER

Chilly living room floor. Embers long dead in the fire. Whisky bottle mercifully still more than two-thirds full.

In the sleeping bag, I caterpillared my way to the stereo. You can't really start a day with Arvo Part. Many have tried, and many a classical DJ has been fired. (At least, I hope they have.)

I flipped through the classical records, but nothing struck my fancy.

"Time for a classic," I muttered to the cat, who, of course, was in Scotland.

I thumbed through my meager collection of twelve inches (the better part of which was also in Scotland) and stuck in "Blue Monday," which would see me through the coffee- and toast-making processes and maybe a run out to the shed and back to roll a thin joint.

Coffee, toast, marmalade, raincoat, shed, Mrs. Campbell taking her washing in out of the rain.

"Hello, Mr. Duffy."

"Morning, Mrs. C."

"This is your fourth day in a row," she observed.

"Yeah, I've been temporarily seconded back into CID for the duration of a particular investigation."

"Aye the murder on the Belfast Road. Your man, the painter."

"Yes," I said. Mrs. C., as always, was very well informed.

"And no, uhm, Mrs. Duffy with you this time?" she asked, knowing very well that Beth and I were not married.

"No, Beth's staying in Scotland with Emma and the cat."

"I hope that there's not trouble in paradise?" she asked.

She unconsciously fixed a loose strand of her still brilliant copper locks back behind an ear. She was a good-looking woman, was Mrs. C, aging well despite the seven kids and the bathtub-gin habit.

"Nothing like that. Everything's fine. Just sorting out a wee joyriding case while Sergeant Lawson is on his holidays."

"If you say so," she said skeptically, carrying the washing in.

I went back inside and ate a slice of Veda bread with butter and lemon curd. If you've never eaten toasted Ormeau Veda bread with Dromona butter and homemade lemon curd, do not despair, because this is the breakfast food that you will be served in heaven.

The rain began, and I listened to it for a while and thought of dead kings.

I found a sheet of paper and wrote:

Barefoot Magnus

by the river
the water flowing backward
I am carried
on the familiar current
to the memory place
where Magnus Barefoot
King of Norway
Earl of Orkney
Lord of the Isles
was ambushed by the Ulstermen
finishing thus the Viking Age
in revenge for Bangor
and Lindisfarne

and the slaughter and the slaves.
Red Magnus, scourge of Europe
from the Russian steppe to Iceland
dead in a sheugh in darkest Ulster
his back arrowed like a hedgehog
his head lofted high on a poleaxe
and then was Magnus buried with honor on a hill
near Saint Patrick
by the River Quoile
for we, men of Ulster, so flawed in many ways
are proficient in ending things.

Not bad for a dilettante. More work required. Obviously.

I slunk into the living room with my coffee, turned on the TV, and immediately muted it again when the news came on. I went to the record player and put on REM's *Out of Time*, a terrific little album with only one dud on side 2. I had heard ominous talk at the HMV in Glasgow that REM had released *Out of Time* only as a novelty LP and that from now on their music would be available only in CD format. Which meant, of course, that I would never buy it.

"I keep telling everyone CDs are a fad," I said to the same invisible cat I had talked to earlier.

I finished my breakfast, had a shave, dressed in a black T-shirt and black jeans, and called Crabbie. He wasn't going to like what I had to say, but I needed him.

"Hello," he said.

"It's me."

"What's up, Sean?"

"You've got to come in to work this morning, mate."

"I have farm business."

"This is a priority. We're on this case. We're detectives again. We gave our word to the chief inspector."

"You gave your word."

"They're paying us time and a half until Lawson comes back.

Double time if it's after hours like last night. That would buy you your new tractor tires or pitchforks or whatever it is one needs on a farm."

"It certainly would come in useful. All right, I'll tell the wife, and if she gives the go-ahead I'll see you in half an hour."

"First order of business is probably to investigate this phone box in Dundalk."

"How are we going to do that?"

"You fancy a trip over the border?"

"No."

"Well, we'll discuss it when you come in. See you in a bit, mate."

I hung up the phone, put on a clean white shirt, pulled on my shoulder holster *avec* Glock 17, and a black leather jacket over the top of that.

Out to the Beemer. I looked underneath it for bombs, found zilch, drove up to Victoria, and instead of turning right turned left toward the new housing developments they were building up there.

It was a bold new world up here, left of Coronation Road and past the graveyard. When I'd first moved here, this was all Irish countryside, but now there was a Presbyterian church, scores of brand-new houses, a new road, and even an integrated primary school (Carrick's first), which had had the radical idea that Protestant and Catholic kids should be educated together.

Also, up here lived a guy we'd lifted for selling stolen paintings. His name was Archie Simmons, and he'd been arrested many times for dealing stolen goods out of his antique shop in Carrick. If he couldn't get stolen art, he'd forge it himself and pass it off as an original. If you ever wonder why there are just so many George William Russells or Jack B. Yeatses on the market, it's down to people like Archie. The RUC had been trying to nail him since the 1960s without much success. The most recent case against him had collapsed because the witness who had accepted a "genuine" Marc Chagall burgled from a manor house in County Down had recanted his story at the preliminary hearing, and Archie had had to be freed. This kind of thing happened all the time. In cases of art theft where there was a paramilitary dimension and provenance issues, the case often got dropped to avoid great embarrassment.

Few people wanted to admit that they'd had a forgery hanging in their living room for years.

Muddy lane, new housing development, big mock Tudor with a Merc parked outside.

I knocked on the door.

A long pause. I knocked again.

"Who is it?"

"Sean Duffy," I said.

"The policeman?"

"Aye."

"What's this about?"

"Open the door and I'll tell you."

He opened the door a crack. He was a tall, skinny old geezer with gray skin, white scruffy beard, and lank white hair. He looked near death, but he had looked like that since the first mug shot I'd seen of him, taken in 1967, so he was probably going to be one of those old dudes who would live forever.

"I haven't done nothing," Archie said in a vague English accent that sounded put on.

"I never said you did."

"Duffy, eh? I heard you jacked it in."

"I have."

"So what are you doing here at this hour of the morning?"

"I'm only working part-time," I said, and explained the circumstances that had led me to his doorstep this muggy July day. "I've got a couple of Polaroids here. What I'd like you to do is identify a couple of Picasso prints for me. Tell me if they're originals and, if so, how much they're worth."

"What do I get out of it?"

"The cops not hassling you for a few months? For instance, over the expired road tax on your Merc?"

"Show me the Polaroids," he said.

I showed him the pictures of the two Picasso prints in Mr. Townes's house.

"Oh, these are nice!" Archie said. "Come in. I'll make you a cup of tea."

I went inside Archie's house, which was stuffed with vases, paintings, and bric-a-brac. If I were a cop on the robbery squad, I could have made two great arrests in the previous twelve hours: last night in the Nazi guy's house, and this morning with all this gear.

But I had bigger fish to fry.

Archie went into the kitchen to make the tea while I flicked on the telly and caught the news. Trouble in Belfast, trouble in Derry—same old, same old.

Archie came in with a tray.

Tea, biscuits, Archie admiring the Polaroids.

"Well?" I asked.

"Like I say, these are lovely."

"Can you tell me about the provenance?"

"Not from a photo. If you could show me the real thing . . ."

"Have you got five minutes? I could run you over to the crime scene."

"Okay."

Beemer down Victoria Road to the Belfast Road. Good morning to the constable guarding the house. Through the RUC DO NOT CROSS tape and into the living room.

I took Archie to the pictures.

"What do you think?" I asked him.

"These are gorgeous."

"Genuine?"

He looked at them for a minute and nodded happily. "Without doubt. A hundred percent genuine article."

"How do you know they're genuine?"

"If the owner of these got himself murdered, who gets to inherit these little beauties?"

"We're actually having some trouble tracking the next of kin."

Archie smiled wickedly. "If you can't trace any relatives, what happens?"

"I don't know. Put them up for auction, I suppose?"

"I'd be interested in bidding in that auction."

"Hold your horses, Archie. Getting ahead of yourself. Are you going to tell me what I want to know, or are you just a big faker like everyone else? Do you actually know what these are?"

Archie bristled, and his voice assumed an odd hectoring Anglo-Irish schoolmaster-y cadence: "During his seven decades of printmaking, Picasso created five major sets of etchings. Fifteen works in The Saltimbanques Suite of 1904–1905, one hundred works in the Vollard Suite of 1930–1937, sixty works in Series 60 of 1966–1968, three hundred forty-seven works in the 347 Series of 1968, and, finally, his hundred and fifty-six works in the 156 Series of 1969–1971. These suites alone total nearly seven hundred individual images."

"Christ, you have all that in your noggin?" I asked, impressed.

"I checked while I was making your tea earlier."

"So what are these particular etchings from?"

"*Le Repos du Sculpteur*. Vollard Suite B 162. Signed. They're actually aquatints rather than true etchings, I believe."

"What is that?"

"A metal plate is covered with an acid-resistant ground, usually varnish, through which the image is drawn with a pointed tool, exposing the metal below. The plate is then immersed in a bath of acid that bites away the metal where it was exposed by the drawn areas that were no longer protected by the ground. After the plate has been "etched" and cleaned, it is ready to be inked and printed—or reworked by the artist."

"So how much—"

"I'm not done," Archie said, warming to his theme. "In the aquatint method, Picasso would draw directly on the metal plate with a black watery ink thickened by the addition of dissolved sugar and gum arabic. The drawing was then covered with an acid-resistant varnish or etching ground and immersed in warm water. This dissolves the drawing material. The plate is lightly rubbed, leaving the bare plate. The protecting varnish will still stick to the plate where the plate has not previously been treated with the ink-and-sugar mixture. A lovely process, which is why he made hundreds of the bastards."

"Hundreds? So not worth very much?"

"Oh, no, quite the reverse. These have become very collectible in the last two decades since Picasso's death."

"How much?"

"Ten grand the pair."

"Ten grand! You're joking."

"Not at all."

"But from what you're saying, it's just a print basically."

"A signed print from a very collectible series. Signed by Picasso."

"Wow. Ten grand?"

"At the right auction, yes."

"What do you think of the rest of the art in here?"

"Completely worthless. Some big reproductions and the, ahem, artist's own stuff."

"How could a hobbyist portrait painter acquire something like this?"

"He must have an independent source of wealth. Don't like to speak ill of the dead, but this guy was a complete hack."

"Are there good auction records for the Vollard Suite etchings?"

"Yes, there are. There have to be. With so many Picasso etchings floating around, the possibility of fakes has always been there. Dealers and buyers insist on a watertight provenance."

"So could you find out for me who bought these two particular—what was that word?"

"Aquatints."

"You could find out who bought these aquatints and when?"

"I could. But the question is, why would I?"

"Again, Archie, it would be helping me out. It would be helping out Carrickfergus RUC."

"Who would then stay off my bloody back until the end of the year?"

"Put it like this, Archie, if you have any trouble with the local cops until, say, Christmas, you can give me a call and I'll see what I can do. I won't help you with anything violent or a domestic, but apart from that, I'll be your man."

Archie liked the sound of that. "I'll get you that info by the end of the week."

"Sooner would be better. This is a murder investigation."

"All right, I'll see what I can do."

My nose told me this was a step in the right direction. We might not be able to find out who killed Mr. Townes, but if we could find out who bought those Picassos at auction, we might be well on the way to finding out who our victim really was.

8
THE PHONE BOX AND THE TAILOR

I told the constable guarding the crime scene that I would have him relieved shortly and ran Archie home in the Beemer.

I went into the center of town and parked the car in front of McConnell and Low real estate agents. I asked about Mr. Townes, and they confirmed that he'd been in the house rental for nearly three months. He'd paid his deposit in cash; he'd paid his rent on time, in cash.

"Don't you have to come up with references, ID, to rent a house?" I asked Mr. McConnell, an excitable young man, who was one of those walking-about, waving-his-arms-around types that you didn't see too much of in Presbyterian Ulster.

"Oh, yes, you do. But that house had been vacant for over a year like so many of the larger properties along the Belfast Road, so we were keen to get him in first."

"But he eventually showed you some ID, surely."

"Mr. Townes was from the Republic of Ireland, so he said that he would bring in his Irish driver's license and references so we could photocopy them."

"And did he?"

"Uhm, let me look through the file."

Of course, the look through the file revealed no photocopied driver's license or passport or any references. Townes had paid his rent early, had charmed everyone in the office, and seemed like a model renter, so no one had pushed him on the ID front. And if they had, the mysterious Mr. Townes would probably have furnished a fake ID anyway.

I thanked McConnell and drove to the station.

I filled Crabbie in on what I'd learned this morning.

Crabbie, who was the polar opposite of the walking-about, waving-his-arms-around type, nodded dourly and leaned back slightly in his chair.

"Bit of a sorry state of affairs that we don't know the name of the victim on day two of the investigation."

"Indeed."

I went to the whiteboard at the front of the interview room and wrote "Quentin Townes/John Doe" in big black letters. Underneath that, I drew two arrows. The first pointed to "Carjacking Gone Wrong Manslaughter"; the second pointed to "Murder." On the bottom of the whiteboard, I wrote, "Phone box, Dundalk. Tailor, Dublin. Picasso prints at auction."

Satisfied, I sat back down again. "Three lines of inquiry, Crabbie. That phone box in Dundalk, his tailor in Dublin, and the provenance of those Picassos. We'll find out who he is, and when we find out who he is, then we'll find out why they killed him," I said confidently.

"Nothing new from forensics or patho. I was just on the telephone to the medical examiner. He's sending over the preliminary report today, but it looks like what it appeared to be last night. Two shotgun blasts a few seconds apart. One in the stomach, then one in the head."

"It smells like a malice aforethought murder to me," I said. "Dumping the car and having an escape bike ready . . . But we'll have to keep an open mind."

"Naturally."

"Toxicology?"

"I put the prelim report on Lawson's desk for you. I assume you'll be using Lawson's office until he gets back?"

"I hadn't thought of that. I suppose I will."

As a part-time reservist, I no longer had an office, just a desk in the main room. But I was lead detective on this investigation now. I couldn't really run a murder case from a cubicle.

"He's still using my chair. That's a Finn Juhl chair the old CI gave me."

"I know. It's a lovely chair. Don't be afeard, Sean. You're entitled to use the office since he's not here," Crabbie said with some measure of satisfaction. Was he feeling it as well? That old hunger for the chase?

I went to the office, sat down in the Finn Juhl chair, and read the tox report, which revealed nothing. No illegal drugs, and only a moderate amount of whisky in Mr. Townes's system.

I confirmed with forensics that the tire tread was almost certainly from a Norton Commando. They were impressed that we already knew that, but they tried not to sound that way on the telephone call.

The additional info forensics had was that the tire was commonly used on Nortons from 1972 to 1977.

I checked with traffic to see if any black Norton Commandos had been stopped speeding at a checkpoint overnight—nope. Alas, you don't get that lucky.

I called up the Northern Ireland motorcycle owners' clubs and asked how many Norton Commandos there were in Northern Ireland, and a guy called Jimmy Wallace told me there were fifteen hundred Norton owners registered with the club in Ulster, and maybe another five or six hundred who weren't registered.

"How many in Ireland?" I asked.

"On all the island of Ireland, there might seven or eight thousand Nortons. It's a very popular make over here. More than in Britain, even."

"How many of them painted black?"

"The majority. In fact, it would be the unusual one that was painted any other color."

"Thanks, you've been very helpful."

I put the phone down and shook my head at the Crabman. "The bloke there says there might be eight thousand Norton Commandos in Ireland. Most of them black."

He shook his head. "That's worse than I was expecting . . . It's always worse than you were expecting."

I filled the chief inspector in on our progress, playing down the information-void stuff and playing up our more promising lines of inquiry.

After our morning coffee break, Crabbie and I drove over to Mr. Townes's house again. I had him wait in the Beemer while I said hello to the constable protecting the crime scene and went inside.

I went upstairs to the master bedroom and found Townes's clothes closet. I grabbed the other bespoke linen jacket from the rack, went downstairs, took the two Picasso etchings off the wall, and took jacket and art works out to the Beemer.

I put them all carefully in the boot.

"What are you doing with those paintings?" Crabbie asked.

"Can't leave them in the house. They're worth a few bob. I'll put them in safekeeping."

"Okay. So where to now, then?"

"Dundalk, I think, unless you have any objections."

"Not I."

"I'll stop in Newry and we can get a bite to eat if you want."

"Okay. Sounds good."

Carrick. Belfast. Newry. A roadside café where we got Ulster fries (potato bread, soda bread, fried bacon, sausage, and egg) and strong brown tea.

"How were the cows this morning?" I asked the Crabman as he lit his pipe.

"Cows are good. You get up to anything in the wee hours?" he replied.

"Actually I did. I wrote a poem," I said.

"About what?"

"A Viking king our ancestors murdered around this neck of the woods."

"You want to tell me some of it?"

"No chance."

Newry.

The stark, beautiful Mourne Mountains and then the stark, unlovely border between Northern Ireland and the Republic, which was swarming with soldiers and police. This was the main crossing point between Belfast and Dublin, and it was always a bloody nightmare.

If there had been any kind of express lane, I could have driven up it, flashed my warrant card, and driven on. But there was no express lane, and we had to wait in the queue with all the frigging civilians.

When we finally got to the front of the line, a soldier with a rifle asked to see my driver's license. I showed him my warrant card.

"DI Sean Duffy, Carrick RUC," I said.

"What's the purpose of your visit to the Irish Republic?"

"Official police business," I said.

"But what is it?"

"It's confidential, sonny," I said hoping that he wouldn't fuck with me. But he was a pale English squaddie shitting himself to be on the border, and only seventeen years old, and he wasn't going to fuck with anybody.

"Okay, over you go," he said.

I drove the Beemer south on the N1 until we got to the outskirts of Dundalk. I got a road map from the back seat, and we examined the town map of Dundalk until we found the Garda Siochana station on the Crescent, right in the center of town.

You could tell we were in the Republic of Ireland now because the police station wasn't surrounded by a bloody great antimissile wall or a sixty-foot fence that was supposed to deter the casual Molotov-cocktail thrower. This was how police stations were supposed to be. An unarmored, inoffensive little red-brick building sandwiched between the distillery and the grammar school. If your cat went missing or you had a break-in, you could just walk into the friendly police station, and the friendly unarmed police officers would help you with your problems. On our side of the border, it was an entirely different story. The police stations were all bunkers, and you had to be searched going in and out, which probably kept many punters away and—silver lining—the crime stats down.

I parked the Beemer, and we went inside (without being buzzed in or searched) and found the desk sergeant, who was not behind bulletproof glass but was, charmingly, behind an actual desk. Friendly ginger-beardy guy in glasses. They were playing music over the speakers, an easy-listening station from Dublin that was currently spinning "'74–'75" by the Connells, a song that always made me kind of depressed since 1975 was my first year in the police—the sort of life change from which there was no stepping back.

"What can I do for you gents?" the desk sergeant asked.

I showed him my warrant card and explained who I was.

"You'll be wanting the RUC liaison officer," the sergeant said in a friendly manner. "I'll take you to him."

Upstairs to the office of the RUC LO, an Inspector Thomas O'Neill, a confident, bullish mustachioed man in his forties. He sat us down in his office and, when the sergeant had gone, asked what this was all about.

I explained about our John Doe and the phone calls to the mysterious phone box on Point Road. He showed no reaction of any kind to our information, and I thought that maybe I was barking up the wrong tree with this angle.

"Does any of this mean anything to you at all?" I asked a little desperately.

"Hold on a minute," O'Neill said. He got up from behind his desk, walked across the room, and closed his office door. He sat back down at his desk and picked up the phone. "Kathy, no calls, please," he said.

"Did you drive out to Point Road this morning at all to have a look at the phone box?"

"No, we came to see you first."

"Good. That's very good. There's a house on Point Road that we have under more or less constant surveillance. I wouldn't want two RUC officers and their northern-reg car becoming part of our operation."

"Sorry, what operation? Who are you surveilling?"

"Brendan O'Roarke lives on Point Road," he said, pausing to see what reaction the name had on us.

I knew who Brendan O'Roarke was, because I'd spent much of the past three years running John Strong. The IRA Army Council thought that Strong was their highest-placed mole within the RUC, but in fact we had turned him and he was a double agent, giving the IRA largely worthless intel while gleaning what he could about the Army Council's future plans.

The latest info we had was that the IRA was split evenly down the middle. O'Roarke was one of the leaders of the "ultra" faction, who brooked no compromise at all with the British. Other prominent figures within the IRA were more amenable to talks with the UK government, especially in light of the recent electoral successes of the IRA's political wing, Sinn Fein, in Northern Ireland. Many in the IRA were coming around to the viewpoint that the way to get the British out of Ireland for good was to win the moral argument for withdrawal as Gandhi had successfully done with the British Empire in India. But Brendan O'Roarke was an old-school hardman whose model was not Gandhi's campaign in India but the campaign of the Irgun in Israel, which, with quite different tactics, had also defeated the British Empire. O'Roarke felt that the IRA didn't need to put out peace feelers; they needed to redouble their efforts to force a weary British public into an immediate withdrawal from the six counties of Northern Ireland.

That was only the beginning of the ultras' plans. Once the British left Ireland, the IRA was to take control of Dublin and form a true people's revolutionary government in Ireland on the Cuban model. Heady stuff and not remotely feasible. O'Roarke and his equally scary brothers were that most dangerous of things in Ireland: romantics.

"Brendan O'Roarke?" Crabbie asked.

"You don't know who he is?" O'Neill asked.

"Never heard of him," Crabbie said.

"Me neither," I said because without John Strong's intel, I probably wouldn't have known the names of any of the current members of the IRA Army Council. Crabbie and I were just ordinary working peelers, not privy to what was going on at the higher levels of the game . . .

"He's the biggest IRA man in town, commander of the north Leinster brigade, on the Army Council for the last ten years."

"Big shit, then?" I asked.

"Oh, yes. He's been to Libya three times in the last five years, if that means anything to you."

I nodded vaguely, although I knew exactly what that meant. Nearly every IRA bomb of the past decade had been made with Semtex from the private stores of Colonel Gaddafi. Libyan Semtex had been found in dozens of bombs all over Northern Ireland, and it was Libyan Semtex that the IRA had used in their assassination attempt on Mrs. Thatcher and that Libyan agents used to bring down Pan Am 235. But I wasn't supposed to know any of that either.

"Have you got the number for that phone box?" O'Neill asked. "And I'll see if it's one of the ones near Brendan's house."

I handed over the phone box number while he went to check.

"Sounds like we've stumbled into a solid lead," Crabbie said.

"Aye, it could be," I agreed.

O'Neill came back less than a minute later.

"As I thought, it's the phone box outside the bowling club."

"Have you tapped it? I'd love to hear what our victim was talking about with this O'Roarke bloke," I said.

O'Neill laughed. "No, no, you wouldn't get a warrant to tap a public phone box down here. It's just not done."

"Oh," I said, disappointed. We RUC men could tap any bloody phone box we wanted—and, thanks to friendly judges, pretty much any home phone too. Down here, though, it was apparently a different story.

"You haven't tapped O'Roarke's phone?"

"No. We haven't, but he can't be sure of that, so he uses several public phone boxes around town."

"And he goes to this bowling club, does he?"

"Almost every day. And he sometimes uses the phone box to call a minicab to take him home from the bowling or into town. Or at least, that's what we surmise because a minicab shows up a few minutes later."

"What sort of bowling? Tenpin?"

"Lawn."

"I thought only genteel old folks played that game."

"Well, Brendan, for one, is not exactly a genteel guy."

"Is he a killer, or more of a man behind the man?" Crabbie asked.

"He's retired from trigger pulling, but he paid his dues. We believe he was one of the shooters at Sion Mills . . ."

Crabbie and I both remembered that incident. A bus full of workers was returning from a textile plant in South Armagh. They were all blue-collar guys, all friends. Masked men from the IRA stopped the van, and the Protestant workers were separated from the Catholics then lined up against a wall and summarily machine-gunned to death. Fathers, sons, brothers, even a grandfather—innocent men whose only crime was to have been born Protestant. A few days later, the UVF murdered a group of random Catholic workers waiting for a bus, and so the cycle of hatred continued on its merry way, atrocity following atrocity as the Troubles spiraled ever downward. The men behind the Sion Mills massacre had never been caught.

"What exactly do you know about this John Doe and his phone calls?" O'Neill asked.

"We don't know anything. All we know is that our mysterious victim only made or received phone calls to that phone box on Point Road, and only that phone box called him. What do you make of that?" I said, handing over the phone records for O'Neill to look at.

"Almost all the calls were made in the morning, when Brendan probably would have been at the bowling club," O'Neill said, handing back the phone records.

O'Neill had missed the next obvious step, so I gave him a nudge. "Do you want to take these records and maybe compare them with your OP logs? Was Brendan at the club or observed making phone calls at the time my John Doe was making calls to Dundalk?" I suggested as gently as I could.

O'Neill frowned. "It'll require a bit of work, that," he said.

I reached into my wallet and showed him the crime scene Polaroid of the victim. "That's Mr. Townes."

O'Neil shook his head. "Doesn't ring any bells."

"But if you wouldn't mind showing the photograph around the station?"

"Okay."

The photograph was already with Interpol, so in theory the station should already have it. But if the coppers here were like the coppers north of the border, you rarely paid attention to those Interpol faxes and alerts.

"We have to continue to Dublin to see Mr. Townes's tailor, but we'll call back here in the afternoon. Will that give you enough to make your inquiries?" I asked, again, trying not to step on toes and being as polite as I could possibly be.

O'Neill was no dummy. He could see that I was railroading him into doing legwork for us, but he didn't mind too much. If Brendan O'Roarke was somehow mixed up in the death of an artist north of the border, it would be more grist for the mill. Sooner or later, the weight of evidence against O'Roarke would be enough to drag him into court for something, anything . . .

O'Neill smiled. "To be honest I've got nothing else going on today. This shouldn't take too long."

"That's great. We're heading on to Dub and we'll be back about three o'clock, I think."

"What's the thing about the tailor, if I may ask?"

I explained the tailor angle, and O'Neill nodded. "That's a good idea. Those old firms generally keep meticulous records," he said.

Thus encouraged, we drove down to Dub.

The Republic of Ireland was clearly booming. What everyone was now calling the Celtic Tiger economy was evident in the drive from Dundalk to north Dublin. For perhaps the first time in two hundred years, young people weren't emigrating en masse; instead, they were getting work in software development and at call centers and at the new manufacturing plants for home computers and mobile phones. Even the road itself was an impressive two-lane dual carriageway that was in the process of being turned into an even more impressive motorway, thanks to money from the European Union's Structural Fund.

We hit O'Connell Street just before noon, and I found a place to park in the Temple Bar.

The tailor's was just off Rankin Street. I got the jacket out of the Beemer's boot and looked ruefully at the Picassos.

If our car got nicked down here, there would be hell to pay.

Crabbie did his Vulcan mind-reading thing. "Car thefts aren't as common as they used to be in Dub," he said.

"I hope you're right, mate."

As we went inside the tailor's, a little bell sounded and we time-traveled back about thirty years: mannequins in tweeds, mannequins in dark three-piece suits, mannequins in blazers and hunting pink and shooting jackets. This was the place where the Anglo-Irish gentry and upmarket Dublin lawyers got their suits made. Maybe the odd rich American in love with the costumes of *The Quiet Man*.

Still, I wondered how they competed with Savile Row. Why wouldn't upmarket Dublin lawyers and the Anglo-Irish gentry just pop over to London?

I quickly found out when I looked at some of the sample prices on the sport jackets.

"Six hundred quid!" I said to Crabbie.

"This suit is a thousand," he replied in amazement.

That was how they competed with Savile Row—instead of undercutting London, they made their suits even more expensive and thus even more exclusive.

An unctuous balding young man intercepted us a third of the way into the shop. He could tell by our shoes alone that we had come to the wrong place.

"How can I help you *gentlemen*?" he asked in an ill-mannered, passive-aggressive tone that I didn't like one bit. You can fuck with me until the cows come home, but no one looks at my comrade in arms, DS John McCrabban, and puts a skeptical underscore on the word "gentlemen"—not on my goddamn watch.

"Detective Inspector Sean Duffy, Carrickfergus CID. I'm investigating the murder of one of your clients," I said, all business.

"And?"

"We have a name that is probably an alias, but it occurred to me that your tailor might recognize the cut of this particular jacket and, if he did, who this jacket was cut for."

The unctuous young man quivered for a moment. "I'll get Mr. Andre."

"Yeah, do that."

Mr. Andre appeared from a back room. He vibed mean-spirited old git from the permanent purse of his lips. He had gelled salt-and-pepper hair, and a thick crease that ran across his brows as if from years of having to look at the fashion sense of his fellow Dubliners on public transport. He was about sixty now, but you knew he'd live till he was a hundred on pure spite alone. "Which one of you is the policeman?" he asked in a posh South Dublin accent.

"We're both policemen," I said. "I'm Inspector Sean Duffy of Carrickfergus CID."

"And what do you want?"

I showed Andre the Polaroid of the dead man. "I know it's not a very good photograph, but I was wondering if you recognize this man. He was going by the name of Quentin Townes."

Mr. Andre shook his head. "I can't say that I do."

"He was probably a customer of yours," I insisted.

"We have so many customers."

"How many?"

"There are about two thousand people in our books. Quentin Townes? Hold on a sec . . ."

He darted into a back room and came back shaking his head.

"I'm sorry," he said.

"All right. Look, I know it's a bit of a long shot, but I was wondering if any of your tailors would recognize the stitching or any other sort of distinguishing mark on this particular jacket. You're the experts, aren't you? It would be really helpful."

Mr. Andre examined the jacket, and a little frown of recognition further knitted his brows for a moment.

"Hmmmm," he said.

"Does it look familiar?"

"Perhaps."

"Wow, you're good. You're maybe the only man in Dublin who could have helped us!" I said because, you know, sometimes flattery works.

"I'll ask Francis to step out. He's our tailor in chief," he said.

He went back behind the curtain, and we heard him yell, "Frankie! We need ya, so we do!" in a decidedly unposh West Belfast accent.

Frankie was a mole-like little man with thick black specs and a mess of curly gray hair. He was wearing a rumpled yellow shirt with brown slacks and black shoes. If they let him look and dress like that in this place, I reasoned, he must be very good at his job.

I showed him the jacket and asked if he could identify it.

Frankie grinned. "Your instincts were right, Inspector Duffy. Every jacket, every waistcoat, every trouser is unique," he said cheerfully in another West Belfast accent. He held a sleeve up to the light, and his smile broadened. "And yes, this is my work. Definitely. I used the 1947 Singer on this one. Oh, yes indeed."

I nodded at Crabbie. Now we were getting somewhere. "Do you think you can find out the name of the person who had this jacket made?"

Frankie thought about it. "It's quite a unique cloth. A lamb's-wool–linen blend. You don't see that much. And the stitching is definitely from the 'forty-seven. I went back to the Singer for two years in the early eighties. 1981–1983, I believe. And the cloth should be in the records somewhere . . . Can you gentlemen wait?"

"We can do that," I said excitedly.

"Why don't you retire to our waiting area. Would either of you care for a cup of tea?"

I shook my head.

"Oh, don't put yourself to any trouble on my account. Only if you're making a pot for yourself," Crabbie said, which was Ulster Presbyterian code for *I am absolutely gagging for a cup of tea.*

"I'll put a wee pot on. Follow me, gents," he said, and led us back to a smart waiting area that resembled a gentlemen's club from another era: ancient leather sofas, old copies of *Punch* and *Country Life*, dusty potted plants.

"Maybe I will take a cup of tea," I said, sitting down on a sofa that had been softened by the bums of the gentry into the most supreme state of suppleness.

"This is nice," Crabbie said.

"I could wait here all day," I agreed.

"Me too," Crabbie concurred. "Although you wouldn't want to get used to all this softness," he added quickly.

Frankie went to the back office, and I grinned at the Crabman. This was proper old-fashioned police work. We old seventies dinosaurs had survived into the 1990s—the age of computers and DNA and smart young men and women in lab coats—but breaking this case would involve legwork, asking simple questions, and hard graft.

A thin, handsome, relaxed young man brought us tea and Jacobs biscuits. We ate and drank, and I leafed through a back issue of *Punch*.

When I finished my tea, I looked at my watch. "He's been gone twenty minutes. Do you think something's amiss?" I asked Crabbie.

"I don't know," Crabbie said. "The files are probably in old ledgers. It might take a while to go through those."

Another twenty minutes passed, and Frankie came back with Mr. Andre and a trim, short older man with gray hair, gray eyes, and a sharp blue three-piece suit. He looked cross, and I could tell from his body language that something was wrong.

"Are you two gentlemen the northern police officers?" he asked.

"We are."

"And you wanted to look at our files, is that right?"

"That's right. Mr. Andre here and Frankie have kindly agreed to help us find out which of your clients had a certain jacket commissioned. Who might you be?"

"I'm Dalgetty. I'm the owner."

"Nice to meet you," I said, standing up and offering him my hand.

He did not shake it, and I was left there looking like an eejit. Dalgetty sniffed. "I'm afraid you'll need a warrant to look at our records," he said tersely.

"A warrant? This is a murder investigation."

"You'll have to get a warrant."

"We're RUC," I said.

"So?"

"So it's going to be a huge hassle for me to get a cross-border warrant. I don't even know what the correct procedure would be, exactly."

"That's not my problem."

"Look, I don't think you've completely understood. A man has been murdered and we want to identify him. We're not investigating you or your firm or anything like that. All we want to do is notify the next of kin that their relative has been murdered."

Dalgetty folded his arms and leaned back on his heels. "It doesn't matter what the reasons are. We hold the privacy of our clients to be sacrosanct. If you want to look into our records, you are going to need a warrant."

I looked at Frankie and Mr. Andre. "You found out the name, didn't you? And your boss won't let you release it to me."

Frankie stared at the floor. Mr. Andre pursed his lips and looked guilty.

"Show these gentlemen to the door, Terrence. Do not let them back into the shop unless they are accompanied by Irish police officers and a warrant," Dalgetty said.

"Bloody hell," I muttered to Crabbie outside. "The bum's rush, that was. Very unpleasant."

"Aye. But what can we do?"

"Nothing," I said, distinctly disliking this feeling of impotence. Was that what it was going to be like after I retired? To be once again a civilian, to be little people . . .

We found the Beemer unstolen, I checked that the Picassos were still in the boot (they were) and had a discreet look underneath for bombs, and we drove off. On the journey back to Dundalk, we talked over the oddness of this little interaction. Neither Crabbie nor I had ever had any dealings with top-flight suit makers before, so perhaps this level of discretion was only to be expected, but still, our peeler radar didn't like it one bit.

When I told O'Neill about it in Dundalk Garda Station, he also thought it was very peculiar.

"I'll get you a warrant if you want," O'Neill said.

"Would you?"

"Would you give us everything you find out that links your John Doe with O'Roarke?"

"Yes! Of course we will. Will a warrant be difficult?"

O'Neill shook his head. "I wouldn't have thought so. If I say it's for cross-border cooperation in a murder case, that should be enough to do the trick. I know just the judge to approach. I'll put a rush on it, and if I'm not busy later on this afternoon, I'll get down to Dublin myself and have a look through these records for you."

"Would you really do all that?"

"Not a problem, Inspector Duffy. If your John Doe was working with O'Roarke in some capacity, it'll be better to know sooner rather than later."

I shook O'Neill's hand. "That would be so helpful," I said, giving him my card and writing my home phone number on the back.

This was progress of a sort on that front, but alas, there hadn't been any luck with the photograph. O'Neill had passed the victim's image around the office, but no one recognized him. He wasn't a local player or a known associate of O'Roarke. Why he'd be calling a phone box outside a bowling club that was a known haunt of a powerful IRA warlord was, therefore, an open question.

I thanked O'Neill and all the boys at Dundalk Garda and went back out to the Beemer. It was raining now and the station car park had flooded, but still I got down on the ground and took the time to look underneath the vehicle for bombs. It wasn't completely inconceivable that the IRA had a couple of operatives or informers working in the police station, and killing a northern RUC officer in the Republic would be quite a coup.

Of course, there was no mercury tilt switch bomb, and we got inside.

On the way back to Belfast, I had a brainwave. "Hey, Crabman, you wanna swing by this famous bowling club?"

"No."

"We could get a look at the phone box and the club and the lay of the land."

"The local police don't want us anywhere near there."

"We won't get out of the car; we'll just drive by, you know?"

Crabbie shook his head and then, after a significant pause, sighed.

"What's that big sigh mean?"

"When you've got a bee in your bonnet about something, I've long since given up trying to persuade you otherwise. Let's go."

I swung the BMW around and we found Point Road. The bowling club was halfway along it, and the phone box just outside on the pavement looked green and clean and benign. Funny sort of place, Dundalk. On the surface, it couldn't have looked more suburban and gentle and dull. But this was where Cuchulainn launched his war against the queen of Connacht; this was where the Vikings invaded eastern Ulster, where the Normans stretched the boundaries of the Pale of Settlement, where Edward Bruce had himself crowned king of Ireland, where the IRA fought the Irish army for the soul of the Free State, and, today, where the Provisional IRA's northern command had its headquarters. Dundalk had strong martial traditions that went back thousands of years. Point Road, however, gave evidence of none of that. Grandfathers pushing baby strollers, women pushing shopping carts, men with pipes and tweeds and flat caps looking at stories in the *Racing Post*.

The bowling club did not exactly seethe with evil either. A well-maintained lawn, a slightly faded club facade with red brick and bay windows, roses planted along the fence.

"Looks pretty mellow to me," I said as we drove past.

"Aye," Crabbie agreed.

"Could we be barking up the wrong tree here?"

"I don't think so. It is very suspicious that our victim would call only this one particular phone box in his whole time in Carrickfergus."

"Very suspicious," I agreed. I turned the car around at the bottom of Point Road and drove past the bowling club and the phone box again. I was hoping for the old prickles on the back of the neck, or something that told me that was the nexus of foulness that had come all the way to Carrick, but there were no prickles.

"Back to Belfast?" I asked.

"I think so."

Dundalk to the border. The usual nonsense at the crossing, and then Newry. Newry to Belfast. Belfast to Carrickfergus RUC.

Up to Lawson's office with the two Picassos. No notes or new developments waiting for us in Lawson's inbox.

Not quite five. No progress on the case, but I couldn't go home yet. Some of the newer lads had heard about our Dublin trip and were keen to hear stories of the old days. I told them about my famous cannonball run to Dublin back in 'eighty-four in my then brand-new BMW 325e. Back then in Northern Ireland, we got the ads for McDonald's and Kentucky Fried Chicken and the other chains, but because of the Troubles, none of those companies had ever set up in Belfast.

"So, lads, there I was doing a hundred miles per hour down the motorway with my siren on, and Matty next to me in the passenger's seat screaming and shitting bricks, when all hell breaks loose and I see the Irish police in the rearview mirror . . ."

Crabbie came in from the bog and looked at me. Only some of that story was true, and his big sour face sucked the wind right out of me.

I finished with less aplomb than I would have liked.

When the other coppers had dispersed, I told him off. "Your face, mate—sucked the wind right out of me."

"We've other actual stories without making up more."

"They don't want the sad stories. The kids just want jokey ones."

And that was true enough. This whole society was suffering from posttraumatic stress disorder, and we weren't even *post* yet.

It was July, so it wasn't close to being dark out, but it was teatime. "You want a lift home?" I asked the Crabman.

"No need. I'm on until the wee hours. I'm duty detective, it appears," he said.

"Jesus, I'm sorry to hear that, mate."

"Oh, it's all right. I've checked with the union rep. It's double time at the full-time detective sergeant rate," he said with some satisfaction.

I did the mental arithmetic in my head. He'd be getting twenty quid an hour just to sit by the telephone. That was okay.

A knock on the door. The gleaming pink face of the chief inspector looking a little morose this evening. "Hello, Duffy, Sergeant McCrabban, I see you're back from your jaunt over the border," he said.

"Nothing escapes you, sir."

"Any developments with our case?"

Our case? Oh, crap, was he taking a personal interest in this one?

"We went down to Dundalk to check up on those phone records, and then down to Dublin to see the victim's tailor. Couple of promising leads there, I think. Excellent cooperation from Dundalk Garda, I must say."

"Good, good. So who was our victim?"

"Well, I'm afraid we still don't know that for sure yet, but like I say, we have a couple of promising leads and I'm sure we'll have this sorted in the next day or so."

"You still don't know the name of the dead man?" he asked, surprised.

"Not yet, sir. But it's nothing to worry about. We have it all well in hand."

"Superintendent MacNeice saw the story on the BBC evening news. He was asking me about it."

"Yes, well, like I say, sir, you can tell him that everything's well in hand."

He gave Crabbie and me a look that I could not quite interpret but that might perhaps be similar to the one adults give to children performing in some kind of Christmas pageant.

"And the victim's killers?"

"Nothing yet from the confidential telephone or the tip lines, but it's *very* early days yet, sir," I said.

Every amateur detective knew the old doggie that if you didn't find out who'd done it in the first twenty-four hours, then it was going to be a tricky one. And this was now hour twenty-four, and we still didn't know either who done it or who was done by it.

"Drink?" I asked the chief inspector, and he nodded, but when I opened Lawson's drinks cabinet it contained only lemonade and Coke. "Jesus," I muttered. "Sorry about this; it's all soft drinks."

"That's all right, I have to head home anyway. It's Cyril's first night of the Robins," McArthur said.

Cyril must be one of his kids, and the Robins must be some Proddy thing, I deduced with my razor-sharp police detective instincts.

"Tell Cyril good luck from me," I said.

The chief inspector left, and I slumped into the chair feeling defeated.

Life, essentially, is about managing defeat. Anybody tell you that? No? Well, you're hanging out with the wrong people from a philosophical standpoint, but maybe hanging out with the right people from a mental health standpoint. You don't want to be around Crabbie and me when things are looking bleak in a stalled case.

I swiveled in the swivel chair and stared morosely out the window.

The gestalt of this bloody case had yet to reveal itself, but I knew that something was up. Something deep. The whole thing with the tailor's shop smacked of something not quite right.

I phoned Peggy on the internal.

"Any calls for me from Dundalk Garda?"

"Nothing, Inspector Duffy. Are you expecting one?"

"Yeah, that or a fax, or something."

"I'll put the call right through if it comes."

Aye, no gestalt yet, but in the absence of hard information one shouldn't waste all one's energy sieving the well-sieved soup.

I opened the window to let the sea breeze in.

I picked up one of Lawson's paperbacks and starting thumbing through it.

It was a book about a policeman trying to solve cases in a rather nice, leafy part of England. The copper wasn't too bright, but he had somehow risen to the rank of chief inspector. All the other coppers weren't too bright either. When I saw that the copper had no idea who Hemingway was, I began to suspect that the writer might be rather posh.

I threw the book out the window and it scudded a wee shite from Internal Affairs who was here to check that we weren't fiddling our expenses. Totally worth the three quid.

I closed the window, stole some change from the vending machine change return slot, and said goodbye and good luck to McCrabban.

Out into the rain.

BMW to Victoria Estate.

I parked outside the off licence and got a bottle of twelve-year-old Port Ellen and a sixteen-year-old Laphroaig for Lawson's office. That would keep the guests happy, and if the guests didn't like peaty, oak-aged, smoky, salty, Islay whisky, then they didn't deserve to be happy in the first place.

I walked to the Victoria Hot Spot and ordered a fish supper.

Victoria Hot Spot did the best cod and chips in Carrick, perhaps the best cod and chips in the Greater Belfast Urban Area. I got the unofficial policeman's discount of 20 percent off.

"One fish supper," Irene said, handing me the packet wrapped in greaseproof paper and the *Belfast Telegraph*.

"Ta," I said, and went back outside into even heavier rain. I looked under the Beemer for bombs and drove up the hill to Coronation Road. I parked the car outside 113 and went inside.

There was a package for me in the hall that Mrs. Campbell had signed for and left inside. It was from Boosey and Hawks—the score for a new work by Alfred Schnittke that I'd inquired about.

I read it as I ate the cod and chips. It was similar to Ligeti's Étude no. 8. Depressing and melancholy but strangely exhilarating too. Schnittke had recently had a series of strokes, and this seemed to be the music one composed when waiting in death's antechamber. It was a nice piece, and I'd half a mind to take it to Bob McCawley in Victoria Gardens, who had a baby grand piano in his front room. Bob let me play his piano when the need arose, and it saved me the bother of keeping one here.

My Maoist barber also had a rather nice piano, but he never let you play in peace. Always giving you a bloody earful about Chomsky or China.

The phone rang in the hall. I swallowed a mouthful of cod and went to pick it up.

"Hello," I said.

"Inspector Duffy?"

"That's me."

"This is O'Neill. From down south."

"Oh, hello, how's things down there in God's own country?"

"Not too bad, Duffy. Listen, I tried you in your office, but they said you'd gone. I hope you don't mind me calling you at home."

"Nah, not at all. Have you got news?"

"I do, but it's not good news, I'm sorry to say."

"Oh?"

"I got a warrant easy enough from old Judge Cleary, who owes me a favor for a traffic thing, and I took two of my trainee detective constables and we went down to Dublin. We found your tailor's shop."

"So what was the problem? Was it closed?"

"It was open for business. I presented my warrant to Mr. Dalgetty, the owner, and he took me to the back office and showed me the books, and unfortunately for us, the records from 1980–1984 were destroyed in a fire. He showed me the burned ledger, and it's completely unreadable."

"A fire? I don't believe it! No one mentioned a fire to us when we were there."

"Oh, there was a fire all right. The books were ruined. He says it happened about a year ago."

"Then why didn't he tell me that today?"

"I don't know."

This was completely bogus. "Did you get the sense that they were covering something up?"

"No."

"Bloody hell, mate. Dalgetty must have been knobbled," I thought out loud.

"By whom?"

"By O'Roarke."

"But why? I mean, you'll find out your John Doe's identity eventually, won't you? What's he got to gain by intimidating a tailor?"

I considered that for a second. "Time. He'll gain time. If it takes us a day or two to find out Mr. Townes's real name, O'Roarke will gain valuable time."

"To do what?"

"I can think of a couple of things. If this is an attack on him, he can martial his forces before the news leaks out that one of his men has died, or maybe he's going to use the time to tidy up any links between the victim and himself . . ."

"Or it could just be a fire in a tailor's shop," O'Neill said pragmatically. They were a commonsense lot down in the Garda.

"Or it could just be an ordinary fire, yes," I agreed. "Well, thanks for traveling down to Dublin for me, brother. You've been a big help. Saves me another journey there tomorrow."

"Sorry I couldn't crack the case for you."

"It's okay, mate. Them's the breaks."

We said goodbye and I hung up.

My brain was in second gear. Booze would help. I made myself a vodka gimlet in a pint glass: three inches of vodka, lime juice, ice, pinch of soda water, stir, hold glass against your forehead for a bit, drink.

The vodka helped me think.

It was obvious to me, at least, what had happened. After we visited the tailor, the manager had called O'Roarke, and O'Roarke had instructed him to burn the ledger with John Doe's name in it.

I called up Crabbie at the station. I told him about the alleged fire. Crabbie was not completely convinced that O'Roarke's fingers were all over this. "Sean, O'Roarke has to know that we'll find out who John Doe is eventually. Ireland is a small island."

The rain outside grew heavier. Sheet lightning danced around the Knockagh.

"He's playing for time. Time to do something. Time to wipe something out so there's no link between John Doe and him. He's doing it right now, as we speak."

I took another gulp of the vodka gimlet. A ciggie would be great about now, but I was off the ciggies.

"Townes must have a house or an office or an offsite storage locker or a garage under another name. Something we missed," I mused.

"I ran a thorough search in all the databases for Quentin Townes and came up with nothing."

"I'm not surprised. It'll be under a pseudonym, or even—" I slapped my forehead. "No, mate, it'll be under his real name, won't it? He'll have a car and a bank balance and passports and getaway cash stored under his real name. A house or a flat here or maybe Dundalk or Dublin, under his real name."

"Maybe that's where he keeps his forged paintings too."

"Maybe," I said. "O'Roarke's minions are probably stripping that flat as we speak, and there's not a damn thing we can do about it. When we do find it, there will no be link to O'Roarke or anybody else."

A long silence down the line.

"Perhaps tomorrow we'll get a bit closer to a solution," Crabbie said.

"Aye, mate, see you in the morning . . . first thing."

"First thing," he agreed.

I stretched out on the sofa. I had the peculiar feeling of being a domino in one of those televised record-breaking domino-toppling attempts. All around me, dominoes were falling, and the line was heading inexorably toward me.

I stared at the phone.

Something told me that it was about to—

Briiiinnnggg, briiiinnnggg. Briiiinnnggg, briiiinnnggg.

I picked it up. "Duffy," I muttered.

"This is Dan Harkness."

Harkness was a Special Branch chief super in RUC intel. Highflier. He had come up with me, but his career had graphed from bottom left to top right in a pretty linear trajectory. Mine, of course, had had its ups and downs and, since John Strong's untimely demise, was pretty much flatlining . . .

"Hello, Harkness, my old friend," I said.

"*Friend* is coming it a bit strong, is it not, Duffy?"

"What can I do for you, Daniel?"

"Duffy, it's more what I can do for you."

"Oh, yeah, and what can you do for me?"

"What is it that you want, Duffy?"

"To time-travel back to 1974 and consider an entirely different career for myself?"

"Nah, what you want, Duffy, is a quiet life."

"Is that what I want, Dan? And I suppose you're going to tell me how I can go about achieving that?"

"Aye, I can."

"Go on, then. I'm all ears."

"How about, for one thing, you stop going over the border without permission from your superiors? How about, for two, you stop going over the border and liaising with Republic of Ireland police officers without permission? How about, for three, you don't stick your nose into Special Branch territory, nosing around serious fucking players like Brendan fucking O'Roarke? Maybe if you did all of that, people like me wouldn't be tempted to take a crap on you from a great height, eh?"

"Is this an official warning, then?"

"No, this isn't a warning, Duffy. This is just a friendly wee chat, that's all."

"In that case, I have to go, mate. I'm a detective on a case and I'm very bloody busy and don't really have time for friendly wee chats," I said, and hung up and walked onto the porch to look at the lightning.

I sipped the vodka gimlet, and behind me the phone rang again. It rang and rang, and eventually I had to pick it up.

"What is it now?" I asked.

Static down the line for a moment before Lawson came on. "Oh, sir! I'm so glad I reached you. I tried calling you at the office, but you were out all day."

"Lawson! Where are you?"

"Tenerife, sir. In, uhm, Spain, sir."

"I am aware where Tenerife is. Why are you trying to reach me?"

"Well, sir, I've heard the news!"

"What news?"

"There's been a murder in Carrickfergus!"

"Murders have been happening in Carrickfergus since the suspicious death of Fergus Mor Mac Erc fifteen hundred years ago."

"Well, yes . . . but . . ."

"But what, Lawson?"

"I was wondering if you wanted me to fly home early. I could do that if you needed me to. The chief inspector called me, and he said I should call you."

"The chief inspector called you?"

"Yes, sir."

"In Spain?"

"He called my father, and my father gave him the number of the hotel where I'm staying."

"*Why* did he call you?"

"Well, he wanted to let me know about the murder and to see if you needed any help with the case."

Lawson was head of Carrick CID, true, but the chief inspector should never have called him about this. I was Lawson's superior in rank, and I had conducted at least a dozen murder investigations. Did he really have so little confidence in me?

I thought back over all my previous homicide cases. In fairness to McArthur, I didn't have a single conviction, but I had found out who had done it in every single capital crime that I had investigated.

"There's no need to come home from your holidays early, Lawson. Sergeant McCrabban and I have this one very much in hand."

"Sergeant McCrabban? Uhm, aren't you both in the, uhm—"

"In the what, Lawson?"

"In the part-time reserve, sir. You're both not—"

"Real policemen anymore?"

"Oh, sir! I wouldn't say that! I would never say that. I just wondered if you needed any help from someone who, you know, is, uhm, *au fait* with the latest investigative and forensic tech—"

"No, thank you, Lawson. We'll be fine. Sergeant McCrabban and I were conducting murder inquiries when you were still in primary school, I believe."

"Oh, of course, sir. I didn't mean any offense. I, uh—"

"None taken, Lawson. Enjoy your holidays. Don't worry, we old duffers won't sully the good reputation of Carrick CID, I promise. Goodbye, Lawson."

Silence.

"Lawson?"

"Yes, sir?"

"I said goodbye."

"I know, sir . . ."

"What is it, Lawson?"

"Well, it was only that when I spoke to the chief inspector, he seemed a bit concerned that you hadn't even been able to positively ID the victim yet."

"These things take time!"

"That's what I told the chief inspector. And he said that if I wanted to cut my holiday short and come back, he would smooth it over with you, sir, but I thought that I should probably check with you first, sir."

Wow, neither of them had any faith in me at all.

I checked my reflection in the hall mirror. Did I look so much older now? Did I project an incompetent vibe? Was it the booze? Was it my reputation?

Lawson, I knew, wasn't a big drinker. Or maybe it was the relative clearance rates: under Lawson Carrick, CID's clearance rates were among the highest of all the stations in Northern Ireland . . . whereas I had run a, ahem, looser ship, sometimes letting petty offenders off with a stern warning.

"Lawson, don't worry, everything's in hand. When are you supposed to come back?"

"Sunday."

"Then come back Sunday. All is well here, okay?"

"Okay, sir. Bye, sir."

"Goodbye Lawson."

As soon as he hung up, I went into the living room, turned off the stereo, grabbed my leather jacket, and went back outside into the rain. I looked under the BMW for bombs and drove straight to Archie Simmons's house.

I parked the Beemer, ran up his path, and banged on his front door.

The light came on upstairs, and I heard him clump down the stairs.

"Who is it?" he demanded.

"Police. Sean Duffy," I said.

He opened the door. "What is it at this time of night?"

"I need answers and I need them now. Who bought those bloody Picassos?"

"Couldn't this have waited until the morning?"

"No, it couldn't."

"Well, you better come in, then," he said, looking at the clock, which claimed that it was five to midnight. Five to midnight, and the real excitement of that particular evening still lay ahead.

9
THE CARAVAN SITE

Archie tied his dressing gown tight about him, covering his whiter-than-white old man's knees.

"Do you want a cup of tea?" he asked reluctantly.

"No, no tea. I just want answers."

A twinkle glimmered in Archie's eyes. "Well, I did some digging for you, right enough."

"And?"

"I found out that the aquatints were sold at an estate sale in Enniscorrey, County Monaghan, in 1987. And what's more is that I happen to know the auctioneer. Charlie Bannion. Old friend of mine from our UCD days," he said.

"And?"

"And what?"

"So who bought the bloody paintings?"

"I don't know, but Charlie will have his record book, and all he has to do is look through it and he'll get you the customer's name. If you're buying a Picasso and you have any intention of selling it in the future, you'll want to make sure the provenance is watertight, so even if you, for example, pay in cash, you'll still give your name and add—"

"Call him."

"Call who?"

"Charlie."

"I was going to call him. I'll call him first thing in the morning."

"Call him now. Old books and old ledgers are spontaneously combusting for some reason in this case."

"It's midnight."

"Call him now!"

Archie could see the look in my eyes.

"He won't be happy—"

"I'm not happy, and you should be more worried about that, trust me. Call him now."

"All right, let me find my book."

He rummaged through his address book and called Charlie. Archie's psychic abilities proved good, and Charlie boy was not well pleased to get the call at this time of night. But when Archie told him it was an urgent police matter, he got slightly more cooperative. Clearly, Charlie, like everyone on planet Earth, had something to hide from the peelers.

I took the phone. "Mr. Bannion, this is Inspector Sean Duffy of Carrick CID. Mr. Simmons has explained the situation to you. I have to tell you that time is of the essence in this particular case. I need to know the name of the person who bought those paintings at the 1987 Enniscorrey auction as soon as is humanly possible."

"But, Inspector, my ledgers are all locked up downstairs."

"Then you'll have to go downstairs, please."

Five excruciating minutes while Bannion went downstairs and started rummaging through his books. He finally found the listing for the Enniscorrey auction and the sale of the Picassos.

"I found the auction," he said.

"Who bought the Picasso?"

"Two thousand Irish pounds each. Four thousand for the pair. The buyer, a Mr. Alan Locke."

"Address?"

"We don't have an address."

"How can you bid at an auction without an address?"

"At a country auction, all you need is the money and some form of identification."

"What was the ID?"

"It was probably the usual."

"And what's that?"

"A driving license."

"Do you happen to remember what Mr. Locke looked like?"

"No, not at all!" He laughed. "This was over five years ago."

"What else does it say in your ledger?"

"That's it, I'm afraid. Mr. Alan Locke. He's your buyer."

"Thank you, you've been very helpful."

I hung up and called Crabbie at the station.

"Carrick CID."

"Crabbie, it's me. I have a name for you. Alan Locke could be our John Doe. Could be another alias, but it might not be. Do me a favor and put the name through all the usual databases. I'll be there in ten minutes."

I thanked Archie and ran out to the Beemer.

Eighty miles per hour down Victoria Road and along the Marine Highway to the station. Upstairs to a not-exactly-joyful (Crabbie didn't really do joyful) but certainly satisfied Detective Sergeant John McCrabban.

He was holding several printouts and puffing his pipe with perhaps more enthusiasm than usual.

"Passport office, MOD records, arrest records," Crabbie said, handing me the papers.

"Photo?"

"On his Irish passport and MOD file. It's definitely him."

"MOD?"

"He was a soldier."

"Was he, now? Interesting."

I looked at the two photos first. One a grainy black-and-white of a young man in a dress uniform with, possibly, Quentin Townes's eyes and nose. Stature seemed to work, and the age worked. The passport photo taken in the 1980s was almost certainly a younger, mustachioed version of our John Doe.

"It's him, I think," I said. "What's your take?"

"It looks like him to me. We only really got to see half the face, but this doesn't look like a bad match to me."

"Same here."

"There's this thing that they do now where you give a damaged body to a sculptor and ask them to reconstruct the face. If we did that, we could compare the completed sculpture head to Mr. Locke," Crabbie said.

"That sounds very interesting. Where did you hear about this?"

"I was talking to trainee Detective Constable Warren before she went off to the CID school. Young Lawson did it on a case they were working on. He's up on all the new procedures and techniques. He's very good, so he is."

Crabbie was not trying to get my back up. Crabbie didn't really do passive-aggressive or snarky, but this praise of Lawson's apparent youthful brilliance was not what I wanted to hear when I'd just uncovered a major bloody break in the case.

"Let me see what else you've got!" I snapped at him, and instantly regretted it.

Crabbie said nothing, but his eyelids drooped a little as he handed me the printouts.

I took the various documents from him and read them fast.

Alan Locke, born in London in 1942 to an Irish mother. No listed father. Mother dies in 1948 of tuberculosis. Custody to an aunt in Dublin. He attends the Friends School in Dublin until at some point, he runs off to England, where there are no records of what he is up to until 1963, when he joins the parachute regiment. He does well in the paras, qualifying as an infantry sniper and serving in Oman, Belize, Germany. He sees combat in Oman and is awarded a Military Cross for "gallantry under fire."

"Was there some kind of war in Oman?" I asked Crabbie. "I don't know anything about that."

"I have no idea, Sean. Sorry," Crabbie said, still a bit hurt by my curtness.

Back to the report.

Locke was honorably discharged from the army in 1971 with the rank of sergeant. No records at all on him in any of the databases until 1972, when he was arrested for driving a stolen car back in County Cork. In 1973, he was arrested for possession of explosives in Drogheda. Both cases were dropped for lack of evidence. In 1975, he was named as part of a conspiracy to assassinate the Irish prime minister (shit!), but again the case was dropped for lack of evidence. In 1978, he moved to London and worked as an art dealer until 1981, when a fugitive IRA man was discovered in his house. He was arrested under the Prevention of Terrorism Act, but again there was no real evidence of wrongdoing and he was released. In 1985, he sold the house in London and moved back to Ireland, where he apparently kept his nose clean as he vanished from the criminal databases yet again.

I put down the papers and clapped Crabbie on the shoulder to break the ice.

"Wow, you did well, mate. Did you see that thing about the Irish prime minister?"

"Indeed. Heady stuff."

"I don't know about sculpting the face of our victim, but what if we took the fingerprints from one of his arrest records and compared them with . . ." I began, but I could see that Crabbie was way ahead of me.

"I've already put in a formal request for a forensic officer to do a comparison. But you know what they're like, Sean: nine-to-five types. I was able to get fingerprint records from the 1981 case, and I compared them to the records of our John Doe. I'm no forensic expert, but they look identical to me."

"I'm sure you're right, Crabbie," I said. "In 1985, he comes back to Ireland from London and then vanishes from the radar. Seven years he's been back here doing God knows what, and for the last three or four months he's been living under the alias Quentin Townes in Carrickfergus. It's fucking sinister, if you ask me."

"Are you thinking he's a player?"

"Sniper? Plot to assassinate the Irish prime minister? Illegal explosives?"

"It looks like he's never been convicted of anything," Crabbie said, always one to give his fellow humans the benefit of the doubt. "Although he's certainly had quite the interesting life."

"Until somebody shot him in the driveway of his house."

Across the incident room, WPC Babcock was marching toward us with a big smile on her face.

"What's her deal?" I asked.

"Well, I asked her to look up Alan Locke's name in all the local property registries."

"Which is exactly what I did," young Babcock said in a cheeky voice for one so young and so low on the totem pole.

"What did you find?"

"Here's something that'll cheer you both up," she said, giving me an address on a yellow legal pad. She was clearly pleased with herself.

"What's this?" I asked.

"Mr. Townes didn't have any other addresses anywhere in Carrickfergus. But a Mr. Alan Locke has a caravan on the caravan site up the New Line Road."

"You're kidding me. A caravan!"

"A caravan." She grinned.

Of course it would be the bloody caravan that nailed him. Recently, anti–Irish Traveller legislation had been enacted to cut down on illegal Gypsy and Traveller campgrounds. Now you needed watertight proof of identity to rent a caravan at official campgrounds in Northern Ireland. Most Irish Travellers and Pavee didn't have driver's licenses or passports, so they could be kicked out of these campgrounds at any time. But if Townes had wanted to park his caravan, he would have needed to produce a proper photo ID for the council busybodies—something that Mr. Quentin Townes didn't have but Mr. Alan Locke did.

"Let's get over there straightaway! Babcock, you're duty officer in charge of the station. Crabbie, you come with me."

Crabbie could see the excitement in my face. He knew what I was thinking. We had to get there first before O'Roarke's goons could get rid of any incriminating evidence.

Evidence of what?

Who the fuck knew?

"What's the address, mate?" I asked the Crabman as I maneuvered the Beemer out of the station car park.

"Lot fifteen, Clifden Park, the New Line Road, which I think is up near Woodburn Forest."

I gunned it down the Marine Highway and up the North Road. It was teeming rain, and the lightning had changed from sheet to fork, spectacularly hitting Kilroot Power Station's chimney in my rearview mirror.

In a minute, we were out of urban Carrickfergus and into the deep Irish countryside from a hundred years ago.

This part of Belfast was like that. The urban recovering war zone ended abruptly in cows, forests, dams, and hayfields from out of a postcard.

We drove up to the top road and found the caravan site easily enough on an unappealing piece of wasteland that had been cleared from the surrounding fields and woods. This seemed to be a site that had been zoned for a housing development that never quite materialized, and gradually the whole lot was returning to a state of nature with giant ferns and nettle bushes and fast-growing trees. There were about thirty caravans in all, most of them white two-person jobs but a few bigger ones for families. Despite the anti-Gypsy ordnances, this was clearly Irish Traveller territory, judging by the number of tethered goats and horses, dodgy-looking cars, and several scrambler motorcycles. The downpour and the hour were keeping any potential rough customers indoors, which was fortunate because coppers sometimes had a hard time walking around Traveller camps unmolested.

The BMW sank into the mud, and Crabbie and I got out into the freezing rain. My watch said two-fifteen in the morning.

"The odd-numbered lots seem to be on this side, the even-numbered ones on that side," Crabbie said.

"What?"

"Odd-numbered ones on this side!"

"Okay."

We began walking through the caravan site. I had the feeling that something bad was going to happen—a feeling that I attributed either to ESP or to paranoia, depending on my mood. It was also geographically dependent. If I had been in Scotland, then it would have been safe to assume that nothing bad was going to happen. If I was in Northern Ireland . . .

I drew my Glock, and Crabbie, thinking along the same lines, drew his revolver. Better safe than sorry. We were both in our civvies, though, which meant no body armor.

"There's lot nine, lot eleven," I said, counting off the caravans.

Lot number 13 was partway into the forest, and lot 15 was presumably even deeper into the edge of the wood.

"I think there's someone there," Crabbie whispered.

"Where?"

"In front of the caravan, just there!"

He was right. A tall man in black was standing outside the two-person caravan in lot 15, looking suspicious.

"I'll go on point; you stay behind me, okay?"

"No. I'll go on point, Sean. I'm wearing a dark coat, and you've got those white sneakers on."

"You're not trying to be a hero, are you, mate?"

"No, are you? Just get behind me, Sean. Come on, be sensible for once in your life," he insisted with a hint of frustration.

"Be careful, Crabbie."

We walked around the nearest caravan, and when Crabbie was twenty-five feet away from lot 15, next to an oak tree, he called me over.

"One man going in and out of the door—tall fella," he whispered.

"Just one?"

"There could be others inside."

"If O'Roarke has sent up a crash team, it could be three or four of them."

"Aye, you're right about that. So how do you want us proceed here, Sean?"

"Well, we're the good guys, so we're going to have to give them a chance to surrender, aren't we?"

"Yes, we are. I think the big, tall guy has some kind of automatic weapon strapped on him."

"Shit. All right. Careful, buddy, okay?"

"You too, Sean."

I stepped out into the rain and approached the caravan carrying the Glock in front of me in both hands. I was nervous. I looked into the woods on the left and right but didn't see any movement.

When I was fifteen feet away from Locke's caravan, I yelled, "Carrickfergus RUC! Put your hands in the air! Put your hands where I can see them!"

The man didn't hesitate for a second. He raised his AK-47, and before I could quite figure out what was happening, he began shooting those big, terrifying 7.62×39mm slugs at us.

I hit the deck (in this case mud, muck, and nettles) and screamed at Crabbie to get down.

The shooting stopped after a five-second burst, and I crawled behind the caravan in lot 13. Crabbie was crouching there beside me with his gun pointed at the caravan's edge.

"Are you hit?" Crabbie asked.

"No. You?"

"No."

"How many of them are there?"

"I don't know. I didn't see. I just dove for the bloody ground. What about you?"

"Same thing. Hit the deck. Big gun, though. Like that time in the flats in Rathcoole. Something of that order," he said phlegmatically.

That time was nearly number up for all of us. This could be too if we squibbed it.

"What do you think we should do?" Crabbie asked.

"You wait here. If anyone comes 'round that corner, shoot them."

"What are you going to do?"

"I might be able to go into the woods and flank them."

"Maybe we should get to the car and order in backup."

"If we go back that way, they'll nail us, won't they? Nah, mate, this is our only chance to—"

A scream of tires and a slew of mud coming at us as a large green Range Rover drove past.

I got to my feet. The caravan in lot 15's door was open, and there was no sign of the man, or possibly men, inside.

"Back to the car!" I yelled to Crabbie.

We ran through the mud and rain to the BMW and jumped inside. I gave Crabbie the radio mic, and he called in a roadblock alert.

"This is Sergeant McCrabban, Carrick RUC. This is a general alert. Stop all green Range Rovers in eastern County Antrim. Suspected terrorists. Suspects armed with Kalashnikov assault rifles."

While he talked to dispatch, I turned the key in the ignition. A rare time I didn't look underneath the Beemer for mercury tilt switch bombs, but this was a moot piece of carelessness as the BMW wasn't going anywhere.

The wheels spun, and the car dug itself deeper into the groove.

"Shite!"

"Try rocking it back and forth," Crabbie suggested, and I knew what he was thinking—his trusty old Land Rover Defender wouldn't have gotten stuck.

We rocked the car back and forward, but there was nothing doing.

"You try it gently in first and I'll push," I yelled at Crabbie.

He scootched over, and I ran around the back of the Beemer. I shoved the arse end of the car, but the wheels just spun and dug us deeper into the muck. This thing was going nowhere.

"No chance!" I yelled at Crabbie, and ran over to one of the scrambler motorbikes—in this case, a Kawasaki 125. I kicked the starter, and the bike sputtered. I kicked again and it roared to life.

"They went that way!" Crabbie yelled, pointing north into the countryside.

I sat down on the bike and selected first gear. The motorbike had no problem at all with the mud. Bloody loved the mud. It slewed through it in a gorgeous S curve, and I drove out of the caravan park and headed north along Woodburn Forest Road.

HANG ON ST. CHRISTOPHER

Left hand clutch, second gear, clutch again and third gear, clutch again and fourth gear. The little Kawasaki was doing sixty mph now and gripping the slick road like a trooper. The rain was battering my face, but I found the light switch and turned the headlights on and that improved visibility a little.

Deeper into the hills through the downpour.

I was soaked to my skin now. Water drenching my jeans and pouring through the gap at the top of my leather jacket.

At least there was no traffic, and nothing on either side of the road but hedges and stone walls, sheep pasture and cattle runs.

Up the New Line Road until it branched left and right. Left was the Carrickfergus Road, right was the Watch Hill Road. Fifty-fifty where they had gone. I took Watch Hill because it looked like the road less traveled.

The Watch Hill Road became something called the Ballyrickard Road, which narrowed to a single lane. We were climbing higher into the Antrim Hills, getting near the village of Kilwaughter.

Wilder country up here, fewer farms, steeper pasture not good for anything but scraggly sheep runs.

Ever ridden a motorbike *fast* at night through the rain?

You can certainly bloody imagine it. Nerves jangling, adrenaline pumping.

The no helmet was an advantage and disadvantage. No protection from the rain, but no steamy visor either.

Higher the road went, but the sweet little Kawasaki 125 loved it.

I turned a bend with the Irish Sea behind me, and there, suddenly, was the Range Rover. Up ahead about five hundred yards.

I had the bastards.

I dropped back and looked at the Kawasaki's fuel gauge. About a quarter of a tank left. I did a quick mental calculation. This thing probably had a one-gallon tank. It was a two-stroke 125, so it probably got about ninety miles to the gallon cruising, maybe seventy-five the way I was running it. Let's say eighty to allow for the little bit of extra the designers always chucked in to save you in a tight spot, and that meant I'd need to catch them in the next twenty miles or so.

Twenty miles was plenty if they were going to Belfast, but if they ran back to Dundalk tonight I'd never be able to follow them there.

The Range Rover turned onto the A8 and began heading south and west toward Belfast.

Yes!

Another thought occurred to me. If they were pros, they'd probably try to ditch the Range Rover in the city and change to another car.

I turned off the full beam on the Kawasaki's headlights and kept what I hoped was sufficient distance behind them not to attract attention. The fuel gauge hadn't moved at all, which was odd. I tapped it and the needle fell all the way to zero.

Bollocks!

No need to panic, though.

Probably just the gauge that was busted. I jiggled the tank beneath me, and I could feel fuel sloshing around in there.

Enough to get me into Belfast?

Maybe.

If they didn't run into a police roadblock, I'd flag down a passing cop car and alert the dozy bugger.

I had thought I was being careful, keeping my distance, not trying to overtake, going easy on the full beam, but they must have made me anyway. The roads were deserted at this time of night, and a solitary motorbike in the rearview just on the very edge of the mirror? Who in their right mind would set out on a journey in this fucking weather? Without a helmet? And hadn't we just driven past a bike exactly like that at the caravan site?

If they'd been more careful or less bold cleanup men, they might have tried to lose me, but as it was, with no witnesses on a country road, they tried something a bit more destructive.

They slowed the car, wound down the passenger's-side window, and gave me a burst of the AK.

Tracer lit up the asphalt, and white-hot supersonic bullets screamed all around me.

"Holy shit!"

I throttled back and slipped the bike into third.

The rear passenger window opened now, and a man in a balaclava began shooting at me methodically with a revolver.

Another burst of the Kalashnikov that tore up the road all around me with white fire.

"Shite!" I screamed as a bullet hit the headlight and ricocheted past my face. It missed me by a good nine inches, but I lost control of the bike, skidded, tried to right myself and missed the curve T. E. Lawrence style.

I tried to pull it back onto the road.

Come on!

Turn you son of—

Leaves.

Thorns.

Branches.

A wall.

Blackness.

Silence . . .

An unknown ellipsis of time.

The return of experience.

The pitter-patter of rain.

The gradual firing up of my consciousness and memory.

Dazed. Dizzy.

"Jesus," I said.

I had no idea where I was.

Car accident.

I've had a car accident in Scotland.

No, not Scotland.

Ireland.

On a case.

A case again after all this time.

I climbed out of the hedge, which had grown up over an ancient stone wall. I was cut and bruised, but nothing was broken and I appeared to be in one piece.

I'd bitten my tongue, and there was blood in my mouth.

I must have been knocked unconscious for at least five or ten minutes, and if they'd wanted to, the Range Rover men could have reversed back and finished me off. But they didn't. They just wanted to get out of here.

And get they had.

They were long gone now.

I staggered into the road.

Lights.

"Hey, hey!" I croaked, but I must have looked a right state, and the lights drove on.

Five minutes later, I tried to flag down a passing car going the other direction, but it ignored me too. A big black motorbike slowed as it got close to me, but then sped up again and drove past.

Total bastard.

I retrieved the Kawasaki, which was covered with dirt and lying upside down in the sheugh. I righted it, cleaned mud out of the spark, and kicked it. It started first time without any complaints whatever. Just try doing that with the Triumph Bonneville I was still trying to rebuild out in my shed.

The front fork was bent and there was muck in the air intake, but it moved.

I rode the Kawasaki slowly back to the caravan site, where Crabbie had called in a police forensic team from Belfast to examine Locke's trailer.

He ran over when he saw me pull up on the bike.

"I lost them," I said.

"Are you all right? Did you take a spill?" he asked with concern.

I shook my head. "I'm fine. I found them and I was trailing them, but they fucking made me in the rearview mirror. I blew it."

"What happened?"

"They fired off a burst with the AK; I lost control of the bike and went off the road. When I got my shit together, they were long gone."

"They shot at you and you went off the bike?"

"Aye."

"Are you sure you're okay?"

"I'm fine, mate. Bit shaken up if I'm honest, but okay."

"Have a seat; I'll get you some tea," Crabbie said with real concern.

"Not necessary. What's going on here?"

"I put the alert out for the Range Rover. Nothing yet."

"Update it, will you? I think the vehicle is heading for Belfast. It was last spotted on the A8."

Crabbie updated the report while I went over to the forensic tent and poured myself a cup of tea and had a couple of their biscuits. My hands were shaking, but the tea helped.

"Anything left inside the caravan?" I asked Crabbie when he returned.

"Nope. Clean as a whistle. I had a look myself while you were in pursuit. They didn't have a key. The handle smashed off and the lock chiseled out."

"What do you think was in there?"

"Guns. A lot of them. You can still smell the gun oil and the nitro, and there are half a dozen gun racks on the wall. No dust in any of the racks. So until recently, and by 'recently' I mean a few hours ago, they contained guns."

I wanted to have a look myself, but the coveralled forensic officers were very territorial.

"What sort of guns?"

"Long racks, so I'm thinking rifles, shotguns maybe. Gun oil on some of the wood. I imagine those boys you tangled with had to come and take the weapons away because they were forensically linked to various crimes."

"I expect you're right," I said.

Crabbie looked at my forehead and shook his head.

"You should get to a hospital, Sean. You're badly scraped up. And look at this. You've hurt your hand," he said with dismay.

"I'm okay. I rode back here after the accident."

"What did you do that for? You should have gone to the nearest farmhouse and called the police."

"Didn't think of that," I said.

He shook his head. "You're probably concussed. I'm taking you down to the hospital."

"No, you're not. We have an active crime scene here."

"That's enough, Sean. Forensics will report their results wherever we are. Come on. I'm taking you to the hospital. I had your car towed out of the mud."

"Look, who's in charge here? I'm not going anywhere," I said, my head spinning.

"I'm in charge. I'm relieving you of operational control, Sean. On account of incapacity. Now, come with me to the car. I'm driving."

BMW to the Shore Road.

Crabbie driving. Riding the clutch as if he owned shares in BMW replacement-clutch suppliers.

BMW to Whiteabbey Hospital.

Docs. Nurses. Crabbie doing the talking. "He's a policeman. He was chasing someone on a motorbike. They shot at him, and he went into a hedge and a bit of wall too, I think."

Wound cleaning.

Bandages.

Tetanus shot.

Head scan.

Head doc: "You took a nasty spill, but you were lucky. Nothing broken. Still, you should rest up for a few days. Avoid stress, and if you get any headaches you should come back and see me immediately."

"Thanks, Doc," I said. "I'll rest up and I'll avoid stress. And, um, what about the pain?"

"See the attending for a prescription. And remember what I said about the headaches."

"I will, Doc, thanks."

When he'd gone, I pulled Crabbie close. "Do me a favor, mate. Get a prescription for the good painkillers. And while you're at it, check with the station on the case."

"No stress, Sean. Leave the case for a bit."

"This isn't stress. I live for this."

Crabbie came back with a script for boring old codeine, and a case update. The initial forensic report on the caravan was that the place had until recently been stuffed full of guns and ammo. And Mr. Locke's fingerprints were everywhere.

Of course, despite Northern Ireland being chock-full of police and army checkpoints, the Range Rover had completely vanished. If it ever appeared again, it would be a burned-out hulk.

When the staff nurse said I was good to go, Crabbie wanted to take me home, but I insisted that we drive back up to the caravan site. We ripped away the *RUC—Do Not Cross* tape, turned on our flashlights, and peered inside the trailer.

Gun racks, all right, and the smell of grease, gun oil, and cordite was overwhelming. In a drawer, we found a dozen spent rifle casings and two paper targets that had the bull's-eyes blown out of them. I passed them to Crabbie.

"Nice wee setup he has here. All his guns and ammo in his caravan. He can separate his two worlds nicely, can't he? We would never have found out about it either except by bloody chance."

"By old-fashioned police work, Sean," Crabbie corrected.

"Indeed, yes. Old-fashioned police work."

I admired the targets some more.

"What are you thinking, Sean?" Crabbie asked.

"I'm thinking what you're thinking."

"And what's that?"

"The hit man got hit."

Crabbie nodded. "It certainly seems that way, doesn't it?"

"Alan Locke was a player. Probably an assassin. Probably working for O'Roarke."

"We can't quite make that connection, can we?"

"Question is, why? Why was he sent north by O'Roarke and living under an alias in Carrickfergus for the last few months? This top bloody soldier of one of the most dangerous men in Ireland. What was the game here?"

"I don't know."

"It wasn't to paint pictures of old ladies and their cats, that's for sure. He was a sleeper agent. Waiting for his orders. And then for some reason, the assassin himself is hit. Hit by another pro who had almost fooled us into thinking he was killed in a joyriding gone wrong. Almost."

Crabbie shook his head. "I doubt it would have fooled any half-decent detective."

"Look around you, mate. Competent detectives in the RUC? In a busy Belfast force, they would have just logged it as such. Aye, Crabbie, it was a good play by this assassin's assassin, and he would have gotten away with it if not for us meddling kids. And then O'Roarke's men come up here to this very caravan to remove the late Mr. Locke's weaponry? Sticks in the craw, mate. If we'd gotten his ID four or five hours sooner, we could have staked this place out or, at the very least, recovered guns that had been used in various murders and robberies."

"Aye," Crabbie agreed sadly.

I put the targets in a plastic evidence bag, and we closed the door and reset the *Do Not Cross* tape.

It was four-thirty in the morning now, and at this time of year that was when the sun would show its face over the Scottish hills. Today, the sun was hidden by gray clouds and rain, but it felt ridiculous to still be on the job at the beginning of a new day.

"We both need to go home and get some sleep. I'll not expect to see you in the office until the afternoon," I said to the Crabman.

A grave look blew across his features. "I won't come in until the afternoon if you promise you won't come in until the afternoon either."

"I promise," I said.

We looked at one another. Someone had fired a machine gun at us earlier. And now we were supposed to go home to our beds and sleep as if nothing had happened.

"It's a stupid job," I said. "A bloody stupid job for men of our advancing years."

"We were almost both out of it."

"Aye."

I sighed and looked at the big ganch. A man pumping hot lead at you will turn the stoniest heart philosophical. "What?" he asked.

"I'd shoot you a *What's it all about, Crabbie*? But there's no point. You'll say we have to discover God's will, and I'll say I'm not even sure there is a God running this charnel house. And then you'll say that if you believed that you'd give in to despair. And then I'll say why do you think I'm so depressed. And you'll say how does your belief in Saint Michael the Protector square with this no-God business. And I'll say well, there's more things in heaven and earth, et cetera. And you'll say well, maybe one of those things is God. And I'll say look around you, mate, does it look like a deity is in charge of this dump? And you'll say this is getting us nowhere, and I'll agree."

Crabbie nodded. "I'm glad we got that sorted."

We started walking to the car and were almost back to the Beemer when one of the older tinker kids came out to accost us about stealing his motorcycle. He was giving me a long diatribe in Shelta and Irish about police high-handedness when I recognized him as Killian, a well-known teenage car thief and con man whose police record was already as long as your arm. He was a joker and a thief, and how he had avoided a long stretch, I had no bloody idea.

"If that was *your* motorbike, I'm a Dutchman. Now, leave us alone. We need to get home to our beds," I said in Irish.

He looked shiftily about him for a moment. "Well, I'm no informer," he said to us in English.

"Go on," I said.

"I don't know anything about the man who was renting the caravan near the woods. Never spoke to anyone, except he told Joshy McDermott, who runs the site, that if anything ever went missing from his caravan he wouldn't be dealing with him, he'd be dealing with the boys from Dundalk."

"By which he meant?"

"You know what he meant."

"The IRA high command over the border."

"It wasn't a threat. It was a promise. You could see it in his eyes. And no one went near his caravan. No one so much as looked in the window."

I could see there was more. "What else?"

"Sometimes, early in the morning he'd come by the caravan and take out a long rifle and go off into the woods there and do some target practice."

I took out my notebook and tried to write this down, but after falling off a motorbike, writing wasn't as easy as it looked.

"We need to know everything about him. You're not grassing on him. He's dead. He was the man who was killed on Prospect Avenue the other night. A man who was calling himself Quentin Townes," Crabbie said.

"But whose real name was Alan Locke," I added.

"He never used either of those names here. He never used any name. But I seen him around town driving that big Jag of his."

"What else did you see, Killian?"

His eyes narrowed. He was no oil painting, and with the squinty eyes he looked a wee bit more reptilian and mean. "How much has it been worth so far?" he asked.

"Twenty quid?"

"How about fifty?"

"How about fifty if you tell us something really good," I suggested.

"The fact that he was probably IRA isn't good?"

"We knew he was IRA already. And we've already been to Dundalk asking about him," Crabbie said, and Killian could tell that Crabbie wasn't lying.

"Something good, eh?" Killian said. "What about the Norton Commando?"

"What about it?"

"It said on the news that the police were seeking the assistance of a man riding a Norton Commando, to help with their inquiries."

"And?"

"What if I was to tell you that a man riding a black Norton Commando came sniffing around here?"

Even my semiconcussed eyes lit up at that one.

"Doing what, exactly?"

"Nosing around Townes's caravan. Didn't see him break in, but you never know; he might of. It was weird. We don't get too many casual visitors or tourists around here, so I noticed him and the bike and he sort of casually walked over to your man's caravan."

"When was this?"

"Not sure, couple of days ago. Way early, when he thought everybody would be asleep. But I wasn't."

"Before the murder?"

"Aye, few days ago."

"You've good eyes, son. You get a reg of this bike?" Crabbie asked.

"Didn't think to. Sorry."

"What did this guy look like?" I asked.

"That I can tell you," he said, and paused.

I took out my wallet and counted out fifty quid. He reached out to take it and I held it back *Rockford Files* style. "This better be kosher."

He grabbed the money. "Now, admittedly, I only saw him from the back—" he began, and I made to grab the cash back, but Killian tucked it into his pocket.

"Six foot one, medium build, gingery-blond hair, pale, probably left-handed because he was carrying his bike helmet in his left hand. A Shoei helmet. He was wearing Levi's and a black motorcycle jacket," he said quickly.

"Well, that's something," Crabbie said, taking out his pipe.

"Not worth fifty quid," I muttered. I gave Killian my card. "If you see him around here again or anywhere else in Carrick, you give me a call. There's another fifty in it for you."

"It's a deal. Hey, Duffy."

"What?"

"Did you hear about the dyslexic guy who walks into a bra?"

I tried to clip him on the ear, but he had already drifted into the shadows.

Back at the station, we filed our incident reports with the duty sergeant and checked the logs to see if the Range Rover had shown up, but there was no sign of it.

The sun was now fully up over Scotland, and the traffic was increasing on the Marine Highway through Lawson's window.

"You know when I took my spill last night, a motorbike rode right past me. A black bike. A black Norton maybe. I was dazed and out of it, but maybe it was a black Norton," I said.

"Bit of a coincidence, eh?" McCrabban said.

"And you don't like coincidences, do you?"

"And neither do you," he said.

"Nope. Can't stand the bastards."

10
DEAD RECKONING

I finally hit the hay at seven-thirty a.m., and woke up four hours later fetally curled in the bed, shivering, discontented, but somehow, oddly, well rested. When I made it downstairs, I tried to call home, but Beth and Emma had left for nursery school.

The answering machine kicked in, and I left a message: "Hey, guys, all's well here. The case is going well. I'm safe. I'll come see you on the weekend if it's not all wrapped up by then."

I knew that the cat was listening to the message with chilly indifference, as was his wont. I stared out at Coronation Road. Rain was pouring out of the gutters and bucketing against the windows.

My back was covered in bruises, and it hurt like hell.

My teeth were chattering.

I tapped the thermometer on the wall. The mercury was hovering around the four degrees Celsius mark. This didn't surprise me. It would never snow at sea level at this time of year, but just about every other type of miserable weather was possible.

Downstairs, wrapped in the duvet. Open the front door. No milk. Didn't understand it. Trevor, the milkman, knew to leave me a bottle of Gold Top every day that I was staying on Coronation Road. And he knew what nights I was staying on Coronation Road, because I lifted the little flag over the milk box. I checked that the wee "Antrim Dairies" flag was raised—it was—but no milk.

"Are you looking for your milk?" a voice asked.

I looked over to the house next door. New neighbor. The house had been vacant for six months, but Mrs. Campbell on the other side said a woman had recently moved in.

This was evidently the woman.

Pretty, late twenties, black hair in a little bob, aquiline nose, blue eyes. She was wearing pajamas and fluffy slippers.

"Morning. Yes, I was looking for my milk."

"Yesterday was the last-ever delivery. Antrim Dairies are exclusively selling through the supermarkets now."

"You talked to Trevor about this?"

"Who's Trevor?"

"The milkman."

"No. Mrs. Campbell told me."

"No more milk delivery *ever*?"

"No more milk delivery," she said.

"And the bottles?"

"I think bottles are over. I think it's all cartons now."

"What'll the kids use for their Molotov cocktails?"

"That's the kind of unintentional side effect that no one ever thinks of."

I looked at her. Those eyes were really something. "If there's no milk, what are you doing outside, then?" I asked.

She waved a couple of letters at me. "There's still the post."

"Yeah, but for how much longer? Have you heard of this thing called email? First the milkman, then the postman. You'll see."

"You're quite the gloomy customer, aren't you?" she said, smiling.

I nodded and reached my hand over the fence. "Sean Duffy," I said.

"Rachel Melville."

"So what do you do, Rachel?"

"I teach English up at the new school. It's an integrated school. For Protestant and Catholic children."

"I heard about that place. What are they calling it?"

"We're calling it the Sweeney School."

"After the cop show?"

She did not smile.

"The barber, then?" I attempted.

She shook her head. "After King Sweeney, who was from around these parts."

Sweeney was the King of Dál nAraide, who ruled this neck of the woods until the Battle of Mag Rath (Moira) in AD 637. If I'd wanted to show off, I could have quoted the story of Mad Sweeney in Irish, or I could have given her Seamus Heaney's translation. I could even have given her a bit of T. S. Eliot's "Sweeney Among the Nightingales."

I did none of those things. Instead, I just smiled and nodded.

"No school today?" I asked.

"It's July."

"Oh. Yeah. The weather. Feels like bloody winter."

"What do you do?"

"I'm a part-time policeman."

"Oh, really?"

"Aye."

"I haven't seen you about much," she said.

"I'm only here six or seven days a month, normally. But I'll be around for the next week or so because I'm on a case."

"Where do you live the rest of the time?"

"Scotland."

"Nice?"

"It is nice."

"Well, lovely meeting you," she said.

"Likewise."

She took her letters and went inside.

Shame about the milkman. I would have left him a tip if I'd known it was his last day. That's what they do to you. With the one hand, they build an integrated primary school almost in your own backyard, but the other hand stops delivering milk to your door. Progress.

Good-looking woman, though. Interesting that in our brief conversation I never mentioned the fact that I had a wife (sort of) and child in that house in Scotland.

I took a step back into the hall and looked at myself in the mirror.

"Got to watch that, Duffy. I know you of old."

Mirror Duffy nodded back and said nothing. Mirror Duffy couldn't resist bragging and muttered, "The silent vertebrate in brown/contracts and concentrates, withdraws/Rachel née Rabinovitch/Tears at the grapes with murderous paws."

The really quite brilliant Anthony Julius had recently spilled a lot of ink in the *Times Literary Supplement* talking about those last two lines. Evidence, Julius suggested convincingly, of Eliot's polite but insistent anti-Semitism.

My spidey senses told me that Rachel next door was a Catholic. I wondered if she was married or single. Another line bobbed to the surface of my postconcussion brain.

"The devious-cruising *Rachel*," I said to myself. "The devious-cruising *Rachel* in her search after her missing children only found another orphan."

I showered, got dressed in a white shirt, navy blue sweater, black jeans, shit-kicking Doc Marten boots.

I made myself fried eggs, potato bread, coffee.

Looked under the Beemer for bombs.

BMW to the cop shop.

No Crabbie, so I sifted the leads and FO drops myself. The Range Rover had vanished. The AK slugs were not a match with any used in previous crimes. There was no further information on Alan Locke. He didn't have a residential address in either the Republic of Ireland or the UK.

I ran him through all the databases, and nothing came up relating to him in the past five years. He'd just more or less dropped off the radar.

No hits on our supposed teenage joyride killers either.

I called Jill Dumont at RUC Operational Research, and after going through a secretary and a bloody assistant, I was put through.

I chewed the fat and asked after her weans and got to the point, but she'd never heard of Locke. She asked why I was asking, and I told her that he was a murder victim in a case I was running in Carrick, and I thought that perhaps he was an IRA assassin.

"Then who killed him?" she asked.

"That's the question."

"Can't be the Protestant paramilitaries—they'd be celebrating the killing of an IRA iceman with fireworks and a lot of calls to the media."

"An IRA feud?"

"Again, calls to the media claiming the hit."

"So who would kill him and not call the media?"

"Two kids who tried to steal his car and things got out of hand, it looks like," Jill said, obviously having pulled up the case notes on her computer.

"It's not that, Jill; it's deeper," I said.

There was a long pause over the phone. "Well, look, you're not usually wrong about these things, Sean. If you get anything solid, I might be able to help you."

I thanked Jill and hung up.

Black clouds through Lawson's window. Black clouds over a gunmetal sea. Other news occupying the front pages now: riots in Derry, riots in Portadown, the looming British and American elections. Not interested in any of it.

In the previous couple of years since I'd had a murder case, the Cold War had ended, Thatcher had gone, Reagan had gone, the Berlin Wall had fallen, and Nirvana had kicked Michael Jackson off the charts, but here in Ireland, the men of violence kept plying their merry game.

I opened my shopping bags and put the whisky bottles in Lawson's drinks cabinet. Now he could at least offer someone a decent glass when they came to see him.

"How do?" Crabbie said, knocking on my door at lunchtime.

"I told you to come in, in the afternoon."

"It is the afternoon."

"Whisky?" I said.

"I don't think young Lawson has—"

"I stocked up for him."

We had a glass of Islay and looked at the vicious black rain squall making its way down the lough. Hail started banging off the station windows.

"If Ireland were anchored off the south coast of France rather than in the North Atlantic, I think a lot of our problems would be conveniently solved by a nice spot of sunshine," I mused.

Crabbie shook his head. "The butter from them parts is shockingly poor. My wife's sister was down there, and she said the butter was *white*. Can you believe it? White butter."

"The cheeses, though, Crabbie, the cheeses . . ."

"Aye, the cheeses," he said thoughtfully. He liked a bit of cheese, did the Crabman.

We chased leads all afternoon, but it was nothing doing.

No Norton. No Range Rover. Zilch on Locke.

The chief inspector arrived when we were gazing at the whiteboard in the incident room. All our blue arrows were pointing at Brendan O'Roarke in Dundalk.

"I heard you found out the name of your victim at last, Duffy," he said.

"We did."

"Any suspects?"

"Still pursuing leads on that front."

"Motive?"

"We're running with the theory that Locke was an IRA hit man, possibly working for Brendan O'Roarke out of Dundalk."

"And the assassin got assassinated?"

"That's our working hypothesis."

"Really?"

"It seems to point that way, sir."

"What happened to the teen-joyriding hypothesis?"

"The teen joyriders are long gone, sir. This is a bit more interesting than that."

"Interesting can sometimes be dangerous," the chief inspector said.

"Well, it's progress, sir."

"Good. Very good. Progress at last. Yes," he said with a strange, unpleasant, conspiratorial look to his face.

"Sir?"

"Hmmm," he said, practically winking at us. You could tell that he wanted us to ask him what was afoot, but this was so obvious that Crabbie and I had no problem telepathically communicating the importance of not asking him anything.

The silence lasted a full minute before the chief inspector blurted out, "Actually, I may be the source of some of your progress," he said.

I raised an eyebrow in his direction.

"What did you do, sir?"

"I called Lawson in Spain. I told him the case was up against a brick wall. And he said he'd see what he could do to help. And now, low and behold, we have the suspect's name and his whole story. Eh?"

I was aghast. Angry. "Sir, our progress has nothing to do with Lawson. Sergeant McCrabban did some old-fashioned legwork yesterday—"

He raised a hand to stop me. "Now, now, Duffy. Don't be flying off the handle because you got a little help from the new broom."

"Sir, I'd be perfectly willing to admit to Lawson's help if he had, in fact, helped, but he didn't. We found the victim's caravan ourselves. From old-school police work."

The chief inspector stood up and headed for the incident room exit. He shook his head condescendingly. "We're all on the same side, you know," he said, closing the door behind him.

I looked at Crabbie. "Do you think he's deliberately trying to get on my nerves?

"No."

"I'm calling Lawson in Spain."

"Don't do it, Sean. He's on his holidays."

"I'm bloody calling him."

I rang the number he'd given me, and they said they'd look for him at the pool. A minute went by, and a breathless Lawson came on the line.

"Oh, sir, is that you? Do you want me to fly home?"

"No. I've a question for you. *Times* crossword. 'Tragic female turning up in boys' school might be reversed.' Eight letters. It's been annoying me for the last—"

"Cosseted," Lawson said immediately.

"How do you get that?"

"If she's turning up at a boys' school, the school must be going coed and if she's a tragic female familiar to *Times* readers you just go through the list, don't you, sir? Helen, Desdemona, Juliet, Little Nell, Tess of the D'Urbervilles. And if you reverse *Tess* and sandwich it between *co* and *ed,* you get cosseted."

And the wee shite had done all that in a second.

"Very good, Lawson. Well, I'll let you go back to the pool."

"Do you need any other help?"

"We may not have your brilliance, but me and Sergeant McCrabban are old hands at this, and we've got some good leads, so I'm sure the whole thing will be settled by the time you get back."

"Are you sure?"

"I'm sure. When *are* you coming back again? Sunday?"

"Sunday evening."

"That's right. Well, we'll have it sussed by then. Enjoy the rest of your trip."

"I will, thank you, sir."

I hung up.

"That backfired a bit on you, didn't it, Sean?" Crabbie said with a slight twinkle in his eyes.

"You've become very disloyal lately."

"Sean, come on. It's like what the chief inspector says. We're all on the same side."

I picked up the phone again and called Inspector O'Neill at Dundalk Garda Station.

"Aye, Duffy, I got your fax. Very good police work. Well done, ID-ing your victim."

"Listen, O'Neill, I want you to do a favor for me."

"What?"

"I want to interview Brendan O'Roarke."

"Why?"

"One of his men got topped and I want to know why."

"We don't know that Locke was working for O'Roarke."

"We can surmise it. It was black-ops shit. He was a trained marksman. An assassin. He tried to kill the Irish PM in the seventies. He was a black-bag specialist living undercover in Northern Ireland, in my manor, and I want to know the reason for it all."

"What do your Special Branch people say?"

"They don't know shit. Look, will you ask him if he'll talk to me?"

"He's got a whole gang of high-powered Dublin, Dundalk, and Drogheda lawyers that look out for him wherever he goes."

"Nevertheless, I'd like to arrange an interview with him whenever it's convenient."

"I'll see what I can do, Sean."

"Thanks, mate."

I hung up and stared at Crabbie's long face until the big hand got its arse in gear and eventually got around to pointing at the "5."

When I went to gather my stuff in the incident room, I discovered one of the Picassos lying on the floor, where it had been knocked down by a cleaner or a clumsy copper. If I left them here, some ganch would knock a hole in them. Same story in the property room with its rising damp. I decided to take them back to 113 Coronation Road for the interim.

BMW home. Radio 3, where I hit paydirt. Arvo again, *Tabula Rasa*. Nice.

Carried the paintings inside. It could only be a temporary solution until the next of kin showed up, but a nice temporary solution. As I understood it, the *Repos du Sculpteur* series was basically a bunch of etchings of a naked bearded guy lying around his studio with a young woman. The two that Mr. Locke had were the sculptor in his bed, and another where he was sitting on a sofa. Presumably, this was an idealized Picasso with his then mistress. I hung them on the living room wall where, with the light coming in from the back garden, they looked fantastic.

Dog barking across the way.

Dog doesn't bark like that unless there's trouble.

Look out the window to see that big bloody skinhead from the other night leaving a bag of burning dog shit on my new next door neighbor's front doorstep. Obviously, this dog-shit bonfire had been aimed at me, but the skinhead was so bloody dense, he'd gotten the wrong house. His mate was waiting for him in a green Reliant Robin, which was maybe the crappiest getaway car ever devised by a human mind.

I marched out the front door and hopped the fence.

"Oi, you! Put that out!" I yelled at the guy, whose name, I remembered, was Pete something.

Pete was surprised to see me coming at him from the side. He hadn't prepared for that.

"Son, you don't have to go through life being this stupid," I said.

"What are you talking about?" Pete asked, standing up to his full height.

"This isn't my house. This is my neighbor's house."

"Isn't this number one-thirteen?"

"No. *That's* number one-thirteen. Now, pick up that bag and take it away with you."

"Or you'll—" he began, and I kicked him in the nuts.

He sank to his knees, and I two-handed clubbed him on the side of the head. I marched across the garden to the Reliant Robin and pushed the three wheeled monstrosity over onto one side.

I went back to Pete.

"Grab the shite and go. And don't come back if you don't want to deal with Bobby Cameron, who lives in that house there and who is a friend of mine."

"You know Bobby?" Pete winced.

"Aye, I do. Now, grab the shite, right your bloody wee car, and fuck off."

Pete slowly got to his feet and went to pick up the flaming bag of dog excrement, which was now a crispy disgusting mess.

"All of it," I insisted.

He cradled it in both hands and walked to his getaway car.

I helped him right the Robin and shoved him inside. "Be gone and don't come back, eejit."

"You're a big fruit, so you are," Pete said as he climbed into the car.

"And you, my friend, are a little pea. A little pea in a green quiver, oblivious to the wider currents. Things are afoot. As of today, no more milk. The post will be next, mark my words. The future is taking us along in its bow wave, son. Forget all this atavistic Nazi stuff, eh?"

"You're a maddo, pal," Pete said as they drove off.

He must have been discombobulated, for he forgot the customary finger and the "fuck you, RUC!"

"Kids today, eh?" I said to the much-calmed dog in the middle of the road.

Back inside.

Pasta. A Lou Reed bootleg from the Berlin days.

A knock at the door.

Rachel Melville.

"Hello," she said.

"Hi."

"What was all that about?" she asked, a little taken aback.

"Oh, you saw that, did you?"

"I couldn't help but see it; it was in my front yard."

"It was nothing. Just explaining the geography and power dynamics of Coronation Road to an outsider."

"Was he trying to put a bag of shit on my doorstep?"

"Apologies for that. He thought it was my doorstep. He won't be back, at least not to your house."

"Does that sort of thing happen often 'round here?"

That and much, much worse, sister. "No, not really; quiet wee street. You'll like it here."

"And yet you're leaving?" she said, gesturing toward the For Sale sign.

"Yeah, sort of have to go. Big house, three bedrooms. All I need is a wee flat down by the water, as I'm here so little."

"You sort of saved me from getting shit all over my feet."

"You could look at it that way, or you could say that I was responsible for bringing that skinhead into your orbit in the first place."

"What did you do to him?"

"It's a long story."

"Well, uhm, look, I was wondering if you weren't doing anything, if you wanted to come over for dinner."

I know what a younger Sean Duffy would have said, but the older one was just that little bit wiser.

"I just made myself pasta," I replied.

She nodded and smiled. A really fetching, groin-tightening smile. "Perhaps another time, then."

"Yeah, another time," I agreed.

She waved and went back next door.

Mirror Duffy: "You still didn't tell her about the common-law wife and bairn in Scotland, did you, Sean?"

No. I fucking didn't.

I ate the pasta, listened to the Lou Reed, and admired the Picassos in the living room. They fit the room well. I put on Miles Davis, and I stood on one foot. I reckoned I was the only person in the world listening to Miles Davis on one foot while looking at an original Picasso.

With, it must be said, a massive hard-on.

Kill the music. Kill the yoga. Go next door and fuck her brains out.

No. "No, no, no."

But maybe.

No.

Phone call.

"Sean, Emma misses you. I was wondering if—"

"I'll be right over."

Outside to the Beemer. Look underneath for bombs. No bombs. Fast down Coronation Road.

So fast I barely registered the stranger lighting a cigarette under the overhang of Mr. Benn's pigeon coop. I noticed him but I didn't process it, because I had other things on my mind just then.

I could have missed him completely because he was very good.

One of the best. And I was going fast. But I registered him and later I remembered him. That wasn't his fault. He was a professional surveillance goon standing a good hundred meters from the house, in shadow, at dusk, but he didn't know that I knew every single person who lived on this street. I knew by heart Coronation Road's geography, history, and sociology. This stretch of road (or possibly the Song Book records of Ella Fitzgerald) would be my *Mastermind* specialist subject. I had made a deep map of this place, and if anything was ever even slightly askew, I saw it.

I didn't process the man then, that night. But I would.

Coronation Road, Victoria Road, Shore Road, Motorway, Belfast, Ferry Terminal, Ferry, Stranraer, Portpatrick, home.

Squeal of brakes in through the back door.

"Emma's asleep now," Beth said.

"How are you?"

"What's that look in your eyes?"

"What look?"

"I dunno. Mad?"

"I'm fine."

"Rapey."

"Rapey?"

"Yeah, rapey. And, Jesus, is that a pistol in your pocket, or are you—"

"Both."

11
THE BREAK-IN

Next morning. Quality time with the fam. The good stuff. Kid being cute at breakfast. Making the missus her sandwiches for lunch. Listening to the chitchat and the craic while Scottish people burbled away in the background on the radio.

Ever read Epicurus? You should. Meaning-of-life stuff. Appreciating the little things isn't the road to happiness: It is happiness itself. The best we're going to get in this world, anyway.

"Joke," Emma said.

"Go on, then."

"Why don't dinosaurs clap?"

"Why?"

"'Cause they're dead."

"Okay, then, here's one for you. What's yellow and hurts when it gets in your eye?"

"What?"

"A bulldozer."

And this time, thankfully, she did laugh.

Good old Sean Duffy. Intimidating skinheads, solving a case, and doing dad jokes over breakfast. This was the good life. Right here. Right now. Didn't need to think about Rachel Melville's hair curling between her—

Walk kid to nursery school.

Hit the bricks.

Ferry terminal.

Toast and a coffee overlooking the cold north water. Ferry up Belfast Lough to the Belfast docks. Back to Carrick, upstairs to office.

Shattered.

Crabbie seeing me screech in, in the Beemer and bringing me a cup of joe.

"Cheers, mate. Any breaks in our case while I was away?"

"Were you away?"

"Aye, wee trip back over the sheugh."

"Glad to hear that, Sean. Family's the most important thing."

"It is. Anything on the case?"

"Nope. Nothing on the car or from forensics or about that bike or anything."

"What *has* been happening?"

"We had an interesting call this morning from a lawyer at the NIO. The Crown Office is asserting its right to Mr. Locke's property in light of the fact that no next of kin or a will is asserting itself."

"No will has been found?"

"Nope, and no one has come out of the woodwork claiming to be a long-lost cousin. At least not yet."

"What about Mr. O'Roarke? Locke's good buddy in Dundalk?"

"Hasn't taken any notice at all. Officially. Yet."

"But unofficially, he was up here with his gang, taking all his guns back."

"That's certainly a possibility," Crabbie agreed.

"The NIO want those bloody Picassos, don't they?"

"I imagine they do."

"They'll end up in some bloated civil servant's office in London, you mark my words," I grumbled.

"Where are they now?"

"I took them home. I found them on the bloody floor of the incident room. Someone had knocked them over."

"If they get nicked out of your home, Sean, the NIO is going to have your guts for garters."

"I know."

The chief inspector was at a conference, so in his absence we didn't have to present a case progress report and could get some real work done.

I called Detective O'Neill in Dundalk. He was a good lad who'd followed through on our conversation. He'd been around to Brendan O'Roarke's house and apprised him of my desire to have a chat. O'Roarke had said he'd think about it.

"Can't we just arrest him and drag him down to an interview room?"

"On what charge?"

"Make something up."

"We don't do that down here," O'Neill said somewhat sniffily.

"All right, mate. Well, thanks."

Another day waned.

Time strayed into the offices and nooks and crannies of Carrickfergus RUC and lingered there. Early 1990s time that hadn't quite shaken off the vibe of the 1980s yet. The Tories still ruled in London, the Republicans still owned the White House, Fianna Fáil still ruled in Dublin, and in Belfast those loudmouthed demagogues Paisley and Adams still represented the people of Ulster.

At five o'clock, I said goodbye to McCrabban and drove home to Coronation Road. The sun was out, and kids were playing kerby in the middle of the street.

Yeah, what I'd told Rachel was kosher. Coronation Road was a safe street now. There had been two attacks on my house in seven years, and that was two too many for Bobby Cameron, the local paramilitary commander. This was his neighborhood, and assassins didn't come onto his street without his say-so. He had pulled strings, and one day the council had shown to set up speed bumps every few hundred yards on Coronation Road. No more boy racers or potential drive-bys now. And after the speed bumps came the new one-way system. You could enter the street only at Victoria Primary School and you could leave it only at the top of Victoria Road. It was a lot more secure, but no system was ever foolproof. When I was staying here, I still looked under my car every morning for mercury tilt switch bombs, and I still left a thin sliver of paper wedged in the bottom of the front and back doors to see if anyone had opened one without my knowledge and was waiting for me inside.

When the paper in the front door wasn't there, I would immediately ask Mrs. Campbell if she'd been over to leave off a parcel, and the like. The five or six times I'd come back to find the sliver of paper missing from the front door had always coincided with Mrs. Campbell letting in a delivery man or the gas man or answering a persistent telephone caller.

Mrs. Campbell, however, *never* came in the back door. Her key was to the front, and she had no need or interest in coming in around the back. Since I'd been living here by myself on my part-time days, I'd *always* come back to Coronation Road and *always* found that little sliver of paper stuck in the bottom of the back door.

But not tonight.

Tonight, when I went into the washhouse at the back of the house to get some turf for the fire, the little sliver of paper I'd wedged in the door wasn't there.

"What the hell?"

I tried the back door. The door was locked, but the sliver of paper was gone. I examined the washhouse floor.

Nope.

The precautions you take to get you through life: always check under your car, embed a lock pick in your jacket sleeve, never sit with your back to a door or a window, and always check the house for break-ins.

I opened the back door, and sure enough, the paper was lying there in the garden. You wouldn't notice it if you weren't looking for it, but I noticed it because I *was* looking for it. I picked it up and examined the piece of paper. Just a random strip pulled from the *Belfast Telegraph*. Could a dog somehow have gotten into the back garden and worried out the paper from the doorjamb?

No, it bloody couldn't. And there were no bite marks.

I went next door and rang the doorbell.

Mrs. Campbell answering it in a housecoat with rollers in her hair.

"Oh, Mr. Duffy! I had no idea it was going to be you," she said, alarmed. "I'm not decent."

"You look lovely, Mrs. C. Look, I was wondering, you weren't over at the house today, were you?"

"No, not I. Why, has someone been in there? Is it the Gypsies? There's a group of Gypsies going 'round, stealing stuff. When you're out at the rag-and-bone cart, their wee boy comes down your chimney and makes off with your TV."

"How do they get the TV up the ch . . . Never mind. So you weren't over today, were you?"

"Not at all."

"Thank you."

I jumped over the fence.

"They have ropes and a pulley, Mr. Duffy. It happened to old Mrs. Anderson at the—"

"See you, Mrs. C," I said. Then I closed the front door, took the Glock out of the shoulder holster, and held it two-handed in front of me while I checked the downstairs rooms. Living room, dining room, kitchen, washhouse . . . all clear.

I went upstairs and checked the bedrooms. Those were clear too. I went into the back bedroom, which served as my office. I looked at the papers on the desk.

Apple PowerBook. Printer. The novel I'd been reading (*Oscar and Lucinda*) upside down next to the computer. From the patterns of dust on the table, it was evident that it had all been moved and then put meticulously (but not 100 percent faithfully) back.

I thought about that skinhead eejit. No, if he had come over to my house to fuck with me, he'd have smashed everything up. Shat on the living room table—that was their style.

I opened the drawer next to the desk. Someone had been through that too.

I stood up and walked away from the desk.

It was the Gene Hackman crapping himself in his apartment moment from *The Conversation*.

Someone had been in here, had gone through all my stuff, and had tried to leave as light a step as possible—and would have succeeded were

I not a paranoid git. They were pros, not the usual clumsy, inept local hoods. If I hadn't been looking, I wouldn't have seen hide or hair of them.

Who were they, and what did they want?

Was it related to the case I was working on right now?

Breaking into my house had been a hell of a thing to do.

Over the back fence and in through the back door when it was obvious I wasn't coming home.

Hmmm.

Ballsy.

What would be their next move?

You wouldn't go through my stuff, read the files on my computer, look through my books and records, and then just leave, would you? No, you wouldn't do that if you were a professional. No, you'd leave a bug, wouldn't you? Possibly on the computer or in the telephone. The computer, I'd be clueless to figure out. If he had introduced a new piece of hardware or a malicious piece of code, I'd never be able to sort that. But the phone was a different matter.

I walked downstairs and unscrewed the plastic mouthpiece from the phone. I pulled out the microphone, and there between the copper wires was a shiny new transmitter the size of a AAA battery.

A bug.

I stared at it for a while, wondering what to do.

If I took it out, they'd realize that it was missing, and they might try a more invasive way of getting me. Whoever *they* were. If they weren't after me personally (and if they were, why not just shoot me?), presumably they wanted to know about the current case I was working on. And a bug in the phone could perhaps lead them on a merry dance of disinformation.

I went into the living room and put on the radio loud to cover the sound of the Polaroid camera as I took a photograph of the bug. I put the camera down and carefully put the bug back into the phone and screwed the plastic mouthpiece back on.

I'd show the pic to Jill Dumont from RUC Special Branch Research, and maybe she'd be able to identify the device and let me know which agency or terrorist organization thought that I was worthwhile bugging.

It was odd. I'd been out of the spook game for almost a year. I had no intel, no secrets that my superiors didn't know. These days, I was a simple part-time policeman with an entirely uninteresting life. I wasn't even CID anymore.

Until this week, that was.

Until Mr. Townes.

Mr. Locke.

Yeah, talk to Jill Dumont.

I walked out to the BMW, looked underneath it for bombs, and got inside. I drove up to Belfast and out to Holywood, where the RUC Special Branch Advanced Intel Branch was headquartered. AIB for short, although all the wags called it the Allied Irish Bank.

I drove carefully and slowly, looking for tails, looking for Norton motorbikes, but there was nothing. Nick Drake was on the radio, but I couldn't even appreciate it I was so worked up.

I showed my ID at the AIB gate and got ushered through several layers of security before getting to Jill Dumont's office. I asked to see Jill, and a secretary told me to wait outside.

I looked at my watch. It was 5:05, and if this were an ordinary RUC department, everyone would have fucked off home by now. But these were Special Branch intel types, and they were used to burning the midnight oil.

Jill and I had come up together in the same class as Dan Harkness, but she and Dan had made the proper prostrations and kowtowed to all the right people, and now she was a chief superintendent in charge of intelligence and strategy. In a couple of years, they'd make her assistant chief constable, and assistant chief constables in the RUC were exactly the sort of people who got made chief constables of the smaller police forces over the water. Knighthood, 200K a year, home in Surrey, pension.

Nice.

Wait a minute: is that what you wanted, Duffy?

No, an easy life in Scotland and my 25K a year pension would do me fine. Would *have* to do me.

Her office was fantastic. Big L-shaped one overlooking the water, and outside it she had a secretary to do her typing. On the desk was a photograph of her and some skinny eejit in a suit, and three blond-haired children.

We shook hands. She'd kept herself trim, and her hair was still a vibrant golden blond cut short and styled into a wave. She was wearing her dark-green chief-super uniform with the pip and crown on both shoulders. Although she didn't want me to see it, I could see the edge of what was clearly a personnel file under some papers in front of her. *My* personnel file, which would make for some complicated reading. The disciplinary stuff, the lack of big arrests, but also Brighton in '84, the Harland and Wolff missiles in '85, and turning that fucker John Strong to work for us . . .

"Thank you for seeing me. I know you're very busy these days," I said.

"It's been a long time, Sean."

"You've done well for yourself," I said, looking about me again.

"Hard labor," she said perhaps a little bit defensively.

"I know that."

"You're looking . . ."

"Like I fell off a motorbike?"

"So what can I do for you today?" she asked.

"It's about that case I'm working on."

"The joyriders?"

"The IRA assassin."

"I hope you're not going to ask for confidential information, Sean."

"If I ask, you'll give it to me."

"Why would we do that?"

"Special Branch bloody owes me. You owe me for Thatcher, and you owe me for Strong," I said bluntly.

She sighed. "You've been told—repeatedly, I imagine—never to mention those two cases," she said.

"I didn't mention any cases. I just mentioned names: Thatcher and Strong."

"What is it that you want, Duffy?"

"I'm being surveilled."

"I often have that feeling too."

"No, I'm really being surveilled."

She sat up in her chair. "An IRA hit team?"

"My gut tells me it's maybe something more serious."

"Something more serious than an IRA hit team?"

"They broke into my house. They were very, very good about breaking into my house. I would never have noticed it in a million years except for the piece of paper I stick in the jamb at the bottom of the back door. It had moved. It had fluttered out into the back garden."

"The wind."

"It wasn't the wind. They've been through my stuff."

"Was anything taken?"

"Nothing was taken. They moved some of my papers."

"Who did, exactly?"

"That's what I want you to find out for me."

"You need the Ghostbusters, not me, Sean."

"How do you explain this, then?" I said, showing her the Polaroid I'd taken of the bug in my phone. "I was wondering if you or one of your minions would know what this is."

She looked at the picture. "Where did you find this?" she asked.

"In my telephone."

"This is in your telephone in your house?"

"That's right."

"What have you done, Sean?"

"Nothing."

"You're always pissing people off. Who have you pissed off this time?"

"Nobody. Look, what is this? Do you know what it is?"

"I know what it is. It's called a CELD-33."

"Catchy."

"It looks like a brand-new one. Brand-new. See that dirty metal bit at the top of it?"

"Yeah, what about it?"

"That's platinum. These things are expensive. A grand each."

"So . . . what? Beyond the capacity of local terrorists?"

Jill shook her head. "Dunno. Probably. And if so, you've been got at by much more dangerous customers than the local terrorists."

"MI5? I think I know how to deal with them."

"I don't think it's MI5. This particular bug . . ."

"Who, then?"

She bit her lip.

"Who?"

"Sean, you have the capacity for getting into deeper waters than you can swim in. My advice to you is to—"

"Strong. Thatcher. A lippy, aggrieved, drunken copper spilling his guts out to the Scottish papers . . ."

"Tell me that's not a threat."

"Not a threat, just something that might happen to a jaded middle-aged copper with a story to tell."

She frowned and then sighed. "The only people I know of that have this type of bug are the Special Activities Division of the CIA."

I waited to see if she was kidding, but she wasn't bloody kidding.

"I'm being bugged by the CIA?"

"Or someone who has gotten access to CIA equipment."

"Why?"

"I don't know. What have you done?"

"I haven't done anything. Not lately. The agent who I was running in the IRA is dead."

She subconsciously tapped my personnel file.

"Yes. I know. I think it's unlikely that the CIA would be interested in your agent unless there was an American dimension. Was there an American dimension in that particular case?"

"No."

"Well, then, I doubt that's it. And a lot of water has passed under the bridge in the last year."

"Why would the CIA be interested in what I'm doing now?"

"What are you doing now?"

"It's this case, Jill. You know it's something to do with this case."

I suddenly wondered if I could quite trust her. We went back, but I hadn't seen her for years, and if Sean Duffy suddenly became a problematic issue in her career path, then Sean Duffy would be gleefully tossed under the next double-decker bus.

"Tell me about the dead guy again."

"He was here under an alias, but we found out that he is a man called Alan Locke, who might be an IRA assassin."

"Yes. That's most unfortunate," she said, and added nothing further.

I stared into her gray, cold, ambitious eyes. "What's the range on one of those bugs?" I asked.

"About eight hundred meters."

"So somebody will be listening in on my phones. And that someone will need to be within an eight-hundred-meter radius of the house?"

"No. Not necessarily. It'll probably transmit to a recording device or a booster. Every time you use your phone, this will transmit the conversation to a tape recorder. The receiving equipment and the tape recorder need to be within eight hundred meters of your house, but the agent could be anywhere. The recording machine might be in the boot of a parked car two streets away from where you live. He comes along once a day, removes the tape, puts in a blank tape, and then goes back to wherever he lives. If it's a booster, he can listen live from anywhere on the shortwave band."

"So chances are, I'll never find the receiving equipment?"

"No. On the old bugs, you could use telemetry to pinpoint where the message was being received. But on these, it's not possible. The signal is broadcast over the shortwave band to anyone with the right equipment within the radius."

"What is this Special Activities Division of the CIA? I've never heard of them."

"Oh, you don't want to mess with those guys."

"Who are they?"

"It's the CIA's paramilitary arm. Very bad guys indeed. Sometimes morally questionable too. I wonder if perhaps one of them has gone rogue and . . ."

"Given high-tech surveillance equipment to the IRA to further the cause?"

"I never said that."

"No, I did."

"Look, Duffy, are you having me on here? Did you really find this in your phone?"

"I really did."

"Well, then, you should report it."

"To whom?"

"To your superior officer. To your divisional officer."

I considered that and shook my head. "You know what they'd do. They'd take the bug out and analyze and tell me what you've told me."

"And by not reporting it?"

"I can lead the person or people bugging me a merry dance if I want. No, not yet. I don't want to jeopardize an ongoing investigation."

"If the IRA has stolen a batch of CIA surveillance equipment, this is something that should be investigated at the highest levels!" Jill insisted.

"And if the CIA *gave* them the surveillance equipment?"

She said nothing and shuffled her papers. I picked up the Polaroid and put it back in my jacket pocket.

"If you're not going to say anything about this, I will," she said.

"No. You won't. If this case fucks up because you blabbed, I'll make sure everybody knows about it."

"If it fucks up and you get killed because the IRA have access to new technology, then what?"

"You can say I told you so to me at my wake."

She shook her head. "You have one week, Duffy, and then I'm calling you on this."

I nodded. "Okay. A week. A man can do a lot in a week. Now, do me a favor and tell me what you know about Brendan O'Roarke."

"Like what?"

"Like everything. I'll wait while you get the files."

"I don't need the files. O'Roarke is a major player. Real hardliner. The realest of the hardliners. His father and mother were both old Republicans. His father fought the British and then Michael Collins and then DeValera. He was interned during World War Two, so he was probably hot and heavy with the Nazis too. Brendan and his older brother, Jim, were the only two boys out of a family of seven. The girls all married and had normal lives, but Jim and Brendan were IRA lifers. Jim is in France somewhere, we think. On the run for a bank robbery in Wexford that resulted in the death of a Garda officer and a civilian. Raising money for the cause, mind you, not for himself."

"And what does Brendan do?"

"Brendan is in the building trade by day, and he's the IRA's north Leinster commandant by night."

"Brendan wasn't in the Army Council a year ago," I said, stating this plain fact that I knew from my agent-handling days with John Strong. John had had to brief the Army Council once a month on what he knew about the latest RUC operational intelligence. But since we—I—turned him, John had been giving them the chickenshit and trying to get actionable intelligence in return. Jill clearly knew all about that, because she didn't bring it up but again subconsciously touched my file.

"Things have been moving very quickly in the last six months," she said. "Big shake-up in the movement. No one really knows why. Or if they do, they're not telling us in Special Branch. Old guard out, new guard in. New guard primarily from the north. Belfast, Derry, and Dundalk men pushing out the old Dublin players."

"A more hardline approach to the war?"

Jill was warming to her theme and becoming a little less tight-lipped. Get anyone on one of their hobbyhorses and they couldn't help but ride that subject . . .

"You'd think that, Sean," she said. "But actually, it looks like the opposite is happening. Again, I'm not privy to all the facts, but it looks like northern moderates have taken over the IRA Army Council. Brendan O'Roarke has been given the job of chief of staff to assure the old guard that the new boys haven't gone completely soft. Brendan's solid. Brendan, everyone knows, is the man who will never compromise."

"Is he a killer?"

"Not him personally. Not since the early seventies. Not his style. He's not a button man, he's an organizer. It was Brendan who cemented the IRA's valuable links to Libya, traveling to Tripoli many times in the early

1980s and securing at least five big weapons shipments from Gaddafi. I don't have to remind you that it was Gaddafi's Semtex that was used in the Brighton bomb, at Enniskillen, and so on."

"Would Brendan have a personal hit man that he was keeping off the books?"

"Wouldn't surprise me."

"To what end?"

"Your guess is as good as mine. Brendan O'Roarke is known to be ruthless. Clinical. And now that he's at the top of the food chain, he can pretty much have anyone in Ireland killed at any time."

"As long as the IRA Army Council gives the go-ahead."

"I imagine they would. Brendan is a very persuasive and scary man."

"But they'd still have to vote on it."

"Yes . . . What are you thinking, Sean?"

"I'm thinking what if Brendan wasn't happy with these new peace feelers? What if Brendan wanted to cement his control of the IRA Army Council and take it over completely? He'd have to eliminate a lot of troublesome people in the north, wouldn't he?"

"It would be very difficult. People like Gerry Adams and Martin McGuinness are very cautious and—"

"He'd have to kill them all at once. Night of the Long Knives–style. He would need hit men in situ ready to go at a moment's notice."

"Hit men like your murder victim?"

"Exactly."

Jill shook her head. "No, I don't see it. And why bug you? Why not just kill you?"

"They want to know how much I know first."

"Hmmm. I'll have to think about all of this."

I got to my feet. "You do that."

She tapped my personnel file a third time. "You're just a couple of years from your pension, Sean. Perhaps consider letting sleeping dogs lie, go back to Scotland and—"

"You're all the same, aren't you? Sleeping dogs. Don't kick up a fuss. Read that personnel file again. Does that sound like me?"

12
THE KILL LIST

I drove back to Coronation Road with more questions than answers. Could the IRA or some other terrorist group really have stolen CIA equipment? Was the American government backing the IRA in some sort of secret arrangement? This seemed very unlikely. President Bush and the British government were tight, but maybe it was a rogue unit or a rogue individual within the CIA.

And would Brendan O'Roarke's personal hit man really be hiding in a nondescript house in Carrickfergus? And who would have the balls to kill Brendan O'Roarke's personal hit man, if not an ignorant and foolish teenage joyrider?

Thirty years ago, the Jesuits had explained the concept of Occam's razor to me. *Explained* here being a synonym for *beat the concept into me with a leather strap:* All things being equal, the simplest explanation is probably the correct one.

Locke was killed by a couple of hopped-up kids looking for a car. True, he was not a portrait painter but an IRA assassin working for Brendan O'Roarke, but even IRA assassins could have their share of bad luck.

But the motorbike . . .

And the bug . . .

I listened to classic FM (late Schubert Lieder, done by the London Symphony Orchestra—excellent) and drank Bass and thought about everything for far too long and then, exhausted, went off to bed.

I found Crabbie at the station early.

I motioned him into Lawson's office, closed the door, and told him everything I knew.

"Are you sure they're bugging you?"

"I'm sure. Jill was sure."

"Could it be that UVF commander who lives on your street? He could have broken into your house and stuck that in your phone."

"I suppose it could be, but Jill says this is a brand-new piece of tech. Unlikely that he could have got his hands on something like that."

We mulled ideas and plans over a glass of Islay, but nothing jumped out at us.

"Until I formally call this in to Special Branch, don't give out any case information over my home phone, okay?" I said.

"Okay. Good idea."

"And here's a wee thing I've been cooking up: maybe, we can use this to entrap our listeners somehow," I said vaguely.

"How?"

"Thinking out loud here. You call me and say there's been a major break in the case at some kind of prepared isolated location. I say great and we drive over there, and we wait for a Norton 750 to show up?"

Crabbie shook his head. "I don't know," he said dubiously.

"Yeah, you're right, it's shite. But let's keep it in our back pocket, eh? There must be some way we can use this to our advantage. We're smart and we're old hands at this game."

Another look from McCrabban that did not exactly inspire confidence.

The hour hand slunk around the dial until it pointed to the big "12" at the top. Lunch of shepherd's pie at Ownies followed by just one pint of the black stuff each.

By four o'clock and with no new developments, I was for heading home. "Well, I guess I'm off, Crabman," I said. "Coming?"

"I can't. I'm on duty again—we've got those trainees in for the night."

"What trainees?"

"They weren't supposed to arrive until after Lawson got back, but they've come early."

"Oh, bollocks. That's all we need. And we have to look after them?"

"So the chief inspector says."

I shook my head. "Fuck 'em. This isn't our job. We're the invisible men. The part-timers. The old geezers in the corner coming in a few days a month to get their pensions. Banquo and Banquo's even more banjaxed ghosty friend."

"The chief inspector had a wee chat with me and said I had to babysit them until Lawson got back."

"Aye, he would come to you. He knows I'd tell him where to go."

"Any ideas what to do with them?"

"They're here right now in the building?" I asked, appalled.

"Aye. That's them over there," he said, pointing through the window to a brown-haired woman with glasses, green jeans, and a bright-red sweater. With her were two spotty youths in bad suits and pointy shoes. Both men had had their hair dyed blond and gelled into spikes. One had grown a soul patch.

Crabbie could see my immediate and visceral loathing for them.

"You go home, Sean," he said quickly. "I'll think of something to do with them."

"They've got plenty of book learning," I said. "Now give them some wisdom."

"Like what?"

"I'll never forget the last words my grandfather said to me."

"What did he say?"

"Stop shaking the ladder, you wee shite!"

Crabbie sighed and shook his head. He couldn't believe he had fallen for this obvious setup. Your guard goes down when you see your mates only seven days a month.

I put on my jacket and walked out to the car. An idea hit me, and I walked back into the incident room, where Crabbie had gathered the newbies for a lecture.

"Sean, what—"

"How about you take our trainees back to the crime scene. I've never been completely satisfied that we found everything that could be found in Locke's house or at his bloody secret caravan."

"Fieldwork. Great idea, Sean," Crabbie said with perhaps faked enthusiasm.

"I mean, just because forensics says they can't find anything doesn't mean *we* have to stop looking, does it?"

"No," Crabbie agreed.

"Are you Sean Duffy?" the kid with the soul patch asked.

"Yes, I'm *Detective Inspector* Sean Duffy. You are?"

"William Mitchell."

The other two felt compelled to tell me their names: Judy something and Patrick something.

"We studied one of your cases on our course," Mitchell said.

"Oh, really? Which case?" I asked.

"The Carrick Castle murder," Mitchell said.

"And what did you learn from that case?" Crabbie asked with a ghastly let's-not-let-this-become-unpleasant fake grin on his face.

"It was an interesting one but, you know, ultimately, Carrick CID let the prime suspect escape," Mitchell said.

"That's what they're bloody teaching you at CID school?" I said, seething. That was how they saw me? That was the sum total of my detective work in the RUC? That I'd bungled a case and let a suspect get away?

"Sean, please, maybe you should head on home," Crabbie said, ushering me out the door before I could have a stroke.

BMW.

Rain.

Marine Highway.

Home.

Neil Young on the stereo. The one about the silver surfer and the aliens.

Vodka gimlet the Sean Duffy way: pint glass from the freezer, the crushed ice, this time three inches of vodka with the ice, soda, and lime juice.

I was thinking about dinner and wondering how Neil Young got his voice that high when there was a knock at the door.

Rachel, the new neighbor.

"Hi, there. What fresh hell have you come to tell me about now? I'm still reeling from the whole milk-delivery thing."

"Well, it's not exactly the last chapter of Gibbon's *Decline and Fall of the Roman Empire*, but my sink is flooding."

"Your sink's flooding?"

"Yup."

"And you came to me because I'm a man and hence you think I know about blocked sinks and things like that?"

"Exactly."

Her lovely gray eyes flashed, and a grin spread itself across her face. She vibed Andrea Corr from the Corrs, one of the few pleasant exports from Dundalk.

"I can't let the side down, can I? Let me see this blocked sink of yours."

Next door.

Water all over the kitchen floor.

Simple blockage in the U bend. Unscrew the plastic washers, remove the U bend, take out a whole pile of gunk, rescrew the U bend, run the water, hey presto, the sink drains.

"That was impressive," she said. "The least I can do is invite you for dinner. Unless you have other plans?"

"No other plans tonight. I'd love dinner."

Spag bol. Standard stuff. Decent red wine from the offy.

The dining room was wallpapered in flowers, and she'd hung a few impressionist posters on the wall. Other than that, she hadn't done much to the house. Not that there was a whole lot you could do—all the houses on the terrace were identical.

"This is terrific food," I said. "Do you make this garlic bread?"

"I did. It's shockingly easy to make. I'm more impressed by the wine. I got this in Carrickfergus! It's from the Medoc. You can get actually get good plonk now."

"Oh, yeah? Not much of a wine drinker, to be honest."

"You're quite the man, though, aren't you? Fixing sinks, scaring ruffians off my lawn."

"That impressed you?" I said self-mockingly. But she appeared to actually *be* impressed by my seeing off those two-bit skinhead hoods.

"You must have some bad qualities," she said.

"Oh, yes! I've recently begun writing verse in my free time," I said.

"Yikes! Me too. Let's avoid that whole minefield, shall we?" she said with a laugh. "I hear you're a music buff," she said.

"I wouldn't say that."

"Mrs. Campbell says you have the biggest record collection in Carrickfergus."

"She's exaggerating. And most of it is in Scotland anyway," I replied, secretly pleased by this.

"She says someone can play you any record in the world and you'll know what it is."

"That's a complete fabrication."

"Go on, then. What's that on the radio in the living room?"

I put down my fork and cocked an ear to Radio 3 coming from the feeble speakers of her ancient stereo.

Shostakovich.

Unmistakable. But which symphony?

She was looking at me, a lovely smile creasing her lips. She was really something. Gray-eyed and long-haired and doughy and feminine, the antithesis of Beth, short-haired, slender.

I took another sip of wine and refilled both our glasses.

The symphony soared and stamped in that way that only Shostakovich can carry off without obvious bombast.

"So, do you know who the composer is? Bear in mind, you could say anything and I wouldn't know if you were bulshitting me or not."

I listened to a few more bars. Yeah, of course, it was his tenth symphony. The one Shostakovich wrote after Stalin's death, or, rather, the one he claimed he'd written after Stalin's death, although in fact most of it was done by 1951, according to his pupil who became his mistress.

Disappointment flitted across her face as she assumed that I, in fact, didn't know. It's a weakness of men—this desire to show off for attractive young women.

You don't need to do it, Duffy. This is just a nice dinner with the next door neighbor. Eat your food and go, mate. Don't give in to the bloody weakness. Wise the bap . . .

She looked glumly down at her plate. I couldn't take it anymore.

"Dmitri Shostakovich, Symphony number Ten, the third movement—the movement where he's kind of homaging Mahler. And I believe it's the Berlin Philharmonic with Herbert von Karajan conducting."

She looked up and grinned. "For real, or are you yanking me?"

The third movement ended, and breaking the between-movements protocol of silence, the Radio 3 continuity announcer reminded listeners what channel they were on and what they were listening to: "It's just after six-thirty, this is BBC Radio Three, you are listening to the 1981 recording of Shostakovich's Symphony number Ten, with the Berlin Philharmonic conducted by Herbert von Karajan."

She put down her fork and grinned. "Fuck me!" she said.

This was a parlous moment. She was beautiful, and we'd nearly finished the bottle of wine.

"I know you're brave, I know you're handy, and now I know you're clever too!" she said, delighted.

"You don't have to be clever to know Shostakovich. Just a little bit geeky."

She reached her hand across the table and rested it on mine.

I let it stay there.

Weak, Duffy, weak.

"You know, there's something I should tell you. I don't know why I didn't mention it the other day, but I'm married. Well, not really married as such. Beth didn't want a wedding, but it's as good as and I've a daughter, Emma. She's nearly five."

Rachel nodded and gave my hand a light squeeze. "I know," she said. "Mrs. Campbell told me everything about you in exhaustive detail."

It would be easier, much easier, if Beth had been in one of her moods or if I hadn't seen her for a week or more. But none of that was the case. I'd seen Beth two days ago and I'd made love to her and I loved her and I therefore had no excuses whatever. None of the excuses men usually give themselves for their flaws.

I walked around the table, and as I did so she stood. I kissed her on the lips and backed her up against the wall.

"Wait," she said, and whisked our plates and the wine bottle from the kitchen table. She lifted her skirt and pushed herself against me. I was hard as a rock.

She wanted me to fuck her on the kitchen table.

Jesus Christ, I'd be a fool to pass up an opportunity like this.

I unzipped my fly and kissed her again. Kissed her big, full beautiful breasts and her soft white belly. She was gorgeous.

She was incredible.

This was a—

I heard the noise of a doorbell above the Shostakovich.

"Come on," she said.

I stopped and listened.

The doorbell again.

I slipped off the table, zipped up my fly. "There's someone at my door," I said.

"Forget it, for fucksake!"

I took out the Glock, walked down the hall, and opened her front door. I looked across the porch to #113 Coronation Road.

Crabbie was standing there with one of the new Scooby gang. He saw me. I lowered the Glock.

"Sean? I tried calling. I couldn't reach you."

"I was having dinner over here. What's up?"

"We found something at the caravan site. Something you should see."

Rachel appeared behind me.

I could feel the utter fury radiating from her.

I turned to her. "I have to go. I—"

"Go, then," she said.

I stepped over the fence between the houses while the door banged shut behind me.

"Will we take my car?" I suggested.

"Brought a police Land Rover. You'll probably need to put some shoes on," Crabbie said coldly.

I grabbed a pair of sneakers and got in the front of the Land Rover with him while the new trainee detective sat in the back. Crabbie said nothing. He approved of Beth. She was a Presbyterian, a schoolteacher. She had given me a beautiful, precocious daughter. She had cooked dinner for him and his wife. She had invited him to her house, and we had all broken bread together there. And even if none of that had been true, it wouldn't have mattered. He liked her.

I caught his eyes in the rearview mirror, and he looked away immediately.

I'd never seen him so pissed off at me.

"Mind if I turn on the radio?" I said meekly.

"Suit yourself."

I found Radio 3 and got the last bars of the Shostakovich, which was sublime stuff but it didn't cheer me up one bit. Made it worse, in fact. Turned it off.

Silence all the way to the caravan site, and then the rain came on again.

The other trainee detectives were waiting for us, standing outside in the wet like bloody idiots. The one with the glasses looked as if they'd fished her out of the river.

I got out and took a hit off my inhaler.

The rain immediately pouring down the neck of my leather jacket.

"Evening, all," I said to the trainees. They were all so young, none of them got the Dixon of Dock Green reference.

"This way, Detective Inspector Duffy," Crabbie said, and I followed him across the muddy campsite to Locke's caravan.

"You found something that the FO team missed?" I asked, amazed.

"Young Jamie found it," Crabbie said.

"In the toaster. He kept it in the toaster," the one with the soul patch said.

Kept what? I wondered, but when I got into the caravan Crabbie showed it to me next to the toaster, nice and safe inside an evidence bag.

It was a piece of A4 paper on which a dozen names and addresses had been written.

I recognized several of the names as senior Republican players, politicians, and activists. Most of them were either IRA or ex-IRA. Some were very prominent people indeed, including ██████ ██████ and ██████ and ██████ ██████.

"What is this?" one of the trainees asked.

"It's a kill list," I said.

Crabbie nodded. "That's what it looks like."

"Ask the kids to go wait in the Land Rover," I said.

Crabbie ushered them to the Land Rover and came back to the caravan, where I was sitting down at the Formica table.

"This will have to go to Special Branch," I said. "They will have to warn everyone on this list that a possible IRA hit man has their name and address."

"That's what I was thinking."

"You know what Special Branch are like. They might subsume our entire investigation."

"So be it."

"What I mean is, they'll take over and we'll be back to the part-time reserve."

"I understand what you mean, Sean. I'm not an idiot."

"I never said you were."

"No, but you've thought it many times."

I looked at him. "That's a terrible thing to say."

"Tell me I'm a liar."

"You're a liar."

He gave me a hard stare for fifteen seconds, then lifted up the evidence bag. "Special Branch will have to be informed immediately. Do you want a lift back to the house?"

"I'm not walking."

"I'll give you a lift home, then."

"You'll report this to Special Branch?" I asked.

"Of course. It would be dereliction of duty not to. These people have to be informed that they've been potentially targeted."

Crabbie drove me back to Coronation Road.

Cold shoulder the whole way.

"Thanks, mate. Hopefully, our betters will sort this one out, eh?"

Crabbie said nothing.

I made to close the Land Rover door, and he gave his head the slightest of shakes.

"Wait a minute, Sean," he said.

"Yeah?"

"You got very, very lucky when you met Beth."

"I know."

"She's a good woman. A handsome woman. Good natured. And a good mother to your daughter."

"I know."

"And a teacher too."

"Yes."

"Saved your wee bairn when they came to kill you that night. Took her in her arms and fled like a good 'un."

"I know. What's your point?"

"You really couldn't have gotten any luckier than that, Sean."

He'd worn me down, and my eyes fell from him and stared at the oil and cigarette butts in the gutter.

"Nothing really happened, Crabbie. Not really. It could have . . . but . . ."

"See that it stays that way," he said, and leaning over, he closed the Land Rover door with a bang so loud that it startled half the mutts on Coronation Road.

I walked up the path.

When Crabbie had gone, I went over the fence and knocked on the door.

Rachel came downstairs in her nightgown.

"Listen, I'm sorry about what happened earlier."

"I am too."

"Duty calls, all that, you know?"

"Yes, I know."

She looked at me closely. "So do you want to—"

"Nah, I should . . ."

"Yes, good night," she said, and she kind of slammed the door too.

I went inside number 113.

I called home, but Emma was clearly having sleep issues and Beth had disconnected the phone. Fuck.

I called my parents in Donegal, but Da was in his bed and Mum was watching a "fascinating program on the Open University about the Chartists."

Who else was there to call?

Crabbie was out of the question, and Lawson was in bloody Spain.

Who else was there?

Nobody.

That's what happens when your friendship circle narrows and narrows.

I looked through my records, but I wasn't in the mood for music.

I sat in the armchair by the fire and poured myself four inches of sixteen-year-old Bowmore.

No point thinking about stupid me. That was a deep well of foolishness to explore, available anytime.

The case, then . . .

Why would a deep-cover IRA hit man have only the names and addresses of other IRA men? What the fuck was going on within the IRA? Was it something to do with O'Roarke's quest for a harder line within the Army Council?

Could he really be plotting a Night of the Long Knives?

Would Special Branch notice the nuance of all this?

Supposedly, Special Branch was the smartest and best of the RUC. But in practice, they had just as many time wasters and fuck-ups as the rest of the police force.

I was on to my third glass of Bowmore when the phone rang.

"Hello?"

"Duffy. Is that you?" the chief inspector asked.

"Yeah."

"Are you okay, Sean?"

Clearly, I'd been slurring my words. Was I drunk? I looked at the Bowmore bottle. Christ, it was a third gone.

"Slight cold, sir. That's all."

"You want to watch that. Summer colds are the worst ones of all."

"Yes, sir. I will."

"I got a call from a Superintendent Clare over at Special Branch. He said that Jill Dumont had ordered him to take an advisory role in this case. That's Chief Super Jill Dumont, in case you didn't know who she is."

I considered hanging up immediately. Chief Inspector McArthur didn't know about the phone bug, and he could blab about the case to my eavesdropper. And McArthur was a blabber, but even half-drunk, I could handle the bastard. Better than hanging up, I'd just intercept him.

"Yes, sir, I contacted Special Branch. This is potentially a Special Branch affair. By the way, did they tell you about the protocols?"

"What protocols?"

"Well, because of the sensitive nature of the document that we found, they've imposed strict confidentiality on the investigation. We, uhm, well, we're not even supposed to be discussing this at all."

"Is that so?"

"Yes, sir, I'm afraid so, sir. You know what they're like."

"I bloody do! They're all up themselves, aren't they? Those bastards. What *are* we allowed to discuss, pray tell?"

"Only the murder case, sir."

"And any progress with that?"

And maybe it was the booze. Or maybe it was . . . no, it was the booze . . .

"Actually, I'm meeting an informant tonight who claims to be able to ID our shooter."

"An informant! That's brilliant. Well done, Duffy."

"It might turn out to be nothing, but you never know, do you?"

"No, you don't. Where are you meeting this informant, if I may ask?"

"The Knockagh Monument at the top of Knockagh Mountain. One a.m. I figure no one else will be up there at that time."

"Not on a night like this," McArthur agreed.

"Like I say, sir, it might turn out to be nothing, but you never know."

"Want any help? My in-laws—"

"No, sir! Don't want to spook him. He only works with me."

"All right, Duffy, good luck. Fill me in, in the morning, yes?"

"I will. Good night, sir."

I hung up. The clock in the hall said it was 12:15. I grabbed my Glock, a pair of binoculars, and a raincoat.

I ran out to the Beemer and looked underneath it for mercury tilt switch bombs. Nope.

I got inside, turned on the John Peel show, and listened to a very hit-or-miss set from the new line-up of the Fall.

I gunned the Beemer along the top road, to the North Road. Up the North Road to the Marshallstown Road and then at a healthy 95 mph clip to the Knockagh Road.

I caught Duffy's eyes in the rearview.

Was this a smart thing to do?

Mirror Duffy was fine with it. Mirror Duffy had had a third of a bottle of whisky and was a complex blend of emotions: guilt, anger, remorse, and humiliation. Mirror Duffy wanted you to take action, and this was action.

That's why you didn't tell McArthur about the bug. Because a move like this was in the back of your mind. You were always going to play this. Break this case wide open tonight, motherfucker.

This wasn't just the booze talking.

No. Not at all. This was the smart play. Completely self-defeating to call in backup. They'd only fuck it up. The eejits down the station? Forget it. Those goons at the DMSU and Special Branch? Amateurs. The only man Mirror Duffy trusted was Crabbie, and nobody wanted to drag him into this.

Solo Duffy it would have to be. Like the bad old days.

13
THE 750 NORTON

I pulled in front of the monument at the top of Knockagh Mountain. The memorial was a massive granite obelisk that had been put up here to commemorate the dead of the two World Wars.

I'd been up here many times since I moved to Carrick. It was a great place to smoke weed and look at the view, and you could see for fucking miles. On a very clear night, you could spot the planes landing at Prestwick Airport near Glasgow to the north, and on clear mornings you could see as far south as the Mountains of Mourne.

But I wasn't here to smoke weed and enjoy the view. I was here to nail a murderer.

It was your usual impetuous, stupid, Duffy-not-thinking-things-through plan.

Duffy, it had to be said, was a man at war with himself. The mature, responsible suburban family man at odds with the dingbat eejit looking for trouble at the first opportunity. I wondered if all men were like this, and I wondered if there was anyone to talk to about it. Certainly not Crabbie—when conversations veered near the personal, you could see that big ganch looking for the nearest exit.

Stuff to work on, Duffy, stuff to bloody work on.

If this little adventure doesn't kill ya.

I hid the Beemer in the shadows near the stone wall next to the sheep field, and then I ran down the Knockagh Lane and waited in the bushes.

I knew he'd come.

You don't break into a peeler's house and bug the phone with a very expensive piece of equipment, and then not come when the copper is about to meet an informant revealing exactly who you are.

He was smart, and he had the moves and access to the best of equipment, but what was going to nab him was old-fashioned police work. Classic fucking sting.

But you know, chickens/hatched, so I immediately touched wood.

I waited for ten minutes, looking at the streetlights in Scotland twinkle across the black water.

It was a still, cold night, and I could hear the fucking bike from two miles away. Was it a Norton? Oh, yes. I wouldn't say I was an expert on motorcycles, but I knew my Triumphs and I knew my Nortons. Who didn't? It was one of the classic binaries I was always on about. Liverpool / Man United. Presta valve / Schrader valve. Beatles / Stones. Triumph / Norton.

Over the years, I'd had countless boring stakeout conversations on the relative merits of the two companies and their machines. It was not a moot point, because although both companies went bankrupt in the 1970s, both were going again in the '90s and making bikes in small but profitable numbers. I was a Triumph guy. The Norton had a reputation for looking good on the outside but breaking down under the slightest bit of pressure. I'd ridden Nortons before, and they were very cool, but I wouldn't trust one to get me to the local chippie. Brando's bike in *The Wild One*?—Triumph. James Dean's motorcycle of choice? Steve McQueen's ride in *The Great Escape*? Which bike did Evel Knievel use to jump the fountain at Caesar's Palace? You get the picture. And which bike broke down repeatedly for Che Guevera as he rode around South America? Fucking Norton, wasn't it? This particular Norton Commando was chugging its throaty, unmistakable way down the B road toward me.

I was amazed at the arrogance of this prick.

Even though he'd been ID'd riding this big black, noisy bike, he didn't dump it. Didn't burn it. Hubris. Yeah, there were eight thousand of them in Ireland, but he was still a cocky bastard.

My watch said 12:35. He was hoping to get here half an hour early and get the drop on us.

He came down the Knockagh Lane at 40 mph and skidded to a stop in front of the monument in the supposedly empty car park.

I watched him park the bike, turn off the engine, and then roll the machine into the shadows.

I watched him look anxiously down the lane and then check his watch.

Yeah, this was definitely my guy. Too many coincidences for it not to be him. He was not only the guy who had bugged my phone, but he was the goddamn murderer as well.

I could just imagine Lawson's sweet, innocent sunburned face on Sunday evening.

You met me at the airport? Oh, sir, you shouldn't have. Well, you can go back to Scotland now, sir; I'll take over the case. Nah, you're too late, Lawson. I caught him. He confessed to everything. Ha, ha. Old dog, new tricks, eh, son?

I found that I had been talking to myself during this not-so-internal monologue. Shit, was I tipsier than I thought?

Time for action.

I drew the Glock from the shoulder holster and walked carefully toward him.

"Carrick Police! Put your hands in the air!"

He spun around to look at me.

"Don't move, arsehole! You're nicked, mate. You're bloody nicked. Put your fucking hands in the air. Now! Put your hands in the air or I'm going to bloody shoot you!"

In my experience, criminals generally surrendered when they were confronted by a cop with a drawn gun. It was better to risk your day in court than get shot dead in the here and now, wasn't it? But this guy was cut from the same cloth as the guys in the caravan park, and I should have foreseen that. Instead of putting his hands in the air, he immediately pulled two semiautomatic pistols from his waistband and shot at me. He was fast and I was momentarily bewitched, but then I hit the bloody deck. And he kept shooting at me. Bullets whizzing all around me in the darkness.

"Jesus!"

The shooting stopped and I looked up. He was running for his motorbike.

"Halt or I will shoot!" I screamed at him.

He kept running.

I returned fire, aiming in his general direction, but I didn't clip the bastard.

And he'd somehow acquired the only Norton 750 on the planet that kick-started first time.

He sped off down the Knockagh Lane while I scrambled to my feet and fumbled for the keys to the car.

The BMW also started first time, but I had to turn it around to get out of the car park.

I drove down the Knockagh Lane at 50 mph, and when I got to the junction I stopped and listened. No bloody motorbike. Left or right, and whichever one I picked on this cursed night would be the wrong one, wouldn't it? Left toward Belfast. Right toward the countryside.

Belfast.

I turned left and drove for half an hour, and of course I didn't find the bike.

Back to Knockagh car park to pick up the shell casings.

How was I going to play this?

Fuck, I was wasted. Shouldn't be driving. Shouldn't be handling a gun. I could get dismissed from the force for this.

How to play it?

No choice. Local cops for this little scene, and Special Branch for the phone bug.

I carefully drove home, made a coffee, and drove to the station.

Crabbie was still there.

Still angry with me.

"Do me a favor, Crabbie, and see if you can contact a Superintendent Anthony Clare. He works for Jill Dumont at Special Branch Intel."

"I'll look him up," Crabbie replied.

"When you find him, tell him about the phone bug in my house and get an FO team to the Knockagh Monument. I tried to lure out our suspect, and it didn't work."

"You went up to the Knockagh, on a stakeout, by yourself in that condition?"

"What condition's that?"

"You're half tore, Sean."

"Am I?" I asked aggressively.

"Yes. Go on home to bed, Sean, I'll handle things here. And when you've had a night's kip, I'll get Special Branch to your house."

"Nah, no time for kip. Let's do it now."

"I think you should go home to your own bed, Sean. For your own good."

I turned suddenly to look at him. "The fuck do you mean by that?"

"Nothing. Get some rest," he said placidly.

"You said go home to your *own* bed. What do you mean by that?"

"Nothing. Good night, Sean," he said, and closed the door and left me standing there in Lawson's office.

"That bastard. That stuck-up, holier-than-thou Proddy bastard!" I snarled.

I poured myself three fingers of whisky and drank it back neat.

I sat down.

My head was swimming.

I took another shot of whisky and got up. I stormed out of the office, into the incident room. One of the night duty constables scurried away, sensing a blowup. Good instincts.

"Where are you, John?" I yelled.

No answer.

"Where are you!"

Again no answer.

"Hide if you must! And yeah, you handle it, pal. You bloody handle it!" I yelled, and banged the table and stormed out to the Beemer to drive home drunk.

"Maybe I'll get lucky and skid off the road into the fucking sea," I said to Mirror Duffy.

But now Mirror Duffy wasn't even there, the sleekit conniving stupid bastard.

14
SUPERINTENDENT CLARE

Discontented, unhappy sleep. How could it be otherwise? I woke up at eight and stared at the rain hammering the windows for a long time.

"You know this is supposed to be summer," I said to no one in particular.

I sat up in bed and listened to the water tumble through the gutters and into the drains.

So many mistakes in this case.

In this life.

The arc was all wrong.

Wrong arc.

Wrong lessons learned.

No bloody lessons learned.

Fuck it.

Coffee. Toast. Black T-shirt. Black sweater. Raincoat. Out to the Beemer. Check underneath. No bombs . . . more's the pity.

No radio today.

Just get in to work.

Upstairs, avoiding gazes, and into Lawson's office, where Crabbie and another man were waiting for me.

"Inspector Duffy, this is Superintendent Anthony Clare from Special Branch," Crabbie said before I came out with a "Who is this fuck?"

He stood up and shook my hand.

"Delighted to meet you," he said.

Superintendent Clare was a lanky, posh-voiced bastard in a well-cut pin-striped three-piece suit. On the stand in the corner, he had parked an umbrella and a bowler hat, of all things.

And here was I with no shower, no shave, and a mayonnaise stain on my raincoat. Lieutenant Columbo would have made a better first impression.

"Would either of you gentlemen care for a drink?" I asked, heading for the drinks cabinet.

"No," Superintendent Clare said. He had watery blue eyes, big nostrils, and the weak chin you'd expect in a toff. No mustache, though—that would have been too much to ask.

Don't ask me how I knew, but I knew he was a fellow Catholic immediately. A Catholic who refused a whisky—what an abomination.

"I've already got us a cup of tea," Crabbie explained.

"Right, then," I said sitting down again.

"So Sergeant McCrabban here has filled me in on the extraordinary document your team found in that Gypsy caravan," Clare began. "We in Special Branch have absolutely no choice but to take this very seriously indeed. This looks for all intents and purposes like a hit list of senior Republican politicians, IRA men, and former IRA men. And that, I'm afraid, comes well within our jurisdiction."

"Yes."

"So the killing of Mr. Locke, and what exactly Mr. Locke was up to in Carrickfergus, will become part of a case that we will need to initiate. Your investigation will need to be subsumed into our investigation, I'm afraid."

"I'm aware of that," I replied.

"Jolly good. I'll have some men come and look through your case files this afternoon. I'd like them in as orderly a fashion as possible by then."

"Okay."

"May I ask you for your interpretation of the situation?" Clare said, softly.

"My interpretation?"

"Yes."

"I do have a rough, er, working hypothesis," I said.

"If you'd indulge me."

"Locke was Brendan O'Roarke's personal hit man lying low in Ulster, waiting for the word to unleash a coup against Brendan's enemies on the IRA Army Council and take it over. Brendan being opposed to all these peace feelers we keep hearing about."

Clare's face went pale. "You seem remarkably well informed for a junior detective."

"All deduction, mate," I said, tapping my head. "That and the papers—you gotta read the papers."

Clare was not fazed by my attempt at glib mateyness.

"So who do you think killed Locke?" he asked.

"Who indeed? The hit man got hit before he could get started. That's thrown Brendan on his uppers, I'll bet."

Clare looked at a collection of notes on his lap. "Now, what's this Sergeant McCrabban said about a phone bug in your—"

I plonked it down onto the table in front of him. "There it is. No idea where it came from."

"How did you find it?"

I took a deep breath and told him about how I had found the bug, and my attempt at entrapment. I expected him to be pissed, but he wasn't.

Clare looked at me and at the device and smiled. "That's really quite good police work. Well done, Sergeant Duffy."

"Inspector Duffy."

"Yes, well done indeed. It's not every officer who acts on their own initiative like that. Some people are a bit stuck in the mud here at regular CID."

"You don't say?"

"I do say. It's nice to see some creative thinking occasionally."

Clare had bought the story, and the rest of his questions were pro forma. Nothing about drunk driving, nothing about drunkenly firing my Glock. Nothing about all the mistakes. He asked me detailed questions about the case files, and when he was satisfied, he excused Crabbie and me from his office. I was a bit stunned to have received praise and positive reinforcement from Special Branch, and if I hadn't been so badly hungover, I might have been a bit suspicious.

An hour after our meeting, a youngish Inspector Gillian Bain and three more Special Branch goons showed up late in the morning and photocopied all our evidence for what was now *their* investigation. Clare and Bain and the goons had a word with my gaffer, Chief Inspector McArthur, on their way out, and when they left with the boxes, the chief inspector came to see me.

We repaired to Lawson's office.

"Drink, sir?"

"Yes. Why not?"

I poured myself a soda, and him a whisky and soda. I was feeling off the drink today.

"Clare was very impressed with you," McArthur began.

"Was he?"

"Yes. He said that he'd like you to keep working the case from your angle if I didn't mind. He's left you all your files and just photocopied the ones he needed for the wider investigation."

"I saw that."

"I take a bit of a different view."

"Oh?"

"I told him that you could work the case until my full-time detective returned on Sunday, but after that you'd have to return to regular duty. I can't afford to pay you to work on a case that another team is now working, can I?"

"But Superintendent Clare asked you to."

"He did," the chief inspector said slowly. "And the compromise I have come up with is that you'll work the case with Sergeant McCrabban until Lawson's return, and then all three of you will return to regular duty."

"Uhm, what day is today?"

"Friday."

"I see."

"As you said yourself, we've already had Duffy's Last Case, haven't we? You don't want to be like Sinatra, do you? A new 'Farewell Tour' every year."

"No, sir. Friday. Well, I suppose we better get cracking, then."

It took me fifteen minutes to find Crabbie up on the roof with a mug of tea, looking at the lough.

He was clearly avoiding me.

"I brought you some biscuits," I said.

"Thank you," he replied politely.

"Whatcha doing up here?"

"Thinking."

"Good spot. Up on the roof between the rain showers. Nice. Get a wee gander at the lough and Belfast."

He frowned. "Maybe we should just keep things on a professional level for now on, Sean. Restrict our conversations to police work."

"Is that what you want?"

"Perhaps that would be for the best. Things were said that were best left unsaid."

"Things were said that were complete bollocks."

"So police work only, please? If you don't mind."

"I don't mind."

I stood there next to him for a while. He cleared his throat. "Was there anything else?"

"Nope."

I went downstairs and closed my office door.

Lawson's office door.

Half an hour later, Crabbie opened it.

I could tell from his expression that he hadn't come to make up. He was all business.

"What's happened?"

"We got a phone call from Inspector O'Neill from Dundalk Garda. They're having a wake for Alan Locke in the bowling club in Dundalk tonight. Apparently, they've discovered an old membership card, and the club members want to pay their respects to him."

"That's interesting."

"I've informed Superintendent Clare about it, but he doesn't think it'll be worthwhile going through all the bureaucratic hassles to send down some men there to mingle," Crabbie said.

"He does things by the book, I suppose."

"Yes."

"And yet earlier, he was praising our creativity in this investigation."

"Indeed."

"You know, you and I could just drive down there and join the crowd and see what we could pick up informationwise."

"Sounds dangerous, Sean. Two undercover policemen at an IRA hit man's wake?"

"In that case, I'll just go down there and nail them on my own."

Crabbie sighed. "You know I can't allow that either."

15
THE WAKE

A man has only so much luck in a lifetime. I mean, I was practically out of the force: a part-timer, filling in paperwork, finding missing cats and bicycles (not that we ever did find the missing cats or the bicycles). You've read Freud. Parapraxis is the specialized, technical name for a bungled or faulty action that nevertheless reveals something fundamental about our deeper selves. The Freudian slip, for example. "Nail them on my own," I'd said to Crabbie. I wasn't supposed to nail anybody. But clearly, I was craving a win after a year of no wins. And poor Crabbie was forced to patrol the dark places with me to sort out *my* issues. Again.

South of the border was where the real bungling would begin.

But we'll get to that . . .

Belfast to Newry to the Border to Dundalk.

Dundalk Lawn Bowling Club.

Crabbie and me in dark suits.

They weren't checking IDs coming in, but they were doing a pat-down search. Back to the BMW, which we'd parked behind a fish shop. We left our guns in the boot and threw our shoulder holsters in there too.

Back to the bowling club.

Pat-down.

"How did you know the deceased?" the goon at the front door asked.

HANG ON ST. CHRISTOPHER

"We knew him through the art world. I have some of his paintings," I said.

The goon nodded. "Why don't you have a seat over there to the left. There are plenty of tables available," he said.

We went inside. Bit run-down and garish. Faded candy primary colors you would normally associate with a scary fairground.

Plenty of tables available. In fact, there couldn't be more than thirty people in here, and most of those looked like old bowling gents come for the free grub. If the goon wanted us to go left, it probably meant that . . .

Yeah. Over to the right of the room I saw Brendan O'Roarke, surrounded by friends and heavies, near the emergency exit and the bar. He was a big mess of a man with gray hair sticking out all over the place, jet black eyes, and pale gray skin. He had big hands, big builder's hands, big throttle-you-around-the-neck hands.

Even from here, you got the sulfurous whiff of the true believer.

"Come on, in you go, gents," another bouncer said. "It's an open bar. There's sandwiches at the back. I would get a sandwich now. It's supposed to fill up."

Within half an hour, his prediction proved correct. Two busloads of people arrived from Belfast, and before we knew it, the place was full of IRA, ex-IRA, and various Republican sympathizers.

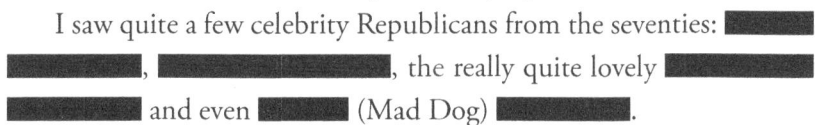

I saw quite a few celebrity Republicans from the seventies: ▓▓▓▓▓ ▓▓▓▓▓▓, ▓▓▓▓▓▓▓▓▓▓▓, the really quite lovely ▓▓▓▓▓▓ ▓▓▓▓▓▓▓ and even ▓▓▓▓▓ (Mad Dog) ▓▓▓▓▓▓.

No one was hiding what Alan Locke had been now. They were proud of him, and they were going to raise a glass in his honor. When the Proddy scum police north of the border finally released his body, they'd have a proper funeral too. Armed men firing volleys over the coffin. The works.

The fact that RUC Special Branch hadn't deemed this wake an event worth attending told you everything you needed to know about Special Branch.

Crabbie and I had been to the bar and got a glass of lager to blend in with everyone else.

181

"So, are you allowed into a Catholic wake?" I asked him.

"Of course," he said dismissively, and then added in a whisper, "Will there be kneeling?"

Presbyterians didn't kneel.

"No kneeling, no prayers, just speeches and drinking and maybe music."

By nine p.m. it was so crowded, it was easy for us to get close to Brendan's table without it being suspicious. Brendan was holding forth on cement making. We drifted away. Booze would loosen his tongue.

At ten, a man I didn't know got up and said a few words about Alan. The man was drunk and mumbled things about the movement and about Alan being a great friend and a great comrade.

When he was done, there was scattered applause, and two fiddles, a bodhran, a guitar, and a set of Irish pipes began to play folk standards.

Crabbie and I drifted in and out of conversations, catching snatches here, snatches there. Close to midnight, I saw Inspector O'Neill and some of his lads, who had also thought to sneak in to see what they could pick up.

I nodded at him.

He nodded back.

We said nothing.

Finally, Crabbie and I managed to get close to Brendan's table again, where Brendan was talking about death by shotgun.

"No, no, all things considered, a shotgun blast to the head isn't so bad," Brendan was saying. "Especially in the old bonce, like. All over in a flash. Stand well back, though. No, that's an easy way to go. Have you heard about this brain-eating amoeba? That's a bad one. It lives in lakes, and if it gets up your nose it burrows into your brain. First thing you know is a headache. Headache gets worse and you go in for a CAT scan. And lo and behold, your brain is riddled with amoeba. No way to get it out without turning you into a vegetable. No cure at all. Only thing to do is shoot yourself."

"Is that why you never learned to swim, Brendan?" a young flunky asked him.

"I never learned to swim, because there were no swimming pools and the sea was too fucking cold."

An older man came by with a tray full of whiskies and handed them out.

"To Alan!" everyone said, and we raised our lagers.

One of Brendan's mates took up the subject now. "There's much worse ways than your amoeba, so there is. Me uncle was in the British army, and he told me what the Japs used to do in Burma. They cut you and stake you out on an anthill. Ants would eat you alive over days. They'd bring you water so you stayed alive while they ate you."

"Fucking British army scum. That's what they fucking deserve," Brendan said. "Only thing worse than the fucking British army is the fucking traitor Micks who work for them."

"I think he's talking about us," I whispered to Crabbie.

"*Ssssh,* for God's sake, Sean!" Crabbie hissed.

"Maybe we should go over there and introduce ourselves."

"Maybe not."

"If I had the cancer, I'd jump off the cliffs of Moher," another of the old stagers was saying.

This brought a round of murmured agreement from the men.

"If you've got the bottle to do it, there's only one way: shoot yourself in the heart first and shoot yourself in the head," Brendan said.

"After you've just shot yourself in the heart?"

"Yup."

"There's no way."

"I've seen it done."

I took this as my cue and broke into the little circle. "What you've seen done, gentlemen, is a murder dressed up as a suicide. There's no way someone could shoot themselves in the heart and then shoot themselves in the head," I said.

"Who are you?" one of Brendan's bodyguards asked me.

"You were talking about the worst way to go? A friend of my father's told me a story once. He worked in the shipyards. He told me that before they launched a ship, they used to put a black cat down into the boiler furnaces to scare off any demons or gremlins that might have gotten on board. He said that one time the apprentice whose job it was to put the cat in there couldn't get the cat to come out before they fired up the boiler. He went into the furnace to get the cat, they didn't realize he was in there, they shut the furnace door and ignited the coal. Poor bastard."

"Who the fuck are you?" Brendan asked me with cold hate in his eyes. It was evident that he knew exactly who I was. He'd seen my photograph. Probably read my file by now.

"Detective Inspector Sean Duffy, Carrick CID," I said, offering him my hand.

He let the hand hang there, and all the other men in the circle looked on me with unconcealed horror and amazement. A policeman had come *here*? To Brendan's bowling club? To Alan Locke's wake? Did I have a fucking death wish?

"Ah, yes, Inspector Duffy from Derry," Brendan said.

"That's right," I said.

I offered my outstretched hand to any of the men in Brendan's circle, but none of them wanted to shake it.

"A nice Catholic boy from Derry working for the Brits. In the RUC, no less," Brendan said, spitting out the words.

"You got all that right except for the 'nice' bit."

Brendan's big bodyguard got between him and me. "What brings you here?" he asked.

"Pay my respects to Alan Locke's friends and family. I'm the copper in charge of his murder investigation."

"You're not wanted here, pal."

"No?" I said, shaking my head.

"This is a private affair, in a private club. You really should fuck off," Brendan said.

"If you value your kneecaps," someone else muttered.

"Or your bollocks," another voice offered.

"I've been trying to have an interview with you, Mr. O'Roarke," I said.

"I'm aware of that. Dundalk Garda have informed me about your request."

"And?"

"I am considering it."

"We all want the same thing here," I said. "We all want to find out who killed Alan Locke."

"Is that so?" Brendan said, his voice dropping to an ominous burr.

"It is so. So if we could talk to you about your friend Alan—"

"I said I was considering it!" Brendan shouted, and suddenly the conversation in the immediate vicinity ceased. Even the music hesitated before picking up again.

Brendan whispered something to one of his bodyguards, who physically picked me up and began carrying me to the exit.

I saw O'Neill's and Crabbie's panicked faces trailing after me.

"All right, goodbye, then. My commiserations on your loss," I said.

The bodyguard dumped me outside onto the pavement. "And don't fucking come back!" he said.

I walked a little bit away from the bowling club until I saw Crabbie and O'Neill.

O'Neill was irked. Crabbie was resigned.

"What the hell was that?" O'Neill asked.

"I asked him for that interview."

"If you want to commit suicide, mate, do it on your patch, okay?"

Crabbie was shaking his head. "Not a good idea to get into *his* bad books, Sean, even if you do live in Scotland."

"I was already in his bad books. He's read my file. He knows I'm from Derry. He's been one step ahead of us ever since Alan got shot," I said.

"Good night, gentlemen, safe journey back across the border," O'Neill said, and slipped off back into the darkness.

Silence in the BMW back to the border.

Silence from Newry to Belfast.

On the outskirts of Carrickfergus, I turned to Crabbie. "Look, I said I was sorry, all right?"

"I thought you were finally growing up, Sean. I'm disappointed in you," Crabbie said.

And those words from that man hurt more than I can possibly say.

16
THE SECOND MURDER

Saturday morning. Coffee. Toast. News on the radio. Overnight, the IRA had left a truck bomb in front of the Europa Hotel in Belfast and blown it up. They'd given a twenty-minute warning, which was sufficient time to evacuate the area, and there had been no casualties. This was the ninth time the Europa Hotel had been blown up since the Troubles began. The second time this year. Anywhere else, this would be a huge news story, but it was story number four on the radio.

Still, it reminded me of something. A wee task I had to take care of.

The last time they'd blown up the Europa, one of the chickenshit details I'd been given was to accompany a DHSS officer to make a notification. The DHSS were cutting some kid off unemployment because he'd been caught working on the Europa bomb site—on the front page of the *Belfast Telegraph*, no less. But the kid lived in a tough neighborhood, and the DHSS were scared about going there in person to tell him. Hence the cops. Hence me.

We'd found the kid's house easily. He was a loner who lived with his gran in the worst neighborhood in Rathcoole, poor sod. An old lady had answered. "Yes?"

"We're looking for Michael Forsythe."

"Michael, it's the police for you."

Forsythe: skinny, handsome, flighty, with wild, dangerous blue eyes.

He'd do well as a paramilitary chieftain of whatever side he chose to join. Better to keep him in regular employment, not cut him off the dole . . . But what did the DHSS care about the long-term good of society? The DHSS officer had informed him that he could either sign off dole forever or face prosecution. Forsythe chose the former path. Satisfied, the DHSS officer split, but I stayed and drank the old lady's tea. I, for one, wasn't going to let this kid fall through the cracks. "What will you do now, son?" I'd asked.

"I can't go back in the army, can I?"

"Why? What happened to you in the army?"

"I stole a truck and they chucked me out."

"Aye, that'll do it."

"And there are no jobs over here."

There certainly were no jobs over here.

"Look, I'm really sorry about this. It's bloody bad luck to get yourself on the front page of the *Belfast Telegraph* and have your benefit officer read it, and that benefit officer be a total bastard. Do you have any prospects at all?" I asked.

"I have a friend in America. In New York. He says he can get me a job."

"Doing what?"

"Bar work."

"Sounds good."

"I've money saved, but I need another hundred and fifty quid for my tourist visa and ticket."

"You're going to work on a tourist visa? Isn't that—"

"It's what everybody does."

"Oh, okay . . . A hundred and fifty quid, you said?"

He nodded. I opened my wallet and peeled off five twenties and a fifty.

"For real?"

"For real. But please don't make a fool out of me. I don't want to see you next week in the Dobbins having a big piss up with your mates."

"I won't. I'll go to America. I'll work for Darkey White. Will you do me a favor, though? Will you look in on my nan from time to time?"

"Sure."

And after that, I forgot all about Michael Forsythe until this morning. A promise is a promise. I dressed, drove to Rathcoole, and called in on his nan. She was a sprightly old lady who went to church, kept flowerpots, and baked. I asked her how she was doing, and she said that she was doing well.

"How's your grandson in America?"

"He's doing very well, so he is. He has his own flat and everything."

"That's good."

"He sent this for you in case you should come by. His friend Tommy brought it over yesterday. Do you know big Tommy?"

"No, I'm afraid not."

She lifted an envelope off the mantel, addressed to "Sean Duffy of the RUC." The envelope contained three fifty-pound notes and a note that, presumably, Tommy had printed out, which said, "Your name has come up in some strange circles, Duffy. I was asked if I knew you and I said no. If you ever come back to America, I'd be careful if I were you."

I looked at the note in amazement.

"Where can I find this Tommy? I need to know about this," I asked the nan, but the Belfast omertà had kicked in. Now she wasn't sure if it was Tommy or Tony.

"Do you have a contact number for Michael?"

Nope, she didn't have that either.

I gave her my number and asked her to ask him to give me a call anytime, day or night. As I was leaving, I shoved the fifties into her money box when she wasn't looking, and made my goodbyes.

I drove to Carrick station, absolutely baffled by this little interaction, and wondered if it could possibly tie into my case.

America?

And what the hell was that Michael kid up to over there?

I thought of the bloody CIA bug. This was all linked somehow. This was spook country shit. And I'd been exiled from spook country. No contacts. No way back in.

I was mulling all this over when the phone began ringing in Lawson's office.

I put down the whisky glass.

"Carrick CID, Duffy here."

"Duffy, it's me, Superintendent Clare."

"Good morning, sir, what can I help you with?"

"Nothing. Everything's very much in hand," he said with the very particular arrogance of a Special Branch detective superintendent.

"So, to what do I owe the pleasure of this phone call, then, sir?"

"Two things, Duffy. First of all, I heard you attended Locke's wake."

"Yes, sir, I thought I could pick up the odd tidbit of info."

"And did you?"

"No."

"I should have made myself clearer the other day. You should always make yourself clear with subordinates lest you be misunderstood. We are in the process of negotiating an interview with Mr. O'Roarke, and this has jeopardized the situation. Apparently, you annoyed the man while he was waking his friend."

"I'm sorry about that, sir," I said meekly.

"You could have got yourself hurt too. The Irish Republic is no place for a detective in the RUC to go gallivanting around."

"No, sir."

"Well, fortunately, the negotiations for the interview are back on track, and fortunately, you didn't get yourself killed."

"Yes, sir."

"All right, then, Duffy. I'll say my goodbyes."

"Wait a minute, sir. You said there were two things we needed to talk about?"

"Oh, yes. There's been a second murder that might possibly be related to our case. I don't think it is, but you have to think laterally sometimes, don't you? Do you know Eileen Cavanagh?"

"I can't say that I do."

"She's in our files. Special Branch files. She's suspected of being involved in half a dozen murders over the last decade. *Suspected,* mind you—never any forensic evidence of a crime."

"What does 'involved' mean?"

"She was the button man. Button woman. She went to Libya in 'eighty-five. Turned out she was a genius with a sniper rifle."

"I see. And now she's dead?"

"Murdered early this morning. I'm at the scene now."

"How do we know this is related to Brendan?"

"It's exactly the same MO as Locke. She was living in South Belfast under an assumed name and an assumed identity. I'm looking at the transcripts of her telephone calls right now."

"She made a lot of calls to a public phone box in Dundalk. Am I right, sir?" I asked.

"You are right. Look, Duffy, I've asked around about you. Wildly contradictory reports, if I'm honest, but a few people I trust tell me that generally you have good instincts. Do you want to come over and take a look? I know it's not really your case anymore, but I thought you'd be—"

"I'll be right over. What's the address?"

Fifty-five Holly Street, South Belfast.

Beemer.

The M5.

Lights on. Siren on. Yeah, I know, you're not supposed to do that, but hey, I was a detective on a murder investigation.

55 Holly Street was a little red-bricked terraced house near the River Lagan. A nice street. University Street. Middle-class street. Number 55 was at the very end of the terrace. There were bloody peelers everywhere: beat cops, Special Branch detectives, forensic officers, even traffic.

So many people, it was actually a bit chaotic.

I found an FO I knew called Damian Shaw.

We shook hands.

"Damian, how goes it?"

"It goes okay. Surprised to see you. Heard you'd retired from detective work."

"I have."

"So what are you doing here?"

"This is very much a one-off," I said, and explained the situation with Lawson, and the shooting of Alan Locke.

"Well, this one wasn't shot," Damian explained.

"What was the cause of death?"

"Are you squeamish?"

"A bit."

"You might want to give this one a miss, then."

"How was she killed?"

"There was a struggle. Looks like the killer broke into the house through the back window, intending to kill her in her sleep, but she woke up and defended herself. She went down fighting. They went at it in the bedroom and the kitchen before he finally beat her to death with an iron skillet."

"None of the neighbors heard anything?"

"House next door is empty, and the house next to that is student accommodation and the students haven't moved in yet."

"Shit . . . Forensics?"

"Unfortunately not. She had a knife, though, so the bastard was lucky."

"What's the working hypothesis? Clare thinks it could be a hit?"

"Nah, I doubt it, nothing so exotic. Burglar thought he was coming into an empty house and he gets the surprise of his life by meeting Miss Ninja here. They go at it and he kills her."

"Not a professional killing, then?"

"Far too nasty a scene for that."

"It's very unpleasant?"

"Oh, yes," Shaw said, impressed.

I took a deep breath. "Better go inside, then," I said.

Up the steps, past more FO men, portable lights and equipment. I saw Frank Payne, my other FO mate, but when I tried to say hello, Frank gave me the fingers-over-lips gesture.

"Superintendent Clare runs a tight ship," he whispered. "No chit-chat, all business."

I found Clare in the living room giving orders to his subordinates. He introduced me to three of his colleagues: a DI Siobhan McGuinness, a DI Michael O'Leary, and a DCI Stan Preston. Both men were younger than I. Both in their twenties or early thirties, by the look of it. Career Special Branch. Going places. Treadmill bodies. No drinking. Sharp suits. Clever. They were the new breed. Analytics men. My type: slovenly seventies-style lazy intuitive coppers were on their way out. Siobhan McGuinness was even younger, twenty-two maybe. Highflier right out of university. Bloody hell.

I watched them go about their work: efficient, organized, professional.

"Nothing yet on your bug, Duffy," Clare said.

"No?"

"My guess is that it's unrelated."

"I doubt that very—"

"You've ticked off some of the local players, and they're tapping your phones to see if they can blackmail you with your gay affair, or something, you think, yeah?"

"Wouldn't they just shoot me, sir?"

"No. Better to blackmail you. Have a man on the inside."

"The bug's pretty sophisticated for local paramilitaries," I said dubiously.

"You can get anything on the international arms market these days . . . Listen, when you've got a moment, I'd like you to have a wee look at the crime scene and give me your impressions."

"I've got a moment now, sir."

"Excellent. This way. Hope you haven't had a greasy breakfast."

"Just whisky."

I followed him into the kitchen.

The body was still there. Eileen Cavanagh's head had been smashed in so hard that her brains and bits of skull were all over the floor and walls. Her face was hanging off.

I wanted to throw up, but I couldn't do that in front of all these Special Branch goons and the FO men.

"Thoughts, Inspector Duffy?"

I bent down, seemingly to examine the body, but in reality to conceal the fact that my eyes were closed.

"We think she heard him coming in the back door and got out of bed and confronted him; the fight progressed to the kitchen, where she managed to grab a knife. Unfortunately, he got the skillet, and in the struggle he was able to beat her to death," Clare said.

I opened my eyes again. There was a kitchen knife in her hand, sure enough. But the handle was gripped for stabbing downward, not slashing or threatening a burglar. The knife had been put there after she was dead. A good coroner might even find livor mortis blood pooling in her palms that proved that.

"I called you in, Duffy, because this is the second IRA assassin to get hit in three days, but I think you'll agree this has more the marks of a burglary gone wrong, yes? Burglar high as a kite, it seems. No professional would leave a scene like this one, would he? I mean, there's brains hanging off the ceiling."

I looked up above my head, and sure enough, there was gore on the bulb and the ceiling. Jesus.

"Well?" Clare said.

I stood and took a deep breath.

"I'm sorry, Superintendent, but I don't think your hypothesis is the correct one," I said cautiously.

"Oh?"

"If she heard someone breaking into her house, she would have reached for the gun that you might still find under her pillow or next to her bed, and she would have stayed in her room and shot the intruder as he was coming in through the bedroom door. She wouldn't go to the kitchen to get a knife. The knife was placed in her hand postmortem."

To calm my nerves, I stood up and looked out the window for a glimpse of the River Lagan beyond the garden. The old Lagan was brown and gray. This Lagan had stretches of blue in it. The elimination of Belfast's entire manufacturing base was at least giving the river room to breathe.

"No, sir, this guy's too good to be heard breaking into someone's house. A house he has been staking out for a few days or even weeks. He broke in; he removed the gun from under her pillow; he woke her from her sleep with a gun in her face. He walked her to the kitchen, made her kneel on the floor, and smashed her head in with a skillet. Single blow. He's very strong, and good at what he does. Then he hit the body a dozen more times to make it look like there was a struggle; then he put the knife in her hands and broke the back window."

"Why?" Clare asked.

"Because he doesn't know that we're onto him."

"Are we onto him?"

"Yes. The pattern is becoming obvious now. All his victims are trained IRA killers with ties to Brendan O'Roarke. He thinks he needs to establish false trails and red herrings in their deaths so Brendan won't get spooked. The joyriders' hijack gone wrong. The woman who confronts a burglar in her own home. But it's too late for all that now. We know, and Brendan probably knows too. Someone is taking out Brendan's operatives before they initiate their coup attempt. Our guy's caution is redundant. He's a pro, but he might as well just have killed her in her sleep."

Clare shook his head skeptically, but I noticed young DI Preston nodding and whispering something to McGuinness, something that made her nod thoughtfully—so at least someone thought I wasn't a crazy old man.

"Anyway, I'll take a look through the rest of the house if that's okay," I said.

"Go ahead."

I searched the house.

Nothing of interest except her record collection, which contained some rare twelve-inch Beatles singles that I very much would have liked to nick, and could possibly have nicked if this were my investigation.

But it wasn't.

I went outside to the FO tea tent and had a cuppa with Frank.

"Gloomy in there, isn't it?" Frank said, gesturing behind him. "Special Branch don't so much as allow you to whistle. I'd rather be working in your manor."

"I'm touched, Frank."

"Don't get the wrong idea. I'm not saying you're a good peeler. I just prefer the working conditions."

"Well, you won't be seeing me for a long time, Francis."

"Why's that?" he asked with some concern.

"Young Lochinvar is back tonight, I think, and he'll be taking over Carrick CID again tomorrow, and I'll be going back to Scotland. Clare only called me in today as a courtesy anyway."

"Aye, I heard you trying to impress him in there."

"I wasn't trying to impress him. I thought his interpretation of the crime scene was wrong."

"Save it for the judge, mate. You want the rest of this smoke?" he asked, passing me the ciggie.

"Nah, you're okay."

"That's right. I forgot you've become a health nut. Oh, well, back at it. Best to Lawson, and I'll see you when I see you, okay?"

"Okay, Francis."

We shook hands and I lingered for a while, but no one seemed to want or need my services.

I checked underneath the Beemer for bombs and drove on home.

17
YOUNG LOCHINVAR'S RETURN

Pale, blond, skinny, eager, smart—Lawson looked exactly the same after his holiday in the sun.

"Spain, you say?"

"Yes, sir."

"Was it raining the whole time?"

"No, sir."

"No, it wouldn't be, would it? The rain in Spain stays mainly on the plain, so I've been told. And you were on the coast."

"Exactly, sir."

"Well, you're the only person I've ever met who has come back from Spain whiter than when he left."

"I did put on a lot of sunblock admittedly, sir."

Lawson was pleased to see me, but I could tell that something was up. And that something was pretty obvious. It was a hell of an awkward situation. Lawson was the gaffer of Carrick CID. It was his department and his show. But now he apparently had to work with Sergeant McCrabban, who was the same rank as he but had a decade of seniority on him. And worse, he had to work with me, an inspector, a full rank above him and with even more seniority.

Lawson let go of my hand.

Here come the fireworks, I was thinking, but Lawson was cut from a different cloth than the other jokers around here.

"Listen, sir, I was thinking about this. Until this investigation runs its course, how about if you reassume temporary command of Carrick CID? I know it's my manor now, but it's going to be a bit weird if I take over this investigation. You're a DI, after all."

"You're a good lad, Lawson. A very good lad. But . . . well . . . there have been a few developments since last we spoke."

I told him about the Brendan O'Roarke connection, about Special Branch taking over the case, about the second murder, about the chief inspector saying that he didn't want to pay Crabbie and me.

"So you see, Lawson, there's not much for us to do here anymore. Our case has effectively been absorbed into a wider Special Branch investigation, and we're out on our ear."

"Oh, I wasn't aware of that, sir. I'm sorry."

"No need to be sorry. Not all of us need closure. Some of us are content with open-textured endings, you know?"

"If you say so, sir."

The office door opened, and a grinning Chief Inspector McArthur burst into the room.

"Lawson! You're back! Well done. Well done!" he exclaimed, shaking Lawson's hand with delight.

"Yes, sir, I'm back," Lawson agreed.

"It's good to see you, son. Good to see you. It hasn't been easy in your absence. But we managed."

"Yes, sir, with the able assistance of DI Duffy, sir."

"Oh, yes, of course. Duffy," McArthur said, seeming to notice me for the first time. "And I suppose you'll be heading on now, Duffy."

I nodded. "Yes, I suppose so, sir. I don't have a case."

"No more overtime for either you or Sergeant McCrabban!" McArthur said, practically laughing with delight. "You should see some of the memos I've had about that from Inspector Dalziel. Whoa!"

"I can imagine, sir," I said.

"Well, I'll let you two catch up. No need to call in on your way out. See you next month, Duffy!"

"Yes, sir."

McArthur left the office with a spring in his step and a happy tune on his lips.

I looked at my watch. "Well, I'll let you get on with the paperwork if you want, Lawson."

"Yes, I expect there's a lot of it, sir . . . Unless you want to go out for a drink, sir? Maybe give Sergeant McCrabban a ring?"

I shook my head. "No, that, er, won't be necessary. Me and John are not exactly . . . we're not on the best of . . . No, er, I have to head home. I'm catching the morning ferry. I better do some packing."

"Whatever you say, sir. How is life over the water, sir?"

"It's a different world, son. Different vibe completely. When I'm done with my time, I don't think I'll come back."

"How long have you got until retirement?"

"Not quite two years and that'll be my twenty."

I know what Lawson was thinking: *By the end of my twenty I wanna be chief constable, not some broken-down part-time inspector . . .*

I said my goodbyes to Lawson and drove home.

Ferry tomorrow morning, it would have to be. Too shattered to pack up all my stuff this evening.

Just drive home and have a cup of tea or take a nap or something.

But in the five minutes it took me to get from Carrick Police Station to Coronation Road, there had been a development in the case.

The phone was ringing as I walked through the door.

"Hello?"

"Sir, it's me," Lawson said.

"Yes?"

"Well, I thought you might like to know that Superintendent Clare's team found a black Norton Commando burned out about a mile from the murder scene in South Belfast late this afternoon."

"It was about time our boy got rid of that bike. He should have done it before now," I said.

"Yes, sir, well, now he has."

"Thank you, Lawson. You best tell Crabbie. It was his case too."

"I will, sir. Good night, sir."

I hung up the phone and turned on the heat. It was raining again and cold. Maybe Crabbie would care about the Norton, but the information didn't move me much now.

Not my case.

Superintendent Clare's case.

Good luck catching this bastard.

This murderer of assassins.

He was good. Very good. I shivered at a recollection of the crime scene and remembered that this guy had been in my house too. Maybe could have killed me in my sleep if he'd wanted. But he hadn't been ordered to kill me. And he was a man who stuck to the plan, wasn't he?

Who else was on *his* kill list?

"Forget it, Duffy. Like you said, not your case. Someone else's problem now."

I was thinking about making that cup of tea when a car pulled up outside the house, blaring the Sex Pistols.

It was 1992. Who played the Sex Pistols in 1992?

I looked out the window to find out.

Oh my God, do these eejits ever learn?

Now I had to make another one of those difficult decisions: gun or hurley stick?

Both, I think. I stuck the Glock down the back of my jeans and went out to the washhouse to get my old hurley stick.

I took off my jacket and shoulder holster, went back in the house, stretched, and opened the front door.

They were piling out of their car now. Nice car. Volvo 240 estate. Orange one. Wasted on them. I like the 240 because you can you look through the headrest when you're reversing. Good Swedish touch, that.

There were four of them.

Pete Scanlon, the paramilitary thug from the other night; Jonty Reed, the Nazi-loving video-recorder thief from the other night; and two more disposable henchpeople, alas not wearing red shirts. They'd obviously come to teach me a lesson I would never forget . . . Or, more likely, they'd come to fuck up my house because they thought I was supposed to be back in Scotland.

I walked down the garden path.

I was so fed up with this whole scene now.

One iteration was okay.

But two?

It wouldn't do. It's a fine line between interesting repetition and boring tautology. Look at the career of Bach or Bob Dylan . . .

I saw the curtains twitch and close next door. She wasn't going to be impressed either, was she?

I yawned.

The sun was still shining in the long Ulster summer twilight. Stray dogs were lying in the middle of the road, kids were playing soccer and kerby. It was a lovely sepia-toned Super 8 suburban dream of a night . . .

Nice.

"Ahoy, there!" I said jauntily with the hurley stick over my shoulder.

"What are you doing here?" Jonty Reed asked, surprised to see me.

Yes, their intelligence had told them I was supposed to be away, and they had come only to fuck up my house.

"I could ask you the same question," I replied.

Jonty looked at Pete uncertainly, but Pete was made of sterner stuff. "We're here to learn you," he said unironically, getting out of the car with a metal baseball bat. Jonty got out of the car too and he also had a bat. As did the other two goons.

It was going to be baseball against hurley. The crossover game the world had been waiting for.

"Come on, then," I said.

"What if he shoots us?" one of the henchpeople said.

"Don't come on, then," I said.

"Fuck it, I don't see any gun," Pete said, and leaped over my fence and swung the baseball bat at me. The bat was very heavy, and it was easy enough to step out of its arc and hit him on the back with the hurley stick.

"Baseball is a very fine game," I said. "But if you're not used to playing it, wielding a heavy bat can unbalance you."

"You're a Fenian bastard, so you are!" Pete said, and swung again.

This time, he almost bloody got me, so I had no choice but to whack him on the top of the head with the hurley. Hard.

He went down like a ton of bricks.

I went for Jonty. Yeah, I know, Gandhi, the Buddha, all that jazz, but I mean, who can resist beating up a Nazi?

He went to swing his bat, but it banged into the car and fell out of his hand. I picked it up. He looked at the hurley stick and looked at me.

"Run," I said.

He took off down the street as fast as his legs would carry him.

One of the remaining henchpeople dropped his bat and took off after him. His mate, however, did not.

He was a big guy. Six-five, 225. Prison tats. Hard man. He looked as though he knew how to swing a baseball bat. Had been swinging baseball bats into kneecaps since he was fourteen.

He stepped away from the car to give himself some room.

"Sex Pistols fan, are you?" I asked him.

"Aye."

"'God Save the Queen'—is that what you were playing? You like that one?"

"It's good."

"You know what the key line is in that song?" I asked him as we began circling around each other in the middle of the street.

"What?"

"You're probably thinking it's 'there's no future for you.' And certainly the Sex Pistols were no strangers to simple statements of nihilism. But I don't think that's it."

"Come here so I can beat your brains out," the big man said, and I circled, carefully, out of arm's reach.

"Maybe you're thinking it's 'God save the Queen: the fascist regime'?

I don't think so. John Lydon understood the difference between oligarchy and fascism even then. I think that was just in there for the rhyme and the fact that it scanned so beautifully. And don't say 'Is this the UDA, is this the IRA?' That's a different song completely; you'll just be an idiot if you say that. No—"

The big guy swung at me, missed, and reverse-swung and missed again but not by much.

"No, the key line is, 'there is no future in England's Dreaming.' You know what the Dreaming is, right?"

"It's something to do with Australians," the big man said.

"That's right. The Aboriginals are an old culture. They're migratory. They follow what they call Dream Lines through a mythological landscape here on Earth. And what Lydon is saying in that song, I think, is that England has to recapture or reimagine its own mythological past so it can have a better future. Man can live in the desert, but he cannot live in a spiritual desert."

"Very interesting," the big skinhead said, and swung his bat vertically down toward my skull.

I dove out of the way and the bat swished through the air and hit the Volvo's roof. The big man was getting too close for comfort. I set down my beloved hurley stick and took the Glock out of the back of my trousers.

I pointed it at him and he dropped the bat and put his hands up.

"I hope I've given you food for thought," I said.

"Aye. You have."

"Great. Now, get on your knees and put your hands behind your head."

The big man did as he was bidden, and I kept the gun on him until the police showed up from the station.

A dozen peelers came because they must have gotten half a dozen phone calls from Coronation Road residents.

Among them was Rachel from next door, who was looking at me with some concern. Next to her was Mrs. Campbell, smoking a ciggie and enjoying the show.

One of the coppers was Lawson.

"Sir, when the alert came through and I heard the address, I came out here immediately. Are you okay?"

"Never better."

"What was it? Some sort of assassination attempt?"

"Nothing so grand. Some local roughnecks who wanted to smash up my house in my absence. They're lucky I *was* here. If Bobby Cameron had caught them doing something like that on his street without his permission, he'd have kneecapped the lot of them."

I thought again of Sun Tzu. And Clausewitz. I could possibly have solved this without any violence at all. That would have been the pure form of the art of persuasion. But Duffy's growth and progress was not a linear graph. Sometimes it dipped below the X axis.

"Well, since I'm out here, I should tell you that Superintendent Clare has offered me a chance to sit in on the interview with Brendan O'Roarke," Lawson said.

"O'Roarke agreed to an interview?"

"Yes. Tomorrow."

I rubbed my chin. "He must be getting worried. All his confreres getting murdered like that."

"Yes."

"And Clare says you can sit in on it?"

"Yes."

"He's not coming north of the border, is he?"

"No, Dundalk Garda Station."

"Well, that's better than nothing."

"I know you were supposed to go home tomorrow, sir, but—"

"Yeah, okay. I'm in if you want me."

"I do."

"I'll call the missus."

"Yes, sir."

"I'll have to change my ferry time, but I can stay one more day. It'll be without pay, though. McArthur says he's cutting me off, the bastard. Is, uhm, Sergeant McCrabban . . ."

"Yes, he says he wants to come."

"Well, in that case I'll definitely come."

Lawson nodded and cleared his throat. "What do you want us to do with these two? Charge them with assault?"

"Nah, no charges, I think they learned their lesson. It was a friendly textual analysis of Sex Pistols lyrics that just got a bit out of hand, that's all."

18
THE INTERVIEW

Cue the dramatic music. The low clouds. Cold north air like a lens of ice. The sun a yellow goblin glow in the east. (Yes, it was still July.) Two Land Rovers in convoy heading for the border. Two incongruous white police Tangi Land Rovers on a country road, driving through the treeless iron starkness of the Mourne Mountains.

Cows, sheep, boggy fields, bleak moorland, stone walls.

Raptors following our progress and curving through the hill country on easy thermals.

Morrigan one of those raptors.

Morrigan the crow.

Goddess of fertility. Goddess of war.

The song of the armor plate. The song of the specially reinforced police Land Rovers' tires. The whir and throb of the fuel-injected eight-cylinder engines. If you could taste a song, this song would taste of blood, sulfur, saltpeter, and, of course, fear.

We were wearing civilian clothes but with flak jackets over the top. We were armed with sidearms and had access to MP5s. This was no joke.

We drove down in convoy on the B219, to the border crossing west of Newry.

Crabbie and I were driving Land Rover 1 with Lawson, two of our trainees (DC William Mitchell and DC Judy McGuire) in the back. The second Land Rover contained DS Anthony Clare and DCI Stan Preston up front, and DI Siobhan McGuinness and DI Michael O'Leary in the back.

I'd been against bringing the trainees, but Chief Inspector McArthur told Lawson he thought it was a good idea, and Lawson didn't want to go against him when he could easily have yanked me out of this little op in the first place. And he was probably right. Good experience for them. Trip over the border. Insight into Garda procedure. A chance to interview a genuine, honest-to-God monster.

As additional security, we were escorted to the border by two armored army Land Rovers, although they would not be allowed to continue down over the border itself. When a British army patrol slipped over the border into the Republic of Ireland without permission, it always ignited an international incident.

The radio crackled, "Border approaching, two hundred yards."

The army Land Rovers pulled over.

The Northern Ireland–Republic of Ireland border had many formal crossing points and many more informal crossing points. We'd decided to cross at one of the informal roads to avoid the border traffic.

We were met on the other side of the imaginary line by an Irish police Range Rover driven by Inspector O'Neill.

We stopped, and I made the necessary introductions.

"Inspector O'Neill, may I introduce Superintendent Clare of Special Branch . . ."

Et cetera.

We all stood around the border looking like idiots for a minute. "Well, shall we go?" Superintendent Clare asked.

"Yes, let's go."

We arrived at Dundalk Garda at ten in the morning.

The interview was supposed to start at lunchtime but we got a call from O'Roarke's lawyers saying that their client had been delayed until two p.m.

We had cheese-and-pickle sandwiches at the station and kicked our heels.

At two p.m., we got a phone call from O'Roarke's lawyers saying that their client was at a construction site and wouldn't be able to make it until five.

At 5:15, we got a call saying that their client was having dinner with his family and now wouldn't be in until six. At 6:05, we got a call saying that O'Roarke was on the way, and at 6:30 we got a call stating that he would be at the station at 7:30.

He actually arrived at eight.

It was completely childish, dicking us about like that. Classier paramilitary commanders wouldn't have done it, but judging from the shit-eating grin on O'Roarke's face as he walked in, he loved it.

The interview room was too small to accommodate all the cops and all the lawyers, so we adjourned to a conference room. And there around a big oval table sat O'Roarke with two Dublin lawyers, Inspector O'Neill, me, Lawson, Crabbie, DS Clare, DCI Preston, DI O'Leary, DI McGuinness, and our two trainees standing at the back with a couple of Garda officers.

Everyone was wearing a proper suit or a uniform except O'Roarke and me. He was dressed as Farmer Giles in flat cap, tweed jacket, shirt, wellie boots, and tweed trousers. I was in my leather jacket, jeans, and lucky Che Guevara T-shirt.

O'Neill explained that O'Roarke was not under arrest but had asked to come here today to help the police with their inquiries. O'Neill started a tape recorder, and immediately one of the lawyers objected.

"No tape or videotape that may be used to incriminate my client," he said in an accent almost as posh as Superintendent Clare's.

O'Neill tried to protest, but I didn't mind.

"We don't need the tape; we just want answers," I said.

O'Roarke looked directly at me. "We meet again, Inspector Sean Duffy of Derry, currently working for Carrickfergus RUC."

"We do indeed."

"So, what is all this about?" he asked me.

"Two people working for you were both murdered in Greater Belfast in the past week. What it's about is the deaths of Alan Locke and Eileen Cavanagh."

"I knew Alan a bit. He did some artwork for me a few years ago. He was in our bowling club. I don't know this Eileen Cavanagh."

"She called you a dozen times in the past month."

"No, she didn't."

"She called you at the pay phone at the bowling club."

"The pay phone?"

"Yes."

"Anyone can call that pay phone. I'd like to see you prove that she called me."

"You've used the pay phone at the bowling club. We've photographs of you on that phone," O'Neill said.

"That doesn't prove anything," the other lawyer said. "You have no proof linking these two deceased individuals with my client."

"Aye, I don't know anything about any of that," O'Roarke said.

"Mr. O'Roarke, these two people who were clearly working for you have been killed. We would like to know why. If they've killed Locke and Cavanagh, who's to say you might not be next?" I suggested.

"I barely knew these people. They've got nothing to do with me," O'Roarke muttered.

"We believe that they were both hit men," Clare said. "And we think they might have been in Belfast under your orders."

The lawyers were outraged by this suggestion. Mr. O'Roarke was a respected businessman. He had nothing to do with the IRA or hit men or anything like that.

"You shouldn't believe everything you read in the *Sunday World*," O'Roarke said. "I'm just a businessman. I keep my nose out of politics. I don't know these people."

"You waked Alan Locke," I said.

"The bowling club waked him. He was a club member."

"Come on, Brendan, don't you see that we're trying to help you here? People are bumping off your guys. Eventually, they are going to move up the chain," I said.

O'Roarke laughed. "Very dramatic, I'm sure. But it's got nothing to do with me. I build houses. That's all."

"Then, why did you agree to this interview?" I asked.

"I always like to cooperate with the police. You seemed really anxious to talk to me, so I thought I would give you the opportunity. But this wild-goose chase of yours is really a bit too much for me. Youse have all got a great imagination, so youse have."

"You've got nothing to contribute to the case?" Clare asked, exasperated.

"I don't see how I could, since I never met Eileen and I don't really know Alan Locke that well."

Brendan poured himself a glass of water from a pitcher on the table and smiled at us all again.

"You're not getting the big picture, Brendan. Don't you see what's happening, here?" I asked him in Irish.

"What's happening?" Brendan replied in Irish that wasn't quite as good as mine.

"Your killers are being killed. Whatever coup de main you were planning against your pals in the IRA is being snuffed out before it gets going," I continued.

"What are you talking about?"

"You sent at least two of your best people north as sleeper agents. Waiting for your orders to execute a plan. But someone has betrayed you. Someone has found out about that plan. You've been outgeneraled. They've killed your soldiers and they're going to be coming for you next," I said in English.

"Who?"

"I don't know. But if you help us, we can stop this war before it gets started."

"You don't know anything, Duffy. You're a fucking amateur. A part-time policeman who is swimming in very dangerous waters," Brendan said.

"My client does not imply—" one of the lawyers began before Brendan cut him off with a gesture.

"I certainly appreciate the warning and your concern for my safety," I said.

"Who said I had any concern for a fucking traitor who has taken the king's shilling?" Brendan said, leaning across the table toward me. "You disgust me. You are worse than the Brits; you are worse than the Prods; you are the lowest form of fucking life there is. A Catholic in the police. A parasite who betrays his own. Now, why don't you fuck off back to Belfast, the whole lot of you!"

His old-man jowls were seething with hatred and anger. He was practically shaking. It was disconcerting to see an older man lose it like this. What was the source of his hate? He hadn't lost any kids to the war. He had a brother in jail and a brother on the run in France, but so the fuck what? He was rich, healthy, respected (or, if not exactly respected, at least feared).

It was strange. I had much more cause to hate than he. They'd tried to kill me and my wife and child. Assassins sent by the Army Council of the Provisional IRA. They had tried to shoot me and threatened to burn me alive. But I didn't hate him or his brothers. Or any of them.

"Why are you still here?" he asked incredulously. When dismissed from his presence, people normally got the hell away from him as fast as they could.

"I was wondering how an old man such as yourself keeps the hate burning inside you. You're shaking. There's spittle on your chin. It's not dignified."

"How dare you speak to me of—"

"I'll speak to you any way I like, Brendan of the Long Arm. *Coimhead fearg fhear na foighde.*"

"This from the man who works for Thatcher!"

"You have to keep up with current events, Brendan. Thatcher's gone. It's Major now."

"It's six of one and half a dozen of the other. We all know who's calling the shots. It's Cromwell come again to Ireland. You know it and I know it. She's worse than Cromwell. She's Hitler come again," O'Roarke said.

I rolled my eyes and said nothing. This was getting us nowhere. Why was it, in conversations with these people, it always came back to the Easter Rising, the famine, or Cromwell?

"Mrs. Thatcher is not Hitler," Superintendent Clare was saying, getting sucked in like a bloody idiot.

"That's what they said about Hitler!" Brendan replied.

I couldn't take much more of this. I got to my feet. "Really? Of Hitler they said he's not Hitler? That doesn't make any fucking sense."

Brendan stood too. He pointed his finger at Clare and me and the rest of us. "I don't know how youse can look in the mirror shaving in the morning. Traitors, the lot of you. Planter scum! Fucking Proddy planter scum!"

"I usually shave at night," Crabbie said deadpan. "No time in the morning, what with the cows and everything."

It was hard to tell with Crabbie whether he was just trying to wind Brendan up. But it tipped Brendan over the edge into a kind of madness. A *teppichfresser*-ing madness, if you want to continue the Hitler analogy. He was bug-eyed and almost literally foaming at the mouth. He banged the table so hard, the water pitcher jumped and fell on its side.

"Interview terminated," one of the lawyers said, and, with some difficulty, escorted Brendan O'Roarke from the room.

After he and his flunkies had left, a still, uncomfortable silence descended on the conference room, punctuated only by the dripping of water from the table to the floor.

"I thought that went well," I said.

"Better than I was expecting, sir," Lawson said, catching my mood.

"Yes, definitely one of the scarier individuals I've met this year," I admitted fifteen minutes later in the pub next door to the police station.

We all sipped our pints and nodded in agreement. In fact, "met this year" was only scholarly caution on my part. He was one of the scariest hardmen I'd ever met. There was nothing but animal hate behind those black eyes of his. The scariest eyes I'd seen in a long time, and I'd met Jimmy Savile and had to throw Roger Waters out of a bar once.

We got a few more beers in and swapped cop stories, and it was close to midnight when we left Dundalk, exhausted, defeated, frustrated.

Get used to those emotions, my little trainee detective chums; they're going to become very familiar to you over the next twenty-five years of your career in the RUC.

19
THE FERRYHILL ROAD

The way back north again. DS Clare in the lead Land Rover with his team, me in Land Rover 2 with mine.

It was raining and there had been some sort of road accident outside Dromad, but it wasn't a problem since the diversion signs were pointing to the Ferryhill Road, which would take us only fifteen minutes out of our way.

In the daytime, this was a lovely part of County Louth to get diverted through. Dozens of little lanes that led down to the River Newry and Carlingford Lough. This was the very place where the great Cuchulainn, Champion of Ulster, tied himself to the boulder and fought off the armies of Meath—if you believed in that sort of thing.

And why wouldn't you?

"Duffy, do you happen to know this part of the world at all?" Clare's voice came on over the radio.

I picked up the mic. "Are you lost?" I asked.

"No. I was just wondering where the border is on this road," he replied irritably.

I grinned at McCrabban. "Only Special Branch could get us lost five hundred meters from the border."

Crabbie nodded and started filling his pipe.

"Do you want me to take lead and see if I can find the border? Or should we go back to the main road?" I said into the radio.

"No! That's not necessary," Clare said. "DCI Preston has just produced a very good one-inch-to-one-mile map. We'll be fine. He knows this part of the country. We have everything in hand now."

"They have everything in hand," I said to McCrabban. "That means we could be here all night."

"Could be," he agreed. "I'm no expert, Sean, but I've bought cows down here a few times. This diversion is very strange."

"Is it?"

"Yes. This is a very narrow road to be on. If we ignore the official diversion and go back to Dromad, there are a couple of different roads that could get us—"

Weightlessness.

Metal.

Light.

Dirt.

My body crunched.

My body folded up.

Blood in my mouth.

Blood in my eyes.

Red out.

Black out.

Silence.

One beat.

Two.

Three.

Screaming.

Alarms.

Blood in my throat. Liquid on my right thigh that might be piss or blood.

Fingers on my face. Someone's hand undoing my harness. Someone dragging me. Two hands on the neck of my flak jacket. A voice calling to me from the bottom of a well. Rain on my face. My legs being dragged across the windscreen. The voice getting more insistent and distinct.

Rain on my forehead like baptismal waters.

"Sean, are you okay?"

"What?"

"Are you okay?"

I was outside the Land Rover's cab. Crabbie's nose was a few inches from my face. It was pouring. We were in a deep sheugh by the side of the road.

I could hear a noise like gunfire.

I looked down at my legs. They hurt like hell, but they seemed to be in one piece.

Water was running down the back of my shirt, and in the darkness it was impossible to tell if the damp under my arms was water or blood.

"Are you okay?" Crabbie asked again.

"I think so. Aye, I'm okay. What's happened?"

"Ambush."

"Ambush?"

"Ambush. RPG and now machine guns."

"From where?"

"Other side of the road. The hill there."

I rubbed my face and looked up the road. The first Land Rover was on its side. Ours was on its roof. They must have fired both RPGs simultaneously. Now they were shooting at us with heavy machine guns and AK-47s. Perhaps a dozen fire sources. Two IRA cells, maybe three. It was a brilliant operation. O'Roarke delays us all day at the police station; then one team trails us from Dundalk, a second team sets up the phony road diversion signs, and finally three kill teams wait for us to arrive on the Ferryhill Road.

A .50-caliber machine gun was chewing up the Land Rover's cab and engine, digging deeper into the armor with every pass. Men were yelling from inside. Crabbie had his pistol drawn, but what he was supposed to do with that against a heavy-duty machine gun, I had no idea. He might as well charge them with a samurai sword for all the good it was going to do.

It wasn't the first time Crabbie and I had been in a Land Rover that had come under attack—shit, we were probably in double figures now—but this appeared to be the last time such a thing was going to happen.

We were well fucked.

"You see Clare or Preston or any of those guys?" I asked.

"No."

"Did they get out of the cab?"

"I can't tell. They're not returning fire, anyway."

We had our bloody own problems. There were three peelers trapped in my Land Rover's main cabin, and eventually the .50-caliber would punch through the armor plate and kill them all. Lawson and that dick with the soul patch and the other trainee with the intelligent eyes—what was her name?

Black sky.

No stars.

"Sean, are you okay?"

"I'm fine. Why do you keep asking?"

"You keep passing out. Are you bleeding?"

"I don't think so."

I tilted my head up into the rain and it cooled my face.

Sitrep.

We were safe in the sheugh for now, but sooner or later the AK-47 men would move in with hand grenades and machine gun fire and finish us off too.

Because we were still on the Irish Republic side of the border, we couldn't expect help from the British army. Even if they found out about our ambush, army helicopters would not cross the border without permission from the prime minister, and he would have to inform the Irish prime minister first. All that would take hours.

"Did you call in a mayday?" I asked Crabbie.

"No time. All I did was drag you out."

I poked my head above the sheugh and looked over toward the vehicle. Bullets were thumping through the windscreen and ricocheting around in there. I could see the radio in pieces on the Land Rover's upside-down roof.

I ducked back down into the sheugh. "Radio's shot to hell anyway... Are you okay?"

"A few scratches. You?"

"I don't know. Am I bleeding?"

"That's why I asked you. Stay still."

Crabbie did a lightning triage. "You seem to be okay."

"Lawson and those others in the cab are going to die unless we can get them out of there," I said.

Crabbie handed me his gun. "You're right. You cover me as best you can. I'll try to get the back doors open."

"They'll kill you."

"I'll be all right. I'll keep low."

"Tell you what, you cover me. I'll try and get the bloody doors open," I said, trying to hand him the revolver back.

"It was my idea."

"I'm your superior officer, you bloody fool!"

"We're both part-time reservists!" Crabbie countered. "And you're the better shot. Cover me in three, two, one."

Crabbie was not exactly Mr. Adrenaline or Mr. Exuberant, so when he did assume an air of command, it was unexpected and you had to pay attention to it.

He crawled out of the sheugh, and I shot at various muzzle flashes with his revolver and my Glock.

When he got to the Land Rover's back doors, he tugged on them as the occupants inside kicked on the warped armor plate.

"Hurry up!" I yelled at him.

The doors suddenly gave way, and all three terrified young coppers came piling out.

"Over here!" I screamed. "On your bellies!"

Lawson, DC William Mitchell, and DC Judy McGuire scrambled over to the sheugh, followed by Crabbie. The darkness protected them, and they made it next to me without getting riddled with bullets.

The terrorists' plan would have been even more effective and deadlier if one of them had thought to bring a couple of starlight flares. Or if they'd had just one guy with a machine gun on the embankment behind us . . . But you can't think of everything, and Brendan's plan was probably going to be good enough.

I patted Crabbie on the back. "Good, work, mate."

He grunted a response and caught his breath.

"Lawson, Mitchell, McGuire, anyone hurt?"

"I'm okay," Lawson said. The others were too frightened to speak.

"Triage them, Crabbie. Let me know if anyone's seriously hurt."

"Will do."

"The other Land Rover?" Lawson asked.

"Up the road there, on its side. Don't know if anyone got out of it or not."

"How many terrorists?" Lawson asked, all business now.

"I don't know. Twelve?"

"Did we cross the border?"

"No, we're still in the Irish Republic."

Lawson's pale face looked grim in the moonlight. "So that's it, then?"

"No, it's not," Crabbie said. "We'll get out of this."

"Crabbie's always right. We will get out of this, okay?" I said.

"Okay," Lawson said, and the other two were still too frightened to speak.

The firing stopped as the IRA men reloaded and regrouped.

"Triage complete. Nobody's seriously hurt, Sean," Crabbie said.

"What are we going to do, sir?" Lawson asked. "Make a run for it?"

"If we leave this sheugh and try to make a run for it, that big machine gun will chew us to pieces," Crabbie said.

"I grabbed the MP5s from the cab," Lawson said.

"You did?"

"Yeah."

He reached down behind him and handed me one of the Heckler and Koch submachine guns.

"You grabbed both of them?" I asked.

"Yes, sir."

"Cool head. Well done, Lawson."

"How many mags?"

"Couldn't get the spare ammo. One each."

"Everyone else have their sidearms?"

"I lost mine somewhere," Mitchell said.

"Everybody else?"

"I've got my gun," McGuire said.

"I've only two rounds left in mine," Crabbie said.

"Here, you take the other MP5," I said, giving Crabbie the submachine gun.

I handed my Glock to Mitchell.

Time for a pep talk so they didn't go to pieces completely. "Everybody has a weapon now," I said. "And we're safe down here in the ditch. If they charge us, they're going to walk into a barrage of hell. Aim for the torso. They'll be coming across open ground. I think we can hold out here for a good wee while. We'll be okay."

There were a few murmurs of agreement.

You couldn't let them give in to shock or panic. If they panicked and started running, the terrorists could pick them off one by one. Crabbie was steady, Lawson was steady, but the kids . . . If I was shitting it (and I was), they must be far worse.

I looked at my watch: 12:15. About two minutes now without a shot being fired. What were they doing?

"Are they reloading?" Lawson asked.

"No, they're pros. That would have taken them fifteen seconds at most."

"So what are they doing?" Crabbie asked.

"I don't know. Changing position? Maybe trying to flank us? Lawson, you go to the edge of the sheugh down there, and if you see anything at all, lemme know."

"If I have a kill shot?"

"Take it."

"I will," Lawson said.

Lawson and I had been in a situation like this in Islandmagee once a lifetime ago, but that time we had three opponents and we actually outnumbered them. This time, they outnumbered us by at least two or three to one.

What the hell was happening with the other Land Rover? Were they dead? Had they gotten out and run for help?

I looked at my watch again: 12:16 and still no firing.

Could the hit teams have withdrawn? Were they trying to flank us?

I poked my head up over the sheugh and looked up and down the road. No movement, no sounds. But there at the first Land Rover, a shadow.

I got back into the trench.

"I thought I saw someone at the first Land Rover," I said to Crabbie. "I think at least one of that lot got out."

"Maybe their radio will be working?" he suggested.

"Maybe." I turned to the others. "Help's probably on the way. Just keep it together for a few minutes longer."

"Should we make contact with them?" Crabbie asked.

"I don't want to shout out and let the terrorists zero in on our voices. I think it's better to keeping fucking schtum."

Crabbie nodded. "I could crawl up the sheugh and make contact that way."

"What's with you and your heroics tonight? You have a wife and three weans. We'll just sit tight. Let the bad guys make the moves."

And that was when the first mortar round landed fifty feet in front of us and exploded in a flash of light and white-hot shrapnel.

"What the fucking hell was that?" Lawson screamed.

"A mortar," I said. "Everyone, keep your head down."

Mortars.

They'd gotten their hands on mortars, and they could just lob them at us all night until they finally found the right range and killed us all in the ditch.

We were fucked now with a capital "F" and a big mortar-shaped fucking dildo.

So this was how it was going to end. If it weren't for Emma and Beth, I'd almost be bloody glad. Dramatic.

We ducked as another mortar round whistled overhead, but this one was even farther off target, missing us *long* by a hundred feet.

They'd shot short and they'd shot long, and their range would get better.

"Wait here, Crabbie. I'll crawl along the sheugh to Clare's Land Rover and see if their radio is working."

"You stay! I'll go," Crabbie said.

I put my hand on his shoulder and our eyes met. I gave his shoulder a squeeze and he nodded.

"If I don't make it back, try to save the youngsters, eh?" I whispered.

"I will. Good luck, Sean."

I crawled along the sheugh, which turned out to be a runoff ditch from the nearby slurry field. I didn't mind the shit and the bog water and the slurry. At least it wasn't a mortar in the bloody back.

When I got to the first Land Rover, I saw DCI Preston bent over the radio set, seemingly in concentration, but when I reached him there was an enormous frothing pool of blood on the ground all around him.

"Christ!"

A piece of shrapnel had somehow missed the body armor on his chest and the metal plate over his heart, hit his armpit, and traveled down into his chest cavity.

"Talk to me," I said, but his eyes were blue and fixed and dead.

I shook him anyway.

I laid him down on the ground and ripped off his chest armor. I pulled open his shirt, but his insides had been bored out by the mortar fragment. The only thing you could say was that presumably, death would have been reasonably fast, either from the impact or from massive hemorrhaging.

I grabbed the radio, but that amazing mortar round that had killed him had also sent a shrapnel fragment into the battery pack, smashing it completely.

I banged the Land Rover's side while random tracer bullets whizzed up all around. "Is there anyone alive in here?" I yelled.

"We're alive!" the two Special Branch detectives said quickly.

"Open the door, crawl out, and follow me," I said.

"How do we know who you are?"

"I'm Duffy. You met me yesterday!"

"You could be anybody. This could be a trick."

"I'm Sean Duffy, Carrick RUC."

"I think that is his voice," one of them said to the other. The female detective inspector.

"He's a Catholic; he could be in cahoots with them. He could have set this whole thing up!" the other said.

Another mortar landed with an almighty flash in the middle of the road between the two Land Rovers. I ducked into the sheugh as glowing fragments embedded themselves into the turf behind me and into the Land Rover's soft underbelly.

"I don't know what you two are doing, but I'm going back to my lads. Preston is dead and Clare is gone. Come or stay; it's up to you!" I screamed into the Rover.

The rear door opened and a gun barrel pointed at me.

"Good, quickly now, grab everything you can in there. Guns, ammo, tear gas—grab it all and follow me. There's a big drainage ditch immediately to your left. The terrorists have mostly stopped shooting. They're firing mortars now. As soon as you come out the door, down onto your belly and into the ditch."

I took a hit of Ventolin while they gathered their gear and crawled to the ditch. They were young, scared, and badly bruised, but in one piece.

"Now back along the sheugh to the others. You'll be okay. What are your names again?"

"Michael O'Leary," the lad said.

"Siobhan McGuinness," the lass said.

"Michael, Siobhan, don't worry, you'll be telling your grandchildren about this one day. Now, come on, stay low and follow me."

Back through the filth of the sheugh on our bellies.

The rain grew harder and turned to hail. It wasn't the hail that was worrying me.

"Sean? Is that you?" Crabbie said.

"It's me."

"Are you hurt?"

"No."

"Only two survivors?" Crabbie asked.

"Preston's dead. Clare wasn't with him. He presumably has gone to get help."

"The radio?"

"Shot to pieces."

"No hope for Preston?"

"None. Died immediately. Shrapnel caught him under the arm, tore right through him."

Just then the mortars started up again.

Closer now.

Better targeted. Two shells fell on the road just ten meters in front of us, and another landed directly on the Land Rover behind us. It blew up with a massive explosion.

We covered our heads as bits of tire and glass and metal rained down like falling stars from the black, unforgiving sky.

"Oh, shit! We're fucked, aren't we?" Michael O'Leary said, his eyes wild behind his cracked glasses. "We're dead, aren't we, sir?" he said, tugging my sleeve. Now that Clare was gone and Preston was dead, I was senior officer and thus in command of the seven of us who were still alive. I took a moment to assess the situation with professional detachment. We were maybe one or two kilometers inside the Irish Republic, heavily outnumbered, completely surrounded. The radio was busted, no one knew we were here, and help wouldn't be permitted to cross the border even if it was apprised of the bloody situation. "Yeah, son, I'm sorry," I wanted to say, but I knew better than that.

"We'll be all right. I think Superintendent Clare has gone to get help," I replied instead.

And if he hasn't, I'll fucking see that bastard court-martialed and fucking shot, I thought to myself.

20
THE MORTARS

Five solid minutes of mortar fire, then silence. Pitch black apart from the starlight and the sickle moon and a dim glow to the north, which might be the town of Warrenpoint.

Rain back to the default border drizzle now.

They hadn't shot at us for ninety seconds. I knew what everyone was thinking. Hoping. *Now they've gone because they don't know our radios are damaged beyond repair. They're getting the hell out of here before the Irish army shows up.*

I looked at John McCrabban. He looked back at me: dour, Presbyterian, sensible. He shook his head. They weren't gone yet.

"They're repositioning yet again," I said. And every time, they got closer.

He nodded, and suddenly there was a sound like *whoommm* and then, in the sky above us, a firework arcing toward the trench.

"Everybody down!"

This mortar round landed on the embankment behind us, embedding itself deep in the grass and exploding with a dull thud.

The next one, a minute later, landed on the tarmac right in front of us, sending shrapnel all over the road.

The next one, a minute later, landed on the wreck of the Land Rover with an almighty metallic bang.

They seemed to have only two mortar tubes, but they were pretty good at aiming the things. (They must have practiced in Libya.) If they got one right in the middle of our trench, we were fucking toast.

"They're getting closer!" Mitchell said.

And he was right. It was dark and the angle had to be very steep, but they were getting really close.

"Maybe we should surrender," McGuinness said.

"Surrender? Come on, it's the Provisional IRA," Lawson yelled.

The IRA never released police prisoners. Cops, they tortured and shot in the head. Soldiers, they tortured and shot in the head. Occasionally, they would release prisoner officers and terrorists from other factions, but never cops or soldiers.

Lawson had taken out a black rectangle from his pocket and lifted it above his head.

"Whatcha doing?" I asked.

"I have a mobile phone. It only works in Belfast and Carrick, but maybe there's a cell tower somewhere," he said.

"A mobile phone?"

"Yeah. For emergencies and stuff."

"Give it a try."

He waved the phone above his head, trying to get a signal on the thing. It wasn't a terrible idea, but it was unlikely that the nearest village even had grid electricity, never mind a cell tower.

Crabbie passed me a canteen of water. I unscrewed the top and took a drink.

"Not even a hint of a signal," Lawson said, putting his phone back in his pocket.

"It was worth a go. Incoming!" I yelled as another mortar landed on the road in front of us.

"If they get one in the trench . . ." Crabbie said.

"I know."

And now they did produce a flare.

A white-phosphorous flare that lit up the whole night like day.

The machine guns and mortars opened up around us in a fresh, well-directed barrage.

"Everyone, stay down!" I screamed over the whimpering.

An explosion almost directly above us. An explosion with a scattering of green stars. I almost wanted to laugh at the beauty of it.

"I don't think Clare is going to be able to get help in time," Crabbie said next to me.

Aye, Clare had probably scarpered and was hiding in a field until morning.

"I think you're right, mate. But we can't get up and run. A single pass of the machine gun really would tear us to pieces."

"We can't stay here, Sean. The mortar has our position!"

He was correct.

Bugger.

When the flare died, I yelled to the others: "O'Leary, McGuinness, get over here!"

The terrified O'Leary was shaking next to Lawson with his hands over his head. McGuinness hadn't heard me.

"Lawson, grab those tear-gas canisters from O'Leary and McGuinness. Gimme them!"

Lawson crawled over McGuinness and Mitchell and found the canisters. Three of them. He crawled back and handed them to me.

"Okay, here's the plan! You lot will crawl north back to the first Land Rover. When you're down there, I'll throw these three tear-gas canisters onto the road and start shooting the MP5. They will obviously fire into the smoke, thinking we're coming out. I'll keep shooting at them, and when I've sufficiently convinced them that we're in the smoke, you lot get out of the sheugh and run down the road as fast as your legs will carry you."

"What about you?" Crabbie asked.

"In the confusion, I'll make my move, crawl down the ditch, and run after you."

"Run down the road? You're crazy!" O'Leary said.

"We don't have any choice. They've triangulated our position with the mortar. Every shot brings them closer. In five minutes, they'll be dropping the shells right on top of us."

"I'll stay with you and shoot that other MP5," Crabbie said.

"No, you run with the others," I ordered.

Crabbie shook his head. "I'm staying with you, Sean," he said firmly, which meant that was the end of the conversation.

"All right, Lawson, you'll take the others and crawl to the first Land Rover, and when you see the smoke and hear me firing you run like fuck down the road. If I'm right, the border is only a few hundred meters that way. There won't be a checkpoint on this road. It'll just be a couple of stone bollards. Get over the border and keep going. Keep going all the way to the River Newry, and when you see a house or a farm, go in and call Newry RUC."

Lawson shook his head and was about to say something, but before he could speak, another mortar round landed on the embankment behind us, just ten feet to our right. It thudded into the damp earth and exploded, throwing muck and huge clumps of turf on top of us.

"Sir, their firing position seems to be on a rise behind the stone wall to the left side of the hill there," Lawson said. "So if we can get to the sheugh on the left hand side of the road, we should be in a blind spot. We could crawl to the hedge there and return fire and help you, sir."

"No, Lawson, just run. You won't be able to hit them. They're elevated, they're behind a wall, and they have a machine gun. Just fucking run, okay? It's your job to lead these men and women to safety. Do you understand me, son?"

"Yes, sir."

"Okay, folks, listen up. Do everything Sergeant Lawson tells you to do, and you'll get out of this in one piece!"

"Yes, sir!" some of them replied.

"Remember, Lawson, down on your bellies all the way to the first Land Rover, and as soon as you see the smoke and us shooting and them returning fire, you hightail it out of there."

"Yes, sir."

He started crawling along the ditch, and the others followed him.

When I was satisfied that Lawson had gotten the two men and two women all the way to the first Land Rover, I handed Crabbie one of the MP5s and put the other in front of me.

I examined the first tear-gas canister and read the instructions. It was longer and heavier than a Coke can, with a pin at the top. You just pulled the pin and threw it.

"How's your arm?" I asked Crabbie.

"Better than yours, I think, I played cricket for Ballymena. Fast bowler."

I had never played cricket in my life, but the words "fast bowler" sounded impressive. I handed the first of the canisters to him. "Just pull the pin and throw it, it says."

Crabbie smiled.

"Listen, Crabbie, about what happened, the things that were said, I, I . . ." and the words failed.

Crabbie nodded. "I understand, Sean. We're brothers, you and me."

"Yeah."

He pulled the pin and impressively tossed the can toward the other side of the street. It ignited in midair, and immediately the road was full of milky-blue tear gas.

I tossed the second canister, with a less impressive arc, and Crabbie chucked the third. Fortunately for us, the wind was blowing from the south, and the gas blew right up the hill where the IRA men were hiding. Immediately, they began firing into the gas cloud.

"Now!" I screamed, and we shot through the magazines on our MP5s. The return fire grew more frenzied, and another shell landed just a few meters from us on the road.

I looked down the sheugh to where Lawson was supposed to be, and he and the others were now running down the road toward the border.

I shot the last of the MP5 into the cloud of tear gas, fire spitting from the muzzle into the grainy dark. I wouldn't hit anything, but it would give the fuckers something to think about.

"Come on!" Crabbie said, and we crawled down the sheugh toward the first Land Rover.

In between coughing and swearing, the IRA men were all shooting into the tear gas cloud fifty meters behind us.

"Let's go," Crabbie said, and we got out of the sheugh and ran down the road.

The border was even closer than I'd been expecting. In two minutes, we were at a couple of cinder blocks and a sign that said "United Kingdom: Road Closed Except for Agricultural Vehicles."

"I would never have taken this case if I'd known there was going to be so much running," I muttered, fumbling in my pocket for the Ventolin.

"Save your breath!" Crabbie said, and took my arm.

We reached the border, ran straight through it and up a hill.

Behind us, the shooting was still going on. The bastards would follow us here if they spotted us, so we had to keep down.

"Sir, over here!" Lawson said from a hedgerow.

"Is everyone all right?"

"Yes, sir. Some of us took a fall, but everyone's okay."

"Well, then, let's go. Single file, foot-patrol stance, at the trot. I'll go on point."

"I'll go on point," Crabbie said. "You take your inhaler."

We jogged down the hill until we reached the River Newry. Not a house or a farm to be seen. Just the fifty-meter-wide river. This part of the borderlands was very confusing indeed. If we went roughly northwest along the riverbank, we'd reach Newry; if we went southeast, we'd be back in the Irish Republic again. If we crossed the river, we'd be in the safe garrison town of Warrenpoint.

"How deep do you think that water is?" Lawson asked.

"Deep, and it's flowing fast. It would be typical if we survived the ambush and then drowned ourselves. We'll head toward Newry. I think it's only a couple of miles up the road."

Newry was a Republican stronghold and would not exactly be a welcoming bastion for a bedraggled police patrol, but there was an RUC station at the top end of town.

"This way," Crabbie said, and I followed him with the others.

We never made it to Newry. Half a mile along the river, we came across an Ulster Defence Regiment patrol who had been summoned out of their barracks by the sound of explosions. They had set up a roadblock and were nervously pointing rifles at us as we headed toward them.

"Who goes there?" a young squaddie asked. He vibed trigger-happy teenager itching to kill someone. That would be another ironic death I didn't want, so I put my hands in the air and yelled back: "We're police. We got ambushed by the IRA just over the border."

"Identify yourself!" another voice yelled.

"We're police! Detective Inspector Sean Duffy of Carrickfergus RUC!"

"An overdue alert's just been posted for you!" the voice said.

And the soldiers lowered their weapons.

And we were safe.

21
THE AFTERMATH

Two Land Rovers blown up and utterly destroyed. One man dead. You'd think that the press would see this as a disaster; but in fact, for reasons I was too stupid to understand, the local papers were portraying it as an IRA failure and something of a police triumph.

I didn't think it was much of a triumph with a man's guts spilled out over the countryside. And it was only relative failure compared to, say, the Warrenpoint Massacre, which took place in 1979 just two miles from where we were hit. In that incident, the IRA's South Armagh Brigade had ambushed a British army convoy with two large roadside Semtex-and-fertilizer bombs. That had been a classic guerrilla operation. The first bomb targeted a British army lorry, and the second targeted the rescue personnel sent in to deal with the first incident. IRA men in a nearby wood opened up with machine guns on the arriving troops and medics. Eighteen soldiers had been killed in that op, and another dozen seriously wounded.

That was a triumphant day for the IRA.

The killing of one RUC chief inspector? It made the headlines in the *Belfast Telegraph,* the *Newsletter,* and *Irish News* but didn't even make it into the first five stories on the BBC news, nor did it make it onto the front pages of any of the English tabloid papers.

Of course, there would be an inquiry four or five months from now. We'd all show up in our shiny dress uniforms and give whatever official version we'd been told to give. Not the truth. Never the truth.

And I knew what was going to happen to the remains of our case. A case like this that involved the killing of a Special Branch detective could not possibly be handled in any way by a part-time CID detective out of a provincial station like Carrickfergus RUC.

Discharged from the City Hospital with only cuts and bruises, I put on a suit and tie and went into the station to await my certain fate.

The fate arrived later that day when Superintendent Clare came by to see me with several new young protégés. I didn't even bother to get their names.

"That was quite something, wasn't it?" he said.

"Yeah, it was."

"Amazing, really, that more people weren't killed."

"Well, one's enough, surely?"

"I'm so glad *your* team made it out, safely."

I had two ways to go here. I could say "yeah" and leave it at that, or I could piss off a Special Branch superintendent by stirring shit: Where the fuck did you go, pal? What the fuck were you doing?

Crabbie was doing his old telepathy trick and giving me a slight shake of the head. *Let it lie, Sean. It's all over and done with.*

"Pity about Chief Inspector Preston," I said.

"Yes. He was a good man. But it could have been a lot worse, couldn't it?"

"I suppose it could, but like I said, one death is enough."

Clare frowned. The local press had lauded Superintendent Clare and me for leading our respective Land Rover crews to safety. Superintendent Clare's picture had appeared in the *Newsletter,* and his bravery commented on.

I couldn't blame him for Preston's death, but as far as I could see, he had abandoned his people "to go and get help."

Help that never arrived.

"Yeah, we made it out safely," I said, and then after a long pause added, "No thanks to you."

"What's that supposed to mean?" Clare said icily.

"You don't abandon people under your command," I said equally coldly.

"I didn't abandon anyone. I went to get assistance."

An icy silence.

Crabbie saying nothing.

Clare saying nothing.

I thought about the future.

Twenty-five months until I could leave the RUC with a full pension. Twenty-six months until Crabbie could leave with a full pension.

Clare was a coward and a liar, but he was a superintendent being groomed to be the poster boy for all the Catholic coppers on the force. He was important, and we were . . . we were nothing.

This was the crucial moment. The moment when I took this further or shut my mouth. The silence was so thick and moldy, you could cut it with a rusty penknife.

Frank Serpico had given a talk at the Royal Hotel in Glasgow a year before that I'd attended with a few Strathclyde Constabulary friends. He'd begun his talk with a quote from Burke: "In order for evil to flourish, all that is required is for good men to do nothing."

But our pensions . . . the future . . .

I took a breath, sighed.

"Of course. Yes, sir, you went to get help," I muttered at last.

"I didn't abandon anyone," he said.

He knew that I knew he had run. But he also knew that I wasn't going to do a damn thing about it. So who was the real coward here? The man who runs away from a gun fight to save his life, or the man who keeps quiet to save his bloody pension?

I looked down at the table. "No, sir, sorry, I misspoke."

Clare nodded slowly.

"I'm glad we got that sorted out. There will be an inquiry, of course. A man died, but since you're based in Scotland now, Inspector Duffy, I don't think it'll even be necessary to make you come over for a long and tedious set of hearings."

I wasn't even going to get to speak at the official inquiry? An inquiry into an ambush of two RUC Land Rovers across the border? Where a policeman had died?

"How will that work, exactly?"

"You'll make a statement and it will be read into the official record.

There won't be any need to drag you away from your comfortable home over the water."

So the fix was in already. Exonerations for everyone—hell, maybe even commendations for everyone.

"No, I suppose not," I said.

"And now I probably should come to the real purpose of my visit here today. As you're probably aware, Special Branch has assumed full responsibility for all aspects of this investigation."

"I know."

"We have all the physical evidence, but I'll need those Picasso paintings as well. They're evidence and they're not in the property room."

"Oh, yeah, of course. Too valuable for the property room. They'll get knocked about in there."

"Where are they?"

"I've got them in storage."

"Bring them over today or tomorrow at the latest while my men are packing up the last of the evidence boxes. We don't want any hint of impropriety."

"What sort of hint of impropriety?"

He could see I was still spoiling for a fight, so he didn't press it. This son of a bitch implying that I would steal a dead man's paintings? Who did he bloody think he was?

Although . . .

He had a few more words.

Boilerplate nonsense.

I listened, let him talk, let him go, watched through the incident room window as he drove away.

I went into the chief inspector's office. "Is the case resolved to your satisfaction? Because if it is, I'm going back to Scotland," I said.

"You removed it from our books, and that's what counts."

No convictions, no resolution, no answers, but it was removed from the books.

I went back to Coronation Road, took the Picassos off the wall of my living room, and drove up to Archie Simmons's house.

He opened the door suspiciously. "What do you want now?"

"Can I come in?"

"I suppose so."

I went inside with the Picassos under my arm. He looked at them and said nothing. I sat down on the sofa in his living room and put the Picassos on the coffee table.

"Cup of tea?" he asked.

"No thanks. Time is of the essence. I've got a proposition for you."

"Go on, then."

"How much to make a couple of copies of these? Really good copies that look like the originals."

"How much are you willing to pay?"

"How much to do the copies?"

"Shall we say, five hundred quid each?"

"You're joking. Five hundred for both."

"Eight hundred for the pair."

"Let's split the difference and say seven."

"Seven-fifty."

"Done. Can you have them made by the end of the day?"

"Impossible!" he exclaimed, his eyes wide.

"What do you mean, impossible? I've seen how fast you work, mate."

"This is a metal etching, not a painting."

"What does that mean?"

"It's an engraving onto metal. It's a whole process. You have to cut the engraving, then do the acid bath, then do the prints themselves. It's not something you knock out in an afternoon."

"How long will it take?"

"If you want to get it as close to the originals as possible, I'll have to experiment with the colors and the process and—"

"How long?"

"A week."

I shook my head. There was no way I could hold off Special Branch for a week.

"Could you have it done by tomorrow afternoon if there was an extra hundred quid in it for you? Eight hundred and fifty quid altogether."

Archie shook his head. But he didn't say no.

I opened up my wallet and counted out seventeen fifty-pound notes. I put them down on the coffee table in the living room.

"I'd have to work all day and all night," he said.

I put three more fifties on the coffee table.

"That's a thousand quid."

His eyes took on a malevolent glint. "You're a bad man, Sean Duffy. What are you up to?"

"Never you mind. Can you do this for me or not?"

"I can do it. I have everything I need here. I've done the process before for a few wee jobs here and there."

"Exact copies, or as exact as you can make them."

"I'm good, Duffy. That's why you came to me, isn't it?"

I went back to Coronation Road and called Portpatrick and told Beth I was booked on the six p.m. ferry tomorrow. She was thrilled.

I hadn't even told her about the gun battle. Maybe she'd never find out about it. The story hadn't made the Scottish papers, and she didn't get the *Newsletter* or the *Belfast Telegraph*. It was possible her parents would read the story, and if they did, I'd tell her that the whole thing was exaggerated by the press, as usual.

"Is your case finished, then? Did you find the murderer?" she asked.

"No. Special Branch have taken over the investigation. But that's almost as good as the real thing."

A day to kill. I drove to Belfast and talked to Terry in Good Vibrations, but he was depressed about the musical direction of the planet, and not in good form.

"Don't you like the stuff coming out of Seattle?" I asked him.

"I'm supposed to be impressed because they finally get punk fifteen years after everyone else?"

"It's not quite punk, Terry; it's its own thing. Beth and I saw Nirvana at the . . ."

But Terry wasn't listening. Terry's method was to discourage new customers by mocking their musical tastes, and to alienate his old customers by telling them they had gone soft in the head for listening to the propaganda of A and R men and John Peel . . .

Back to Carrick.

I dined alone at a new Indian restaurant out on the Belfast Road that was pretty good.

Sleep. Bed.

Next morning, the Special Branch team was still packing up the boxes, but they were nearly done.

I drove to Archie's house.

"Do you have those Picassos?"

"Yes, but they're not completely dry yet."

"I need them now."

Blow-dryer.

Archie not happy: "This is a farce, so it is. It's humiliating. Unprofessional."

I took the fakes to the station. Clare was there for the last of the stuff and the signing of forms.

I gave him the fake only-just-dried Picassos.

"Extraordinary," he said. "They look so fresh."

"Yeah, well, don't put your big grubby fingers on them. Apparently, they're worth a few grand each."

"More than that, surely."

"No, they're just prints. He did hundreds of them. I want a bloody receipt for these. I wouldn't want to see a profile of Chief Constable Anthony Clare in the *Belfast Telegraph* and notice these behind him on the wall in his living room," I said with a jocular tone.

But not *that* jocular.

"I'll type it for you," he said.

"When? I'm leaving today."

"Hold your horses. I'll do it now if you want."

"Please."

I took the CID-headed paper and put it in the typewriter.

Transfer from CID Property Room Carrickfergus RUC to custody of

Special Branch. Receipt for two Picasso etchings. Vollard Suite B.162. Signed by the artist.

Clare signed it, and I photocopied the receipt and made him sign the photocopy too.

We said our goodbyes.

When the Special Branch men were gone, Crabbie gave me a funny look.

"You're up to something. I can always tell when you're up to something."

"I'm not up to anything. I just wanted to see those pictures safely taken out of our hands."

I gave him a big hug, which he, of course, hated.

"I've a ferry to catch. I'll see you next month, mate, okay?"

If Lawson didn't need us, it would be back to traffic and admin for the pair of us. But that was okay. One month closer to a pension.

"If we're in on the same days, you'll come up to the house, won't you? Helen always enjoys having you over, and the boys miss their Uncle Sean."

"Dinner? I'll do it."

He stared at me and put his big, meaty paw on my shoulder.

"I know you, Sean."

"I know you do."

"I think I know you as good as anyone."

"That might be right."

He shook his head. "It's over, Sean. It's not our case anymore. It was never going to be our case. As soon as it got complicated, it was always going to get kicked upstairs."

"So what—"

"So you have to let it go. You have to promise that you won't go back to Dundalk or do anything else stupid."

"I'm on the ferry tonight, mate. Finito."

"Good. I'll see you next month."

Touching, that.

Crabbie worried about me.

Crabbie worried that Sean Duffy was going to do a Sean Duffy. But what could I do, exactly?

I went in to say goodbye to Lawson.

"I'm off. I'll maybe see you next month."

"Oh, sir, uhm, you left two bottles of liquor . . ."

"You're head of CID, Alex. When someone senior comes in your office, you offer them a drink. That's what men do. Okay? Keep those bottles, and when a higher-up comes in, offer them a drink. I should have told you this before now."

He nodded. "Thank you, sir, I'll do that . . . Are you off to Scotland?"

"Aye."

"And the Locke case?"

"A good old SEP."

"Someone else's problem?"

"Exactly."

I drove down to Larne and caught the ferry.

Larne to Stranraer.

Stranraer to Portpatrick.

I saw the next door neighbor I had beaten the shit out of a year earlier. He had another new car. Protective of his cars, this bloke.

He saw me.

"How do?" I asked.

"Okay."

"New car?"

"Aye, but I don't mind if it gets the odd scrape. It's only wheels to get around in, after all, isn't it?"

"Yeah," I agreed.

I went inside and distributed hugs and presents.

Later, after dinner.

"I saw our neighbor outside. He's got a new car. Everything all right now with him?" I asked.

"Yeah, I saw the new car. I remember what happened last year, so I took preemptive action," she said.

"Did you?"

"Yes. I said I hope I don't hit your car again! And he laughed. And then he came over in the afternoon. He couldn't have been nicer. He brought a big bunch of flowers, and a Lisa Simpson doll for Em. Remember last year, you wanted to threaten him?"

You don't know this, honey, but I nearly fucking killed him.

"Yeah, I remember."

"Threatening people isn't always the answer. Some people are just nice. They make a mistake and they realize it's a mistake, you know?"

"I'm very glad. Oh, I almost forgot. I got something for the living room. That space opposite the fireplace."

"What?"

"I think you'll like this."

"What is it?"

I went to the car and brought in the Picassos. "Original Picasso screen-prints. Got them from an old friend."

Beth's face lit up.

"Originals! Aren't they worth millions?" she said suspiciously.

"No. Unfortunately not. He made a couple of hundred in this series, so they're not worth that much. Still, lovely, aren't they?"

"Yes. And they'll look terrific in your den, I think. They're a bit too scandalous to put above the fireplace in the living room."

Later still, after Beth and Emma had gone to bed.

I looked at the Picassos on the wall.

I had no guilt about it.

Locke had no next of kin. It would go to the Special Branch property room, where it would remain for two or three years while Clare's investigations got nowhere.

They'd lie in that property room for years until someone nicked them or they got destroyed.

Eventually, ten years from now, some eejit clerk at Special Branch might remember them and they'd get auctioned, and the money would go to the Treasury.

Fuck the Treasury.

And fuck Special Branch.

And fuck this case.

22
THE LAST INTERVIEW

Middle of the night. Cold sweat. A noise in the living room. Gun under pillow, check on Beth, check on Emma, walk down the hall.

Living room overlooking the black sea. A man in a balaclava sitting on the sofa, holding an AK-47.

"Well, this is overly dramatic," I said.

"Aye, it's not the Odessa Steps sequence, but it'll do. Do you know how easy it was to get in here?"

"What do you want to do, kill me?"

"That's not a serious question, is it? If I wanted that, you'd already be dead."

"So what do you want?"

O'Roarke took off his balaclava. "You're naive, Duffy. Do you think twenty miles of sea can protect your family from a mishap?"

"What's my family got to do with it? I didn't come after *your* family."

"No. But we're different men, aren't we?"

I sat up in the bed, completely awake, drenched with sweat. I hyperventilated for a minute and a half before my breathing regulated and I calmed down. I removed the Glock from underneath the pillow and sat on the edge of the bed for some time. I took a hit on my asthma inhaler and went into the living room. There was no one there. I cleared the house and checked on Emma. She was sleeping deeply. Even the cat was sound asleep in his basket.

I sat down next to him and stroked his head.

"You won't protect us, that's for sure," I said.

He purred, grew irritated with the stroking, and tried to bite me.

Music would wake the whole house, so I turned on the TV, but it was that dead time when nothing was on but the Open University. I turned it off again. I was restless, troubled. My subconscious knew something that I hadn't quite processed yet.

I had made it personal with O'Roarke.

I was on his radar now.

I was a legitimate target.

As a Catholic policeman, there would always been a bounty on my head until the day I retired—hell, even after I retired, but few gunmen would take the trouble to come over to Scotland to off one Fenian peeler.

But O'Roarke would, wouldn't he?

I'd annoyed him.

And he'd tried to get me and squibbed it.

And he would try again.

Damn it.

I poured myself a glass of Bowmore and opened the French doors.

Salt and cold and a sea breeze that was coming from the north. I was still spooked, so just to be on the safe side I went outside onto the street. Quiet. The lights on both neighboring houses were out. It was so quiet, I could hear every curl of the sea on the shore.

Into the back garden with its view of the North Channel.

And there across the water was the Kilroot Power Station chimney, and the lights of Whitehead and north Down. The angle isn't quite right to see Coronation Road, but with a good telescope you could see Carrickfergus Police Station. In fact, you can even see Lawson's office window.

This stretch of water was nothing to a man like Brendan O'Roarke, and finding out my home address would not be difficult for him.

I sat down on one of the garden chairs damp with dew. I rested the Glock on the glass tabletop.

I never get dreams like that, and it had unnerved me.

O'Roarke wouldn't do the actual killing himself. He'd send one of his assassins if he wanted me dead. If he could spare one of his assassins, because someone had been going around killing those very assassins, getting closer every day to killing O'Roarke himself. One way of looking at it was to think that the person was doing me and everybody else who wanted peace in Ulster a favor.

But that's not quite the way I looked at it.

They'd committed a murder.

On my patch.

And he'd killed a cop right in front of me.

And if I still could, I'd bring the bastard down for it or help Lawson or Special Branch bring the bastard down.

I'd protect my family, but I'd bring him down.

I finished the Bowmore and had no more reflections or insight or anything else. I just didn't know what to do, and for someone who'd had a little bit of power for eighteen of the past twenty years, this feeling of impotence was new and unpleasant.

Have to get used to it. When I retired properly, I'd be handing in my gun, and although I got on well with the Dumfries and Galloway cops, I knew they wouldn't tolerate a rogue peeler in their parish, so I'd have to be on my best behavior. No gun, no bullying the neighbors, no heroics. There were millions of us forty-year-old men going to seed in contemporary Britain. Getting fatter, getting slower, complaining about the music.

"Fuck it," I said, and went back to bed.

The next morning, Emma got me up and I made everyone scrambled eggs and toast with butter and marmalade. I kissed Beth goodbye and walked Emma to kindergarten.

A few of the other parents nodded at me as I walked her into the playground, but of course, in that Scottish way, no one tried to engage me in conversation.

I went back to the empty house. I put on Radio 3 and tidied up.

The Scottish day: warm with a pink sky like crab apple blossoms, and a highland breeze bringing pine and hawthorne and all the Pictish consonants.

Radio 3 was in the middle of a Brahms marathon, so I switched to Atlantic 252, one of the pirate stations broadcasting from the Irish Sea. They were playing "These Days," which was a nice little song only partly ruined by Nico's weird tone-deaf singing.

I turned off the radio and sat in the quiet living room.

I picked up one of Beth's *Wooden Boat* magazines and started flipping through it.

Beth had circled a listing for a River Nile tour that was taking place in October: "Join us for eleven incredible days exploring the Nile's finest ancient maritime attractions with renowned Egyptologists Colleen and John Thompson. This century-old paddlewheeler remains a symbol of the golden age of river travel and carries her passengers in belle epoque luxury and comfort . . ."

Beth had underlined day four of the tour, which was a "visit to the boat yard servicing an active fleet of Aswan feluccas."

The phone rang.

"Hello."

"Hi," Beth said. "What are you doing?"

"Nothing. Reading."

"Whatcha reading?"

"*Wooden Boat* magazine," I said. "You've circled the Nile cruise thing."

"Oh, my God, doesn't it look incredible?"

"Well . . . could we afford it?" I asked, thinking of the grand I had just spent forging two Picassos for the Special Branch property room.

"I think so. I have a few shares that I'd like to get rid of."

Beth, I knew, came from money. But how much money she had was not something I had pressed her about too deeply. We had a joint account, but she still had money in her building society and she had her shares. For all I knew, these shares could amount to a couple of hundred quid or fifty grand . . .

"Well, if we've got the money, would we all go?"

"Of course."

"What is a felucca, anyway?"

"It's a shallow-draft sailing boat with usually two lateen sails."

I held the phone away from my head and thought about it. Maybe not a bad future, Beth leading me from ancient shipyard to ancient shipyard. Forget Ulster. Forget the war. Develop other interests. My obsession with O'Roarke was in danger of becoming Melvillean.

"Is that why you called?"

"Oh, no, I almost completely forgot. You got a call from a Bob Urquhart, from the Dumfries and Galloway police. They've confirmed your range time for ten this morning."

"I'll head over there now. Give me something to do," I said.

"Yes, that's what I was thinking, if you're determined not to take up golf."

"I am determined not to take up golf."

"Okay, then. Must dash. Bye, sweetie."

"Bye."

I hung up the phone.

Beth worried about me on my downtime. She worried that I would get bored having nothing to do twenty-four days out of the month; hence the hints about golf and reminders to go to the range and trips to Egypt . . .

I went to the range and shot paper targets.

Targets don't shoot back at you.

But range time can often be clarifying.

"Beth. I'm sorry about this. I have one loose end to tie up. Have to go back to Ireland, but I'll probably be back tonight, I promise," I said making it sound casual.

The ferry to Belfast.

An easy passage over the chilled out Irish Sea.

The drive from Belfast to Newry.

Over the border yet again.

Through the Mourne Mountains to Dundalk.

The bowling club. No sign of our boy.

"Brendan's not in today?"

"He is not," a caretaker said.

"Where is he?"

"He's at home."

"It's that big house on Point Road, yeah?"

"No he moved from there. On the Shore Road now, you can't miss it."

Brendan's big house on the Shore Road. A big modern job overlooking the water. A red-brick castle with a turret at the back, and everything.

I parked the Beemer and took a deep breath.

Do you really want to do this?

I don't know.

I walked up a gravel drive and rang the doorbell.

Brendan answered it.

"Saw you coming through the TV camera," he said.

"Can I come in?"

"Sure. Follow me to the lounge."

I went inside.

It was like a Ken Adam set from a late sixties Bond flick with maybe more high key spotlights. Brendan had a full bar off to one side, and the oversize speakers for his stereo setup might have given Ozzy Osbourne pause.

I sat on a white sofa next to a white rug over hardwood floors. Brendan handed me a bottle of Guinness Extra Stout and a bottle opener.

"Do you need a glass?" he asked.

"Are you using a glass?" I asked cagily.

"Of course. I'm not a barbarian."

"Then I'll take one."

He handed me a milk tumbler, and I tilted it three degrees from the horizontal and poured in the Guinness.

There was only a moderate head, which seemed to mollify Brendan a little. I was a traitor copper from the north, but at least I could pour a pint of beer like a man.

"Huh," he grunted.

We sat in silence for a minute.

"Nice finally to have a drink with one's real enemy. Not Man City, but one's *real* enemy," he said.

I knew he was looking at me. The peat fire crackled. A cat rubbed itself against my legs. From upstairs there was a strange, muffled thumping that could be anything from the boiler playing up to an informer being beaten to death with a blackjack.

"You find you need a fire in July?" I asked.

"It's freezing here all the time. House is too big. Can't heat it."

"Blame the builder."

"I am the builder."

"I know."

"I heard you're a bit of a music lover," Brendan said.

"I can take it or leave it."

He rummaged through the record stacks, found the album he was looking for, and took it out of its sleeve. He cleaned it with an antistatic brush and carefully moved the needle to the fifth track.

"What do you think of this?" he asked.

It was Ella Fitzgerald singing Rodgers and Hart's "Blue Moon" over a full string orchestra. When the song was over, he carefully lifted the needle from the turntable and put the record back in the sleeve.

"That was very—" I began, but Brendan cut me off.

"Not yet!" he said.

He put on another record. It was "Blue Moon" again but a different version. Slightly slower, with only a guitar. The voice was unmistakably Julie London's. One of my grandmother's favorites. I hadn't heard this particular track before, although I was familiar with London's version of "Cry Me a River," which my grandmother had played over and over.

When the song ended, Brendan put it back in its sleeve and sat down again.

"Which did you prefer?" he asked.

It was probably a trick question. You'd be a fool to go against the great Ella Fitzgerald, who had one of the sweetest voices of the twentieth century, but just this time I'd actually preferred the London version.

"The second one. Julie London."

"Not the first one?" he asked.

"No. Ella's got a beautiful tone, but somehow Julie London just nails this song."

Brendan smiled with satisfaction. I had given him the correct answer.

"Yes," he said, and finished off his Guinness. He got up, went to the kitchen, and came back with two more bottles, but just then his wife, Elaine, came down the stairs.

"This is Sean Duffy, from the north, originally a Derry man. Sean, this is Elaine, my wife. She's from Fermanagh."

We shook hands. "Lovely part of the world, Fermanagh," I said.

"It is," she agreed. "How's he treating you? He can be a bit odd with visitors."

"He played me two versions of 'Blue Moon.'"

She looked horrified for a moment. "Not Elvis and Mel Torme?"

"No. Julie London and Ella Fitzgerald."

She sucked in her breath. "And what did you say about them?"

"I said that Ella Fitzgerald had a beautiful voice, but for some reason, I liked the Julie London version a little better."

She smiled and patted me on the shoulder. "You dodged a bullet there."

I smiled at Brendan. I'd dodged quite a few of his bullets. And his bloody mortars.

"Well, you boys chat. I'll see about lunch. Do you like sandwiches, Sean?"

"Love 'em."

When she'd gone, I finished the bottle and put it on the tabletop. "I looked for you at the bowling club."

"I don't go every day."

"What makes you tick, Brendan?"

"I'll tell you."

He told me.

The poor man did not depart from his well-beaten track: evil Brits, Thatcher, the famine, Bloody Sunday, and so on.

I wondered after a time if he had forgotten to whom he was speaking. This was the boilerplate one churned out for visiting Irish American dignitaries, not inspectors of the police from either side of the border. Did this traditionally wearisome diatribe ever impress anyone?

Finally, he even got bored with it himself and stopped.

He had made me angry now. This man had killed one of my colleagues. A kid, really. A frightened kid. And he was giving me bloody music exams and talking crap about Cromwell as if I were some dim-witted Kennedy just off the plane from Logan?

"What was the purpose of this visit, Inspector? To warn me or to threaten me?"

He had me there.

I didn't know the answer.

"I wanted to let you know that I am not investigating you. I'm off the case. Our paths won't cross again."

"Then what are you over here for?"

"I had a dream you came into my house to kill me and my wife and child."

"I wouldn't do that."

"Wouldn't you?"

"No."

"No, but you know people who would. Who would do it for you if you gave the word."

"So what is it that you want?"

"I want your promise that you won't come for me or for my child or for my wife. Especially not them."

"And in return?"

"We leave each other be."

Brendan thought about it.

He stared at the fireplace. The turf logs charcoaling white.

"It's the fucking Tories. North and south. We're playing into their hands. They want the working classes at one another's throats because they know that if we're ever united, it'll be the fucking Tyburn gibbet for the lot of them."

Brendan's face was red and he was getting all worked up again.

"Do you have any kids?" I asked him.

"No. I had a son. Didn't make it. Leukemia. This was a long time ago. It's curable now. His type. Curable, but not then."

"I'm very sorry to hear that."

"Do you want another record? If you guess this one, I'll be very impressed."

He put on "Music, Maestro, Please" by Tommy Dorsey. It was obvious from the third bar. I pretended it was a hard one and only told him what it was at the end.

We had a third bottle of Guinness, and he walked me to the door.

"I won't come after you," Brendan said. "I had my chance and I blew it. Every dog has his day."

"Who do you think's been killing your people?" I asked him.

"I don't know. But something tells me it's not local."

"Spooks?"

"Maybe. I thought you were off this case."

"I am. I'll get in trouble if I start nosing around."

"Sean Duffy is born to trouble as the sparks fly upward," he said, paraphrasing the book of Job.

He offered me his hand and I had no choice but to shake it.

Outside the house, I wiped my hand on the back of my trousers.

"Cop killer," I muttered, and spat.

I drove to the Garda station and let them know I'd been by. They weren't pleased to see me. Very few people on this island are pleased to see me. But these people were getting sick of my ugly mug around the place. Who was this high-handed RUC goon who kept coming into their parish to tell them their business and point them in the direction of a bad man?

An RUC goon who had gotten himself blown up on the wrong bloody side of the border, creating an international incident.

An RUC goon who had—according to the files—somehow fucked up a prosecution against a Finnish national that the Garda had arrested on a murder rap and transferred into this goon's custody. I was a walking disaster area. And what's more, I was a part-time, nearly retired burned-out walking disaster area. They were so annoyed with me in Dundalk Garda that I wasn't even offered a cup of tea.

I got the message: See ya later, lads, on the other side of the river.

23
KILLIAN'S INTEL

You know the old trope about the detective who solves the case but can't solve his own life? You've seen that one a million times. So have I. Suicide and alcoholism in the RUC aren't occupational hazards, they're actual career pathways in the brochure they give you when you join: admin; forensic; community policeman; detective; riot squad; station drunk number 1; station drunk number 2; quiet guy who shoots himself and is missed; loud, annoying, wife-beating guy who shoots himself and is not missed.

Glad to be out of it.

Glad to be across the sheugh.

New world over here. Cold turkey on the ciggies. Down to a lunchtime drink and a couple in the evening. Still the occasional spliff, but trust me, it does more good than harm.

The night ferry.

My own bed.

Morning.

Daughter curled on the sofa in a gold-colored blanket. Pale, beautiful, wild-haired like an Irish princess in exile in a foreign court.

Soldiers and boiled eggs for her this morning. "These floppy bits of toast with butter all over them, these are called the soldiers."

"I know that."

"And the eggs. The boiled eggs. Do you know what they are?"

"They're not anything. Its eggs and soldiers. The eggs are just eggs."

"The floppy bits of toast are the soldiers, but the tough-looking hard-boiled eggs, now, they're policemen. See how they're all lining up together? There's probably a riot about to happen. The soldiers will run, you'll see, or panic, but the cops—the cops will stay calm and still."

Emma listened politely to this and then picked up one of the silver teaspoons and cracked down in the middle of one of the eggs. She peeled off the excess skin and shell and dunked the soldier in the running mess.

"Looks like you're enjoying it," I said.

"Yeah."

"As long as you don't think hitting the policeman was the best bit."

"No, Daddy, of course not!"

I dressed her and walked her to school.

Walked home along the cliffs. Thought of Dirk Bogarde walking along these very cliffs in *Hunted* (1952), directed by Charles Crichton. Bogarde tries to escape his murder rap by fleeing to Ireland, just over the horizon.

Ireland lurked there in the mist.

I ignored it and walked home. Another day listening to records and staring out the window at the water. That's what you did on off days: make breakfast, walk Emma to school, go for a walk, sit in the living room and watch the sea. Wait. Wait for what, exactly? Waiting is its own reward, say the Zen masters. "Why are we waiting?" chant the fans on the Liverpool Kop.

Fingers reaching for the telephone dial.

Crabbie's home number.

"How do?"

"Sean, what about you?"

"How's the farm?"

"It's good. Milk subsidy went up by five pence."

"What does that mean?"

"They give us five pence more per gallon."

"Who does?"

"The EEC . . . the Europeans."

"And what do they do with the milk?"

"I have no idea."

"It's the Germans who are subsidizing this whole milk-buying business."

"Aye."

"They buy all the Irish milk and French butter and Italian grapes."

"Aye."

"To keep the farmers in jobs."

"Aye."

"And I buy a new BMW every couple of years to keep them in jobs, so in effect, it's me that's buying all that milk, isn't it?"

Crabbie knew me well. Too well. "What's on your mind, Sean? Is it the case?"

"No. I just wanted to chat."

"You have to let it go, Sean. It's Special Branch's case now. The tiny bit of the investigation that's left in Carrick is Lawson's case now. They're all Lawson's cases now."

"We have to let this one go?" I asked semirhetorically.

"Aye, Sean, we do," Crabbie said firmly. "We're the wee dog chasing the post van. Even if the post van stops for us, what can we do but bark at it? We're not real peelers anymore."

"That hurts."

"Does it? It shouldn't. It was the choice you and I both made. We make choices and we live with them."

"Since when did you get so wise?"

"I've always been wise; it's just that you never listened to me before."

"You're hitting me with too many truth torpedoes too early in the day, mate. I'm going to have to go."

"Take it easy, Sean. Buy a dog and then walk the dog. Play a round of golf. These are your golden years. And if you're still bored, I could do with a hand bringing the yearlings in."

"I think I'll pass on that. Later, mate."

"Later."

Coffee. Digestive biscuits. *Murder She Wrote.* It was the one where Jessica visits Fiona, a friend of her late husband, in Cork, where the family runs a traditional wool garment business. Cousin Ambrose is about to take over management of the factory and move the site to Dublin—too far for the local villagers to keep their jobs. Ambrose is found murdered in the local church. Unfortunately, the local Garda copper DS Terence Boyle doesn't have the wherewithal to figure out the murder, but Jessica is somehow able to put the whole story together. I won't spoil it for you if you haven't seen it. (And if you're unemployed and stuck at home most days, you *will* see it.) I got the murderer at the twenty-eight-minute mark, but then, I was a better copper than DS Terry Boyle, who was perhaps somewhat handicapped by the fact that he clearly had never been to Ireland in his life before this visit to the fake County Cork of the Hollywood back lot.

Phone ringing.

"Hi, sweetie, how are you?"

"*Murder She Wrote.* Jessica's in Ireland. I got the murderer before she did. Intuition, really, rather than deduction."

"Uhm, well done, Sean. Look, the sun's supposed to come out later . . . And there's the market on downtown."

"Don't worry, I won't sit in the house all day, I promise. There's nothing on till *Countdown* now, and you know that Gyles Brandreth rubs me the wrong way."

"Well, that's good. Remember what Dr. Havercamp said. A good brisk walk—"

"I remember. I know, I'll go for a walk. I'll walk the cat on a leash."

"I'd like to see you try. There's the bell. Better go. Love you, Sean."

"Love you too."

Later.

The market was a very good place to pick up records. It seemed the whole country was switching to CDs and CD players, so entire record collections were being sold on the cheap.

The market was the big weekly event in Portpatrick, and people came in from all over Galloway and parts of Ayrshire too. Today was even crazier because it coincided with the quarterly horse fair, and when I got to the top of the hill, I saw that the little village was a teeming souk of Travellers, traders, and tourists.

I almost went back to the house, and that, of course, would have been the end of the case. No Iceland, no Knock, no Delaware, no answers. No dance with death, either. But Gyles Brandreth was on bloody *Countdown,* so I didn't go back. I walked down the hill into Portpatrick.

I waded through the people, horses, and school-ditching kids until I saw big Mike Moffatt at the record stall, looking pleased with himself. Mike was six feet six and nineteen stone. Bald and bearded, he was one of those characters who only ever wore a white T-shirt and stovepipe jeans, no matter the weather. A Geordie not afraid of the bloody cliché.

"New records?"

"Nothing that would interest you."

"Well, maybe next week, then, Michael," I said, trying to beat a hasty retreat.

"Not so fast, Duffy. Some Gypsy kid was looking for you. Says he's got some information about a case. He knew you lived somewhere in Portpatrick and he knew you'd be down my record stall, so he left a note for ya. Smart kid."

"Let's have this note, then."

Big Mike shook his head. "Nah, mate, quid pro quo. Buy a record and I'll pass on the note."

"Fuck that, I'll find him. I'm sure he's over by the horses."

"Maybe he is, maybe he isn't. Here, take this Cliff Richard Christmas album. Fifty pence to a good customer such as yourself."

I forked over the fifty pence and got the record and the note.

The note was a sketch of a horse and the numeral "2." Two o'clock at the horse fair. Killian was illiterate, then, but that didn't mean much; a lot of tinker kids were illiterate.

I Oxfammed the Cliff Richard record and headed over to the beach. There wasn't an Irishman born alive who could resist a Gypsy horse fair, so the note had been superfluous. And sure enough, I found Killian with various uncles and cousins racing field hunters and Shire horses along the strand.

Even though we were across the sheugh, it probably wouldn't do his reputation any good to be seen with a peeler, so I just gave him a nod when he turned a big brown chestnut mare near me. Our eyes met, and I went over to the improvised shabeen tent, which always seemed to spring up at these things.

Killian met me as I was scoffing risible chips and a good poteen.

"What is it?" I asked him.

"Can we talk somewhere more private?"

"My house is just over the hill."

"You lead, I'll follow."

There were some crims I wouldn't want to know where I lived (especially if they knew I was going to be on vacation and the house would be empty except for an unreliable watchcat) but Killian had a weird honor code that would never allow him to exploit the knowledge of my address for personal gain.

I walked back up the hill and toward the cliffs. An election was coming up, and a sign near the house said, "Vote Tory to increase the dissonance." It did my heart good to see the word *dissonance* on an election poster. Over that little stretch of water, election posters were cruder and uglier, and if there was a big word it was a big word from the Book of Revelation.

Killian trailed me to the house.

I went inside and put the kettle on, and when he saw that the coast was clear, he came on in too.

"Tea?" I asked.

"Milk, no sugar," he said.

"No sugar?"

"It's what I grew up with. And goat's milk."

"We only have cow's milk."

"That'll do.

"I saw you riding that big mare. You handled her well without a saddle or a bit."

"I was riding horses before I could walk."

"I'll bet you were. What does a big old mare like that sell for?"

"She's not old. That gray on her flank is her natural color. A year old. Fourteen months. She's a high-blooded animal, not a workhorse. If you're looking for a trotter for your wee girl, I could get you a bargain."

"No, I'm not yet. What's brought you to see me, Killian?" I said.

"I have an opportunity in New York. Mate out there. We both know you, it seems."

"This mate of yours . . . he's not called Forsythe, is he?"

Killian raised an eyebrow but neither confirmed nor denied it.

"That's one of the reasons I've come to see you. I could do with a bit of start-up cash for flights and such," he said.

"What makes you think you'll get cash from me?"

"Something tells me I'll be leaving here with some dough," he said with an air of satisfaction I didn't like at all.

I made the tea, and we repaired to the living room. He was a big lad, with big hands and a long, gormless face with oddly penetrating, intelligent dark eyes.

"Nice place," Killian said.

"Thanks."

"Good little setup you have here. You're a peeler over there, but here you're away from the nightmare."

He was perceptive, this kid.

"Away from the nightmare but not away from the nightmares," I found myself saying.

"You should go to a therapist. I'll bet you can get one on the NHS."

"What do you want to tell me, Killian?"

"Well, remember you said if I spotted that Norton Commando rider again I should let you know? That there might be a reward in it for me?"

"You're four days too late," I said. "We found that Norton burned out in an alley in South Belfast. And no recoverable evidence from it."

Killian nodded. "How much of a reward we talking about, here?" he asked.

"Like I said, we found that motorbike—"

"You found the motorbike, but you were looking for the rider."

"Shit. What do you have for me?"

His eyes became sly, cautious, sleekit.

"Spill it, son," I said.

"Prelims: you're not interested in a bit of petty larceny, now, are you? From a professional standpoint?"

"Was it in Carrick?"

Killian smiled. "It was well out of your jurisdiction. It was at the airport. That's not even the RUC, is it?"

"No, it isn't. That's the Belfast International Airport Constabulary. Whatever you did at the airport is not my concern."

Satisfied, Killian continued. "So I'm running a wee team at the airport. Distraction and lift with my cousin Kate, you know how it is."

"Sorry, what are we talking about here?"

"Kate's a redhead. Sixteen going on twenty-five. Distraction and lift. Standard stuff."

I had never heard it called this before, but it was easy enough to grasp what he was talking about. "Your cousin distracts male travelers at the airport by asking about a gate or a flight or something while you steal their bag or their wallet?"

Killian shook his head. "I don't do the lifting. It's a three-man job. Kate distracts them, I keep watch for the peelers, and Luke, me partner, he gets accidentally jostled into the mark by the crowd and lifts whatever he can and he hands it to me. If it's a wallet, I strip it of its money and leave it on a seat. Someone'll turn it in, and the mark's usually so happy to get his passport and credit cards back, he doesn't give a shit if the money's gone. Kate is the key. She's so fucking innocent, they never associate her with the wallet going missing. Nine times out of ten, they actually think they left it there on the seat."

"Nice little arrangement. And what if it goes wrong?"

"Almost never goes wrong. Luke's so deft at the lift and the handover that if they catch him, he doesn't have the wallet on him. It's already with me."

"*Almost never* is the key phrase, I'm guessing here."

Killian nodded. "Almost never. And yesterday was one of those almost-never days . . ."

"I'm listening."

"So yesterday we're doing the morning rush-hour flights at Belfast International and we're doing a healthy business."

"What's a healthy business?"

"We have a hard limit of ten marks in a session and then we call it quits and go. The airport police are fucking eejits, if you'll pardon the expression, but even eejits catch on eventually."

"What happened?"

"We were on mark number eight and we'd taken over four hundred quid. Healthy score, you know? And I let Kate pick the marks. She's an old hand and she can weed out the troublemakers and the undercover cops. And she starts doing the old song and dance to this guy, asking him for gate thirteen, and Luke takes his wallet and I get ready for the handover, but this fucking guy, I can't believe what I'm seeing, he grabs Kate by the wrist and has her on the ground and with his other hand he has Luke by the wrist and has him on the ground. Christ, he's fast. Nobody's that fast. But he is. Amazing. So they're on the ground and the airport fuzz come running over and I'm about to get the fuck out there when I look at his face and it dawns on me that I've seen it before."

Chills. Fucking chills down the spine, man.

"Motorcycle Man."

"Motorcycle Man."

"Are you sure?"

"I never forget a horse or a face."

"So what did you do?"

"So instead of legging it, I kind of join the crowd around the cops and Luke and Kate. And they're doing the right thing. Protesting that it's all a mistake and they're innocent, but the airport peelers aren't listening. And I'm watching the guy and his face is unusual. He's just caught someone lifting his wallet and he's not triumphant like you would expect. He's annoyed; he's annoyed at himself. He's made this big fuss and everybody's looking at him and he's pissed off."

"What happened next?"

"You might well ask. So the lead peeler comes out, plainclothes guy, and he opens his notebook and the uniforms are cuffing Luke and

HANG ON ST. CHRISTOPHER

Kate, and then suddenly Motorcycle Man gets all apologetic and picks his wallet off the ground and he says, 'I'm so sorry, I dropped my wallet. These two had nothing to do with it.' All this in an American accent. And he looks at Kate, and Kate knows he's letting her go, so she doesn't kick up a stink. But the peeler's not buying it. The peeler's going on about Gypsy pickpockets and how he's seen Luke before around here and all that shite. But the guy is insistent. They had nothing to do with it; there's no crime been committed here; you have to let them go. And the peeler finally can see that there's no percentage in arguing it out, and if the guy's not going to press charges there ain't gonna be no case, so he lets them go. And the guy—this is the good bit—he apologizes to Luke and Kate for their trouble and gives them twenty quid each to get a cup of tea."

"Are you sure about the American accent?"

"Quite sure."

"So what happened next?"

"Luke and Kate scarper before there's any other trouble."

"But you don't."

"No, course I don't."

"What do you do?"

"I wait until all the fuss has died down, and I follow him first to the coffee shop and then to the departure lounge and finally to his gate."

"So where's he going?"

"He's flying to Knock."

"Knock."

"He takes Aer Lingus Two-Twenty-Two to Knock."

"That's what you've got for me?"

"That's what I've got. How much is that worth to you?"

At some imperceptible point in the story, the language of our conversation had switched from English to Irish, and a request for money in Irish doesn't quite have the brutal ring to it that it has in English.

"I'm not sure I can do much of anything with this. Aer Lingus flights to the Republic only require boarding passes with a name on them. You don't need to present an ID or passport to fly to the Irish Republic," I said.

"So you check the names."

"It's going to be a fake name, isn't it? Give any old name when you book the ticket, and if you're as cautious as Mr. X . . ."

Killian smiled "But you're going to check it anyway, aren't you?"

Yup, he knew me, this kid. "How many other passengers? What type of plane?"

"Dash Seven, I think. No more than ten passengers."

"I'll get my wallet."

24
BELFAST–KNOCK–SHANNON–INVERNESS–REYKJAVIK–JFK

You know me. Always keen to explore a lead, especially if it's in an out-of-the-way locale with almost no chance of bearing any fruit, and especially if I'm picking up the tab from my own pocket. What is that? Dedication to the job? An unquenchable thirst for justice? Or an eejit semiretired copper with too much bloody time on his hands?

All of the above, probably.

I called the airport and got the manifest. Eight passengers for the Belfast International Aer Lingus flight to Knock. Five male passengers. No ID required for this flight, but four of those passengers had a name that showed up in UK or Irish records. One passenger's name on the manifest was John Smith.

He wasn't even trying.

Either that or he was just having a laugh.

It was three p.m.

I picked Emma up from nursery school. "I have a new joke, Daddy."

"Go on, then."

"There are two cats: an English cat called One Two Three, and a French cat called Un Deux Trois. They are in a contest to swim the English Channel. Which cat won?"

"I don't now."

"The English cat. Because the un deux trois quatre cinq."

I laughed and she laughed, and it was a lovely moment.

Beth wasn't stupid. She could tell I was heading out before I even broached it. I had laid out the leather jacket with the escape kit in the sleeve, and I had cleaned my .38.

"What's going on?" she asked.

"Lead on a case. A tip-off."

"You're not a full-time detective anymore, Sean. Isn't it Lawson's—"

"No, this was a tip-off for me personally. I have to go."

"Where?"

"Belfast Airport and then Knock in County Mayo. Do you want to know more?"

"Is it IRA? Is it dangerous?"

"No and no."

"When do you leave?"

"I have to leave now. It's a hot tip."

Beth nodded.

She got it.

She knew me.

I wouldn't let it go.

I'll never it let it go.

Beemer to Glasgow Airport.

I flashed my warrant card so that I could take my weapon on the plane.

"Are you on an official investigation, or is this a—"

"It's an official RUC investigation."

Glasgow to Belfast International.

"DI Duffy, Carrick RUC. I'm going to need to look at the security tapes from yesterday."

Two hours of scrolling through the tapes, and I had a blurry image of passenger John Smith. Six feet one, twelve stone, sandy hair, white shirt, no tie, brown sport jacket, brown trousers, black oxfords.

Last flight of the night to Knock.

A lecture from the airport fuzz: "You won't be allowed to use your weapon in the Irish Republic. You must report immediately to the local Garda station and—"

HANG ON ST. CHRISTOPHER

Yeah, yeah.

Eleven p.m. A Dash 7 turboprop aircraft. I was the only passenger. I'd been to Knock before. Twice. And I wasn't even a good Catholic.

An Cnoc, meaning *the Hill,* or, more recently, Cnoc Mhuire, "Hill of (the Virgin) Mary."

As boring and poor and damp as every other village in this part of County Mayo until August 21, 1879, at approximately eight p.m., when the Virgin Mary, together with Saint Joseph and John the Evangelist, appeared to fifteen of the villagers for over two hours during a rainstorm. The villagers had not read David Hume on miracles, nor were they surprised by the Virgin's pale skin or her ability to speak Irish.

The shrine grew in popularity throughout the twentieth century, and eventually an airport and a new church were built. By the time of Pope John Paul's centenary visit in 1979, Knock had become one of Europe's major Catholic Marian shrines, alongside Lourdes and Fatima.

A million visitors a year now, either to give thanks or to beg for Our Lady's intercession.

As I said, I was an old hand.

Airport to the village by taxi. A visit to the basilica, where at this time of night (midnight) in the cold drizzle there were still two nuns and the mother of a severely handicapped boy in a wheelchair. Everyone was praying except, probably, the boy in the wheelchair.

I crossed myself and thanked the Virgin and John the Evangelist and Saint Joseph and Saint Christopher the protector of travelers and Saint Michael the Archangel, the patron saint of policemen.

"*Ave Maria, gratia plena, Dominus tecum. Benedicta tu in muliéribus, et benedictus fructus ventris tui, Jesus. Sancta Maria, Mater Dei, ora pro nobis peccatoribus nunc et in hora mortis nostrae. Amen,*" I muttered to myself, and walked back down the hill.

I ignored the new church, which was an architectural monstrosity, and headed straight for the hotels. There were quite a few hotels in Knock now, and it took until three in the morning before my printout of the airport security camera footage bore fruit.

"Oh, yes, that's Mr. Daley, an American gentlemen," said the night manager of the Holiday Inn at Carrowmore.

"Is he still here, by any chance?"

The concierge shook his head. "No. But you only just missed him. He checked out yesterday morning. Or rather, the day before yesterday since we're after midnight now."

"Rental car or airport?"

"Oh, he was flying out. We had to call him a taxi."

"What time was that?"

"First flight out. Seven in the morning."

"He say what part of America he was from or what he did for a living?"

"Oh, no, Mr. Daley kept very much to himself."

"I'll need a taxi to the airport."

Knock Airport at 3:30 a.m. Every shop closed, no flights due in or out until nine, security reduced to two men and a dog.

But if you kick up enough of a fuss, the people will come.

After a few hours, I found Mr. Daley's face on the security tape of a noon Aer Lingus flight to Inverness. There wasn't another flight from Knock to Inverness until noon today, but there was a nine a.m. flight from Shannon Airport. The man matching Mr. Daley's description had called himself John Williams on this flight. No ID had been required on the flight from Knock to Inverness, but John Williams was the name on the ticket.

Need to rent a car and drive to Shannon and fly to Inverness.

"How far is it from Knock to Shannon?" I asked the bleary-eyed man from Hertz.

"I think it's about a hundred and fifty kilometers."

"What's that in real money?"

"A hundred miles."

"So about two hours?"

"No, the roads aren't good, it might take you nearer three."

I was there in one hour forty minutes, in a Toyota Corolla whose suspension would never be the same again.

Shannon to Inverness.

Now, why the hell would Mr. Williams go to bloody Inverness?

I sat at the airport and thought about it.

Williams or Daley or whatever he was called was a good Catholic.

He killed people, clinically in cold blood, but he was a good Catholic, and before he had ended his mission he had gone to Knock to seek compassion from the Holy Virgin.

And then?

Then he would either go back to Belfast and continue to do what he had been doing, or . . .

He'd go back to America.

Why Inverness rather than Belfast?

Because he was careful. He wanted to jump from airport to airport, from identity to identity, to shake any pursuers off his tail.

I took the photos I had to every desk at Inverness Airport, and finally someone recognized my traveler.

Williams had flown out of Inverness last night on Iceland Air 134 to Reykjavik on, get this, a US passport. His name, apparently, was Brian Smith, and he was from Philadelphia.

When I called the embassy, it turned out that there were more than a hundred Brian Smiths from Pennsylvania, forty-three of whom held valid US passports. But when they faxed me the passport photo pages to the airport police offices at Inverness Airport, none of the photographs matched.

"When's the next flight to Reykjavik?"

"They're not very often. The next one isnae until six o'clock tonight."

"Book me on it."

I couldn't take my gun to Iceland, so I had to leave it with the police in Inverness.

I called Beth and Emma and explained that the lead was taking me to Iceland.

I had a feeling the trail was going to go cold there. Mr. Smith was a very cautious man indeed, and no doubt, in Reykjavik there was yet another identity waiting for him.

"Be careful, Sean," Beth said. "It sounds like you're following a very dangerous man."

"It's Iceland. I don't think there's been a murder there in ten years."

"Well, don't be the first."

"I won't, and I'll bring youse back something. Something Icelandic."

Time to kill in Inverness, but I didn't feel like sightseeing, so I just stayed in the airport until flight time.

I called Lawson.

"Carrick RUC, this is Sergeant Lawson," Lawson said.

"It's Carrick CID and you are Detective Sergeant Lawson. How many times do I have to tell you?"

"Sir? Where are you?"

"Don't worry, I'm not in the building. I'm safely in Scotland. Inverness Airport. Do you want to know why I'm in Inverness Airport?"

"I have a feeling I'm not going to like the answer, sir."

"Is Crabbie in today? He should be in on this call too."

Lawson found McCrabban and put me on speaker.

I told them everything: Killian's lead, the man's multiple identities and passports.

"What are you thinking, Sean?" Crabbie asked.

"I'm thinking what you're both thinking. He's a fucking iceman from America who has been brought in to terminate O'Roarke's crew. Someone from outside the movement brought in by O'Roarke's rivals so there is no possibility of this coming back to bite anyone in the arse."

"So you're thinking the assassins got assassinated by another assassin before they could assassinate anyone?" Lawson said.

"I maybe wouldn't have used the word *assassin* so much, but that's exactly what I'm thinking."

"Who is this guy?" Crabbie asked.

"A real cool pro. I'm guessing mafia or something. Perhaps ex-CIA 'cause of the tech. Definitely a top guy, though."

"He sounds like he could be big trouble," Crabbie said.

"Don't worry, lads, I'll be careful. If I find him, I won't be able to do anything about it but report it to the local cops, so this is where you come in, Lawson."

HANG ON ST. CHRISTOPHER

"Sir?"

"We're going to need to act fast on an international arrest warrant. Prep the paperwork, will you?"

"Yes, sir."

"Good. I'll keep youse in touch."

I bought a Walkman tape player/recorder and took Iceland Air 134 to Reykjavik.

Flight half-full.

I landed at Keflavik Airport four and a half hours later.

I did my usual routine. I introduced myself to the airport police, showed them my ID, and explained what I was about. Everybody spoke English—better English than mine in several cases. The cops accompanied me as I showed Smith's photograph to all the airline desks, but Reykjavik was a busier airport than either Knock or Inverness, and no one remembered our boy.

I checked flights out of Reykjavik under the name Brian Smith, but of course, no one matching that name had left in the past twenty-four hours. No one with the name Brian Smith had gone through passport control.

The security footage from passport control was no help either. Several flights had landed at once, and hundreds of men had come through roughly matching Williams's height and build, but none that looked exactly like him.

He had switched identities again.

This, it seemed, was where the trail went dead.

Smith could be any one of hundreds of men flying anywhere.

It was all really rather brilliant. This was how a professional lost a tail. Multiple flights, multiple identities before continuing to his final destination.

Two days of this, staying at the airport Hilton, looking at grainy CCTV tapes, eating Hafragrautur (oatmeal and water) for breakfast, and cod and chips for lunch and dinner.

Sympathetic local peelers, a good airport bookshop where I found Louis MacNeice and W. H. Auden's *Letters from Iceland*.

The hotel room. Night. A bed. A table. A desk. A lamp. Some nice stationery. A Bible in Icelandic, which began with *1 Í upphafi skapaði Guð himin og jörð. 2 Jörðin var þá auð og tóm, og myrkur grúfði yfir djúpinu, og andi Guðs sveif yfir vötnunum. 3 Guð sagði: "Verði ljós!" Og það varð ljós.* Too much bloody light, in fact. Through double curtains at midnight, the sun had still not quite set. I read one of MacNeice's bits from *Letters from Iceland,* which was typically Ulsterish in its gloomy portents but which got my mood perfectly:

> *So I write these lines for you*
> *Who have felt the death wish too.*
> *But your lust for life prevails—*
> *Drinking coffee, telling tales.*
> *Our prerogatives as men*
> *Will be cancelled who knows when;*
> *Still I drink your health before*
> *The gun-butt raps upon the door.*

I pulled back the curtain and stared at the annoying twilight. This was all bloody pointless, wasn't it? It wasn't even my case. I got up, dressed, and got a taxi to the airport. I went to the Iceland Air information desk to book a flight home, but there was no one there. There was no one in the entire airport apart from a couple of sleepy security guards and a cleaning crew.

I walked around looking at the closed shops and restaurants. There is something beautiful and depressing about an empty airport with its harsh lighting and its implicit message that to go is the great thing, that *here* is the place you should not be.

Buses to Reykjavik ran every twenty minutes day or night, rain, shine, or snow. I was leaving Iceland today come what may, and I'd never seen anything of the place.

I went outside.

It was 4:25 a.m., but of course the sun was up.

The bus driver, a suspiciously cheerful lady with curly red hair, asked me in English where in the city I wanted dropped off.

"I don't know. Anywhere, I suppose. I just want a quick look 'round. I'm flying out this afternoon."

HANG ON ST. CHRISTOPHER

"I will drop you at the Rat House."

"That sounds like my kind of place."

A twenty-five-minute run through what appeared to be a volcanic wasteland until we hit the outskirts of Reyk. Pretty, colorful houses that weren't at all like the tin shacks of MacNeice and Auden's day.

The bus driver dropped me at the Ráðhús Reykjavíkur, which turned out to be the city hall and visitors' center.

There were plenty of people around: elven, athletic, handsome people in T-shirts and light jackets. A grubby dark-haired, unshaven, smelly Mick in a leather jacket, black jeans, and Doc Martens looked well out of place.

I walked to the harbor and the city center.

People said "good morning." It was that obvious. I said "good morning" back.

An attractive, friendly city on a lough, filled with attractive, friendly people. It was Belfast's northern evil twin. No, Belfast was the evil twin and Reyk was the good twin.

"Good morning," a gorgeous silver-haired lady walking a dog said.

"Morning."

"Good morning," a pretty young jogger said.

"Morning."

"Good morning," a fetching young couple pushing a pram said together.

"Morning."

I was starting to hate this town.

I found myself at the Hotel Borg on Posthusstraeti.

I went inside.

"Good morning, sir, how can we help you?" a bright young thing asked at reception.

"Is the bar open?"

"No, I'm sorry, but the bar won't be open until noon. Are you a guest at the hotel? We start serving breakfast at seven."

My head hurt, and all this "good morning" shite was giving me dyspepsia.

"Can I get a coffee at least?"

The bright young thing smiled, shook her head, and repeated: "I'm sorry, sir, we don't start serving breakfast until seven."

I'd given up the smokes; otherwise, this would have been the perfect place for a consolation ciggie. My hand reached in my jacket pocket anyway and brushed not against my cigarette packet but against the envelope containing Mr. Smith's photograph from Belfast International Airport.

I put my warrant card and the photograph on the reception desk.

"I'm a policeman from Ireland. You haven't seen this man, by any chance, have you?"

The receptionist frowned. "Hmmm," she said.

"Hmmm, what?"

"That looks a lot like Mr. Wilson. He comes here two or three times a year. He just checked out yesterday."

Holy living fuck.

"Do you have a forwarding address for Mr. Wilson, by any chance?"

"Yes, I think so."

She rummaged in her files for a moment.

"Emmet Wilson, Twenty-Two Ferry Street, Middle Bay, Virginia 22432, USA."

"Thank you very much," I said, writing the information down in my notebook.

"Would you like me to make you a breakfast reservation?"

I thought about what Michael Forsythe had told me. My name had come up in some weird circles in America.

Michael was trying to warn me off. His mate Killian was sending me the other way.

But America was where I needed to go. Now.

"Sorry, what?"

"A breakfast reservation?"

"Oh, no thanks, I have a plane to catch."

25
MIDDLE BAY

The Hertz desk at JFK.

"We don't have any BMWs, Mr. Duffy. We only have American."

"What's the fastest car you've got?"

"Fastest? Carol, this gentleman wants to know what—"

"Yeah, I heard. Tell him we've got a Buick GNX on the south lot. It's the high rate and an extra twenty dollars a day for the insurance premium."

I'd never heard of a Buick GNX, but when I got to the south lot it looked okay, and it was painted black which is always cool.

I studied the map carefully and drove from Hertz's south lot onto the Belt Parkway. I got almost all the way to Rockville Center before I realized I was going completely the wrong direction. Swing a U-turn and back past JFK again. Over the Verrazzano-Narrows Bridge across Staten Island, and an intersection with the 95. I-95 to the 235, and the 235 all the way to Wilmington, where I stopped for gas and a Coke and cheeseburger at the Wendy's next to the gas station.

It was fun driving on a continental landmass. In Ireland you could get only five or six hours away from your problems. Here you could drive to bloody Alaska if you wanted to.

I got another Coke for the ride.

Down through sleepy Delaware to the township of Middle Bay.

Right on the Chesapeake here. Sand dunes, scrubby trees, boats, crab and lobster shacks. It was the sticks, but I guessed we were just within the outer limits of the commuting distance to Washington, DC, which seemed to be about thirty miles away on the other side of the Chesapeake Bridge.

I drove through the town. Nice place. An idyllic suburban community from a movie—from the first act of a Spielberg flick that establishes the deceptively anodyne vibe before the bad shit goes down in acts two and three.

I found 22 Ferry Street, which was a three-bedroom house overlooking the water. I don't know about American house styles, but this one looked old—nineteenth century or perhaps even older. Its ancient timbers had been freshly painted white. A white picket fence enclosed a garden with a well-trimmed lawn and rosebushes. Unlike several of the houses on the street, there was no American flag flying from the porch, but in one of the upstairs bedrooms you could just make out a folded Stars and Stripes on a window ledge. The car parked outside was a dark-green Porsche 911. The house was only a short walk away from a wooden jetty where a small boat was moored.

I drove by slowly, turned at the end of the street, and drove past again. Little café about two hundred yards south of the house. I parked in the shade of what might be a maple tree, and went to the café to get a cup of coffee and a sandwich. They didn't have any sandwiches, but I got myself a blueberry muffin.

I put my Walkman on and waited for about three hours listening to a classical music station coming out of Baltimore (four boring Beethoven pieces I'd heard a million times, and a completely new—to me—Handel symphony). The man came out of the house at just before six o'clock and got into the Porsche.

He was much more conspicuous than I was expecting. All those bloody eyewitnesses back in Ireland really could have helped me nail him, because once seen, he wasn't easy to forget. He was taller than the CCTV footage would have you believe (six-two, perhaps) and very pale with close-cropped sandy hair. His posture was ramrod straight, and there was a bounce to his step. He was wearing a red plaid shirt tucked into dark-blue jeans, and white sneakers. He exuded confidence, professionalism, and togetherness. He'd stand out in Northern Ireland or England but perhaps not so much here. There was an easiness to him that I found irritating. If I'd killed a woman in cold blood just days ago, I wouldn't be that easy.

He didn't appear to have a concealed weapon on him, but there might be one in the car's glove box, for all I knew. The Porsche pulled out of its spot and drove toward the center of town. I followed at a discreet distance and kept on him as he pulled into a supermarket car park.

He got out and went into the supermarket. He came out fifteen minutes later with a grocery bag, which he placed in the passenger seat of the Porsche. Back to the house. I parked in the spot under the maple tree.

The lights stayed on until just after eleven. I leaned the seat back as far as I could in the Buick and tried to get a few hours' sleep. Tomorrow, I'd have to find a hotel nearby, but tonight I wanted to keep my quarry close.

Four or five hours' broken sleep, and I woke at five-thirty when the café opened for business. Croissant/coffee/bathroom. I took a bathroom break, washed my face and hands, and carried the food back to the car just in time to see my man come out in shorts and T-shirt. He turned right and ran along the trail that skirted the Chesapeake. I walked up to his house and read the name on his mailbox. John Wilson. A phony-arse name if I ever heard one.

I returned to the car and waited until Mr. Wilson came back from his jog at six-thirty. He showered, shaved, and came back out to the Porsche wearing a short-sleeved blue shirt, no tie, tan pants, and brown shoes.

I followed him over the Chesapeake Bay Bridge, past the US Naval Academy, and into the outskirts of DC. Early enough so that there was little traffic, and he drove fast on the stretches of two-lane road. The Buick turned out to have a lot of pickup, and I had no problem discreetly keeping up with him.

Great little car, this, and I found myself patting the dashboard as it made its way easily through a red light where I could have lost him.

"Buick GNX, eh?" I said to myself. Never heard of it before, but I'd remember it.

DC was a nerve-racking experience with its traffic and strange merges and exits. The Porsche drove fast at ten miles per hour above the various speed limits, and Mr. Wilson arrived at his destination at 7:30 sharp. The destination was CIA headquarters in Langley, Virginia. I was only mildly surprised by this.

I made sure I saw him drive through the gate, and when I was satisfied, I headed back to the Chesapeake Bay Bridge. I found a motel on the outskirts of Middle Bay and checked in. Thirty bucks a night, a swimming pool, cable TV with forty channels, and comfy beds. I ate well in a local diner that served crab cakes and hash.

For the next two days, I watched John Wilson leave for work at 6:50 and followed him over the bridge and all the way to Langley. On the third day, I followed him to the bridge, but as he drove on, I found the last exit and circled back to Middle Bay.

Lucky Che T-shirt, leather jacket, sneakers, gloves.

I walked to Wilson's house and slipped around the back.

I zipped my leather jacket and quickly scaled his back fence. Up the garden path, on the alert for dogs. No dogs. I took out my big lock pick kit and I was through the back door in under a minute. I now had eight hours or so until he'd be back, which would give me all the time I needed to figure out exactly who Mr. Wilson was, who he worked for, and what he was doing in Northern Ireland.

26
CHEZ MR. WILSON

The back door opened into a little room full of boots, outdoor clothes, a fly rod, and a landing net. I looked for a burglar alarm box, but there was no alarm. We were safe out here in the boonies—why would you need such a thing?

I took from my pocket the pair of latex gloves I'd bought at a local drugstore, and carefully put them on. I removed my shoes and left them in the mudroom. I walked into a back kitchen that had recently been remodeled. There were a dozen different boxes of pasta on the shelves, and homemade spaghetti sauce in the fridge. There was also what appeared to be a homemade cheesecake. Wilson was something of a gourmand.

From the kitchen, I walked into a formal dining room that had a large polished black ash table and chairs arranged beneath an ancient-looking silver candelabra. The silver had recently been polished, and there wasn't a speck of dust anywhere in the dining room. The dining room walls were painted sky blue, and hung on them were framed French railway posters of the 1920s. It was an attractive room but strangely characterless.

The adjoining living room also had several French railway posters, and a large television set with a video recorder underneath. Of more interest was a CD player with a large selection of CDs in a stack next to it. Wilson's musical tastes perhaps left something to be desired: Phil Collins, the Eagles, Van Halen, Journey, ABBA, Air Supply—fairly mainstream stuff that did not really tax the musical imagination. Although after my experience in O'Roarke's house, I found that I had become a little less tolerant of music snobs.

There was a bookcase in the living room, filled mostly with cookbooks, histories, and a few self-help texts about managing your time better. I flicked through a few of them, but no hidden letters or anything else of interest came out.

The next room was a sort of study, or perhaps a place for contemplation. A desk, a chair, a rug. On the wall was a large crucifix, and in a corner alcove there was a shrine to the Virgin Mary. Interesting.

Up a floor.

A bathroom at the top of the stairs, which revealed not much. Mr. Wilson used an electric razor and preferred brushing his teeth with Colgate. In a little stand next to the toilet were the current issues of the *New Yorker* and *Guns and Ammo*—not a natural combination. This eclecticism intrigued me.

Five bedrooms upstairs, not the three I'd expected. Tardis-like, the house was bigger than you expected from the outside. Only one bedroom in use, though. No sign of wife, kids—anything like that.

The bedroom at the back of the house had been converted into an office. There was a balcony in this room, with a view across the Chesapeake to Kent Island. The office had a desktop computer and a black metal filing cabinet. The cabinet was secured with an ineffective little lock.

When I opened it, there was nothing inside.

When I turned on the PC, it was password protected. I tried to guess at passwords for a few minutes but had no luck. This was not my forte.

I checked in the office drawers and in other rooms in the house, but it slowly dawned on me that there was going to be nothing particularly personal at all in this house. Just as it was for Mr. Townes back in Carrickfergus.

I looked under the bed for a shotgun, but there was no shotgun, just a pair of slippers.

On the office desk there was another stack of books. A few recently published novels and one massive book on art criticism.

Jesus, had I gotten this case wrong after all? Had he killed Quentin Townes because he didn't like the poor man's paintings?

No.

The art book was coincidence or research or something. My theory of the case was correct.

I sat at the desk and opened the art book at random and read: "All the world has drained out of Rothko's paintings leaving only a void. Whether it is the void as glimpsed by mystics or merely an impressively theatrical emptiness depends on one's expectations. In effect, the Rothko chapel is the last silence of Romanticism."

Huh.

Well I guess I learned *something* from this case.

Rothko. I'd have to look into him.

Behind me, a voice said, "Howdy."

I turned around fast, and there was Wilson, pointing a suppressed Heckler and Koch MP5 at me.

"Okay, motherfucker, lie down on the floor and put your hands behind your back. I've just had a new carpet fitted in here and I don't want to shoot you, but I will."

I did as I was told. He handcuffed me behind my back, frisked me, removed my wallet, and tugged me to my feet.

"Walk," he said.

"Where to?"

"We're going down to the basement."

"I don't like the sound of that."

"You shouldn't," he said.

27
THE BASEMENT

I had no play. I walked downstairs and found that the door in the hallway leading to the cellar was open. I walked down the shaky wooden stairs into an unfinished basement: concrete floor, washer, dryer, boxes. He unfolded a garden chair and had me sit on it. He sat opposite.

He took out a pack of cigarettes and lit one.

"Smoke?" he asked.

"I've sort of given up."

"No kidding?"

"Two years now."

"I've been trying to give it up, but I can't do it. What did you use? The patch? Gum?"

"Sheer tyranny of will," I said.

He laughed and drew on the ciggie. He looked at my driver's license, warrant card, and credit cards. None of it interested him. He knew who I was already.

"When did you make me?" I asked.

"On the very first morning you tailed me. What on earth possessed you to get a black Buick GNX?"

"I asked for a fast car and that's what they suggested."

"You stuck out like a sore thumb, man. I think they only ever made a couple of thousand of those things."

"I didn't know that."

"You don't do well when you're not on your home turf, do you, Duffy?"

"I do okay."

"The FBI practically deported you in 'eighty-two. What were you thinking coming back over here for anything more than a tourist jaunt?"

"I thought that was all water under the bridge."

"No water under the bridge, Duffy. When *you* enter the country, all sorts of alarm bells go off. I probably would have made you anyway even if you hadn't been driving a black Buick GNX."

I nodded. "Maybe I will take one of those cigarettes."

He lit one and put it in my mouth, and I breathed in the gorgeous, comforting Virginia tobacco of a Marlboro red.

"Why Iceland?" I asked.

"I always go there when I go to Europe. Reykjavik Station is one of our hubs. I change passports there. And then usually again in London. Is that how you found me? The hotel? You went to every hotel in Reykjavik with my photograph from the airport?"

"Something like that."

"That's good police work. I should have figured you'd do something like that . . . Well, now that that route's blown, we'll have to figure something else out."

"Yes."

"So what happened this morning? You doubled back when you got over the bridge?" I asked.

"Yeah. This is exactly what I figured you do. Either yesterday or today. You're very predictable."

"Oh, dear."

"Don't be depressed. These are very deep waters for the likes of you."

"The likes of me?"

"A cop, even a maverick cop like yourself. This is way above your pay grade."

"So let me ask you something, Mr. Wilson, if that is indeed your name, what gives you the right to go around killing Irishmen and women?" I asked.

"What gives me the right? That's your question?"

"Yeah."

"You followed me. You know where I work. You know who I work for."

"That doesn't answer my question. What gives you the right—"

"Shut the fuck up," he said, taking the cigarette out of my mouth and stubbing it on the floor. He shoved the barrel of the MP5 into my cheek.

I desperately fingered the secret pocket of my leather jacket, but I couldn't pull back the Velcro patch covering the lock pick or the razor blade.

I had prepared for exactly this situation, but I hadn't bloody practiced it.

Shite.

Oh, Duffy, what kind of eejit are you? Remember the seven "P's": proper preparation and planning prevents piss-poor performance. I gave it another go and another, but try as I might, it didn't bloody work. I couldn't get the Velcro off and I couldn't get the lock pick out, which meant there was no play and he was going to be able to shoot me like a slab of meat. Bloody deserved it too. This was what came of sticking your nose in. Few, very few, coppers had the persistence or the money or the stupidity to follow a lead like this all the way to America. For what? Truth? What was that thing that Dr. Creery told us from *Paradise Lost*? "Truth never comes into the world but like a bastard, to the ignominy of him that brought its birth." Ha! Yeah, that was it. Fancy me remembering that from thirty years ago. The most boring class in the school. Me sitting there next to the great Cormac McCann, who went on to become *the* IRA master bomber, me getting picked on for talking, and Cormac getting told to explain what our conversation was about, and him standing up and off the cuff talking about stressed and unstressed verse and the advantages of the Senecan and Ciceronian styles. The look on Dr. Creery's face—priceless.

I smiled.

Wilson took a step away from me and lowered the MP5. He had me completely in his power, and he knew it. "What are you thinking about now, Duffy?" he asked triumphantly.

"Milton."

"Milton who?"

"John Milton."

"Where does he fit into all of this?"

"He doesn't. He's a dead poet."

"I know that," he said.

"Do you?"

"Yeah. English major."

"Which college?"

"I'm asking the questions. I'm going to go upstairs to get something. Don't move from the chair. If you move from the chair, I'll consider it a breach of trust and I'll have to shoot you immediately lest you do anything else to put me in jeopardy. Do you understand?"

"I won't move."

"Don't," he said, and went upstairs. I spent the next three hundred seconds trying to unhook the Velcro patch in the left sleeve of my leather jacket, to no avail whatever. I'd had it sewn too deep in the sleeve, and my fingers couldn't reach it.

Wilson came back five minutes later with an ominous-looking sheet of black tarpaulin. He had changed weapons to a Glock, which had also been fitted with a suppressor. He spread the tarpaulin on the concrete floor around the chair. Blood can sometimes sink into concrete if it's sufficiently porous. And then you'll never get it out.

"Oh, I have to get one more thing," he said, and went back to the basement stairs. He paused halfway up. "Remember, if you move a goddamn inch out of that chair, I'm going to kill you immediately."

There was no play anyway. The basement was below ground. The only way out was up those noisy, creaky wooden stairs.

Shit, shit, shit.

I thought about Beth and Emma. Never seeing them again. This was the ultimate price of selfishness. This American adventure, this desire for closure, this desire to know. Curiosity/cat.

Wilson came back downstairs again with a mug of coffee and an ashtray. He lit another cigarette. "I won't offer you another cigarette, Duffy. You weren't lying. You've given up. Ever since your police medical in 1989—the medical where your doctor—Dr. Havercamp, I believe his name was—diagnosed you as asthmatic and, quote, borderline unfit for duty, unquote."

I tried not to act surprised. Americans were always impressed with European sangfroid. "Were my files entertaining?"

"Extremely. For an amateur, you sure have the capacity to get yourself mixed up in a heap of shit."

"Maybe I'm jinxed."

"Well, I'm not the one handcuffed to a chair in someone else's basement," he said.

"No."

He took a sip of his coffee.

"You could have made me a hot beverage."

He shook his head. "Better safe than sorry. Can't have you flinging it at me, breaking my good china."

Good china. Americans didn't say that. Maybe he'd spent a lot of time in the UK, or maybe he had a British mother or grandmother.

"'The mind is its own place and of itself can make a heaven of hell or a hell of heaven.' *That* John Milton," he said.

I wondered why he was trying to impress me. What purpose would it serve if I was going to be food for worms in another five minutes? Maybe that was his thing. Let the guy know that not just anybody was taking him out. He was special. He was good. He studied your file beforehand. He had memorized a whole bunch of old poems at his Ivy League school.

"Better to reign in hell, than serve in heaven," I said, finishing the quote.

He nodded and took another sip of coffee. "I read that in your file too. You're well educated and, it must be said, a bit of a showboat."

"What else does it say?"

"Have you read it all?"

"Not allowed."

"Lot of fascinating stuff.... Well, until about a year or so ago, when you moved into the part-time police reserve, whatever that's supposed to be, and then it goes mysteriously quiet. And I don't like quiet. We don't like quiet."

"Who's we?"

"I think you know who *we* is... Anyhoo, a few phone calls, a few emails, and eventually *we* get another file about Sean Patrick Duffy, semiretired policeman."

"And what does that one tell you?"

He smiled and took another sip of his coffee. "You see, that one is the one that gives me pause. Because in that one, we're almost colleagues, you and I."

"This is no way to treat a colleague," I said.

"*Almost* colleagues. A true colleague would not have flown across the Atlantic Ocean and come into my home. A true colleague would have made a phone call, ascertained the fact that fundamentally we are all on the same side, and left it at that."

"Are we all on the same side?"

"Yes, we are."

"That's a relief. I thought maybe you were going to kill me."

"No, you're right. I am probably going to kill you. I'll certainly kill you if you don't answer all my questions," he said without cracking a smile.

"Why?"

"Why what?"

"Why would you kill me?"

"You're a rogue element, Duffy. Coming all the way here. Breaking into my house? You realize that the work I do cannot be jeopardized by someone like you."

"What is the work you do?"

"Like I say, I'm asking the questions," he said, pointing the gun at my forehead again.

"Take the handcuffs off, and I'll tell you what you want to know."

He shook his head.

"You wouldn't really kill me in cold blood."

"As you can probably imagine, this basement is adequately soundproofed. I even improvised a range down here at one time. This wouldn't make any noise at all."

"If I start screaming . . ."

"I won't let you start screaming. And one of the advantages of living in the country is that everyone lets you be."

"I wondered what you were doing out here at the end of a long commute."

He nodded. "Most everyone else lives within the Beltway. But I don't like to hang out with everyone else. I like to be away from DC and Langley and all those flags at Arlington. When you drive past this house, you probably think *retired schoolteacher* or something like that."

"You don't think *wet-work technician for the CIA's Special Activities Division*."

He shook his head. "No, you don't think that. So no one bothers me and I can do what I like. If I kill you, no one will hear it, no one will know about it, no one will know you were ever here, and tonight I'll take my boat out onto the water as I often do and no one will notice me drop a couple of garbage bags over the side in the darkness."

"What about the car?"

"I'll dump that in South Baltimore."

"I told my sergeant back in Carrickfergus that I was coming here."

He shook his head. "Not to this address," he said in a let's-not-play-stupid-games voice. "This is a classic Sean Duffy lone-wolf op. You've got form, buddy. And it wouldn't even matter if you did tell him. There's no evidence that you ever arrived here, and there won't be any forensic evidence that you were ever in my house, I can assure you of that . . . Now that that's settled, it's question time. How, *exactly*, did you find me? I thought I'd been very careful."

"A kid made you at Belfast Airport. An informant of mine. And I followed your trail from Knock to Inverness, to Iceland."

He groaned. "I never thought anyone would go to all that trouble. Don't you have anything better to do?"

"Not really."

"Tell me precisely what you did, so I can make sure I never make that mistake again."

"I showed your photograph to the receptionist at the Hotel Borg, and she recognized you immediately because you'd complained that the curtains didn't close over all the way in your room."

He groaned again. "Getting sloppy in my old age."

"And she had your name and address. Your real name and address after a whole bunch of pseudonyms, which I then immediately shared with the RUC Special Branch."

He shook his head. "No, Duffy. No, no, no. Everything was going well. You were telling me the truth and I was believing you and we were building rapport. And now you make me do this."

He put the gun and the coffee cup on his table, walked behind me, locked my head in his left arm until it was rigid and unmoveable, and then he pushed a gloved thumb into my right eye. He knew exactly what he was doing. The pain was excruciating.

"And that's only a taste," he said, sitting back down and picking up the coffee cup again. "Now, just the facts, Duffy, just the facts and we don't have to have any more unpleasantness."

My eye was throbbing in pain.

I took a half minute to get my breath back.

"I can't breathe. I need my inhaler. It's in the inside pocket of my leather jacket."

"I want you to breathe. At least until you answer all my questions," he said, reaching into the pocket to get the inhaler. The shoulders unbunched and the sleeves rolled down my arm.

The secret pocket was now accessible.

He put the inhaler in my mouth and I sucked deep.

"Better?" he asked.

I nodded.

"Now, who else have you told?"

"Nobody. The Inverness police knew I was going to Iceland, and the Icelandic police knew I was looking for someone. But I didn't name you. Your name is only on my notebook back in the motel," I said, speaking loudly enough to cover the sound of Velcro ripping as I took the lock pick out of its secret compartment.

"That's it? You haven't told anyone else my name?"

"I haven't."

"That's what I thought. That's your MO. Lone fucking wolf. You know what happens to lone wolves in the wild?"

"They get really sad at the annual wolf picnic when it's time for the wolf wheelbarrow races?"

He smiled at that one and then shook his head. "They starve to death, Duffy. Wolves need the pack, and without the pack they are nothing. I'm not a lone wolf. I have an entire organization, an entire country behind me," he said.

I put the lock pick into the handcuff.

And this I had practiced. I had done this a thousand times. You can unpick a set of handcuffs with a paper clip if you practice hard enough. And with a dedicated lock pick?

I coughed to cover the sound of the cuff unclicking.

"So what's the plan? Are you going to kill me?"

"That would certainly be the most straightforward solution," he said. "You're a very irritating man, and you're going to cause us nothing but trou—"

Before he could finish the sentence, I sprang forward, and with my left hand I tipped the coffee mug into his face and with my right hand I grabbed the Glock off the workbench. Wilson was Company, and not just Company but SAD and therefore trained in all sorts of dark arts; he'd be faster than I and sharper than I and he'd probably get the gun back off me if I didn't act immediately, so I shot him in the left ankle and kicked him off his chair before he could do anything.

"The next bullet goes into your brain! Facedown on the floor, hands behind your back!"

He complied and I cuffed him with his own cuffs. I examined the ankle wound. He would need a screw or two in the subtalar joint, but I had missed the artery that runs down the front. He wouldn't bleed to death, but he would be hurting. Good.

I took a wallet out of his pocket. His credit cards, CIA ID, and driver's license all said that he was actually someone called Kevin Donnolly, aged thirty-three years. He tried to get up, but I wasn't going to let him pull the same arsey-varsey shit on me.

"Just stay lying on the floor, pal. Get yourself really comfortable. I've got some questions of my own."

"I'm not telling you anything," he said between gritted teeth.

"You think I won't kill you?"

"I know you won't kill *me*."

"Let me tell you about a case that wasn't in my files," I said, and explained how I had killed Freddie Scavanni in more or less cold blood.

"But he was a bad guy; we're on the same side," Donnolly protested.

"Are we? I'll need to be convinced about that. And besides, there are other things apart from killing that could be done to you. Have you ever heard of a Belfast six-pack?"

I explained to him what a Belfast six-pack was. Bullets in the ankles, the kneecaps, and the elbows. It wouldn't kill him, but he'd be a desk jockey for the rest of his days in the CIA. He was sufficiently convinced by the Belfast six-pack that I felt encouraged enough to press record on the Walkman. The blank tape spooled, and the light for the internal mic came on.

"Now, first of all, is Kevin Donnolly your real name?"

He didn't answer.

"I've got your ID right in front of me."

"Yes," he grumbled.

"Where are you from, Kevin?"

"New York City."

"DOB?"

"Seven/seven/sixty-nine."

"And who do you work for?"

"What does it say there?"

"The CIA."

"That's who I work for."

"What do the neighbors think you do?"

"They think I'm a bureaucrat in charge of fertilizer inspection at the Department of Agriculture."

"That job is so boring that actually, I'll bet you they all think you're in the CIA."

"Perhaps."

"What were you doing in Ireland?"

"I'm not at liberty to say."

I pressed Pause on the Walkman and shot the floor two inches from his face. When his yells had died down, I pressed record again.

"What were you doing in Ireland?"

"Wet work."

"And in plain English?"

"I was contracted to take out a man and a woman."

"What man and what woman?"

"Alan Locke and Eileen Cavanagh."

"Which you did."

"Which I did."

"Why?"

"It's complicated."

"Try me."

"You're not authorized to know."

"Maybe not, but you're going to tell me anyway," I said, shutting off the tape recorder and putting the barrel of the gun behind his kneecap.

"All right! All right! Put the gun away. I'll tell you."

I turned the tape on again.

"Speak."

"Brendan O'Roarke," Donnolly said.

"What about him?"

"Alan Locke and Eileen Cavanagh were assassins working for him."

"So?"

Donnolly sighed. "For the last year, the British, Irish, and American governments have been in negotiation with the IRA Army Council about an end to the Troubles."

I had to conceal a gasp. This was news to me. Not even a hint of such a thing had leaked into the press.

"Continue," I said.

"In a few months or early next year, the IRA is going to announce a ceasefire and a cessation of military activities. In return, the British are going to set up a power-sharing assembly and begin the release of all IRA prisoners."

"They've agreed to this?" This kind of offer had been on the table since the 1970s, but there had never been any traction before.

"The IRA Army Council is split. Seamus and Brendan O'Roarke are two of the most powerful hardline holdouts."

I understood it all now.

"Brendan O'Roarke had been in the process of organizing a coup d'état in the Army Council, and the CIA was asked to stop him?" I asked.

"Not quite. We have not yet been given permission to operate on the soil of the Irish Republic, so we can't hit O'Roarke directly . . ."

"But O'Roarke's assassins in Northern Ireland were fair game?"

"O'Roarke set up a team in Northern Ireland in anticipation of taking out three of his rivals in the IRA Army Council. He was planning a midnight coup. The Brits and Irish couldn't possibly be involved in taking out these assassins. Far too hot for them. So they asked us."

"And you said yes."

"The Agency said that it would look into it."

"You did more than look, mate."

"O'Roarke's plan was a good one. With ***** ****, Liam Flaherty, and ****** ******** dead, the O'Roarke brothers and their followers would become the majority faction on the Army Council. Any deal with the British would be scuppered. Peace would be put off for twenty years at least."

"The Troubles continue well into the next century."

"Exactly. But we've taken out the assassins. O'Roarke's enemies are safe. And now everything is in place for a successful conclusion to the negotiations. With O'Roarke's three most trusted and dangerous hit men in Northern Ireland dead—"

"Wait. Three?"

"One of my colleagues took out the final member of O'Roarke's team last night in Derry."

"Shit. So what happens next?"

"I can't tell you the rest."

"You can and you will. I'm not a blabber, and you know it. But I have to know it all."

I put the gun in his ear. When that didn't work, I kicked him in the ankle.

"All right! Stop!"

"Talk."

"You can't breathe a word of this, Duffy," he said between gritted teeth.

"I won't."

"We have a team in situ in Paris who are on the trail of Seamus O'Roarke."

"And another team for his little brother, Brendan?"

"It's the only way."

"Back to my original question. What gives you the right to go around killing Irishmen and Irishwomen?" I asked.

"We have the full cooperation of the British and Irish governments. At the highest levels."

"How high a level? The Home Office?"

"Higher. On both sides of the Atlantic. And in France. Executive level."

"Oh, I see."

I was way out of my depth here.

I took a deep breath.

"Would you really have killed me?"

"Yes."

"Why?"

"These negotiations are too important. They cannot be jeopardized."

"Why the trip to Knock, to the Marian shrine there?" I asked.

"What I'm doing is the right thing to do. But still, taking men's lives—"

"A woman's life too."

"You need to make penance, don't you?" he said.

"And do you think you got forgiveness?"

"What I'm doing is for the greater good. You can see that."

I took the tape player and stood up.

"Where do you keep the rope?" I asked.

28
A SORT OF ENDING

Better the anticlimax. The disappointing theme in the minor key after the timpani, trombones, and tubas. A solitary violin reprising the melody until the scratching stops and silence overwhelms the music.

I examined Donnolly's wounds and made sure they weren't life threatening, and then I tied him to the heating pipe in his basement. I gave him a water bottle, a pack of Ritz minis, and a pot to piss in and told him that once I was back in Ireland, I'd call the police to come and rescue him. He asked me to call not the police, but a number at the CIA.

I wrote down the number.

"So you're not going to kill me?" he asked.

"I'm a cop," I told him. "I'm not habitually in the execution business." I showed him my Walkman. "And this tape will discourage you from getting into the execution business with me. If any sudden accidents happen to me or my family, copies of this tape will be sent to the *Guardian*, the *Washington Post*, the *New York Times*, the *Nation*, and the BBC."

"You'll blow up the peace process?"

"To protect my family? Bet your arse."

"You need to uncuff me."

"Fuck that."

"I need to show you something in my safe."

"The safe?"

"The safe."

"Just tell me where it is and the combination."

Upstairs. The den.

Safe behind a picture of the Virgin on the wall.

The combo, 33L, 44R, 44L.

The red file. The second one from the top.

Inside, there were photographs of my house in Portpatrick. A photograph of a girl curled on the sofa in her golden blanket. The Irish princess in exile in the foreign court.

I took the file downstairs.

"You know where I live! You've had goons scouting my house?" I said, furious.

Donnolly nodded. "Go home, Duffy. Forget everything that happened here."

"I can't do that."

"For the sake of your little girl, do exactly that."

I showed him the tape. "It seems we're at a stalemate here. If I go public, bad things will happen to me. If bad things happen to me, this tape goes public."

"Stalemates are okay. A stalemate has kept the peace in Europe for forty-five years. Peace is coming, Duffy. Don't fuck it up."

"Don't you fuck it up either. I'm not a man to be trifled with."

I looked him in the eyes to make sure he believed me, to make sure he'd tell his superiors not to mess with me.

I paused on the stairs and looked at him. "A 750 Norton? Seriously? Everybody knows you can't trust a Norton."

I went upstairs and locked the front door. I drove the Buick to Dulles and booked my ticket. I bought a Lisa Simpson doll for Emma and fancy chocolates for Beth.

DC to Glasgow direct.

Flight touching down at three in the morning. A bleak, dark, wet Scottish morning, but a morning in the UK, where the CIA would not be able to lift me so easily.

I'd be as good as my word, and later on today I'd make multiple copies of the tape I'd made, and give them to my family solicitor with instructions to send to the media in the event of my untimely death.

I went to a bank of phone booths and called Donnelly's supervisor at Langley.

"Who is this?" he asked.

"It's the man who tied Kevin Donnolly up in his basement in Middle Bay, Virginia. I've left enough food and water for a day or two, but he'd appreciate it if you came and rescued him as soon as possible," I said, and hung up.

I found the BMW unscathed in the medium-stay car park.

I drove through Glasgow until I found a phone box.

I sat in the car in the rain, thinking.

No, you don't get to murder Micks on my watch for free.

Not *completely* for free, anyway.

The phone box was covered in ads for prostitutes, and it reeked of urine. Standard stuff for this part of town.

I dialed Brendan O'Roarke's number.

"Who is this? You know what time it is?"

"They're going to try to hit you in the next two weeks. Vary your routine. Leave the bloody country if you can. They're coming for you. This is not a joke."

"Who is this?"

"A concerned citizen."

"I recognize this voice."

"Don't say any names."

"I won't. Is this a warning, then?"

"It's a tip I heard, that's all. Watch out, and tell your big brother to watch out too."

I hung up.

Aye, I don't hold with Brits and Americans going around killing Irishmen.

And maybe it was for the greater good, but at least I'd done my due diligence.

All I could do.

He wasn't going to vary his routine. Or if he did, it would be only for a day or two. Complacency would kick in and the goons would kill him. They'd kill him and his crazy brother in France. Good riddance, really, nutcases like them.

Back out of the fragrant phone box, into the Scottish rain.

Rain from a low-pressure system that was moving quickly through western Britain, bringing heavy precipitation that was bouncing off the pavement. Of course, the black BMW 325i didn't mind the rain at all. Sitting there waiting for me like a demonic familiar.

Presents in the back seat, raincoat in the passenger's side.

Glasgow to Portpatrick is a comfortable two-hour run down the motorway and the A77. An hour and a half if you don't mind risking the traffic police.

I did it in fifty-nine minutes.

No cops, no hassle.

The house quiet.

I went in through the back door and up the stairs.

I checked on Emma and tiptoed into the bedroom. I stripped and slipped beneath the sheets.

"Is that you back?" Beth moaned, half in and half out of sleep.

"Yes."

"Did everything go okay?"

"It all went fine."

"Did you keep your receipts?"

"Receipts?"

"So the police can reimburse your meals."

"I forgot to do that."

"You should have kept your receipts," she said, and went back to sleep. I lay there for a bit and then went downstairs to make a cup of coffee.

I removed my wallet containing my battered Saint Christopher medal and the lucky postcard of Saint Michael (the patron saint of peelers) trampling Satan, by Guido Reni.

Coffee and a slice of toast with butter and marmalade.

I went into the living room, stoked the embers in the fireplace, and as a reward for my endeavors poured myself a glass of the twenty-five-year-old Bowmore.

Peace is coming, Duffy. Don't fuck it up.

I sat in the easy chair and looked out at the water. Now that the rain had blown through, it was a calm, clear day. From the house on the cliff, it was only twenty miles across the narrowest bit of the Irish Sea to the lighthouse in Whitehead. A little farther to the left, I could see the power station chimney at Kilroot, and a little beyond that lay Carrickfergus and Belfast.

So near and yet so far.

We were safe here.

Donnolly knew where I lived. The company knew where I lived. MI5 and -6 knew where I lived. But they wouldn't come for me. I knew how to keep my mouth shut.

Jet, the cat, appeared from wherever he had been sleeping or hunting—his only two modes of existence.

"Hey," I said, and he acknowledged my presence.

I rubbed his neck, drank the coffee, ate the toast, sipped the whisky.

It got boring.

To hell with the minor key, the anticlimax, and the silence. I looked through my Chess Records Howlin' Wolf singles collection, found "Spoonful," slipped it out of its sleeve, and carefully laid it on the turntable. I got up and examined the Picassos on the wall.

I liked them a lot. And I liked Chester (Howlin' Wolf) Burnett singing Willie Dixon's words and telling it exactly like it was:

> *Men lies about little,*
> *Some of them cries about little,*
> *Some of them dies about little,*
> *Everything a fight about a spoonful,*
> *Just a spoonful,*
> *That spoon, that spoon, that spoon, that . . .*

I opened the door to the back garden.

A Turner smear of red in the eastern horizon. The sky, the color of a robin's egg, was frozen with expectation. Night had been vanquished. Nothing could stop the day. The Earth was spinning on its ellipse around the local star, and the morning would come . . .

Was coming . . .

I watched the cat stretch and begin a fresh patrol.

I looked through my notebook and removed the last twenty pages, ripping out everything I had learned in the previous fortnight.

I read through the pages, dropped them on the fire, and watched them curl and burn.

I drew a line through the poem I'd written. It was too obvious. Too on the nose. Poetry should make you work a wee bit.

I sat back on the chair and listened to the music and drank.

Howlin' Wolf singing. Otis Spann on piano. Hubert Sumlin on guitar.

Perfect.

I finished the whisky.

The sun was climbing over the North Sea now.

Britain was in light, Ireland in darkness.

But, who knows, maybe not for much longer.